PHILIP E. BARUTH

The Dream of the White Village

A NOVEL IN STORIES

R.N.M., INC.
WINOOSKI, VERMONT

Book Design by Anne Linton, *MacWorks,* Winooski, Vermont
Cover Photographs by Natalie Stultz

Library of Congress Catalog Card Number: 98-65692

ISBN 0-9657144-1-1

Published by:
R.N.M., Inc.
Champlain Mill
Winooski, Vermont 05404

PRINTED IN THE USA

To one of the world's most
crucially important people
— my mother, Diane Fountain —
this book is lovingly dedicated.

ACKNOWLEDGEMENTS

My thanks also to David Huddle and Bill Lychack at the *New England Review,* for publishing the first two sections of this book and, in the process, encouraging me to write the rest; similarly, to Paula Routly and Pamela Polston at *Seven Days,* who published some bits of this and let me see how it played around town; Anne Geggis and Sona Iyengar, my friends at the *Free Press,* who helped me research the church burnings of the 1970's; and to Rick Barba, T. Alan Broughton, Joseph Chaney, Margaret Edwards, Huck Gutman, Elizabeth Inness-Brown, Mary Lou Kete, Willow Older, Philip Pochoda, Sid Poger, Allen Shepherd, Nat Sobel, Melissa Tedrowe and Kari Winter for either providing raw material or reading the manuscript in its rough form. I'm perhaps most indebted to the six people who actually produced this text: Jay Rogers, who sold it; Mike DeSanto and Renée Reiner who read it and bought it, Daniel Lusk, who edited and oversaw, and Anne Linton and Natalie Stultz, who designed and photographed. Thank you all.

The Dream of the White Village is unquestionably a work of fiction. Nothing in it is true, no detail, no person and no event. Even where I've borrowed a street name, or the orientation of a cannon in a particular park, or some scrap of local political history — even there what appears on the page has been irrevocably changed by its immersion in fiction. This Burlington is not meant to be definitive, only my own. I've rerouted some streets and maybe a ferryboat. Windows have been added where characters need light by which to read; in such cases, the sun may have been moved as well. I hope you'll accept these revisions insasmuch as my intention — always — has been to create a more involving narrative for the reader.

— PB

How can the poem and the stink and the grating noise —
the quality of light, the tone, the habit and the dream — be
set down alive? When you collect marine animals there are
certain flat worms so delicate that they are almost impossible to capture whole, for they break and tatter under the
touch. You must let them ooze and crawl of their own will
onto a knife blade and then lift them gently into your bottle of sea water. And perhaps that might be the way to write
this book — to open the page and to let the stories crawl in
by themselves.

— John Steinbeck, *Cannery Row*

And with Footers beside him, and Martin trailing with an
amused smile, Billy went out into the early freeze that was
just settling on Broadway and made a right turn into the
warmth of the stairs to Louie's pool room, a place where
even serious men sometimes go to seek the meaning of
magical webs, mystical coin, golden birds, and other arti-
facts of the only cosmos in town.

— William Kennedy, *Billy Phelan's Greatest Game*

Contents

This book is set for the most part at a time in the early 1990's when demographers and statisticians had begun to talk about a second Mason-Dixon line, this one in the upper northeast corner of the country, running straight through New England.

According to the people taking the polls, respondents in the lower New England states — Connecticut, Rhode Island, and Massachusetts — were increasingly dissatisfied with and anxious about their own surroundings, yet continued to believe that New England itself, as a geographical region, as an historical entity, was "special" and "uniquely desirable." Those answering the same questionnaires in the upper three states — Maine, New Hampshire, and Vermont — tended to believe very strongly both in their immediate surroundings and in the larger concept of those surroundings. Everyone still believed in New England, that is to say, but New England seemed to have contracted, slowly and without any warning of any kind, disappeared nearly half into itself like a drought-struck lake.

This book is set in Vermont. It was the state most strongly associated with traditional New England by a majority of respondents in each of the six states. The book begins in the six-month period of one year in the early 1990's when Burlington, Vermont, had its AIDS Outreach clinic and its truly best and least expensive Chinese restaurant fire bombed. Also destroyed in the fire that gutted Number One Chinese was another store directly abutting it, a video store called Hot Shots. It was a relatively new store, which had distinguished itself from others in town by renting a selection of pornographic videotapes, and some of the fire investigators believed that whoever set the fire planned for both buildings to burn.

It was arson, and it was arson done in such a way as to advertise that it was arson: arson for arson's sake. The police stated it as a confirmed fact, and their certainty started the town talking about the original arsonist years before, in the mid-1970's. Everyone was worried that it would start all over again. Because Burlington had a history of set fires, fires no one could solve or understand and that seemed to rise up out of a mute, bodiless anger. It was one of the town's more disquieting secrets, and it was hidden in almost exactly the way a large family hides a short strain of mental illness.

And yet for all of this, for all of it, Burlington was a sassy and almost absurdly beautiful place to live. It was a traditional white-church town with pronounced wiseass tendencies. The people returned a Progressive mayor for twelve years, and then sent him to Congress, where he is still the only Independent. The city threw in with Central Vermont Railroad and bought a wide stretch of lakefront property and turned it into an urban preserve, pointedly off-limits to developers, and again it was almost laughable how beautiful the waterfront greenbelt and promenade turned out to be. Lake Champlain lay at the foot of the town, a somehow shy yet vast and exquisite lake. There were cobblestone streets and horse-drawn carriages for the tourists. A small coterie of craftsmen made furniture more or less by hand and sold it to no-nonsense types from Brooklyn and Stamford up to see the foliage; IBM had a manufacturing plant just through the woods in Essex where they turned out memory in millions of semiconducting chips. There was good, loud local music. Teenagers were heavily pierced, painstakingly tattooed, male or female, or set up with blond dreadlocks, and even then they looked rosy-cheeked and fundamentally understood by their parents. There was clean air and bold linen-white clouds and blue skies that hit you like an absolute slap across the face when you walked outside. It was a finch-sized town with a condor's heart, and it was just a big time being there, being in Burlington.

• • •

There are three central thoroughfares in town, Main Street, College and Pearl, and all three run in parallel from the top of College Hill down to the lake. But Pearl Street is what it's all about. It is the one street that tells you, in its slow roller-coaster descent to the water, all you need to know.

If you begin at the top of the Hill — even, say, with the black iron statue of Ira Allen, Ethan's shrewder brother, that stands in front of the University — you have the mill town of Winooski at your back. Winooski, despite its unremitting hard work, remains the awkward stepsister city, grouped around woolen mills that no longer spin anything and which have been only incompletely re-envisioned as health clubs and shopping malls.

Burlington will be spread out directly in front of you. Down and to your left is the town's affluent side, including the best shops and the priciest homes, the cool brick structures of South Williams and South Willard and South Union. Down and to your right are the more luckless and lackluster business ventures and the Old North End, stark rows of houses on streets that are often narrow and comparatively treeless. The Old North End is where you can still buy a three-bedroom house for a song because what few stabbings and assaults the town has take place mostly in the bars and houses of that maze-like section. It is what passes, in Vermont, for a wrong side of the tracks.

Pearl Street is the dividing line between the town's hemispheres, and for that reason alone it is a study. Like the border towns in Texas and California, Pearl Street is savvier and less given to illusion than what lies on either side of it. Heading down to the lake on Pearl you pass Church Street, the cobblestone pedestrian mall; Pearl's, the redoubtable and the only gay bar; the community college; the Social Security Office; the Cathedral of the Immaculate Conception and the Episcopal Cathedral; Bove's Italian Cafe, Anthony's Italian Foods, and M&M Italian Market, a little Bermuda Triangle of pasta and chianti that smells even in winter of garlic and grilled sausage; and finally a short row of tall Victorian houses just at the foot of the street, the last two or three of which are halfway houses, single-occupancy dwellings for people who qualify, in one way or another.

That's as far as you can drive, but if you walk across Battery Street to Battery Park, you are looking out over the water and squarely at the Adirondack Mountains of New York. You pass a brass monument commemorating the year cannon barked at British ships trying to take Fort Ticonderoga on the New York side. When you get to the very edge of the park, the western-most point, there is a low rock wall, and if you look out over this wall you are looking down three hundred and fifty feet or so at the waterfront park itself, what the excitable *Burlington Free Press* likes to call the Queen City's crown jewel.

Directly beneath you is an oversized rectangle of grass kept meticulously mowed. It's a large free space where people run their dogs and throw frisbees and where visiting French-Canadians have their picnics, spread their cloths and wine and cheese. In the hot months of the summer, a tall white Camelot-style tent will be erected in its center.

That green rectangle is bounded by lights and bike path and flowering shrubs, and at night, from Battery Park almost directly overhead, it looks like God's own pool table, set down with great care in the flat space beside the lake. The boat house stands at one corner pocket looking like a carousel barn; the sharp new Coast Guard station makes up the same-side corner, while the opposing length has the Little Saigon Restaurant at the far end, and a small patch of condominiums at the near, because for all of its good intentions the town has been too polite, finally, to slam the door completely on its developers.

A suicide or a drunk who raced his car down the length of Pearl, ignoring the lights and picking up raw momentum, could conceivably leap the rock wall of Battery Park and arc out into space and finally come to rest, some three hundred feet down, in the side pocket.

This giant's pool table at the very butt end of Pearl Street is the last major thing you need to know about Burlington, because it tells you more clearly than anything else the physics of the place and the people, and consequently how its stories should be told. If you watch that rectangle of grass on a sunny May afternoon, sooner or later you'll see everyone in town make their pass through it, along the waterfront path and then up and over the grass. They'll see five or fifteen people that they know, and they'll link up for an instant. They'll bat the breeze, they'll observe the rituals. And in that sense there's no way to tell the story of one Burlington individual or even of one family, because the path and angle of any one person depends on how they glance off at least ten others, on what direction those ten others came from and what precisely pushed them on their way.

Given a surprisingly short interval of time, any two people in Burlington, according to these pool table physics, will
make contact. Or kiss, to use the technical term. And that
kiss will alter everything in the small world beyond recognition, endlessly renew the need to study the set-up. So the
story of the Masseau family — and the fires that went unre-
flected in polls showing the yearning for what Vermont no
longer knew itself to be — can only be one of the unseen
angle and the vertiginous carom into the lives of others, and
the families of others. It can only show to what an extent
family itself is chance collision. And like the story of any
game, it can only be one of choosing up, and taking sides.

The Present: 1993-1994

Maurice Masseau

The three most famous restaurants in Burlington were three of the least elaborate, and it's fair to say that the two qualities were not unrelated. Bove's Cafe, an Italian restaurant near the foot of Pearl Street, was famous county-wide for its weekend all-you-can-eat spaghetti and for its raw garlic white sauce. It was a place where families waited in a line snaking out the door on Friday night, even in winter. The families stood with drunk, courteous college students, and everyone was more or less glad to wait because that's what you did there, and the place made absolutely no pretensions, but was simply Bove's.

Another, the Oasis Diner, was the once vital but now murmuring heart of the Democratic machine in Vermont. It was packed with silver stools, fried eggs, and contemplative old men. Campaigning governors and presidents drank coffee there, but increasingly less often. Because the food was dynamite and the cramped silver car of the restaurant photographed very honestly, it took the nation as a whole lurching to the right to weaken its outsized, perennial hold on fame.

The last of the three was Nectar's Lounge. Nectar's had two halves, one a slow-moving diner and the other a dance club dominated by a huge leather horseshoe bar. Nectar's was famous for gravy fries served through a small window onto Main Street. If you had a dog, you could walk by that window and the fry cook would hand out a lump of pastrami molded like a robin's egg. "My sense is that's a pastrami dog you're walking," the educated cook would say. Nectar's was famous because an obscure local band named Phish had played there on Thursday nights before going on to become a nationwide phenomenon in its own right. Like Bove's, Nectar's celebrity was inseparable from its lack of ambition. Beer was cheap, there was never a cover charge, and if you got tired of the noise you could climb the stairs to the Metronome on the second floor.

Maurice's nightly organizing routine wasn't cast in stone but it was well-practiced. He ordinarily began at Nectar's, in the restaurant half, at about eight o'clock at night, eating whatever was on special, shepherd's pie or hot roast beef sandwiches. The cooks and the waitresses knew him, and he could serve himself coffee without anyone thinking it odd. He'd eat and read the *Free Press,* running his eye over the crime log and the local news. When he'd finished, he'd put in an hour on the bar side of the building, talking with people at the horseshoe before the band began and killed the possibility of conversation. If he found anybody inter-esting, a real prospect, he might stay and spring for a few beers.

If not, he'd climb the stairs to the Metronome and sig-nal one of the bartenders; they'd step together through the emergency exit out onto the dark roof and smoke a joint, looking out over Main Street and the distant purplish mass of Lake Champlain. Even in the dead of winter they'd stand out there and smoke.

Invariably, Maurice got a rush of enthusiasm looking out over the bars and the pricey Burlington shops, even at the knots of well-dressed college kids who at street-level rubbed him the wrong way.

During those overlook moments, it was as though the town itself recognized the sense of ownership he had felt most of his life. Maurice felt it as an inheritance and an obligation and had since his father's funeral, which, because

Chris Masseau had been a police sergeant, was attended by the mayor, the chief of police, and one of the state's two senators. Twenty-one guns were fired over the lake that day, fired right straight at New York's Adirondack Mountains. Maurice could remember standing in Battery Park beside his metal folding chair, overlooking the waterfront and hearing the eulogies, looking down on wheeling seagulls. Beyond his stunned grief, he had felt light-headed and destined, and guilty for the pleasure he took in it. It was a prescient sense of ownership. Although he had never told anyone, not even his older brother Reuben, Maurice had decided with the crack of the guns that he would be mayor, when he was older and the wind blew right.

In his dreaming, then and since, he had never considered national or state-wide office. The sense of intense longing was concentrated, just city-sized.

When he and the bartender finished smoking, and Maurice had flicked the roach out into space, they'd come back inside. The bartender would pour Maurice a free pint, and he would look over the prospects in the upper, quieter bar. Maurice preferred to spend more of his time in the Metronome, although it seemed always to attract less of his kind of people than Nectar's, people with local credentials and common sense and the desire to keep the city clean, traditional.

Between nine-thirty and eleven o'clock, he'd work the pool table and the elbow of the bar next to it, getting to know people, sounding them out, gauging how they saw the world. This was Maurice's job, and it came naturally to him. He had a prodigious gift for searching out the like-minded and for making them feel found.

Winnowing the bar crowd in that way, he'd find a few guys here and there each week who would then wind up at bigger events — fish-offs and cook-outs in the summer, deer hunts in the fall — and who would drift into membership in a group that was less an organization than a set of common desires that could not always be publicly expressed. It had no real name, this group. But the newcomers' names would wind up on telephone trees, and they would be called before close elections. Some of these newcomers would blend into the less patient wing of the group, and they might find themselves six months later in the back of a pick-up running without its lights and its license plates. They might steal lawn signs put up by rival candidates, or they might go further, perform some of what Maurice's brother Reuben liked to call direct action, depending on how much and how soon people felt comfortable with the newcomers.

And so this group had two faces, one set behind the other and neither of which was ever shown to the public.

It had all begun as griping resistance to the Progressives, who were always talking about the rich getting richer and who swung the city far to the left in the eighties, pumped up everyone's tax bills to pay for social programs. Neither the Republicans nor the Democrats seemed to be able to make any headway against the Progressive coalition, so some people had eventually put their heads together. It started as just a few men with a little bit of clout. In fact, Maurice's father had joined the group when the meetings were eight guys going camping.

But while the Progs occupied the city government and grew fat, the group also matured. Only recently, they had helped defeat a popular Progressive mayor who supported health coverage for the partners of homosexual city workers. It was regarded as an inexplicable upset, and the papers sputtered foolishly about the hubris of the Progressive grassroots leaders.

It had taken all of fifteen hundred votes, good organized votes. All politics are local, quoting Tip O'Neill, but in Vermont, with a state population at less than three-quarters of a million, nobody needed Tip O'Neill to tell them anything.

Maurice was not the only unofficial organizer, but he — and his brother Reuben before him — was responsible for the twenty-somethings, the bar crowd. They were his people. He knew them all like they came straight from a catalogue: the young stonecutters from Barre and the privileged students they tried to stare down, the alternative types with rings in their eyebrows and studs in their tongues, vegetarians and crunchy granola types, the occasional skinhead and the bleeding hearts whose minds could never be changed, the kind who walked in walk-a-thons.

Maurice knew them, and he knew how to avoid wasting his time. For mingling and watching and shepherding the odd one here and there, he received two hundred and twenty-five dollars a month as well as the use of a small one-bedroom apartment in Burlington's Old North End, heat and most utilities included.

And when the time came, maybe in ten years, he would emerge as the youngest mayoral candidate in the town's history, and inexplicably he would win.

• • •

Maurice knew for a fact that when the time came he would be backed to run for mayor of Burlington, this because of a pool game that was played on February 3, 1986, when Maurice was twenty-one and his father was four years dead. It was during the interval when his father's memory was still freshly sainted, midway between being actively lamented and all but forgotten.

The game was played at the New Social Club in Winooski, where Chris Masseau had met people and conducted business dealings unknown to anyone but himself, the concerned parties, and his old patrol partner, Avery Yandow. Yandow had retired from the police force the year before Maurice's father was found slumped at home against one of the kitchen cabinets, the victim of a massive stroke.

After his early retirement Avery Yandow made full-time what had always been his strongest part-time passion, running the New Social Club and keeping its membership properly select. He was a small, bandy-rooster type, no more than five feet four, a diminutive frame below a prematurely wizened face. Only in his late fifties had silver hair and clipped beard taken away the air of childishness that had haunted him his whole life, the boy-sized aura that made him a person more given to anger than he might otherwise have been.

Avery Yandow had a simple policy concerning membership in the Club: *No bums, no scums.* He wore sport coats with nylon shirts beneath, tall-heeled black boots, and he seemed finally, in the cragginess of late middle age, to be able to relax a little in his own smallness.

On the Wednesday night of the game, Maurice had been out walking on the Burlington waterfront. It was one of those rare, perfectly still nights in deep winter. There was no wind from the lake at all, and so Maurice had stood for about a half hour at the boardwalk railing, smoking cigarettes, kicking at the railing to keep warm, and putting his various dreams into rough order. He flicked his cigarette butts out toward the prow of the hulking Plattsburgh ferryboat, frozen tight for the winter. By ten-thirty, he was cold through and possessed of what at twenty-one he could only consider a genuine vision.

Maurice showed up at the Club around ten minutes of eleven. He came into the entryway, stamped the snow from his feet and picked up the small phone mounted by the heavy wooden door, was buzzed in. Inside, about twelve men were spread around the bar. Two others were poking through a game on the smaller of the club's two pool tables. The walls of the club were white-washed plaster and dark wood paneling. It always had a mixed air of family room and board room.

Avery had his cousin's son working the bar and was himself sitting in the next small room, where the big-bellied tv set in the corner showed women with unnaturally large breasts in small swimming suits wrestling in a plastic pool filled with mud.

Maurice sat down on the couch facing Avery's couch. His thawing fingers felt like they were on fire. The sound on the set was turned nearly all the way down, as Avery wasn't concerned to hear the play-by-play. He nodded to Maurice, turned back to the set.

"How's the young blood this evening?" he asked.

Maurice took off his thermal headband. "The young blood has got a hell of an idea kicking around in his head tonight, Avery. What do you think about that?"

Avery's eyebrows pushed up. "Don't know. Guess that would depend on who thinks it's a hell of an idea. Just the young blood? Or folks who make a point to know better?"

Then Maurice had plunged into his case, talking a streak about this ward and that ward, who at the Club could pull a thousand votes in the New North End, the people who owed his father and whose markers Maurice now claimed, talking about actually making the changes that his father and the rest of the group for whom the New Social Club was the visible arm had been talking about making for years. He talked about everything except the thing that surrounded him the whole time like thick perfume: the sense that he belonged to the city and the city belonged absolutely to him.

When he was finished, Avery — who hadn't moved the entire time, but had merely nodded or chuckled skeptically or both — cracked his fingers in a loud, showy gesture. "You want to be mayor of the Queen City of Burlington. That's the idea, more or less," he said with a yawn.

Maurice leveled a stare at him. "That's right, Avery. Say nine, ten years from today. You help me and I could win. I have absolutely no doubt about that." It was both flattery and the truth. Avery had more say than anyone about how the people affiliated with the Club would vote, and he was the main organizer for the Club's smaller and stronger shadow group, who met there every few months after hours, with the doors locked and no one being buzzed in, member or no.

And the memberships of both groups had been growing, slowly and unfailingly, over the last decade, growing like an ivy. It was not absurd to think that in a few years they could elect a mayor. If and when that happened, it would be in part because Avery had said yes as opposed to no.

"Mayor Young Blood," Avery joked.

"That's right."

"Well, listen now, Maurice. Don't you think there might be some people ahead of you in line? People been doing their part and paying their dues and might feel like they were a little bit more up to the job?"

"I pay my dues, Avery. Have since I was a kid. You know that. And I've done more than one job for you. I'm not saying I want it now. I'm saying I'll keep working hard, getting out the vote, bringing people in, and I'll do my part. But I'm just asking if when the time comes you'll do this for me." Maurice ran a hand over his goatee, trying to get part of what he felt into words that would carry some weight. "I just feel like I have to know that that's what I'm working for. Among all the other things. I gotta feel like that's a specific investment I'm making. And in exchange it would be an investment for you, for everybody. That seems fair to me."

"What's Reuben think about this little plan?"

"I didn't tell him," Maurice said. "He kibbitzes too much."

"Mayor," Avery repeated wonderingly, out loud but to himself. "His Honor, the Boy Wonder."

Maurice felt his anger flicker up, but he put it down, and said as casually as he could, "The youngest mayor of Burlington ever, Avery. The Masseaus are history-makers. Always have been. As you know."

Although his voice was even, Maurice's reddish brows were pulled tight and Avery seemed to sense where the anger was and what it was about. He would have seen it often enough in himself, the sore spot, the flash point. Avery pulled at his own short beard. He chuckled again. "You still shooting pool these days, you and your brother? You used to shoot pool at one time, I remember."

"Reuben doesn't really play good enough that you could say he actually *shoots pool*," Maurice said with a straight face. "But I still play now and then. Sure I do."

"You play about every night, son. Even I know that."

"Goddam right," Maurice said, face still impassive.

"Well, then let's settle this the way your dad and I settled every argument we ever had that made any difference. Best man on the table is the best man period, and fuck all the talk about what's fair and what's owed anybody and all the other horseshit." Yandow was a recognized amateur pool player, and he had won tournaments in the state. He and Maurice's father had shot in doubles tournaments together, all up and down the Atlantic seaboard, Maine, New Hampshire, Connecticut.

Maurice couldn't help himself. A smile transformed his face. "You want to play for whether or not you'll support me. When the time comes."

Yandow nodded, a smile pushing up through the beard. He scratched at his hand. "Play you for Burlington, young blood. At least a good shot at it, when the time comes, like you say. One game of straight to a hundred. You win and we'll do it up right. Get you on the ward council, maybe from there to city council, at a certain point, of course. You got to be twenty-five at least. You lose, though, and I'm gonna stop off your organizing money for the next two months to teach you a lesson about how big your little britches actually are."

Maurice's smile faded slightly. Two months pay was four hundred and fifty dollars. And he knew for certain that it was a debt Avery wouldn't forgive; Avery was known as secretive and occasionally cruel, but he had extraordinarily strong scruples about wagers and people who welched. He'd once broken a cue across the shin of a member who couldn't pay off a bet because he'd drunk up all his money. The drunk wasn't buzzed back into the club for a full year, almost to the day.

But Maurice felt that he needed the promise as much or more than anything he could remember. It was a part of how the vision went together. And so almost immediately he began to play the game the way his father had taught him. He squinted an eye and began shaking his head sadly.

"You haven't played me in a long time, Avery. I'm *even better* now. And if I remember, I was about good enough to beat you when I was fourteen. Dad always told me not to, though. You know, watch out for your ego."

"That's all right, son." Avery narrowed his eyes and chuckled again, turning back almost reflexively to the television, where the mud wrestling had been replaced by women's volleyball. He said lazily, "It's always a help to shoot on your own table."

They did in fact play on Avery's table, an eight-foot slate that Avery had donated to the Club on the condition that it be locked in a smaller room off the bar to which he held the keys. That room was known as the cloak room, for what it had once been as well as for the sound of it, which Avery liked. Mostly he opened it for the smaller, more select meetings, but he was also always on the lookout for games with some drama. Now he made a small show of taking his cue from its rack on the wall, fitting it together, taking some talc from the dispenser. He applied it carefully, like a salve, to the inside curve of his hooked thumb.

Maurice picked his own cue from those hanging near the door. They were nicer than the cues in the main room. "You want a spot of some kind, Avery?"

"Spot?"

"Well, there's quite an age difference here. I mean, your eyesight is, I'm sure, not in the twenty-twenty range anymore. I'm willing to consider some kind of handicap."

Avery smiled and said nothing, but with the cue in his hand and the balls clicking into the rack, he began to walk a little straighter and higher in his boots somehow. The smile was window-dressing; his eyes had taken on a dispassionate, vaguely clinical expression that could not more clearly have signaled his intention to win as quickly and as cuttingly as possible.

Maurice won the lag, and they were into the game. From a weak break Maurice managed a run of four balls, then sat in one of the two armchairs as Avery stalked around the table. His stance over the ball was tense, eyes wide and flipping even wider as he finally pumped the cue hard. His shots struck the backs of the pockets hard and fell in; there was no sense of touch as such. It was an exercise, each shot, in exactitude and control. And, less clearly, it was an exercise in pay-back, a long-tended and meticulous revenge against whatever the array of balls symbolized for him.

"Watch it, Avery, *damn*. Smoke coming from that cue. You're shooting the power stick tonight. The wind off the table is fierce."

Avery said nothing, stalked to the next shot. Maurice watched him run nine and thought that his style was even more pronounced now than it had been when Maurice had played him as a kid, in the cellar while his father looked on. Even then he had thought Avery played like a man who hated the balls and killed them with the pockets.

"Take a breath," Maurice said, as Avery lined up a long shot. "Don't overwork yourself."

Avery squinted down his cue. "You talk like your father. He always thought he could talk himself into being a better shot too. Or me into being a worse one. Always start running off at the mouth when he saw me start to heat up." He sank the second to the last ball, and waited while Maurice racked the other fourteen. He grinned at Maurice. "Never worked, son. I used to beat the man stupid night after night."

They continued to play for the better part an hour. Some of the men from the bar drifted over when they heard that Avery was playing Maurice in the cloak room.

No one said anything to either of the players, but they stood outside the door looking in and talking to each other about what shot they would have played and why. No one said anything to the players because they knew that it was a game with something at stake, something big enough for the room to have been opened in the first place.

Only Avery's cousin's kid said anything. He stuck his head around the door, waited for Avery to make his cut, then asked, "Beer, Avery?"

Avery shook his head silently.

The kid looked at Maurice. "Sure," Maurice said. "Put it on Avery's tab."

"Put it on my tab and you're looking for another job, kid," Avery remarked quickly, and then went back to shooting. When he missed, Maurice stood and made a shot, but so falteringly that he backed the cue ball right up behind the four ball, snookering himself.

He cursed out loud and pointedly did not look at the faces in the doorway. He looked up at Avery but Avery had his eyes down on the balls. All Maurice could do was try to leave him blind as well. He nearly did, but not quite, and Avery dropped six more in quick succession.

It was only when Maurice was behind forty-six to sixty-six and getting the hot prickle of defeat in his cheeks that he realized something. He realized that he was playing Avery as though his father was in the next room, having a beer at the bar, as though Maurice Masseau was still Chris' boy and liable to get corrected on which shot he selected from the field. It hadn't occurred to him because the game had been going so fast, but he was playing like he was *hoping* his father would come in and crab over his stroke, like his scratching the cue ball could both lose him his shot and restore his father to life.

It was playing with Avery, in this room that could be Maurice's own cellar if he closed his eyes, that threw it all back at him four years after the funeral.

So he began something comforting and senseless. As he walked to his shots, he said in his mind over and over and over again, "Your father is no more. Your father is no more. Your father is in Heaven and is no more." It was a nonsense version of something the priest had said at his father's funeral, that afternoon in Battery Park, and it came up in his mind out of nowhere. It was a chant, a rasp of white noise, and suddenly he could hear himself think below it, in the place where he talked to himself about how to put his shots together. He began to feel the cue ball again, to know where it would roll and why.

He ran the rest of the rack, eight balls, and then crushed the new rack open like a walnut.

Maurice was in the low nineties, and Avery in the low eighties, when Avery finally cracked and resorted to a little talking himself. "Playing like a regular adult," he said loudly and appreciatively when Maurice handled a tough kiss. "Shooting a man's stick," Avery added, smiling inscrutably beneath the silver beard. There was no way to tell, really, how much of it was meant as goading and how much as honest opinion. But it occurred to him that maybe Avery was also conjuring or unconjuring something with this game.

"*Oh* yeah," Maurice answered. "Oh yeah." He took the time to chalk his cue, because nine times out of ten it was chalk or choke. He saw the end of the game then, saw it shine up at him brilliantly. "Shooting for the city," he said quietly, and then he touched off his shot.

James

On August 12, 1870, the novelist Henry James took a little packet steamer from Fort Ticonderoga to the theoretical water boundary of New York State, and then passed over into the Vermont half of Lake Champlain. He had been traveling and writing up his travels, and he was bored with mountain vistas and panorama. The movement from steamers to stagecoaches and back again had grown tiresome. He had his head down and his gaze focused on the lake itself. He examined its physiognomy. "It is narrow for a lake and broad for a river, yet it strikes you more as a river," he mused.

It was only the dueling mountain ranges — Adirondacks on his left, and the Green Mountains of Vermont on his right — that pierced James' boredom toward the end of that day. "The vast reach of the lake and this double mountain view go far to make Burlington a supremely beautiful town. I know of it only so much as I learned in an hour's stroll, after my arrival. The lower portion by the lake-side is savagely raw and shabby, but as it ascends the long hill, which it partly covers, it gradually becomes the most truly charming, I fancy, of New England country towns."

In his hour-long stroll through Burlington, Henry James managed to see several things very clearly. He saw what he called the "civic greenness and stillness and sweetness of the place," and he made it plain to his readers that it had touched him genuinely, if briefly. He described the houses of the town: "pleasant, solid American homes, with their blooming breadth of garden, sacred with peace and summer and twilight." He was supremely pleased with the town as he had conjured it, and he felt no need to investigate or elaborate further. The town was New England itself, and New England was peace, and a civil twilight quiet.

Henry James added only that as he stood in the muddy street at dusk, the city's tired laborers passed him in couples, their speech a mingling of Yankee inflections and Canadian French.

• • •

About an hour after dusk, almost exactly one hundred and twenty-three years later, James Craig was riding the last ferry across Lake Champlain from Plattsburgh, New York. The ferry rode low in the water, and looked to him almost exactly like a hand plane shaving across the surface.

James was in the process of moving from Southern California to Burlington. His rented station wagon sat beside him, blocks shoved carelessly under the front wheels. The car was filled with everything he owned, the nose of it pointing out from the ferry toward the black land mass of Vermont. There were a few other cars on the ferry, and all of the people were out on the deck because of the heat, but no one spoke to James and he spoke to no one. The ferry whistle sounded.

He was in his second year of running away. Two summers earlier, his wife had told him that she needed time to work things out. In a way, her leaving him had been of a piece with the way things had always worked between them. She'd come up to him at a dance their senior year in high school and talked for a few minutes and then put herself in his arms, and he'd been stirred by the certainty in her embrace. Until that time he'd been the sort who sat in the back of classes silently, worked two jobs and knew nothing of any importance about women, dating, social life, love. It wasn't until she chose him that he realized how desperate he was for it.

She changed him in various ways. It was a polishing process, and they both enjoyed it. He was tall and his arms were already strong from carpentering and working with cars; she took him to the new indoor mall and bought him shirts that showed off his build, and it was a revelation to him that the blank mass of his body could be attractive in that way. She drove to his house one night at three in the morning with a bottle of Boone's Farm Strawberry Wine and coaxed him out his window and into a field across the street. It was his first love affair, and he married her the next year.

By the following June, when she was considering how to tell him she needed time away, he was still racing home from work, checking his hair in his rear-view mirror before going into the house to see her.

By that August it was all but over. She called the apartment and told him that the marriage was a mistake. She felt as though she was too much of his life, and that the responsibility was too much. He called back and argued, and then pleaded, let weeks go by, and then called and pleaded again. It wound up with him signing papers at a Burger King near the old apartment. And then he'd moved as far away from Hartford as he could, to California. But he'd never let it go. Half of the money he earned as a finisher he applied to their credit card bills, to show her he was still handling things even if she'd momentarily lost the sense of them as a couple.

But after a year and a half in the foreignness of Southern California, James was moving back east. It hap-

pened to be Burlington because it was close but not quite
Connecticut, and he had an uncle nearby, in North Hero.
So when the ferry rounded a darkened point of land and
came into view of the scattered lights of Burlington, he was
already looking to it for certain things. They were needs he
couldn't have expressed aloud to himself — companion-
ship, home, passion, something like vindication, belonging,
and a renewed sense of being embraced and told that he
mattered. He didn't know it about himself in any explicit
way, but he sensed that he didn't have the strength to move
again by himself, to start over in a new place from scratch,
if this move didn't work. The spray was in his face as he
looked at the lights. They marked the limits of the town the
way Christmas lights suggest a porch.

Almost immediately James noticed a larger, pulsing
orange light. It was in the lower left-hand quadrant of the
implied Burlington, and it was moving in the way that only
fire moves, like a fluid. At first he thought that it was a bon-
fire, maybe for the end of summer. But the murmuring
behind him grew louder, and as the wind shifted he could
smell it strongly, a charcoal smell. As the ferry slid closer he
could make out the waterfront, the dock on King Street,
and up and a good ways beyond, the swaying fire and its
orange glow. Sirens drifted over the water.

When James drove off the ferry, he could see what
looked like airborne ash in the halos of the streetlights.

The next morning he had pancakes with local syrup and
read the papers with his aunt and uncle. It turned out that
it was the Vermont AIDS Outreach offices that had burned,
on Elmwood Avenue, near the bottom of Pearl Street. The
investigators said that the fire was so intense that filing cabinets full of confidential information combusted from the
inside. James read the classifieds. The fire lingered almost

not at all in his mind, except as a piece of carpenter's prag-
matism, a possibility to keep an eye out for: the thing would
need to be re-built.

• • •

James' grandfather had told him once, when he was very
young, that pool was the only honest game known to man.
You couldn't cheat because everything was out there on the
table, on the felt and under the lights. A ball went down or
it didn't. He had learned later that his grandfather was
speaking only from his own gentlemanly understanding of
the possibilities. James had been cheated many times since.

He met Maurice on a Thursday night about five months
after coming to town, in a bar called the Metronome in
downtown Burlington. The bar sat atop another bar on the
first floor called Nectar's; the upper bar was quiet, nearly
always, and people were serious about the pool game. Very
little lag between shots. He didn't have to ask people to call
their pockets. Pool there was not an opportunity to pose,
and he enjoyed the feeling — fairly hard to come by otherwise — of crisp strategy in the games. Most people played
a few shots ahead in the upper bar. People planned, moved
the cue ball around.

James held the table for a while that night. Maurice
was the sixth person he played: a very pale twenty-six or
twenty-seven-year-old with a reddish moustache and goatee that connected in a perfect thin oval around his mouth.
The rest of the face was cleanly shaven. His crew-cut head
was covered with a slightly oversized black baseball cap.
His eyes were black as well, and his expression sober. He
kept his long dark-green wool coat on. He looked vaguely
Irish, vaguely inner-city. It was a look James had seen

before, but couldn't place.

Maurice came up to him when the balls were racked and he had picked a cue for himself. "Maurice," he said sticking his hand out. It looked sickly white poking out of the dark overlarge sleeve of the coat.

"James."

"All right if I call you Jimmy, James? Is that okay?"

James hesitated, tempted to say no. "Sure," he found himself saying.

Maurice shook his hand and smiled suddenly. The seriousness lifted cleanly and completely off his face, and James couldn't help but smile back. "Jimmy, I have come to end your reign. I am here to end it completely, at a stroke. With these hands."

"Fine," James said, poker-faced. He knew the strategy, knew it was possible to get talked out of his own game. But he couldn't resist adding, "It's a free country."

"It's a free country," Maurice repeated to himself softly, eyes wide, nodding his head. He had two small gold hoops in his left earlobe. "I like that. That's catchy. That's thinking that takes you somewhere. Your break, isn't it? Winner breaks here, I think. And you are the winner, at this point."

As James chalked his cue and leaned over to break, he could hear Maurice repeating it to himself just audibly, stressing a different word each time: "It's a *free* country," he said admiringly, chalking his own stick, "it *is* a free country. I like that. That works. The whole *country*, all of it. Free. I like that."

James kept his head down, stroked the cue ball hard, but it was off somehow, and he got nothing on the break. Maurice looked over the table, picked a shot and bent to it, but just before he was about to shoot he stood back up and smiled again. He held his hands out in front of him. "With these hands, Jimmy," he said again, apologetically, nodding.

James smiled, took a drink of his draft. He watched as Maurice walked around the table, from shot to shot. The long green sleeves of the coat would pull back and his thin white wrists would protrude, stroke the cue, then retract back into the baggy darkness. He talked his game. "I came down too far," he would say aloud, clucking his tongue, "now I'm gonna have to show my stuff. I hate having to show my stuff so early in the night." And then he would work a clean bank shot, snapping it. Then again: "Now, *this* looks tough. Some tough, tough shit, this little guy. Jimmy, do you think this shot is beyond me? Do you think this one spells trouble? Jimmy?" He waited for James to answer.

"Not really, no," James said finally.

"Not really, or no?"

"No."

"Confidence," Maurice said, nodding. "You know I'm a shooter, don't you?" He bent over the shot, and it seemed from where James was standing that he was a few degrees off the direction he needed. "You know I'm a player. Of course you can see that right off."

James moved a bit to his left. From there, he could see that Maurice did have the cue just a bit out of line. Maurice narrowly missed the shot. He said nothing, pulled back and sat scowling on a high bar stool, pulled himself into the small tent of his coat. But just as James drew back to shoot, Maurice said blankly, "You know, having confidence in somebody is like kicking them in the goddam head. Screws that person up."

James followed through, letting the talk go in one ear and out another. That was the only way to play with talkers. He made four balls slowly and carefully.

"Screws them *up.* Up, up, up. Uppity up."

Working the cue ball back up the length of the table, James could suddenly see the end of the game. It laid itself out in his mind like a building plan, angles and lengths.

"Best way is to have nobody have any confidence in you at all," Maurice went on. "Then everything you do is literally amazing. You get out of bed and it's a miracle. People are bowled over if you put on your underpants and socks by yourself. Brush your teeth."

James boxed himself in making his fifth ball, could go nowhere with the sixth. He wanted the game too badly. That was the other problem with talkers, even if you stayed silent. It wasn't so much that they made you want to win as that they made you terrified to lose to them. He missed his shot but buried the cue ball — legally, but defensively — behind his last two balls.

The cautiousness wasn't lost on Maurice. He was grinning to himself. He chalked his cue, tapped it against the overhead lamp, a large thick-plastic replica of an ice block, with a bottle of beer frozen inside. Maurice began to look at the bank shots, considering each possibility quickly and efficiently. "Where you from, Jimmy?" he asked as he looked them over. A man coming into the bar slapped Maurice's shoulder as he passed.

"Connecticut originally. But I've been living out in California, Southern California."

"Whereabouts?"

"You know Long Beach?" James asked. Maurice nodded. "Well, right south of there. About twenty minutes, half an hour from L.A. A town called Costa Mesa."

Maurice shook his head, pointed out the shot he intended with the tip of his cue, tracing the projected path of the cue ball. "Costa Misery, you mean. Jungle in that part of the world," he said in a low voice, looking up for a second from sighting the shot. He looked serious. "Jungle-jungle, out there in the Sun-Belt. You were lucky to get out." He made the bank shot, the cue ball following the path he'd laid out as though it were notched in the table. "That's the war zone, out there. That's what they call the jungle-jungle."

And then he botched the last shot, a fairly standard cut. "Shit, no," Maurice said, covering his eyes with his hand, massaging his temples. Again James had had the clear impression that his aim had been maybe five degrees off. Not many people would have seen it for what it was. He was cheating, almost invisibly, to lose.

James immediately began to cheat to lose back. His shots started to nick the corners of pockets, bounce in and out of pockets, close enough to real errors that it took three shots before Maurice — occupied with his own talk, and with missing his own shots — realized that they were both just finessing.

He scowled at James when he realized. He pulled his black baseball cap lower, then smiled brilliantly, and again James felt compelled to smile back. It was obviously an act, a polished little bit, but it managed to release some frag-mentary, authentic charisma. The smile rewrote the faint meanness of the black eyes and the goatee. Maurice point-ed at him with his whole arm. "We are two very bad pool players, Jimmy. Who's worse? That's the thing now. Who is the worst of the two of us. Who literally can't play for shit, you or me. I say it's me."

James smiled again. This was the type of game he enjoyed most of all, one which drew everything into its own contracted orbit, in which personality spun as well, people put english on themselves. Anyone watching would've thought they couldn't play to save their lives.

Maurice shot and narrowly missed. The eight ball bounced back and forth rapidly in the mouth of the pocket, like a pinball, before popping out. James was impressed. It was an incredibly difficult miss to pull off.

Maurice turned to James and said very deliberately, "*Darn* it."

• • •

Later James turned to find a full beer waiting beside his nearly empty glass. The young woman bartending nodded toward the pool table, where Maurice was talking and shooting with a group of airmen from Plattsburgh Air Force Base. "That one's on Maurice," she said. She bit her fingernail, looking at the pool table. "But you can leave the tip if you want," she added a little more softly and sarcastically. "He doesn't tip. At all." She adjusted her black stretch top. "I mean ever."

James put a dollar out on the drink rail. "Allow me."

She was just picking it up when Maurice sat down beside him. Maurice noted the exchange of the bill, gave the bartender a hard look, squinting at her. Then he turned to James and said, "You have to be careful about feeding the monkeys in here. That one in particular. You think you're getting in good with them and next minute they're on the bottom of the monkey cage throwing their shit through the bars at you."

The woman smiled broadly, uninsulted. She twisted her dark hair up behind her head briefly, playing with it, then walked slowly away. Maurice watched her go, frowning. "Old flame," he explained. "Cold flame now."

"Thanks for the beer," James said.

"No problem. That game we had was the only fun I've

had playing in here in a month. These people are stiffs, I'm telling you. They have to slam everything. *Slam.* Crush the ball."

"I know. You get tired picking the ball up off the ground for them."

Maurice nodded slowly, eyes on the pool table. "Yes, Lord. Gotta slam everything. Have to have the macho noise when they shoot. Have to have it." His face had worked itself into the scowl again, as though the people playing pool, or the half of the bar he could see, were offensive to him. Without looking at James, he said, "You know, there used to be an English king named James. Wildman king of England."

"There was more than one."

Maurice turned to look at him, appraisingly. He nodded. "Exactly. Well, the one I mean was the one that got kicked out of London for being Catholic. He took the royal seal with him." He lifted his own beer, touched it to his lips, and when he set it down the level in the glass was roughly the same. It might very well have been his first drink. "Then he threw the royal seal in the Thames River on his way to France. He deep-sixed it."

James considered it. "That's real class."

"Bet it is," Maurice said. "What a bunch of bigots, running the guy out for being Catholic." He shook his head, drew his baseball cap way up on his head, exposing his neat red crew-cut hair, then reseated it just over his eyes. "I mean, *I'm* Catholic." He pointed abruptly at the bartender standing at the far end of the bar, talking to an older woman. "She's Protestant. We went out. What's the problem?" He smiled a little, to cue James that he was joking. "What are you, for instance?"

"I used to be Lutheran."

Maurice nodded agreeably. "See? What's the big deal? Your family was probably German or Dutch or something somewhere down the line. Scandinavian."

"German," James put in.

"Right. German. There you go. And we all live together in perfect harmony. No worries. I'm telling you, those English," he raised his glass for another tiny sip, now unable to control his grin, "are all a bunch of worthless goddam bigots. I literally *hate*," he started to laugh, and James laughed, seeing where it was going, "I literally hate every single one of them." He fingered the thin cross-bars of beard that connected his moustache and goatee. "No, seriously, what are you doing in Vermont? You know it gets cold here, right? You know it snows and shit."

"Yeah, someone told me already," James answered dryly. "I'm a carpenter, mostly a finisher. I went out to California two years ago because they build all year round, more jobs. That's what everybody said." James snapped his fingers. "Then the bottom fell out of that economy, and it looked like things were picking up over on this side of the country." It was the short version of the story, with his fractured marriage left out. He glanced involuntarily at Maurice, to see if the absence of it was visible to him.

But Maurice simply nodded. "So why not Connecticut again?"

James looked at him again. Maurice seemed really to want to know. He was waiting for the answer, the bill of the baseball cap pointed right at James. "I have some cousins up here in Vermont. I started out up in North Hero where they live. Of course it turns out there's not much work here either. But then I got a job down here in Burlington a couple weeks ago. It's better in the city. North Hero is stuck out there in those little islands."

Maurice was nodding to himself, eyes closed. "It's getting to be an old story," he said seriously.

"What is?"

He opened his eyes. "Migrating all over hell for work. For a nice place to live. A place where people aren't sacked out all over the street. And it always comes back to family, and where people belong. Everybody's going back where they came from. Everybody needs to go back to wherever in the world they came from, save us all a lot of fussing and fighting." He had his hands pulled up inside his coat sleeves, and the sleeves themselves mouth to mouth. The lack of hands made his white face float in the expanse of green coat. "Family in the north country. It's what guys like you and me are going back to." He jerked his head suddenly toward the bartender. "Did she tell you I didn't tip her?"

James glanced at the woman, thought about whether or not to answer. "She said you never tip, actually."

Maurice nodded knowingly, raised himself up on the stool, half-standing on the struts. "Hey, Alison!" She turned, very politely. "Give this guy back his buck."

She crossed her arms. "Why?"

"Because I tipped you. Give it back."

Alison snorted. "That's *your* story," she said and went back to her conversation, studiously avoiding Maurice's glare. She and the older woman suddenly broke into laughter. He came back down onto the barstool, frowning again, then turned and gave James the quick, big smile again. "You have to love it though. She's so — I don't know — so light and sneaky, you just have to love her." He looked up at the clock. "I gotta go, it's almost midnight. I have to make my rounds." He stood, put his bar change in the front pocket of his jeans. "So James, what are you doing Saturday afternoon?"

James swallowed, wiped his mouth. "I don't know yet," he answered. "Why?"

"Because a whole bunch of guys get together over in Winooski every few months and hang out, drink beer, bullshit. You know. Every once in a while somebody gets wound up and starts talking politics. It's a good time. You know where the trestles are, you ever hear of the trestles?"

James shook his head. "I'm living in Winooski now. But I never heard of it."

Maurice put on his gloves, began to punch his palms with his fists, seating them. "It's a cool place. If you want to go, I'll pick you up. I live over there too. Where you living?"

"Franklin. End of the street, ninety-five Franklin."

Maurice nodded, eyes closed. "Ninety-five Franklin. I'll stop by like two o'clock, unless it's below zero out. If you want to go, great. If not, don't worry about it. But it's a good group of guys. Like a softball league, but without the softball. Some fun shit goes on." He stroked the cross-bars of his moustache absently with his gloved hand. "You must not know many people in town yet."

James shook his head. Maurice scowled again, then yelled down to the other end of the bar. "Alison! Come here for a second."

She came slowly down, wiping her hands on a towel. Maurice turned to James. "James, this is Alison. Alison, James. Alison, don't mess with this guy. He's named after a king. A very old, bad-assed Catholic king."

"King James," Alison said, drying each finger. "You know, I like your bible."

Maurice smiled once more at James, patted his shoulder. "There, now you made a new little friend."

• • •

It snowed much of Friday night, and though the plows were out late and then early, the roads were still layered Saturday morning with snow and road sand, churned together into a slick tan paste. Slow-moving cars threw up small wakes of the stuff as they passed James' apartment. By two o'clock the sun was shining, but the temperature was low enough that the snow-cover shimmered without melting. It was disorienting to James, the tumbled masses of snow everywhere he looked, collected overnight from nowhere.

He waited by the living room window of his upstairs efficiency apartment. The room was furnished with a black futon mattress — now neatly folded into a couch — a small lamp standing on a squat red two-tiered tool box, and a digital clock. It was the first time since moving to Winooski that James had been invited to anything. He almost couldn't admit to himself how glad he was, and he told himself that Maurice was drunk, that Maurice wouldn't remember, or that he wouldn't have liked the people there in any case.

"Who are they?" his wife would have asked, not suspiciously, but out of curiosity. She'd have been glad. She had once told him, "Jamie, I can't be your only lover and your only friend, too." She would have been straightening the house, checking the clock. "Did they say two o'clock?" She would have moved pillows. "Who are these people again?"

His nose against the chilled window, James answered the impression of her aloud. "Just some guys I met the other night, good guys," he said cryptically. He gave her Maurice's line, teasing her. "Like a softball league, but minus the softball."

At twelve minutes after two, an old Dodge Dart made

the turn onto Franklin Street. As it swung around, James could see a man crouched behind it, hanging from the bumper. He was using his boots as skis, leaning with the curve. As the car passed the house, he stood and let go of the bumper simultaneously, so that he slid to a quick, stylish stop about three feet from James' cleared walk. The car continued on, seemingly unaware.

Maurice shook himself once, all-over and violently, like a dog. Snow and bits of sludge flew from the baggy green coat. He re-seated his baseball cap. James met him at the door, blinking at the glare off the snow. There was no wind, though, and it wasn't bitter. "Your Highness," Maurice greeted him, shaking his hand.

"Call us James," James said.

"Call my ass James," Maurice came back. "Your name is Jimmy, and don't you forget it." He started them walking back up Franklin Street. "I'm the only one that gets to have a fancy-pants formal first name. Can you believe my mom named me Maurice?" He looked over at James, baffled. "That's a black guy's name. Or a French guy. Or, like maybe a black French guy. It's ironic, me with a black French guy's name."

"I saw you ride up," James said. "Did you know that guy in the car?"

"Nope."

"Seems like a good way to get your leg run over or something. I mean, what happens if you slip under the tire? The guy driving doesn't even know you're there."

Maurice dragged his hand against the bulging snow-bank, began to pack a handful of snow together. "We used to call that skitching when we were kids. Skiing and hitch-ing. Nobody gets run over. What happens most of the time is your legs go out from under you and you get dragged before you remember to let go." He sidearmed the snow-ball at the stop sign on the corner, but missed it. "Once I came out of this bar in Burlington and the temperature'd dropped like twenty degrees, and there was this massive windchill factor. My buddy and I were just *piss* drunk. Nobody'd stop and give us a lift. So we caught this truck's bumper, and rode it all the way into Winooski, both of us scared if we let go we'd just freeze by the side of the road."

"So it's a survival skill, then," James said, joking.

"Bet it is." Maurice's pale face was serious. He drew up another gloveful of snow, packed it. "You have to have con-trol over your environment. Always, always. You gotta be able to move around, no matter what's going on with the weather, with anything. Look at the Revolutionary War. We won because we could move around, in the woods and shit. Look at Vietnam. They had tunnels. We had guys that couldn't move." He looked over at James, poked the shoul-der of his jacket with a finger, a little didactically. "That's what's wrong out in L.A. The cops can't move. That's why they call it the jungle-jungle. Vietnam times two."

He was scowling again, and James let the subject drop. They walked down a short hill, turned onto a small highway that led toward Essex Junction. They passed a long, large, brick woolen mill that had stood idle for years before being refitted as an upscale shopping mall called The Champlain Mill. The banks of snow reached nearly above their heads as they walked. A sander passed heavily by, following the track of the earlier plow, road sand being thrown from the rear of it like seed. As they passed a small row of squat, Cape Cod-style houses — like little fortresses with their chain-link fences, enclosed porches, and drab storm win-dows — Maurice steered him into what looked like a dri-veway but was in fact a small alleyway.

"This way, Highness," Maurice said.

The alleyway became a dirt track that took them back behind the row of houses, into undeveloped woods that opened on the left into a small graveyard. Headstones poked out irregularly from the cover of shining white snow. Beyond it, the dirt road dropped down into a turning circle surrounded by high-voltage equipment, generators, power-lines, massive winches stuck out over the Winooski River. Two cars were parked in the circle. Beyond them a sign read, *Green Mountain Generating Plant, Gorge 16.*

Maurice pointed to the sign. "That always kills me. They numbered the gorges."

"How else are they going to know where they're supposed to show up for work?"

"The boss says, 'You know that huge goddam gorge over by the railroad tracks? Well, you're working there today.' Numbers are just for people from out of town."

They took a small trail, marked with fresh footprints, past a fenced-off generator and through the trees. It dropped down suddenly onto railroad tracks. In the distance, James could see a large green wrought-iron bridge. "We go this way," Maurice told him, starting toward the bridge. "You know what Winooski means, in Indian?"

James shook his head, panting a little. He could feel the cold tingling all along his legs.

"Onion," Maurice said. "You believe that?" He pointed over toward the river. "The Indians used to grow onions here. I can't remember if it was the Abenaki Indians or the Winooski Indians. Not that it matters a whole hell of a lot. Six of these Indians, half a dozen of those. But whoever, they were into the onions big time. River of onions. You ask me, they should have just called the town Onion. Onion, Vermont. It fits better I think. Winooski sounds like shit, in my opinion."

"Maurice," James asked after a second of walking. "Why were you trying to lose when we shot the other night?"

Maurice finally threw the snowball he'd been polishing and packing. It struck a large tree trunk, and left a perfect circle of snow stuck in the bark. "Once I got up there, I saw you were one of these guys who comes just to play pool. You didn't know anybody. You could sit there for five or six hours and never ask anybody to dance. So if I beat you, you're one of those shy guys who's going to sit around bummed out for an hour, waiting to get back on the table. I can spot a loner from twenty miles off." He took off his glove, wiped his nose. "I was amusing myself, being nice."

"That's *your* story," James said, smiling at him.

They walked beside the tracks. James could hear both of them breathing in the snow quiet. Gradually the steep banks on both sides of the tracks dropped away; the land flattened out. And suddenly James could see others walking toward the bridge, some from the tracks on the far side of it, others coming up slowly through the small trees and brush from beside the river. Some in pairs, some walking singly through the bare trees. All young men, in variations on the same outfit, wool hats or head bands, fat leather gloves, jeans, dun-colored boots working through the snow. For a moment it was like seeing a herd of big animals laboring on the snow, working through to some distant shelter.

He heard people on the tracks behind them. Two men came up in a moment, one wearing a ski mask and a red and green neon ski jacket, the other dressed much like Maurice, down to the black cap and the neat oval of facial hair. They were running down the middle of the tracks, jumping from tie to tie. "Make way," said the one with the neon jacket. "This train's coming down the track."

"What's up, Maurice," the other one said.

"There's going to be plenty of beer, you guys, you don't have to beat everybody there," Maurice yelled as they passed quickly by. "It's not a goddam race."

They both giggled, and the first one began to chant, "I *think* I can, I *think* I can, I *know* I can, I *know* I can." The second one picked it up until they passed out of earshot.

Maurice shook his head and spat on the ground. They continued until they had nearly reached the upper bank of the river. James could see that the neat tracks in the center of each tie stopped right before the iron bridge. "We go down here," Maurice said. The footprints trailed down over the side of the concrete pilings that supported the bridge. Maurice jumped down first. Even though they were built together like stairs, each of the pilings was too large and too long a drop to be used comfortably. James had to climb down, holding on with his gloves while his feet found the piling beneath.

He came down into a large shadowed space protected from the snow by the overhead bridge. There were already fifteen or more guys standing with beer bottles in their hands. Directly in front of him was Gorge 16, a stunning cut in the hills with the Winooski River some two hundred feet below the end of the concrete platform on which he stood. There was nothing between him and the river. The twenty square-feet of concrete beneath the bridge might as well have been a diving platform.

Behind him a smaller piling and the large concrete wall running up to the bridge formed a natural altar shape. And that wall had been covered with grafitti, swirls of red, green, blue, violet, and shapes, the names of rock groups, obscenities and the words *Love* and *Peace* and an exaggerated drawing of a naked woman and a man, facing not each other but outward. Spilling out of the man's mouth were the words, *I Demand Head!* On one side of the makeshift altar were ten stacked cases of beer. A man with a neat black beard was pouring out charcoal into a pile on the other side. He had a small wire grill that stood over the pile on three legs, and a fancy set of barbecue tools. There were two tall stacks of plastic-covered packages of steak.

Maurice came up holding two open bottles of beer. He handed James one. "Let it snow," he said. "We have arrived."

"Should I put in some money or something? I mean, for the food, or what?"

"It's free," Maurice told him. "It's all donated. We got a butcher up in St. Albans who donates the meat, and a couple of guys with liquor stores kick in beer."

James took a drink, then asked, "Why? I mean —" he couldn't think of another way to put it "— why do they do that?"

"Advertising. Community spirit. What goes around comes around," Maurice said, running a gloved finger over his moustache. "It's an excellent group of guys," he added. "Look at that." He pointed to two blue recycling baskets off to the side of the altar, green bottles already being neatly stacked in one, discarded styrofoam in the other.

• • •

For the next hour or so the young men continued to scramble down the pilings, one or two at a time. They all wore sturdy boots, thick gloves — some puffy and camouflage-colored, like alligator hands — and steam shot from their mouths and nostrils. First their feet would appear, in the air by the bridge overhead, then they would jump to the first piling, still slick with snow and frozen tracks. They would either sit down or get on their hands and knees to negotiate the next few descents. People standing by the fire would yell to them, and they would yell back, clumsy in their parkas and camouflage snow suits, careful of their balance, eyes on their feet.

The dark figures moving over the huge frozen blocks of concrete fascinated James. There was a sense of timelessness and ritual, some druidic flavor to them there on the slabs. They continued to come until there were more than forty, standing above the river, talking about sports and job lay-offs and a local school tax referendum. And yet, seeing them sliding over those giant steps, he was also reminded of television shows and movies he had seen as a child, like *The Land of the Giants* and *The Incredible Shrinking Man*. The actors in those shows always ran through laughably fake sets of giant furniture. They held up pencils or needles that were supposed to be giant-sized, but were obviously hollow, made of balsa wood, ridiculous.

• • •

James was standing in a small knot of people eating steak sandwiches. They were all having some trouble managing paper plates and food and bottles of beer with gloves, and the temperature too low to sit. The young man in the neon ski jacket was there, and the near-clone of Maurice.

"President, Vice-President, and the First Lady, they're all out in this lifeboat, after Air Force One crashes in the ocean," began a man in a sleeveless jean vest over heavy white thermal layers. "They're all out there in the drink."

"Yeah, they're all out there," the man in the neon ski

jacket said.

"So all the sudden, there's a big huge wave — *big* huge mother wave — and the lifeboat capsizes. All three of 'em go overboard." He took a bite of his steak sandwich, chewed briefly, then asked through a mouthful, "Who gets saved?"

No one answered. The almost-Maurice suddenly dropped the remaining heel of his sandwich into the snow. He bent and retrieved it, blew ostentatiously on it. "Blow the germs off, and it's good as new," he said.

"The whole country gets saved," the man in the jean vest finished, laughing and then coughing at his own joke. He wiped the corners of his mouth carefully with his knuckle, trying to avoid getting steak sauce on his sleeves. "Goddam country."

Another man in the group spoke up. "Wouldn't help. Even if the whole Congress went overboard. It's the system. It's screwed up."

"It was a joke, dude."

The man shook his head, putting a clump of orange barbecue-style potato chips into his mouth. He chewed them, shaking his head as he did so. He cleared his mouth with a drink. "Well, then it isn't funny," he said finally.

"What do you do, man?" the guy in the neon jacket suddenly asked James.

Before he could answer, he heard Maurice's voice from somewhere behind him. "That's James, Ricky. Just moved to Vermont. First-timer."

Ricky nodded, looking over James' shoulder. "James," he began again, with a little more friendliness. "What are you doing for work? You working now?"

"Carpentry. I got in with this place over by the airport makes book shelves, furniture." James took a drink, crumpled his paper plate against his thigh. "You know, authentic Vermont-design kind of crap. This place does all mail-order business."

"Where'd you move in from?" asked the guy in the jean vest.

"I was up in North Hero, but before that I was out on the West Coast. California."

Ricky looked interested. "Where in California? I got a brother who's living out by Berkeley, just below Berkeley. He's in San Jose. He's a computer freak."

James looked around for a garbage can. "Southern California, right south of Los Angeles."

There was a pause, and then he heard Maurice's voice drift lazily out from behind him again. "You know, Ricky, the place where they crucified those three cops for roughing up Rodney King."

It was as though a circuit had been closed. Everyone in earshot began to talk more animatedly, more heatedly. It began to circulate as a common topic, displacing the sports talk and the complaining about the deteriorating old North End of Burlington, the end of the days when you could walk by yourself at night.

"You're right they got crucified," Ricky said, spitting on the snow. "For beating on a fucking PCP-addict, who's legally drunk, and driving like a maniac."

"They told him like five times to stop," put in the Maurice-clone. James watched him say it and suddenly remembered where he had seen the look before: a music video, a year or two ago, by a white rap singer who'd faded in and out of popularity. "They were yelling at him over the loudspeaker. Asshole kept running away."

"What kills me is, they needed a home *video* to tell that he got his ass beat. I'll tell you what. You fucking don't stop when they tell you to stop, and you try and pull your big-ass black shit on ten or fifteen cops, and I'll tell you what. You got your ass beat."

"Right," the guy with the jean vest said, "screw the video. Your ass is grass."

"You're right. They swarmed his Negro ass. I don't care how big you are."

"They use that swarm technique. Those cops train together, man. That's it."

"I'm black, I'm proud, I'm screaming out loud," some- one from another group called over, laughing. "I'm black, I'm proud, I'm screaming out loud."

They were all leaning in around him, putting their remarks to him because he had lived there, he was the touchstone. James' mind went blank for a minute, listening to it gain force. On the edge of the crowd, someone was pantomiming the beating, pretending to bring a nightstick into the face of the man next to him. James just looked at them, at their strange sudden zealousness. He continued to crush the paper plate smaller in his hand, until it looked like a small, deformed snowball.

"Hey," he heard Maurice say loudly, after a moment, "give James some fucking air over there. You're brutalizing the guy. He's not resisting arrest."

• • •

It broke up about a half an hour before dusk. Maurice and James walked back through the woods, by the cemetery, got out onto the highway. James could barely feel his feet. The highway had been perfectly plowed and sanded. The snow- banks looked like they had been cut cleanly with a huge knife.

"We know snow removal up here," Maurice commented.

Maurice talked on and off the entire walk back to Franklin Street, about what an excellent day it had been, for a winter day, and what a good turnout. "Sometimes in the summer we don't even get that many," he pointed out. "It's an excellent organization," he said again. "Everybody's organizing these days, except for people like us. What kind of thing is there for you if you're young and you're a guy? All of our social clubs bottomed out. They all went by the wayside with the Elks. Who wants to hang out in a place like that, except old men? It's important to have some strong organizations, that can work for you." He kicked a piece of ice, which skittered crazily on the polished, packed snow. "To preserve things. And we have other stuff going on. Word of mouth stuff. Not just parties, but more serious stuff. Not everybody gets the word, if you know what I mean."

It was nearly dark when they reached James' house. He was exhausted. He had a feeling of lassitude, and loneliness, and told himself that he was worn out from the walking and the beer.

In a way that sometimes happened, James found himself half-pretending that his ex-wife was not in Hartford but waiting inside, watching for him through the curtain of the upstairs window. He examined himself and Maurice through her eyes. He looked for her in the window. The pretense depended on a dim, alternate history, in which they had never finalized the divorce, in which she had not been able, finally, to maintain the measured telephone voice that had worked them through each of the various stages.

Maurice stopped him as he was about to go up the snow-dusted front walk. He put a hand on James' sleeve.

"So James, let me ask you something, just between you and me." He took off his gloves and blew on his fingers, rubbed them together. "What's your real take on King and those three cops? You never said."

James felt emptied out. He remembered the first time he had seen the King video, in a California bar with two people from work, people he hardly knew. It was just after the divorce. They had all three of them been shaken by the endlessness of the beating. James drove the three of them home, watching for police cruisers, irrationally terrified that he would be pulled over for drinking and driving, made to get out of the car.

"What's your take?" Maurice asked again.

James coughed into his fist. He wanted to say what he thought, but he couldn't. He hated himself for standing mutely, steam passing out of his half-open mouth, but he could tell that to say it was to fall immediately back into the silent fringes, where no one knew him, or invited him. He couldn't say what Maurice wanted to hear, but he couldn't bring himself to say what he didn't want to hear, either.

"Well," Maurice said after waiting, nodding to himself, looking up at the moon. It was nearly unshadowed, round, clear and bright. He seated his calfskin gloves, pulling them down daintily with his thumb and the tip of his forefinger, like a gentleman. "Then good night sweet prince."

Alison

Alison was picking up a small stack of four ones — four ones she'd been monitoring for twenty or thirty minutes, trying to tell if they were tip or bar-change — when it began again, the need. Four clean dollars in a pile didn't come along all that often, and as soon as it was clearly left, clearly *waiting*, she took it with her left hand while looking the other way. She was only looking the other way out of some vestigial modesty. But the hand with the money accidentally brushed a hurricane glass, long and fluted, and it shattered quietly into the ice bin. It was a piña colada. There was no color, even, to telegraph the fragments. It all gleamed up at her, some of it harmless and some of it, maybe, not.

Alison picked the big pieces out, all she could see, and when she'd done so, she brushed damp hair off her forehead with the back of her hand and looked around. Nobody'd seen. It was a Tuesday, and the few people in the bar were caught up in their own trite, individual addictions: sipping gin, shooting pool, darts, searching robotically, vainly, for available women in the nearly all-male crowd. Tuesday was almost always addicts only. Nobody'd seen. She glanced at the pool table toward Maurice, and he was there making friends, oblivious.

So she kept pouring drinks, something she'd never done before. The bin had to be emptied, wiped down, and refilled if you broke a glass in it. That was gospel. Now every time she filled a glass with ice and made a drink she felt like the psychopath in a Hitchcock film. People accepted the drinks from her hand. "Thanks a lot," they said.

"Alcohol's a poison anyway," she told one guy out of the

blue as she handed him a Chivas and Coke. "I should be giving away rusty nails for swizzle sticks. It's not like it really
makes it any more dangerous."

He looked her over. He didn't even bother to ask what
she meant. "I'll keep that in mind," he said. He looked
around mechanically. "What's your name," he asked.

"Watch your ice," Alison said, smiling, pointing down
into the amber liquid.

He took a sip, showing her his dimple. She knew what
he was going to say before he'd put it together himself.
"Okay, Watch-Your-Ice," the guy said, "whatever you say."

● ● ●

Finally, though, she couldn't keep going with it. It was too
random. There was an idiocy and a lunacy to it, and she
dumped the bin in the alley behind the Metronome, wiped
it down, and made the four trips with the ice bucket that it
took to re-fill it. She got back the five glasses she'd poured
with the old ice by offering the people fresh drinks.

But all of it touched off something particular inside of
her. It was a need to cause change. It was disgust with the
sameness, the smugness of the small city, which, because it
was the largest and the most liberal in the empty state, was
unaware of its own bloodlessness and mediocrity. It was an
urge to smear the air with what was wrong. She was gra-
cious enough, in some part of her, to see these feelings —
when they cropped up every six months or so — as an unex-
pected inheritance from her mother, but in Alison's mind
they were also precisely what set the two of them apart, in
addition to life and death. Alison *did*; her mother had never
done.

By the time she left the Metronome, at a little after

three a.m., the need had swelled to include everything she saw walking home. Classical music was still playing from overhead speakers; it drizzled down on the heads of the few panhandlers standing and stamping under the neat awnings of gift shops. She found herself wondering where the main stereo system for the mall was located, how to get at it.

On Pearl Street, she passed Pearl's, the city's only true gay bar. It was a standard, two-story white frame building, with shuttered windows, discreet. Two women came out the door, turned and came up the street toward her. They were hand in hand, maybe twenty or twenty-one, heads cropped very close and with blazers and hiking boots. Alison could hardly believe them, the daring anomaly of them in the quiet little street.

"Right on," she said to them as they passed her.

They turned and one of them smiled quizzically, put a hand on top of her dyed-black hair. "What'd you say?"

"You guys are excellent," Alison said, walking backward in the dark.

"We know," the other woman said.

"But thanks," the first one put in before turning around.

• • •

Burlington was the dream of the white village. White people moved through the streets in small, pale groupings, families and day-tourists from Montreal and knots of children who knew one another from school. Everyone was clean. Everyone seemed to wear glasses and neat khaki pants, pressed skirts. To Alison, everyone looked smart and rich.

And on the upper end of Church Street — the brick-and-cobblestone pedestrian mall, politely closed to traffic

— stood a white church with a steeple that rose up into the blue sky like the hugest, boldest, most sterile middle finger Alison had ever seen. Some days as she was walking up the mall she would just look around her at the people shopping and the young kids clumsily smoking cigarettes on the laquered green benches. She would just marvel that they couldn't see it. It was a fuck-you that was too big and too fundamental for them to see. All the outlying villages, Hinesburg, Jericho, Richmond, had their steeples, but not like Burlington. When the stereo-enhanced bells went off at noon, Alison could hear them from her apartment window, down Pearl Street, almost to the lake. Eight tones, four descending, then the same four ascending in reverse. Every day, every day. She heard it in words as well as tones: Our — Town — *Shut* — Up; Shut — Up — *Our* — Town.

It was the dream of the white village, and it had been her mother's dream, too. Before her death, Alison's mother had been a fairly widely published poet (or "poetess," as she'd insisted her flyers read). She was known for most of her adult life as Vermont's second-most-famous female poet, and the fact that she was being lovingly and firmly shoved into line behind all of the male poets and a woman who wrote nothing but tepid nature verse seemed never to bother her at all. She had a small gazebo out behind their old house where she sat for hours in the summer, writing. By the time she died she had the face that some middle-aged white women get: pasty, doughlike, as though life had taken the tanned, sharp young woman in Alison's baby photos and methodically unbaked her.

One Sunday morning when Alison was six, ten years before the death, her mother had woken her gently. The room was cold and dark. It was four-fifteen in the morning. "Get up," her mother whispered. "Quick. Don't be scared, little baby. It's all right. But get up. Don't think. We have to go catch someone."

Alison pulled on clothes, complaining in a hushed, whiny voice. Her mother stood at the doorway, in the square of light, clicking her tongue. "He's only there for another half hour," she said in a lilting voice, "then he flies off home. You're gonna miss him because you're such a slow shoe-tier."

They parked the car beside the VFW building and walked a block to Church Street. Her mother looked up and down the length of it. "Nope. We missed that part. He's down by Main Street by now." She had Alison's hand and she swung her arm, as though they were on a holiday. "You are just gonna love him. He's just beautiful," she whispered.

They walked down the mall under the streetlights, between the rows of expensive shops, which even at six had seemed to Alison designed for people other than her and her mother. As they passed Bank Street, her mother glanced left, then pulled up short. She caught her breath and swung Alison around. "There he is," she said softly. Alison looked, saw nothing until her mother pointed to it. It was a street-sweeper, a large green tank of metal with twin iron forks extending from the cab like tusks. Circular brushes were moving underneath it, noisily, just barely visible. A small side light threw a careful spot of illumination at the point where the revolving brush met the gutter.

Alison just stood there in the dark. Her mother walked her closer. "Look at that man," she said over the swishing noise and the diesel exhaust.

Alison looked at the driver, a large man with white hair and glasses. He was leaned way over, watching the spot of light, driving by watching his brush and the curb. He might have been ice fishing, sitting blandly over a hole in the ice, for all the enthusiasm she could see. Occasionally he'd lift his head, check his bearings, and then lean over the lighted gutter again. Once she saw him spit on the street. Gum wrappers and cigarette butts blurred with the coming of the brush, vanished.

Alison's mother looked at Alison. She shook her head, almost at a loss for words. "Every time I see him I can't believe him," she said.

A poem came out of it, one drafted that very morning when they got back to the house. All of Alison's complaints her mother turned into apostrophe, to the early hour, to the humble machine, to the driver with the bleak, diamond-cutter's eye. "The Clean Streets" appeared in a prominent national journal under both their names. It was the first of five or six things for which Alison would never forgive her.

• • •

There was a time when dating activists was her activism. It was when she didn't know how to make things happen. So she found Maurice, who was always organizing, drawing people into something shapeless and magnetic and impen-etrable that he would hint about even as he held it always just out of her reach. But she'd gotten tired of the allusions to gatherings she wasn't invited to attend. Maurice was a two-month one-night stand.

But John, Alison's first real boyfriend, was a teamleader for Greenpeace, and when she was nineteen she'd joined the organization herself, started helping him plan actions. He was twenty-seven. He *looked* like an activist: muscular, tanned from work, black hair, black eyes, outrage and anger that would rise up suddenly like a shot of steam.

The first action they executed together was the last. It

was a smokestack on the south side of Burlington, an older chemical factory — Greenpeace had samples from the ground and the air, all showing lead and iodine concentrations way above legal limits. But it was stuck in the courts; the stack kept pouring smoke. So John had proposed the idea, and the leadership in Boston went with it.

They scaled it, she and John, in the middle of the night.

It was laughably easy at first: over the plant's security fence, across the unlit work yard, up the wide old iron ladder bolted to the stack. She could remember John looking back at her as they climbed, making kissing motions with his lips. In his black t-shirt and shorts he was almost invisible. She slapped at his leg with her rust-smudged hand.

There was only one frill, as John called it, one real obstacle. About three-quarters of the way up they came to an iron gangway, the swinging hatch padlocked. Alison would have used bolt-cutters, but Greenpeace was strict about property damage. Instead, they used climbing ropes, climbing out from the stack and then up, out, over, and onto the gangway. Hanging from her hands and two safety ropes, two hundred feet up, her small biceps absolutely taut, Alison felt a surge of energy like nothing she'd ever known. It was July, and the air was so clear the stars were bursting out. John grabbed the back of her olive-green sweatshirt and helped haul her up. She felt the cool night air sweep onto her bare back and under her arms.

As he helped her get her footing on the gangway, John rubbed the small of her back, while she wrestled the sweatshirt back down and wiped the long dark hair from her eyes.

"Nice back," he said, grinning down at her. The whites of his eyes and the stars continued to leap out at her. The feeling of accomplishment, action, deed ran through her like laughter.

"That was so —" Alison held onto the cold railing — "just so *fucking* cool," she said, jumping up to half-hug him. "Oh my god. John, this feeling is like — I don't even know." She swung around to look at the Burlington lights, neat and peaceful. "It's like taking a huge giant-step over everybody's head who says you can't do it. You just do it. You just climb up the ladder and say screw it. You're up here and they're just looking up at you. You just get it done."

"You like it, then." John smiled expansively. His teeth glowed white in the gloom of his black hair and tanned face. He rubbed the small of her back again briskly. "You like this kind of thing, a little bit."

"Yeah. I like it."

"I can see that."

Alison pointed below them to the security shack. One window was lit up, but it seemed empty. "Can they see us from there? I mean is there enough light up here?"

"No. No one can see us, Al. We are invisible. We work in dark and silence. We could moon the city of Burlington and nobody'd see until dawn." John spit over the edge of the railing, and the spit disappeared, made no sound. "Let's hang the banner first," he said, trying to sound competent — using what Alison called his teamleader's voice — but excitement and breathlessness bleeding through.

"Check," Alison said, giving him a quick look.

They unpacked his backpack, taking out the oversized roll of painted white canvas. It was almost as big and thick as a tire. She wondered briefly if she could have climbed the gangway or the security fence with it strapped to her.

"It looks like a huge roll of toilet paper," she whispered. "Economy size."

"Just make sure you don't drop your end."

"Check," she said, with a little more open sarcasm this time. Holding the metal bracket, they began to feed the banner down behind the gangway so that it inched down the brick face of the stack. A brass weight at the end pulled harder the further it moved away from them. When it was unrolled and hooked to the gangway, Alison bent over to look, but she could read only a swirl of individual letters in the dim light. Only the Greenpeace photographer, who would be on the street at first light, would catch the entire message for the papers: *This Stack Releases Unsafe Lead and Iodine — Call 911.*

They had handcuffs to secure themselves to the structure — to keep the stack shut down for as long as it took the police to cut them off — but John said they might as well wait an hour or so. "Sometimes I wait till the cops get like five feet away and then cuff myself," John bragged softly, putting his arm around her. "They go ballistic."

They were both kicking their feet over the edge of the gangway. John looked around, chuckling to himself. "Be wild to have sex up here," he remarked.

"Yeah," Alison said automatically. She was looking at the tracery of lights across Lake Champlain. It was New York State, the dark land mass across the water.

He chuckled again softly, kissed the ridge of her ear. "You like that idea, don't you?" he whispered.

"What idea?"

"Doing it up here. You like that idea, you little animal. Don't you."

"Who said?" She felt his hand come up the back of her sweatshirt, cool and rough against her skin. He pulled idly on her bra strap.

"You said."

"I said it'd be wild. I was agreeing. I didn't say I felt like going for it right *now*."

John pulled a set of handcuffs from the backpack and dangled them in front of her. "That's not what *I* heard," he sang in a teasing voice.

Alison patted his cheek. "Well maybe you weren't listening right," she turned back toward the lake, then added, "teamleader."

"Tell me that climb didn't get your blood going."

"No, it definitely did. It was the best thing I remember. I swear."

"Tell me it doesn't make you want to — I don't know — celebrate, and touch and grab each other," he touched her lower lip with his finger, "and roll around and —"

She laughed. "Okay, then, it doesn't."

John smiled, hung his head and shook it slowly. "Little Miss Repression. You just committed a political crime, babe. Get with it. Sex in public is the least of your worries, even if we got caught. Which we wouldn't. And besides *flagrante delicto* looks excellent on your resume."

"John," Alison began to wrap her hair into a ponytail with an elastic, "just try another channel. Just look at the pretty lights."

He shrugged his large, pointed shoulders. "Suit yourself." He cracked his knuckles, paused to inspect a small scrape on one of them. "We'll be in the slammer tomorrow. Maybe until Tuesday. State-enforced celibacy. Gather ye rosebuds is the way I look at it."

"Don't sell yourself short, John. Maybe you'll get lucky in the slammer."

Even as it came out of her mouth, something told her not to say it, some vague premonitory sense. John looked like he'd been struck in the face. He breathed through flared nostrils for a second. Then he locked one end of the cuffs against the gangway, and Alison flinched at the sound of it ratcheting shut. John let the other cuff dangle like a chrome crab. He laced his fingers together. "Excuse me," he said carefully, "but there is no reason to be a bitch. Is there? Is there a reason to be a bitch? Just because you hauled yourself up one little local smokestack. No need. Just say you're not interested."

"John —"

"Say you're not interested. That's all you have to say. Say it."

She turned toward him, in almost perfect disbelief. Her mouth was hanging open. "Just *what* the hell is up *your* butt tonight?"

He looked at her like she was a mental patient, just staring at her. His face was red now beneath his curly black hair, and suddenly — almost as though her mind were a police sketch artist, distending, augmenting, comparing — she saw that his cheeks and his neck would turn fleshy and his activism would turn conservative finally. His teamleading then would yield nothing different than her father's, a sales manager in Phoenix with a younger wife who cooked and sold real estate and wrote no poetry.

"*My* butt?" John said finally, as ominously as he could manage.

It wound up with him handcuffing her wrist to the gangway, and then stepping back quickly to avoid the whistling swings of her fist. But after five minutes or so of trying to force her to apologize, he unlocked her anyway, obviously scared of the implications. By then he was apologizing and threatening at the same time, half-pleading with her. By then Alison was crying from frustration but still enough in control to avoid screaming at him.

She unhooked the banner before he could stop her, and

the brass frame hit the ground with a distant clank. The hundred-and-twenty foot roll of white canvas curled after it like toilet paper. It was "Clean Streets" all over again, she had realized wildly while she was swinging at him, and she was absolutely goddamned if that message would appear in the *Burlington Free Press* under both their names.

It was sometime during the long climb back to earth, though — the climb without John's help, the tougher climb during which his spit hit her twice square on the crown of her head — when she realized that not only did you have to write your own messages, but that writing messages wasn't enough. You had to make things happen: your own perception, your own plan, message, your own event. And six months later she'd met Cheryl-lin, who'd almost immediately become her best friend, and whose sexuality and blood and culture were all subject to change, effective weapons in their own right.

• • •

The lower half of Pearl Street, from the Church Street pedestrian mall to Battery Park overlooking Lake Champlain, was the bum knee for the entire town. It was what kept the image the town had of itself from biking or jogging into reality. Lower Pearl had the Cosmetology College, the Social Security Office, the tiny, dogged Community College, the Employment Assistance Program, the gay bar, and finally a cluster of halfway houses — made-over Victorians with bad paint and porches — poised right across the street from the lake. The young women on lower Pearl had different hair than women anywhere else in town. People were always waiting patiently for the state offices to open, people in motorized carts and full-body braces, smoking, frighteningly ambulatory, metal frames running everywhere, or people just stood, momentarily stunned and nibbling their cigarettes, touching their own faces.

Cheryl-lin lived in the last halfway house, in the attic. She had four windows, all with different spectacular views of the lake. It was an apartment she'd got by the rawest patience, waiting a year and a half in seedier rooms for more transient tenants to cycle through the house. Because she cooked, the church group that ran the house let her stay even after she'd been on the wagon a year. Sometimes in the summer or spring the two of them would sit in the attic at sunset and talk, the windows opened out all around them like a crisp color brochure. Alison would complain about men and the whitebread texture of the town, Cheryl-lin talked about men or women, depending. They would eat Karmelcorn and let the mountains knock them out.

Alison knocked at the front door of the halfway house, and after a long minute a man with a green knit cap and a darker green peacoat opened the door. He wore the peacoat sometimes even in the summer. He recognized her and waved her inside. He didn't say anything, just moved away from the door.

"Hey, Leon," Alison said, closing the door behind her. The lobby of the house smelled of garlic and ginger. Cheryl-lin cooked most of the time. "How goes it?"

Leon rubbed his nose with his fingers, then spread his hands. His eyes were saggy and red beneath fierce black brows. Alison always had the impression that he was about to focus, suddenly take charge, but it never happened.

"Cheryl-lin home?"

"Yup." Leon walked away from her toward the communal dining room, his steps slow and deliberate. He looked back. "She's up there," he said helpfully. He had the news-paper spread out on the large table, completely covering it. He walked to the table and began examining different parts of it, as though it were a table-sized jigsaw puzzle.

There were two cramped spiral flights of stairs to the attic, and Alison took them very fast, pushing off the wall with her right hand as she spun upward. When she got to the attic door, she knocked but didn't wait for the answer. The last miniature flight of stairs brought her up into the center of Cheryl-lin's room. Cheryl-lin was sitting at a van-ity table next to the open bathroom door. She had on a blue silk prize fighter-style dressing gown that Alison had given her for Christmas one year. "I just have to do my blood," she said.

"You were supposed to be ready."

"I'm ready except for checking my blood."

"You're not even dressed."

"Can't dress until the blood's done." She was bent over a small white plastic box. She looked up, deadpan. "Ipso facto," she smiled slowly, "is what they call it, I guess. I'm sure you understand." While Alison watched, she pricked her finger with a tool from the box, squeezed a drop of blood out onto a test strip. A digital reading came up on the face of the box. Cheryl-lin muttered to herself while she closed up the box and threw away the disposable strip.

"What's the deal?" Alison asked.

"My sugars are, like, off the scale." Cheryl-lin looked straight at her for the first time. Her eyes were dramatically wide, and she ran her hands through her black shocks of bangs. Her face Alison had come slowly to think of as the most beautiful face she had ever seen — clear brown skin and almost lidless eyes, the epicanthic folds of the eyes small, ingenuous, wondrously affecting. "Completely off the map. I mean, something is screwy. I must be incredibly strung-out about something." Cheryl-lin took down her insulin kit from the shelf above the vanity. She broke open a new syringe. "I think it's my father's birthday, is the thing. It's like" — she was shaking her head slowly, looking for just the right phrase — "*coming up.* You know, you get that feeling. That the feeling's coming. That you're not a good daughter, you're not a good human *being*," she filled the syringe and said out of the side of her mouth to Alison, "you can avert your eyes now."

Alison watched, as she always did. The needle went into Cheryl-lin's thigh, quickly, and in another second was in a large green corked wine bottle on the shelf that held twenty or twenty-five used syringes already.

Cheryl-lin flicked a finger over the spot on her thigh, erasing it from the conversation. "Just that ancient guilt. Like you're horrible. It eats up my sugars." She got up and went to her small walk-in closet, disappeared. There was the sound of hangers sliding.

Alison sat down in a small rocker with an embroidered seat, facing the lake. It was her seat. She folded her hands in her lap and looked out on the distant white surface for a certain black dot. When she found it, and concentrated on it, the insurgency and discontent came back up inside her like something bodily, something in her muscles.

"So are you going to get him anything?" she asked Cheryl-lin.

"Not even." There was a sound like shoes being kicked off against a wall. "I don't think there would be any way to do it minus the sarcasm. I really don't."

Cheryl-lin's father was an analyst for IBM. After her mother had moved back to Taiwan, Cheryl-lin and her father had had horrible, quiet fights, stamina fights, at the dining room table of her father's house. And one night when she was sixteen her father had simply proposed that she move out. Their lifestyles, he summed it up, clearly would never again dovetail. She had changed too much, her name least among the changes. He supported her with bi-monthly checks for a year and a half, until her eighteenth birthday. Then nothing. In the year following Cheryl-lin had spent time in three or four substance-abuse programs. A lot of the time in the low-roofed apartment at dusk was spent marveling about their mirrored histories — mother-less at sixteen, fathers turned legal fictions at eighteen — and their statistical chances for growing up whole.

"That fucking car is still out there," Alison said, rocking slowly.

"You're so unforgiving about that car. It's a promotion. It's nothing personal."

"I take it personally." Alison focused her eyes on the lit-tle black spot, sitting in the middle of the vast, snow-cov-ered lake. It reminded her of ants in sugar; it gave her that same sudden queasiness. "Ever since last night I've been getting that feeling again. Really bad. It's bugging me now."

"What feeling?"

"Like something has to be done. By me. These people in this town, they're all so —" Alison broke off. She gave a very, very quiet scream. "So absolutely pat."

Cheryl-lin stuck her head out of the closet. "Just stay away from my syringes. I'm serious, Alison. You do your thing, but use your own stuff. Use your own blood."

"You know, you remind me of that about once a week. I don't know if you knew that, but that's what it is. About once a week."

"I'm serious. Don't touch my needles." Cheryl-lin came out of the closet, and stopped in front of the rocker. She was wearing black velvet pants, a pale green turtleneck covered with a fawn-colored vest. The clothes hung perfectly on her.

"Quite beautiful," Alison said.

Cheryl-lin turned sideways, accentuating her height, slenderness, shot a hand through her bangs. "You think it's all right?"

"You don't need my advice." Alison got up from the rocker. "What's the big deal anyway? Is there someone you're trying to impress or something?"

Cheryl-lin ignored the question as she picked up her coat and gloves, then led the way down the miniature steps to the second-floor door. "You know," she said, fishing for her keys, "you get so uptight about this town, people in this town, but just look out that window. How many places do they have halfway houses with a view of the water?" She pulled the door shut behind them and locked it. "Where else can an alcoholic rehabilitate with a view of the water? Don't say Pittsburgh, or L.A. or New York because it's not happening there. Not by a long shot."

"Just wait."

"For what?"

They made their way down the cramped spiral stairs. "For this corner to get sold out from under you," Alison said. Cheryl-lin laughed. "You think I'm kidding. There's already two or three of these old corner houses up for sale. You watch. Some developer with a heart will come along and plan a big set of newer buildings and then — surprise — it'll turn out he doesn't have a heart at all, and all these old co-ops are going condo and post-modern."

They came out into the dining room, where Leon was still propped up over the paper. He looked up at them with mild interest.

Cheryl-lin took a black beret off the coat rack and seated it on her head. "Leon, tell Anne she's supposed to cut the vegetables for tonight. Don't cut them for her again, please. She's not doing her share."

Leon looked back down at the paper. He rubbed the back of his neck. "I'm not eating tonight," he said.

"But tell her that anyway for me, okay? She gets back at four, tell her I want to start cooking at six and I'd appreciate it if she had the vegetables cut."

Leon nodded, almost to himself. He would cut the vegetables for Anne, a fifty-year-old chronic alcoholic, in any event, because Anne would ask him to cut them. Leon was the only person who'd been in the house as long as Cheryl-lin. In those five years, Cheryl-lin had lived with two women and one man, and Leon — in spite of once walking in on Cheryl-lin and her first live-in girlfriend making out in the tv room late one night, the television gone to snow — Leon had never batted an eye. He hadn't wanted the attic apartment, even though he'd had seniority over Cheryl-lin when she moved into it. He had never said why, except to point out that it wasn't what he was used to.

"Okay, Leon?" Cheryl-lin asked finally. "Will you communicate that to her?"

Leon looked up, eyes red. "Of course," he said, and went back to his reading.

• • •

Sometimes Alison would remember driving with her mother, to and from poetry readings in Barre or Montpelier, once in Windsor. The square, red Nova would sluice through the hills, like a single drop of blood accelerating through large expanses of white snow-cover. Inside the car her mother would be talking, always talking. Some nights she told Alison how to make poems. Once she put her hand against the frosted windshield and made a hand-print.

"Now watch what happens when I take my hand away," she told Alison. The print scaled over slowly, molecule-thin planes of ice appearing, imbricating. "Now you make a poem out of that for me." She unsnapped her purse, brought out a cigarette with her free hand, lit it with the car lighter. "You tell me how you see it, what happens." A silence rose up with the smoke. "Think about what that makes you feel like. Say to yourself that makes me feel like what."

When Alison thought about it now, sometimes she — the older Alison — would drop down on the cold wind-shield and look in through the palm print. She would clutch the racing drop of blood and look in at the two of them sitting in the silence, immobile, in the front seat. *You,* she would say to her mother, *shut up. Stop the word games. It's play. It does nothing for anyone in the world of physical consequence. It's Scrabble made sacred.* She would watch her mother drag politely from the cigarette, leave a ring of coral lipstick. *And slow down. It's not a race.*

You, she would say to the small Alison who sat in silence, the smell of the bottled smoke already mixing with her own sour emptiness of poetry, *wake up. Wake your little ass up.*

• • •

Her first scenario was the most dramatically successful. It was eight months after she'd met Cheryl-lin. The two of them used to go walking down by the water, along a patch-work bike path that took them past defunct oil storage tanks and rusted warehouses. And at two or three places the water was oily, stagnant, as though there were some hidden spring of petroleum under one of the old tanks. Mayoral candidates would mention the problem, then leave it for a second term.

It had come to her like an inspiration, whole and perfect. She took a handful of Cheryl-lin's syringes from the green corked bottle, while Cheryl-lin was showering; she went to the University hospital and managed to steal a pair of surgical gloves from a wastepaper basket; she put all of it with a pad of used cotton balls into a plain white institutional garbage bag, and at three in the morning in early May she planted it at the shoreline beyond the bike path. The bag she tore open and scattered along with the contents. She poured mud and oily water over it all like a baptism.

The next morning she called the *Burlington Free Press*. She got a reporter from the Living section.

"Hi," she began, "I was jogging this morning down by the bike path and there's a whole bunch of washed-up crap down there, medical waste and stuff. I thought you might want to take a look at it."

"Who's this," the reporter asked.

"I can't say, I called in sick to work. I wasn't supposed to be out jogging. But there's needles down there and everything."

"What?" the reporter asked.

Finally, she just hung up on him, her heart kicking in her chest. But two days later the Vermont section ran a fairly large story about the waste, and the editorial page ran letters the day following. And with no resistance from anyone or anything, money was freed up at the federal or the state or the city level, and yellow cranes and backhoes were suddenly crawling like huge, good-hearted dinosaurs over the shoreline. Alison and Cheryl-lin would watch them when they took their walks. Massive old tanks were cut apart with oxy-cetylene torches and folded up like tents.

Cheryl-lin almost stopped speaking with her when Alison finally got so full of the sense of accomplishment that she confessed. It was in the attic apartment, and the sun had fallen just enough so that when Cheryl-lin whirled on her, Alison could see only the shadow of an expression, panic, anger.

"They had my blood in them!" Cheryl-lin yelled at her. "What if — what if they analyze it or something? They can do that, they can type it and stuff. It might as well have my goddam driver's license in it."

"Cheryl-lin," Alison said, pulling back a little from the heat of that expression, "it's Burlington. They're not going to analyze it. It's burnt by now."

"But what if they *had*."

"They didn't."

Cheryl-lin sat back in her chair, pulled herself all the way into it, including her long legs. She was silent for a moment, angrily silent. "What if some little kid or some-thing stubbed his toe on one of those things, or, stuck one in his eye —"

Alison made the mistake of laughing, more from the tension than anything else. "Nobody was gonna stick one of those in their —"

"You know, Alison," Cheryl-lin was out of the chair and in front of her face again, kneeling up in front of her, "when you're a diabetic you learn a lot of things, like that you're going to have to bleed on a plastic strip three times a day every day of your life, and you might go blind anyway. And that you can wake up in the hospital with guys just standing over you, talking about sports. But the first thing is that your needles have to go where they belong. They always go where they belong. If you're going to be my friend you better fucking learn it too." She looked at Alison, eyes wide. "Now say you're sorry."

"I'm sorry," Alison said. She kissed Cheryl-lin's flat brown cheek. "I really am sorry."

Cheryl-lin started to cry suddenly, inexplicably, and they sat in the half-dark for a few minutes while she did. Alison hugged her for a while, then stopped, sat back again on her heels. Finally, Cheryl-lin cleared her throat. "Thanks anyway, though," she said thickly. She reached over for a tissue from her bookshelf, blew her nose.

Alison pushed some of her bangs away from her face. "For what?"

"For the very clean water."

"You're welcome," Alison said.

• • •

The day was clear and sunny, and warmer than it had been for over a week. People were everywhere, sitting in snow-sculpture chairs and standing with cups of expensive coffee, students and tourists. In the winter the locals seemed to fade away. You could find them, like den animals, crowded in two or three of the town bars, but it was only in the summer that the part-timers didn't absolutely rule the streets.

"Watch this," Alison said, as they came around the corner onto Church Street. A man was coming toward them, walking beside his wife, who was pushing a small, plush stroller. Alison walked into the man's path, looking off to one side, and would have bumped him but the man stepped briskly to one side. "Sorry about that," he said pleasantly.

"No problem," Alison answered. When the couple had rolled the stroller by, she turned to Cheryl-lin. "You see that?" she asked.

"What, did I see you almost run into that man and his baby? Yes. I saw that."

"No," Alison said, smiling faintly, "I'm talking about the absolute lack of honesty."

"Missed it, babe," Cheryl-lin said. They passed a store that sold Third World clothing, and Cheryl-lin stopped to run her hand along a chrome rack of Guatemalan dresses standing shining on the ice. "I'm listening," she said over her shoulder, hands combing efficiently through the prints.

"It was obviously my fault, right? He was walking along, and I got in his way. Simple. And he knows it. But he makes a big point out of moving, just about *skipping* out of the way, and excuses himself for being in *my* way. When he knows all along."

Cheryl-lin pulled out a dark green dress, laid it along her body, craning her head back to look at it. "Just exactly how ethnic does this look on me?" she asked.

"Cheryl-lin, come on," Alison said, taking the dress and rehanging it, "you're already late. She's got your charge card number, you know. There's probably a penalty charge for every half hour you keep them waiting."

They started back down the mall, avoiding small children running with their hats thrown off and their coats hanging open. Cheryl-lin took Alison's arm. "So, sorry, you were telling me what a nerve that guy had to avoid running into you."

Alison saw small glances at them, then polite eye-shifts, and it pleased her somehow, to be in possession of the answers to questions that people passing were asking themselves. "I'm just saying that the guy was working with this complete image of himself. He has this image going that can't be compromised, this kind of Bing Crosby *Holiday Inn* Vermonter —"

"Say it loud, girl!"

" — this kind of maple-sugar-sweet rich small-town white folk, just getting high on life in the great white north, cross-country skiing, and on his own goodness and charity and shit. To grandmother's house we go, all day, every day." She looked over and saw that Cheryl-lin had rolled her eyes up, but she kept on, working it out for herself as she went. "Read my mom's poetry some time. There's a little shelf in the library. Just read one. Believe me you'll see what I mean. Bunch of smiling pod-people, Yankee pod-people." She bit her thumb nail, thinking. "And all the real feelings — all the territorialism and the meanness and the prejudice, all that gets secretly stored. But it's in there somewhere, all that rot, working underneath —"

Cheryl-lin waved briefly to a young red-headed woman coming out of the bagel store. The woman smiled and waved back, then held her hands up above her head, smiling brilliantly and looking at the sun. "I know," Cheryl-lin yelled over, "isn't it amazing? It's supposed to be like this all week!"

" — and you think it's funny," Alison went on, "but you're the one who suffers most from this kind of shit. Because everybody's operating with you through about three or four layers of fear and mistrust, and then filtering it all back through the maple syrup."

"I happen to like maple syrup," Cheryl-lin said firmly.

Alison steered her left suddenly, around the corner to PhotoShoot Glamour Photography. "I like maple syrup too. As a topping, as a treat. Not to swim in."

"That's a very comforting philosophy you have," Cheryl-lin said as she went through the door. "This pod-people deal. You must rest well at night."

Inside, PhotoShoot looked very much like a beauty salon — with a girl of about fifteen being made-over in one of the three swivel chairs — but with much bigger mirrors and a rack of glitzy costumes beside a closed door marked *Studio*. The air smelled of perfume, cosmetics, nylon. Blown-up photographs hung on every wall. A woman with tight jeans and styled white hair met them at the door. She glanced at the clock. "You must be Cheryl-lin," she said, holding out her thin hand.

"How could you tell?" Alison asked as Cheryl-lin shook hands. The woman laughed, along with the young woman styling the high-school girl's hair.

"Don't mind her," Cheryl-lin told the woman confidentially. "She's my press flack. I pay her to be a little bit rude and obnoxious."

"I didn't notice at all," the woman said, still smiling.

"Where's Susan?" Cheryl-lin asked, turning around.

"Susan actually is sick today —"

Cheryl-lin's face fell. "You're kidding."

"— yeah, she called in sick." The woman shook her head sympathetically. "I know, she told me that you set it up with her. But she called this morning and told me everything you wanted, so I'm sure I can get you some shots you'll be happy with."

"Well, as far as what I wanted, I *wanted* Susan," Cheryl-lin said.

"I know, I know," the woman said, face still pained. "But — I hope I don't sound conceited here — but I am the owner, and I taught Susan everything she knows about a camera." She pointed to a swivel chair and a mirror ringed with frosted bulbs. "Why don't you have a seat and we'll just do some touch-up makeup on you."

Cheryl-lin sat down and looked at herself in the mirror. Alison took a seat by the window. Cheryl-lin caught her eye in the mirror, then made a face.

"Now, tell me again what kind of photo this is," the woman said as she picked up a fat cosmetics brush.

"A passport photo."

The woman looked quizzically at Alison, as though to make sure.

"She's going to Taiwan," Alison explained.

• • •

Cheryl-lin had four shots taken in a green silk gown, with her straight black hair held back in a shining costume tiara; four shots in an elaborate white boa, shoulders bare; four in a man's black silk cutaway, her hair hanging straight, hands clasped confidently over her knee; two in a leather bomber jacket; and one dressed as she came, velvet pants and fawn vest, smiling with perfect candor at the camera.

After about four or five minutes, Alison could see that the disappointment had worn off. Cheryl-lin was lost in the modeling. The owner would adjust the camera, ask her to move her arm or her face, and Cheryl-lin would do so, an odd, radiant expression on her face. "I like that look," the woman would murmur from behind the camera. "This time try smirking, just a little. Like you know a joke, a secret joke."

"Secret joke," Cheryl-lin said softly, looking at the camera.

At one point, when Cheryl-lin was changing out of the tuxedo coat and scanning the racks, the woman asked Alison, "Why didn't she go to the booth at Woolworth's for a passport photo? I mean I'm not saying she *should* have, but most people do."

Alison shrugged. "One, because she's who she is. You'd have to know her. But according to her she says she refuses to go meekly into the Far East. She wants them to know at the border what they're dealing with. And she's gonna see her mom for the first time in like ten years. Her mom was kind of a bitch about it, before she said yes. That's in there somewhere." She shot a look over at the rack. "Plus, I don't know if you noticed, but she likes to model."

"I noticed," the woman said. Cheryl-lin came walking back in the bomber-jacket, her face a little harder, tougher. She had her hands thrust in the pockets. Alison could see that she was prepping the next role.

"Ready?" the white-haired woman asked brightly.

The woman's stationary camera had a parallel video set-up built into it. When they were done shooting, she popped a diskette from the side of it. She took them to a sleek computer monitor at the other end of the shop. "Now what's on this disk," she explained as the machine powered up, "isn't exactly what your pictures will be like. Your eye contact was to my camera. But the difference is almost nothing."

One by one, the fifteen digitalized pictures of Cheryl-lin came onto the screen. She had a knack for catching the eye of the viewer. Each photo was vivid, engaging. There were no throwaways, none with closed eyes or awkward posture. The owner went through the brightly colored shots one by one, smiling at the two of them periodically, or throwing in a compliment. When they had gone through them all once, she had the computer call up all fifteen at once, a small army of Cheryl-lins, row over row.

"I like the ones in the tiara, surprisingly enough," the owner said to Cheryl-lin.

"They're not bad," Cheryl-lin answered critically. "But

— I don't know," she bit her lip, glanced at Alison. "That might be a bit *much* for Taiwan."

"What about the green? I think the boa shots are maybe a little flamboyant too, although they'd make great promotional shots. You should think about modeling."

"That is exactly what Susan said." Cheryl-lin narrowed her eyes playfully. "Are you sure that's not just some PhotoShoot line?"

Alison stood behind Cheryl-lin's chair, listening to them joke, and out of nowhere a feeling of envy and despair crept over her. Almost like a blush, she could feel it passing over her skin. It was the first time she could remember a feeling like it. It was connected indirectly to the different poses, to Cheryl-lin's changeability and the way in which she could live — daily — a mild, uncaring opposition to everything around her. The photos popping on and off the screen, in pairs and groups of four, were like a manifesto of indomitability. Alison was jealous somehow, she had to admit it to herself. And in a more naked way she envied her the coming passport, that would take Cheryl-lin to see her mother. Borders could be crossed, duties could be paid. Great spaces could be nullified. Finally, Cheryl-lin would open a Taiwanese door and there would be her angry mother.

• • •

Alison was walking across the lake, the next time she really knew what was happening. The Adirondack Mountains of New York were standing crazily in front of her. The moon was up and clear. It was sometime after three in the morning. She was headed for the long, arcing jetty of rock that marked the limits of the harbor.

The snow had a thin crust of ice and powder. It was just

heavy enough to bear her weight for three-quarters of a step before collapsing, jarring her each time. She knew she was walking slowly, and that it would be twenty-five minutes or a half an hour before she reached the car, but it didn't matter. Every few minutes she would look down and watch her legs work, independent of her.

The afternoon had caught her and pulled her down. When she left Cheryl-lin — who had a dinner party with some friends from the University multi-cultural affairs program — she went and had a beer with a friend of hers tending bar at the Chicken Bone. It was a lark, being in a bar so early in the afternoon. Everything seemed new and relaxing. Even the regulars, hunched over drinks already, were amusing. She enjoyed playing darts for the first time in a long time. She found herself flirting with almost everyone. When Nate was done bartending, they went to the Daily Planet and had another few drinks. They ate chicken-wings at the bar for dinner.

There had come a moment where she was thrilled to let herself slip down into it, the conscious wasting of the day. She went to the Metronome, where she could drink for free. When it closed at two, she stayed after hours with Cheever and the new cocktail waitress, and helped them clean a little. She'd taken a hammer, a can of red spray paint, and — for some impulsive reason — a staple gun with her from the utility room when Cheever said they had to go. She refused a ride home and started the gliding downhill walk to the lakefront. Now she was walking out on the lake. The things she'd taken were heavy in the pockets of her coat. Inside her pocket, she had her hand gripped around the handle of the staple gun.

Once Alison clambered over the jetty wall, she could see the car. It was sitting midway between the jetty and a small island off in the distance to the left. From there she could see that it wasn't a black car but chocolate-brown, crusted with snow and ice. It had been driven out onto the ice January first as a promotion for a local car dealer. You could sign up at the dealership to register a guess as to when it would fall through the ice. Every piece of the car had to submerge. The winner drove home a duplicate sedan. Alison assumed the other would be hauled out and junked. And that was what offended some sense of rightness inside her, the flippancy of the loss, the vulgarity, and the eye of the town turned toward that massive waste like a carnival or a strip show. With people going hungry, they were tossing cars in the lake.

She had no idea what she planned to do. She reassured herself every so often, looking down at the swishing motion of her legs, that she would know when she got there.

But when she came up to it, cold and sullen, snow drifted around the tires, nothing came to her but a diffuse, sodden sense of pity. The car was a closed-circuit of uselessness, created for nothing, destined for nothing but shattering ice over dark water. A methodical part of her had been considering options while she walked: shooting the tires, smashing windows, painting a message that would remain in people's minds even after the thaw. She had thought about stealing a Keri-Sun heater and lugging it out behind the car and switching it on full, so that by sun-up the car would have burst through the ice. No one would win. Now none of the ideas held. They would do nothing, except lay more indignity on the brown machine half-buried in snow.

There were old footprints all around the car. Alison tried the doors but they were locked. The walk had upset her stomach, and she thought of lying down inside. Finally, she forced herself to throw up — a little but enough —

after walking behind the car to put it between herself and the town she could feel expectantly behind her.

She sat on the snow, laughing at herself and where she was. There was absolutely nothing but the car, emptiness. The stars were leaping out at her again. She wondered how much sugar was in her blood. Cheryl-lin knew every moment, she forced her own blood to give up its secrets.

When she could stand, she came around to the hood of the car and cleared most of the snow off with awkward sweeps of her arms. And then she climbed up onto it and lay down. She lay with her back against the windshield, legs splayed out in front of her.

She knew she couldn't fall asleep, and so she said things aloud to herself periodically. "You're just the old brown whore," she said to the car, thumping her gloved hand down on the hood. "What I need's the pimp. That's who needs something done to him." Once she rolled over and tried to peer through the windshield. She took out the staple gun and held it against the glass. "Slow down," she warned. "It's not a race. The roads are still slick some places." When her words had dropped away in the sharp air, she added, "It's not a race, Mom."

• • •

Alison opened her eyes, realized she had been asleep and felt fear surge over her. And in that same instant, it came to her, the inspiration she'd been expecting. It was like a craving and a logic. She saw that she'd been starting outside herself. Things had to happen with her first, inside her. She shoved off the hood and stood on her stiff legs, got her bearings.

She looked toward shore and found the uniform lights

of the Radisson Hotel. To the left she could see the jutting observation platform of Battery Park. And just beyond that she imagined the halfway house, the warm, dark attic.

She pushed off and started the labored walk back toward Vermont. The cold air hurt her lungs. But somehow she was lighter now, and if she held her breath, she could walk over the crust of ice for ten or fifteen feet without tumbling through.

• • •

Alison let herself in as quietly as she could. She had had a key for the last year and a half, but duplicate keys were against house policy and she wasn't supposed to use it except in case of emergency. She came into the faint glow of the television in the front room. Leon and Anne were sitting on the couch in front of the screen, and they looked up at her as she came out of the entrance-way. Anne was a large, sullen woman in sweatpants and slippers. Alison had the quick, certain impression that they had started months before in opposing chairs, moving imperceptibly closer, and more, that this was as close as they would come to one another — divided by one cushion — for who knew what reason.

Leon glanced at her, then at Anne, whose glasses shone with the glow from the screen. He seemed unsurprised by the key, the late hour. "She's up there," he said without being asked.

The stairs hurt her stiff, cold legs. It almost hurt her arms to steady herself against the walls. She came up into the center of Cheryl-lin's dark room, and it was like coming into some sacred ceremony of sleep. She froze until she heard Cheryl-lin's light breathing, then she forced herself to move silently, to walk slowly, her body tensed.

Cheryl-lin woke as Alison was kneeling down. She came half upright in bed, almost violently.

"Cher, it's me! It's me, Alison, calm down," Alison whispered.

There was a pause, then Chery-lin fell back on the bed. "What are you doing here?" she whispered loudly. "What's wrong? Are you okay?"

"I'm fine. I'm cold." Alison knelt by the bed, feeling herself shivering. She could barely make out Cheryl-lin's face. "I'm fucked in the head tonight. I'm fucked up."

"Where have you been, you seem all —"

"I'm screwed up."

"Were you at Metronome? How did you get all wet?"

Alison brushed her hair back with her hands. "Can I sleep with you? I don't want to go home. I'm exhausted."

"Fine," Cheryl-lin said after a pause, moving in the gloom toward the wall, "but change out of those clothes. I just did my sheets. You can put on one of my t-shirts if you want."

Alison unlaced her black boots, pulled them off. Her jeans were crusted with snow at the bottom. "Where do you want me to stick my jeans?"

Cheryl-lin's voice drifted up. "Just throw them on the heater by the window."

It was maybe the third time since she'd known Cheryl-lin that Alison wondered if she was watching her as she undressed. She pulled off the jeans, saw her own white cold legs, and she wondered if Cheryl-lin was seeing them with eyes already adjusted to the dark. She looked at the shape of herself. She took off her sweater, her vest, her t-shirt, and then, piling things on the embroidered rocker, her bra, her earrings.

Alison got into bed, almost overcome by the cold, the fatigue in her legs.

"You're shivering like crazy," Cheryl-lin whispered at Alison, putting her arms around her. Cheryl-lin was in a t-shirt, almost hot against Alison's skin. "Don't you want to put something on?"

"I'm fine," Alison said. "I got on my birthday suit."

"Nothing personal but don't put your feet on me. They feel like ice cubes."

Alison drew her feet back, rubbing them together. She felt warmth beginning to overcome the shivering. "I've turned into one of my own drinks. Minus the shards of glass."

"You were at Metronome, weren't you?"

"Yes," Alison whispered. "For a little bit." She reached out her foot and rested the sole of it on Cheryl-lin's leg. Cheryl-lin yanked her leg back. "Or who knows," Alison went on, "maybe with the shards of glass."

Cheryl-lin turned over to face the wall. "Look, girl-friend, this isn't an after-hours party. Let's try to remember that I was sleeping when you woke me up."

There was a silence until, after a few moments, Alison heard Anne passing very slowly up the stairs and onto the second floor. She heard Anne's door close.

She moved closer to Cheryl-lin, careful to keep her feet behind the rest of her body.

"Thanks for letting me stay."

"You know you can always stay."

"I know," Alison said. She pressed in against Cheryl-lin's long, straight back. The need was as strong in her as she could remember it; it was inseparable from the feeling that she was short of breath, and from the colored dots moving in the corner of her vision. She could feel the desire for happening and change moving closer to actual events, reaching a point of overlap. She put her arms around Cheryl-lin and leaned forward. She kissed the back of Cheryl-lin's neck, softly and quietly. There was no response, and after another minute she kissed the same spot but more fully, tasting the kiss. She moved her hand to the curve above Cheryl-lin's hip, and again she touched first experimentally, then allowed herself to feel the warm flesh through the cotton.

Cheryl-lin rolled over to face her. "What are you doing?"

Alison could see her face more clearly in the dark now. "Nothing."

"It doesn't feel like nothing."

Alison felt herself blush, but she came forward and hugged Cheryl-lin. "I mean nothing bad. I mean, I want —" she hesitated, then ran her hand slowly underneath the thin t-shirt, resting her hand on the small of Cheryl-lin's back, "— I want to, if you want to," she whispered. "I'm serious, Cher." She moved her hand back and forth over the smooth skin.

"Alison, if you've had a couple of drinks and want to come over here and —"

Alison squeezed her tighter. "Don't be mad, Cher," she whispered urgently, "just don't be mad at me. I thought about it, I know I want to." She brought her lips up to Cheryl-lin's ear, kissed the skin beside it and then, feeling herself fall forward into the event, took the long lobe into her mouth.

Cheryl-lin pushed her away. "Alison, what is your *prob-lem* tonight?"

"What problem, I'm —"

"You're coming on to me in a fairly big way, is what

you're doing."

Alison was silent. There was the sound of Anne's door on the second floor opening, the sound of the bathroom door closing. Water moved faintly through the pipes.

"I mean, I'm asking you what's the matter."

Alison leaned on her elbow. "Nothing is the matter."

"Then why are you acting like a guy who says he just wants to sleep with you and then starts rubbing up against you?"

"I love you," Alison said softly.

Cheryl-lin was backed against the wall, and she brought the blankets down into the gap between them to keep the draft out. "I love you too," she whispered. "But since when does that mean making out?"

"I want to."

Cheryl-lin paused. "Well, what if I don't want to?"

"Don't you?"

"No," Cheryl-lin said. "I don't. Partly because you're my best friend and partly because you don't. And partly because I never thought about it before."

Alison looked her in the eye. "I do, Cher."

"No, you don't. You want to shock yourself, or somebody else, or whatever you call it when you get in that mood where you have to make something *happen*." Cheryl-lin suddenly got up and went to her dresser. Alison heard her shake out a cigarette and the flare of a match lit up the room, then everything went black. Cheryl-lin stepped over her, carrying an ashtray, sat down tailor-fashion. Abruptly she got back up and went to the dresser. She took out a t-shirt and threw it to Alison. "Here, put that on." She stepped by again, sat back down.

"Why? I'm fine."

"Because I don't want your breasts staring at me all

night, that's why." Cheryl-lin began to smoke silently, shaping her ash against the side of the ashtray, her face clearly illuminated every time she took a drag. "I'm so goddam awake now I can't believe it," she said finally.

Alison put the t-shirt on, pulled her long hair free with one hand, lay back down. She was looking at the windows, the four squares full of the darkest color of blue, black violet at the edges. Neither of them said anything. Anne returned to her room a floor below. When Cheryl-lin had finished the cigarette she put the ashtray on her nightstand and got under the covers. She lay on her back, and then turned to Alison.

"I'm going to hug you," she said.

She put her arms around Alison. "I'm sorry I can't, if you really want to, if you're not just kidding. But I don't think you do. I think you're thinking about other things, about political things or personality things. Or — I don't know — I just feel like you're wanting to do it just to change. And I can't do that for you."

Alison put her hands on Cheryl-lin's clasped hands. "You change all the time. You change whenever you want. You told me that time that you liked the fact that nobody could ever classify you."

"I know."

"I want to try that."

"But that's not why I do it." Cheryl-lin yawned. "That's not why I am the way I am, that's just a by-product. That's just a positive consequence. I sleep with who I sleep with because of who I am. I mean, who I want is part of who I am, not —" she stopped to think for a second "— not who I want to be in the world, necessarily. It's not about *deciding*. Or politics either."

Alison still had her eyes focused on the windows. She

felt like crying but she knew that she couldn't or wouldn't. "Everything is about politics."

"Not love."

"Love and sex most of all. Love and sex more than fucking anything."

"Well," Cheryl-lin's voice came softly from behind her, "maybe not friendship then. Maybe that's my point." Cheryl-lin coughed, and Alison could feel the small spasm pass into her own body.

"Is that okay?" Cheryl-lin asked.

"Whatever," Alison said in a monotone.

"Don't be like that."

"I'm not being like anything."

There was a pause. "You're warm enough now? Alison?"

Alison nodded mutely. Then after a moment she said, "Really, I'm okay, Cher. I'm not mad. I'm just thinking."

"Excellent, girlfriend," Cheryl-lin whispered. "Because I'm beat. It's just about sleep or die now." She pulled her arm out from under Alison, but didn't roll away. Alison could hear her breathing, the slow, forced regularity of someone who is determined to sleep. Alison could feel her still, very lightly, pressed against her. In spite of everything she'd said, Alison wasn't sure about that touch, that pressure. She wasn't sure whether she felt reassurance at the touch, or some excitement or just mute, bodily approval. It did something to the need and to her discontent, but she couldn't isolate what exactly. She concentrated on it, like a game for bringing sleep. *This makes me feel like what,* she asked herself in the dark.

Maurice

Reuben "Reebok" Masseau,

You're still in jail, brother. You are still in the can. It's been almost ten months now. I can't believe it's double figures. I still start walking out to the car at least twice a day to head over to your house and then I realize 1) you're not home and 2) you're still in jail. So I'll sit on the hood and have three or four cigarettes, one after the other. Then most of the time I go for a long ride anyway. It's been so blazing hot here, about all you can do is go for long, fast drives or go push a cart around the supermarket, take a fake list. Look like a shopper.

I just never thought you'd do any time, really, Reuben. I swear it never even crossed my mind. I always thought you were too smart. I thought you'd get a four-year suspended sentence [no time], 500 hours community service [a few Pancake Breakfasts at the VFW], $3000 fine [I would have taken up the collection for you], and a lecture from the judge. And then we would go to Champion's and get a pitcher and talk about what an uppity bastard the judge was, and scope women and listen to people do the karaoke. I thought you'd beat it, right up to the very last second.

Well, one thing you can count on: you will be out in two years, first parole hearing. Believe it. I mean it, believe it. I've got the machine working. Anybody with any kind of literary skills is working on a letter for you. We should have fifteen or twenty of those ready in another month or so. And I went over to St. Mike's the other day, and I went

down the list of your professors. I had quite a few cozy little chats in people's offices. Some of them were glad to
help, but some held out for something. Some were little
suckerfish.

Do you remember a guy Cleveland, a Poly Sci guy? He
said, "Yes, I remember Reuben very well. I read about that
fire in the paper. He got six years ultimately, didn't he, for
arson?" And I said, "Yes, ultimately, even though he didn't
do it. If you knew him in college, you know he's not that
kind of person. He's gotten a bad deal." Cleveland's looking
at me through his little glasses. Behind him he's got the
books he's written fanned out on a shelf, all nuclear war
stuff. He's got his hands crossed on his paunchy gut. "The
Reuben I knew was capable of pretty much anything," he
goes.

So I laughed. I figured what the hell. We both started
laughing.

And then I said, "That's exactly the kind of letter I'd like
you to write — detailing his good points," and we both
started laughing again. And I told him that there were some
people picking up your legal expenses, and they'd give him
a small honorarium. "Exactly how small?" he goes, just like
that. So he's on the payroll now. I should get a draft letter
next week. And then I've got some other stuff cranking,
low-profile. I have an appointment — jump back — with
our beloved Congressional Representative himself in three
weeks. Your favorite. See what a hot-button you are on
everybody's agenda?

His secretary didn't remember me at first. I said, "I
spoke with him last year about the fixed-rent housing pro-
ject. I had a meeting with him about that issue."

She still didn't get it. "The Congressman's schedule is
very full while the legislative year's in progress." I said, "Ask

him if he'll see me. Give him my full name." She called back the next day. And all the sudden my name had a *Mister* in front of it. "Would the 21st of June be all right, Mr. Masseau?"

I still remember the first time I went in to see him. You were in Boise on that handshaking tour, or you'd have gone. Avery Yandow set it up for me. I went in and started telling him what I thought about those fixed-rent apartments down by the lake, what we all thought, that they were just government-sponsored condos for welfare cases. That it was just creeping Socialism. He just sat with his hands folded, looking at me. You know he gets that super-serious look, with those big thick glasses. I was a little nervous, but it felt good too, letting him know what was what, letting him know people had their eye on him.

You know that voice you get sometimes, Reuben, like you're totally cool, and totally well-informed, but there's something nasty back behind it? You used to use it on guidance counselors and home-ec teachers and people like that, and I used to think to myself, *just excellent.* Like a newscaster with a knife, cool, very cool, cuttingly cool. That's what I gave him that day in his office, and you could tell he wasn't expecting it from someone my age. He definitely called around, checked my credentials. Definitely. People told me.

But you will remember which way he swung on fixed-rent. And that was something he *gave* a shit about. So two years maximum. Because he definitely does not give a shit about you, so he shouldn't be shy about a goodwill gesture. All I'm going to ask is that he put in a good word. And like I say, we'll have the letters and community testimony and all that other fun stuff.

• • •

So that's everything I've been doing right, Reebok.

Now I'm going to tell you what I've been doing wrong [surprise, surprise]. I wasn't going to mention it, since it's over and done with, but I've been thinking about it all night, and I'm just going to tell you. If you hear about it, I'd rather you heard about it from me. Believe me, I've drawn all the wonderful lessons out of it. So please don't give me the big brother bullshit. I'm only telling you because it's bugging me and you're in jail and you won't be able to throw it back in my face.

We go back about six months, to one night in the Metronome. It was right before the last big pow-wow out at the Trestles. It was just a few months after you'd been taken into custody. I was out making the rounds and so I hit the Metronome around 10:30 or so. You know how it is the last two or three days before one of those big introductory meetings — you're looking to shill anybody in, and they'll sort themselves out or in later.

So there's this guy on the pool table named James, and the first thing that strikes me about him is that he looks like you. Not exactly, but enough so that the whole time I'm shooting against him, I'm continually tempted to say, "Hey, Bok. Check this shot out." He was a little bigger and beefier than you, but your face and your real short brown hair. It wasn't you but it was like a walking marker for you. He was interesting, this guy. So I started doing the talking routine while I'm shooting, trying to rattle him ["Sometimes you have to run your mouth to run the table" — Dad, 1975]. He was one of these loner/loser types, but nice.

So I brought him in. Bought him a beer, listened to his tale of woe. He's a migrant, just like everybody else. He'd been out to California for work, Connecticut, then back here, anywhere, construction guy. I introduced him to

Alison at Metronome, and talk about seeing the hook set. She was looking good that night, I'll give her that, but basically I think this guy hadn't said hello to a girl in two or three years. King James, I started calling him. This guy James actually knew who I was talking about. He'd obviously been to school.

And so I brought him out to that afternoon at the Trestles. We hiked in together and I saw people doing double-takes, thinking it was you and me walking in like always. That spot always reminds me of what there is in this state that's worth fighting for — the old iron train tracks over you and the river surging below you, and those tall rock chasms, covered with snow and blue ice.

I brought him out there but I couldn't tell shit about him, couldn't tell where he stood on things. And it wasn't me either: I had these four airmen over from Plattsburgh Air Force Base and one Coast Guard boy, and in about a half an hour I had a very clear bead, four no's and one definite yes [the Coast Guardsman, a Georgia boy]. But this guy James was inscrutable. He's one of these very, very quiet guys. Even when the conversation started to get serious, he was quiet.

Somebody started talking about how the Abenaki Indians want more land, and it all started rolling around to the main issue of who controls the land, who built Vermont and zero-growth and zero-support for trash migrating up from New York and Boston. And the whole time I'm watching this guy — like watching a deaf-mute version of you, Bok — out of the corner of my eye, and he's not reacting. First I thought, this is some politically correct pud-puller and inside that silent little head he's feeling superior and thinking what a bunch of racists he's got himself into. Then he'd go get another beer, smile at somebody, and I'd think, no, he's just settling in. It's like he's settling into the reality of ideas he's had all his life. He's getting a sense of who he is again, and what belongs to him and people like him.

Okay, here's where I start to do things incorrectly. We go to last month, end of May. I figured that it was time to shake that same group of first-timers down again, see who was who. So I had the four of them meet me up at Metronome: two brothers from Colchester John Petrie brought in, that Coast Guard boy from Georgia, and this guy James. James almost balked at the last minute. I called him up, asked if he felt like playing pool, fucking around a little. I could feel him turning it over in his mind. There's this dead silence.

I felt like saying, "What the fuck *else* have you got to do, you Gomez?" But I said, "Hey, Alison was asking where you were these days. I thought you two were on your way to being friends."

More silence. It was like he was talking it over with no one.

"What do you say, Your Highness?"

"Sure, I guess," he manages, finally. I felt like saying, "Well, *thank* you, James, I'm touched, truly." The guy had no sense of who was doing who the favor, no sense at all.

You have to imagine this scene. The two brothers are into doing shots, that's all they want to do is shots of tequi-la — two dark little Italian guys, in tank-tops, popping back shots, and hitting on the bartender (not Alison — I thought James was going to leave when he saw she wasn't around). The Coast Guardsman is a six-and-a-half-footer named Balfoort with a big nose and who sounds like Jerry Lee Lewis, and all he wants to do is shoot darts. His arm reached up to about six inches from the board. You know that big plastic block of ice with the beer bottle inside that hangs over the pool table — I saw this guy Balfoort full-on punch it the night I met him. Lifted it up on its chains like it was the heavy bag, air-hammered it. *Strong* fucker, with a wild streak. And James. James only wants to shoot pool, and since he's pissed about Alison not being around, he's playing sharp. We're trading games, if you can believe that. He was winning as many as me, just as many.

And I'm running between all four of them, making sure everyone's having a good time. I'm watching everyone's alcohol content. Gabe and Mike, the Italians, I'm even having to slow *down* a little; Balfoort's just about right; and James I'm putting down free drafts for because he's not into it, he's sipping. I figure he needs five beers in him, minimum.

About 11:30, I tell them we're out of there. I had the payoff set up for midnight sharp, so I had about a half hour to get them over there. "Where now," Gabe says, leaning against the bar. Both he and his brother have a little sheen of sweat on their faces. They must have had seven, eight shots each. They were the kind of short guys who work out a lot and keep sneaking looks down at their pectorals.

"Bigger and better," I say. Balfoort sticks a dart right in the frame of the window beside the board. He sticks it in deep and on purpose, you can tell. "Wouldn't have to go much," he says, pouring the last of his beer down his throat, "this place is deader n'fuck." The guy's from some little wide place in the road in *Georgia,* and he's ragging on *our* bars. I didn't say anything though. Burlington does suck on a Tuesday, for the most part, let's face it.

James comes over to me and asks, kind of quietly, "Think you could drop me home? I'm kind of beat." I'd picked all of them up in my car. Imagine that.

"James," I said, shaking my head, smiling, "you refuse to

have fun. You look me right square in the eye and you refuse."

"It's not that, I —"

"You refuse. Why don't you just relax for once in your life? Have a little fun. Get roaring drunk. Break somebody's arm. You work in that mail-order plant all week." I play-slapped his cheek. "Just give it another hour. I'm willing to bet we can show you how to have some fun. You are in for a shot of fun therapy."

"Chill out," Balfoort says, making like he's going to pop James in the arm.

"Yeah," Gabe goes. "You're messing up my aura." He turns to Mike. "You believe that? He's messing up everybody's aura."

I called Joanna the bartender over. "Our auras are screwed. Pour us each out a shot of something, will you? Something medicinal."

She poured us Kamikazees. James wasn't going to drink his, until I made it a toast, until I stopped and waited for him to touch glasses with me like everyone else. "To Burlington," I made it, "the land of the free." I touched glasses with James again. "And the home of the what, James? What do you think? Home of the what?"

He looked around at all of us, and I could tell he didn't want to be odd man out. I could tell he'd had enough of that in his life. He wanted to be liked, to be ordinary. There was a part of him that wanted to cut loose.

"And the home of the babes," he says suddenly, even smirking a little.

"That is my *boy*," Balfoort says, putting his long stick arm around him.

• • •

So three days have gone by, Reebok. I broke off the other night, and I haven't been able to make myself get back to it. It's not that I'm so worried about what you'll think — although I guess I am, some. I always wanted you to think I was smart, that I could be a tactician instead of a loose cannon. I'm not the guy I was at fifteen now, Bok. I'm not. I did a very good job organizing while you were out in Boise, everyone said that. And I'm doing a good job now. I don't know what it was. I think it was that I wanted James to be all the way in. Or maybe just because he reminded me of you. Whatever.

Anyway, I got them all out in the Fairlane that night and lit two little pin joints, got them passing in opposite directions. I was drumming on the steering wheel, just tooling around Battery Street, out into the new North End, cruising back. The cottonwood trees had all split open a few days before, and the air was full of that white fluff. It looked like snow in the headlights. You'd see it up in the glow of a streetlight, lashing by, and you were convinced it was snowing. If you held your hand out the window, you could just about make a pollen snowball. But it was hotter than a bitch out. "Action, action, we want action," I was saying. "Action, action."

"What about Sh-Na-Na's," Mike said from the back seat.

"Bunch of old people dancing to fifties music," Gabe shot back. "Bunch of jailbait in braces and push-up bras. And not even that on Tuesday night."

I looked up at the mirror, caught Balfoort's eye. "Too bad we're not in Georgia," I said. "Then we'd have no problem. That town you're from. Action out the ying-yang there, I'm sure."

"Bet your ass," Balfoort says, adjusting himself, trying to

get comfortable with his head ducked, shoulders hunched. He gives a huge belch. His head's lolling a little bit, either because he's too drunk or too tired to hold it up straight. "Fuck or fight there, whatever you want. Bremen is the town for it. Just say gimme, gimme."

"Sounds like real edge-work. Real sex and thrills. Kill or be killed stuff."

"Bet your ass."

Mike sticks his finger into my neck like a gun. "Take this car to Bremen, Georgia."

Gabe starts chanting. "Action, action, we want action."

Both joints are gone now. Twelve minutes to midnight. I had it working, Bok, you have to admit. It was Mission Impossible timing. "So you guys want *thrills,* then," I said. I smacked my own head. "Oh, shit, I didn't know *that.* Excuse me. I can get you some thrills. That's not a problem."

Mike coughs the word "Bullshit" into his fist.

I started angling down toward the waterfront. The lake's dark, just a few lights here and there, lighthouse winking somewhere over in New York. "You guys wouldn't know a thrill if it bit you on the balls," I said, dropping down College Street, turning onto that access road that runs parallel to the bike path and the boardwalk. We glide by Little Saigon, that Vietnamese place that opened last winter. There's only one or two streetlights down there, and the light from that restaurant and that set of little apartments down at the far end. Other than that it's quiet. Just a big strip of forest and a couple of deserted factory buildings. You remember, we used to do donuts on that road in the wintertime.

When we get to the end of the road, I swing the Fairlane around in the dirt — Mike and Gabe and Balfoort are sliding all over one another in the back, swearing — and then I shut it down. We're sitting there in the dark, the nose of the car pointing up the dirt road to Little Saigon. That white pollen is falling all around us, but really slowly, like it's falling through water. Looking at it falling and rolling into fat white balls on the road beside the car only made you more aware of the heat. The wind was hot when there was a wind. The pollen glued itself to your skin if it hit you.

"What the fuck is this?" Gabe says, looking off toward the string of lights that mark the boardwalk. "Where's the bigger and better?"

I turned around in my seat to look at all of them. James was sitting next to me, looking like he was lost, like he didn't know where he was. The three in the back are drunk drunk, their faces are getting slack. "Attention please," I said. "There is a secret stripper bar in South Burlington that only I know about. You have to know someone to get in. They go down to nothing, they take off their g-strings. Everything. It's the only stripping around here south of the Canadian Border." That's true by the way, Bok. Steve Misiaszek opened up this after-hours club in this warehouse he had sitting vacant. Word-of-mouth only. He just runs it like a card club, basically. "The women all look like Playboy models. They lap dance, they do massage, but basically they just get off on stripping. I talked with them about it. It genuinely makes them horny. They'll do whatever you ask them to do."

James turns and looks out the window. It's not like he's uninterested or disgusted, but he's not going for it. The other three are brightening up. Maybe that's why I wanted him all the way in, Bok. You couldn't pull the same strings with him as with everyone else. He's got strings, but sometimes you pull on them and nothing happens. There's a brain.

"There's a stripper there on Tuesday nights, strips until

three a.m. Sindy Cinammon, her name is. She's nineteen. She's got like —"

Balfoort smacked the back of my seat. "Well, go, man! What are we sitting down here for *diddling* ourselves, go up and give the secret knock and let's go!"

"Secret knock, secret knock!"

"Maurice," James says, looking at me.

"Secret knockers," Gabe starts yelling, "secret knockers! We want secret knockers!"

Balfoort's arm snakes between the seat and the door, loops around my throat. He starts playing like he's going to choke me. "Secret knockers!"

"First, we play a thrill game," I said, opening my door. I step out and lean my head back in. "You said you wanted thrills. First we loosen up."

They all get out of the car, lurching around and slamming the doors, then they come around to the hood. James is still silent, not having a good time at all, but he reaches up all of the sudden and grabs a big chunk of white fluff falling by his face. Wherever a current of wind blows, it puts together little mummy shapes of the stuff against your feet, and they go rolling down the dirt road, mad little mummies.

"This game's called Chase the Seagulls. You ever see a dog tear into a bunch of seagulls? That's what we're going to do. In a minute —" I pointed toward the only streetlight between us and the flat brick outline of Little Saigon, "— a little flock of seagulls is going to come walking right toward us, and we're going to fucking chase them. Chase. We're going to scare the living shit right out of them. Chase their funny little asses."

Balfoort's bent over, hands on his thighs, trying to clear his head. He's pulling in deep breaths through that big hook nose of his. "So we're gonna chase some Christ's sake birds, right up the goddam —"

"These are special seagulls. These are special Vietnamese seagulls. They speak only bird language. They're the kind of birds that sneak into town unofficially and start taking the waiter jobs and the dishwasher jobs. The guy that owns that Vietnamese restaurant only hires Vietnamese gulls. I used to know a bunch of people that waited at that restaurant when it was Eileen's Place. Then this Vietnamese boy bought it. Now just those goofy little gulls wait there. We're going to give them a run for their money. When was the last time you fuckers really ran?" I started stretching my arms, my legs. "When was the last time you got up off the goddam sofa? Really ran, I mean? I mean can you run? At all?"

Mike is looking down toward the weak light. "I ran track. So did Gabie. More than you did, I bet. We ran 440. We can run."

"Chase the seagulls," Balfoort muttered to himself. He kicked a rock with one long sneakered foot. "Vietnam," he said.

"Can you fucking run *now,* is what I'm asking. Or are you gone to fat, over the hill, middle-aged? I can sprint faster than all of you, definitely. No doubt."

I saw the waiters then leaving the restaurant, just the black-and-white shadows of them, about to walk under the streetlamp. "We're not biting, remember. We're chasing. No biting. But chase those fucking seagulls. Chase those skinny bastards until you see them fly over the trees. You ready, you bunch of pussies, you fat fucks? Are you ready to chase?"

Now they're all looking down the chute toward the streetlight.

And then the waiters hit that light, three of them. They glowed for a second. All three were wearing black pants and shoes, white, white, white shirts. All of them with the same greasy black hair, pollen falling down on them. You could hear their goofy little voices. One of them had a little take-out box hanging from his hand. They walked into the street-light, and they did look like half-assed seagulls. The waiters at Little Saigon finish around 11: 30 but they hang around and punch out at midnight to soak an extra half hour. Bob Burghoff tends bar down there twice a week. He told me they wait by the time-clock every night, like clockwork.

"On your mark," I said.

James is squinting at the gulls in the distance. He looks like he's trying to focus on them, trying to see through the dark.

"Get set, ladies!" I yelled. Gabe and Mike are smiling now, shoving at each other, and Balfoort's got his long legs set, like he's standing in starter's blocks.

I grab James by the shirt right behind his shoulder, and shove him forward as hard as I can. "Go! Go!"

And then we're running. I'm running as fast as I can, because I know the rest of them aren't going to open up until they see me open up. I'm sprinting, my feet are kick-ing up dust and gravel and the pollen falling in front of me gets whipped away from my face as I fly into it. Sweat's working over my forehead. I can see Balfoort beside me, and Mike and Gabe are already a little ahead of us, strain-ing, but we're together still. We're cutting through the dark like a pack of hunting dogs. All we needed was somebody up on the bluffs to blow the horn.

The Vietnamese boys know. You can see it. They know we're not out jogging. They know we're not going to whip past them. They know we're running *at* them. You can see them stop, and palsy around a little, and then the two brothers start yelling something I can't make out, some-thing foul, and the waiters start flying back toward the restaurant. You can see their little white socks circling around like crazy in the dark. And we chase them, under the trees and down the dark little road.

Until I realize James is gone, and I draw up short. He's not even following us. I turn around and look back. He's kneeling down in the dirt and gravel about 50 yards back, like he fell down on his knees and he can't get up. He's got his head down.

I could not fucking believe it.

This is the bad part. I totally forget about the chase. I start running back toward him, half-sprinting. I felt like somebody'd lit a flare inside my chest. I couldn't believe he was dogging us. And as I come up on him I see he's got his head down on his chest, and he's crying. He's not sobbing, but he's crying — I could hear him — and he's just got his arms hanging by his side. He won't even look up at me. I remember thinking to myself, what in God's name is he bawling about?

And then I hit him, Bok.

I made a fist and swung backhanded at him. I caught him right at the temple, and his head rocked over. "You fucking pussy!" I started yelling. "I said run!"

His head came bouncing back up like a tether-ball, and I hit him again, again backhand, and this time I hit him so hard with the back of my fist he went right down, fell on his side. I think back on it and I can't remember what all I was thinking. It's blank. I hit him so hard I sunk my own knuckle, I found out later. If I hadn't missed his temple and caught the bony part, I'd have killed him for certain.

"Get up!" I kicked him in the back. "Get the fuck up!" Dirt was sticking to his face all around his eyes and his mouth, and some pollen. He still had his eyes closed. He looked like an insane guy. "God*damn* you," I yelled at him, and all the sudden I could feel myself almost crying. I'm nearly crying and kicking him. I was yelling all kinds of things at him, raving at him. I have no idea why.

And about a minute later the rest of them came running back, and they grabbed me, and got me back to the car. It was a good thing too. I almost think I could have killed him. I really think I could have. We left him there, which was really stupid, but we did. And that was all of it, fortunately. I never heard anything more about it. Nothing in the paper. So that's it. Surprise, surprise.

I know exactly what went wrong where. I shouldn't have even had him along. I know it. I shouldn't have wanted to have him along, if he didn't belong. I shouldn't have even stayed in touch after the Trestles meeting. Those big meetings are designed to get rid of people like him early, so I wasn't using them for what they're used for. And I shouldn't have gone off on him, definitely.

I've figured this all out for my own little self. So like I said, don't even give me one of your precious lectures, Bok. I mean it. I don't need that shit from you anymore. Ever.

• • •

Whoa. Just reread all this. A long, long letter. Again I've been out to the bars, keeping all the connections fresh. Never let it be said that I wasn't willing to sacrifice for the political future of my state. Forget what I said there before. I just miss you, Reebok, that's all. It feels like part of me went to jail, the good part. It's so hot and humid out here now, nobody can think or act straight. It's just a burning, crazy, global-warming summer. I just got the little partial cast off my hand. You have no idea how sweet it is to be able to scratch your hand after three weeks of plaster-cast.

But I'll bet it's really super hot in there. I shouldn't be

complaining. Remember, though, two years max. I have the machine working. Letters, affidavits, good words from the powers that be, everything. Gary Andrews is a guard up there now, and he tells me he can drop this right in your cell to you, uncensored. Door to door service, and totally private. I sealed it up with red wax, so there should be a big, royal Masseau seal on the back. If it's broke open, let me know. But it won't be.

You know what else I was thinking about driving back from Metronome tonight? That time when you, me, and Billy Messing were out in Parson's bean field. We'd dug a big pit and thrown in all of the old aerosol cans from the back shed, covered all of it with gas and lit it. We were back about twenty-five or thirty yards from it, dug down in a little half-assed foxhole, watching the flame and the black smoke and heat waves wilt the plants around the hole. You had your new repeater BB gun.

And you whispered to Billy, "Messing, go see if they're ready to blow." And when he said no way, you put the BB gun on him and made him walk out there and stand over the pit, and we laughed our asses off when they started to pop and he took off through the rows. I can remember so clearly, I was so glad and — I don't know, *proud* — that you made him do it, and not me. That was the first time I felt like we were related, like you were my big brother.

I don't know what else to say, man. Maybe when I come up next week we can talk about some of this. You can lecture me if you want, I probably do need it.

I miss you, Reuben.

Your bro,

P.S. Let me know if you need anything. We should be

able to get you stuff, if you need anything. All right. Watch out. Don't drop the soap.

Cheryl-lin

The Airport Limousine turned out to be a very late-model Chevy van, with two long rear passenger seats bolted down like pews in the space where, possibly, a waterbed had once been mounted. The driver came out into the curling snow and took her bag. He didn't ask if she would like it taken, but he gave a short, eyes-down nod at the bag to avoid surprising her. He started to lift it with his right arm, obviously thought better of it and came down with his left, getting a grip on the leather with both hands.

"Bulky," he whispered, half to her and half to his hands. It was 4:50, almost an hour before sunrise, dark, chill, windless pre-morning. The street's houses were dark. The compulsion to whisper was nearly absolute.

The driver was a short, ungainly man in a baby-blue parka. The bag, for its part, was tear-resistant seal-brown leather; it was oversized, and a significant piece of technology. She could carry a large wardrobe, hanging dry-cleaned and folded, wrapped over and around the blunt objects — shoes, library books and small appliances. The massive cavity was reinforced by a fairy skeleton of titanium. It was heavy luggage that demanded respect from the handler, and Cheryl-lin always used the bag's pop-out rollers and leash, even in light snow.

But the bag seemed to engage men — almost immediately and almost invariably — in a kind of closed contest in gravity. She started to say something in the way of a warning, then simply watched the driver heft and swing it, landing it on his knee. From there he muscled it with his dropped shoulder into the space behind the rear-most pew.

His boots slid backward on the fresh snow, once, then twice. When he absolutely had to, he drew in a rush of air through flared nostrils, teeth clenched. It was how a single man might load a hearse, in the snow, if the pressure was on.

"Are you all right?" Cheryl-lin whispered, the suggestion of a giggle escaping her, as he slammed shut the large rear doors.

The driver turned toward her, flushed. "Say what now?"

She spoke up, talking over the falling snow. "I was hoping you hadn't *herniated* yourself. The bag," she pointed to the rear of the van. "You know. I think it could potentially rupture somebody." She almost giggled again. "Really badly."

He gave her a little look. "Pretty heavy bag," he said grudgingly.

Cheryl-lin was almost to her door when her feet shot out from under her. She grabbed blindly for the handle, almost within reach, and went down with a bang of her shoulder and temple against the passenger side of the van. She could see a milky patch of ice where her fall had cleared the surface snow. She started to get up, then realized almost immediately that putting any weight on her legs would send her skittering again and that — in one of the more-or-less routine abasements of early February — she was going to have to crawl a few feet. The driver had made his way back around to her side of the van and, when he saw her down, gingerly stepped toward her. He was short enough so that in his parka he seemed only to reach and not to bend.

"Don't touch me!" she said suddenly, catching sight of his gloved hands. "It's all ice over here. Don't!"

"I won't."

"Why didn't you *tell* me this was all," Cheryl-lin managed to tilt her head and catch him for an instant with her wide-open eye, "ice and slippery and dangerous and," her damp black bangs fell over the eye, "and *shit* over here."

"I didn't know. You can't know." He stood next to her, obviously worried about his own liability, helpless and watching, like a gymnastics coach. "Not in this kind of snow. It rained last night. It froze. It's all buried."

She found some stable snow with her hands and drew her legs up under her, preparatory to standing. "I'm getting my balance. Just don't help me." She rose slowly, putting a snowy calfskin glove to the side of her head. She made it to her feet and stood there, hand to her temple, mouth open and eyes tightly shut, jaw muscles working as she probed with the pads of her fingers.

"I'm not," he told her.

"Yes, well, thank God for the small things."

"You're okay then?" he asked, cocking his head to look at the side of her head.

"Yes, I'm okay. Yes. Let's get going. I don't mean to be bossy, or anything, but I have to get out of this town before I do something drastic." Cheryl-lin took her hand away from her temple, then suddenly began to laugh, a high, almost strangulated laugh. It squeezed off into a giggle. "Yes, I see *much* better now actually. So let's go. Another minute in Burlington and I'm going to — I don't know — be one of those people that go in and shoot up the post office."

The driver was already moving back around the van. Cheryl-lin moved to the passenger door with great deliberateness, opened it, stepped up and in. The driver started the van and pulled slowly out into the dark street. Soft country music drifted out of miniature speakers mounted in the doors. The cab was warm and close and comfortable.

She could hear the muffled power of the large engine. The driver seemed competent, checking his mirrors, then his speed. His baby-blue parka looked brand new, and she had the quick sure sense that he was proud of it.

She broke the silence. "Sorry I, um, was freaking out back there, a little bit. It's just that I have this plane to catch in Boston, and with the weather like this here I'm kind of worried about getting in there on time for the connection. So, sorry."

"Hey," the driver said magnanimously, "you hit your head."

"Really hard too. That *really* hurt."

"Got your bell rung," the driver said, obviously more comfortable with the situation now. "That ice was laying for you. Laying in wait." He glanced down at her tall black patent leather boots, the two-inch heels. "Just for the future," he ventured after a pause, turning his gaze out the window, "you might want a little more traction, winter time. You ought to get over to the Timberland outlet. There's sales about now." It was friendly advice, and it was at the same time, she could tell, introducing the improper foot-ware into evidence in any future civil action.

Cheryl-lin looked out her window. She had lived in Burlington for the bulk of her life, sixteen years, and she resisted the temptation to say something truly sarcastic. She restrained herself, in deference to the quiet cab, the sure movement of the van. "Yes, well. Thanks for the tip," she said finally.

"Sure," the driver said. He drove for a second. "Time's your flight leave here?"

"Six-twenty-six. But I have to grab something to eat too."

He looked at a small stick-on clock on the dash. "Plenty

of time."

Cheryl-lin nodded. She brushed some sludge off the glossy side of her boot, then snuck a look at the driver's boots. "You know," she put in, unable finally to let it alone, "actually, I have about six pairs of heavy Eskimo killer-weather stomping-around boots — I have one pair that when I put them on and lace them up you can't even *see* me — but I figured since I was going to be in planes and airports for the next day and a half, where you feel like a prehistoric creature walking around in winter boots," she brushed her bangs away from her face and gave him a small smile, "I thought I'd suffer for fashion." Her hand went to her face again, checking for swelling.

"Where you heading to?"

"Taiwan."

The driver looked over at her, looked her over, quickly but completely. He took in her straight black hair, flat cheeks, her brownness and the careful folds of her eyes, and she all but saw the word *Chinese* settle in the air between them.

"Do you mind if I have a cigarette, by the way?" she asked, to divert him. "I could just really use one. I'll roll down the window a little bit."

He smiled, showing uneven — almost snaggled — teeth for the first time. He quickly hid them behind his lips again. "Mind a lot more if you didn't," the driver joked, pulling his own pack from inside his unzipped coat. He shook one out for himself, took it with his lips, replaced the pack, found his lighter and lit it, all with his right hand. His left, along with his eyes, continued to drive the van.

He lit her cigarette before sliding the lighter back inside his parka. They both smoked in silence for a moment, and she felt the air of comfort and competence re-establishing itself. It came up again with the smoke. They crested the hill and passed the tall brick spires of the University, the bare trees on the common. Cheryl-lin found herself looking at the snow-covered paths, and out of nowhere she felt a swelling of both affection and regret, both out of proportion in strength, as though this were the last time she would ever see the campus. She had always been at home there, had gone to countless parties there and had never been a student herself, for the dimmest of reasons. She put it out of her mind, smoothed her thin black eyebrows with her forefinger.

"So how come you're going to Taiwan?" the driver asked. "That is a hike, Taiwan. That's definitely some frequent flyer miles on that one."

"I don't have time to tell you all the reasons before we get to the airport," she said. "Believe me, there are a few." Her voice rose up into the high, strained chuckling, and she cut it off by waving her hand dramatically in front of her. "But I'll tell you a couple if you really are interested to hear it. Do you know Muddy Waters, the coffee place on Main Street? By that vintage clothing store with the anorexic mannequins in the window?"

The driver nodded. They were stopped at a traffic light, and he began to rub at the windshield, trying to clear the steam from it with his splayed hand.

Cheryl-lin carefully ashed her cigarette out the cracked window. "Well, I went in there last night with some friends, for a going-away party sort of thing. And I hadn't been in there five minutes and I noticed this couple, sitting over in the dark by the back wall, holding hands. You know, newly-wed-style holding hands. And I thought, 'Oh hey, there's Mark with some girl, *fine*, I can handle this,' because I realized that it was someone I used to live with a long time ago, like five years ago. And it all ended on not so bad terms anyway, so it wasn't like it was any major deal. So okay, *fine*, I wave to Mark, and he turns and waves, and the woman he's with turns and who is it but this woman Carla, who I never lived with but who I dated for about three solid months. And that did not end on really good terms because she still to this day owes me four hundred and fifty dollars that she borrowed to get her engine rebuilt." She looked over at the driver, caught a look on his face. She started to laugh, brushed her bangs back. "Look, you were the one who asked, so —"

"No, hey, that's your —"

"So, I mean, this is part of the answer. It's all part of it." Cheryl-lin cleared a space on her own window with her fist. She looked out, recognized a squat hamburger place called Al's French Fries. It had arches, now layered and mounded with snowfall, giving it an alpine flavor. They were about halfway down the business strip that led to the airport. "Anyway, this whole sort of going-away party thing turns into me sitting there wondering if — you know — are they *talking* about me? Are they sharing nasty *stories* about me? Are they both, like, so ashamed that they went out with me that they're both desperately trying to keep the subject off me and on something else?"

"Come on," the driver put in, chivalrously and openmindedly, "who could be ashamed? You're not some dog. Don't give me that."

"Well, thank you, yes, it's nice to know that I'm not some dog at least."

"Sure," the driver said.

"It's not that I don't love this town. I do, I think it's a very sane and a very healthy place to live your life. The quality of life is really, really phenomenal. I mean I can walk on the streets at night and feel like I'm going to make it back to my apartment. I do love it. I love the people and the places, but the drawback is that it's so absolutely and horribly fucking small that you have to love them seventeen or eighteen times every day. It's like some Greek mythological torture after a while, the same sweet old man taking your money at the gas station turns out to be the usher at the movies, and your friend's uncle. Then he turns up sitting next to you at some Italian restaurant. Or you start going out with someone and you find out day by day all the incestuous little ways you're *already* related to them, I mean like you once — I don't know — you once French-kissed their aunt or something at some coming-out dance or you saw their father go into a motel with some teenage girl. Or you once had a one-night stand in their apartment before they lived there. Or just seeing the same people day after day, winter, spring, same. Fall. Doesn't matter. Same."

The driver was hunched forward, concentrating on the road, eyes squinting through the snow, which had begun to fall more heavily in the last few minutes. "Yeah. I know what you mean. I mean, not about French-kissing the *aunt,* but —"

"And that's just the most general of the reasons," she went on. She ran a hand over the legs of her slacks, checking the creases. They were only a mile or so from the airport, and her mind had already begun to distance itself from this driver and this van, and had moved outward to the crowded airports, the humming, hollow-bodied plane, and Taiwan as she remembered it from the perspective of a five-year old.

"One of the other reasons is I'm sick to death of waiting tables three nights a week, and forcing myself into a submissive posture every time I enter the restaurant. And another is that I live with a houseful of crazy people, too. And after a while that gets to you, no matter how nice they can be or you can be. It *gets* to you."

"You want to talk crazy people," the driver said. He squinted, nodding grimly. "Try my house. I have five kids, all between ten and eighteen. Four girls, on the phone, in the bathroom. Nail polish bottles. Everywhere. And going out on dates, two are now. Piercing *everything*. Bellybuttons. Eyebrows. Crazy-looney."

Cheryl-lin shook her head. She smiled knowingly. "Take my word for it. These crazy people are different."

"Yeah, how?"

She held the smile and raised her eyebrows. "Because they're really crazy."

They were stopped at the last major intersection before the airport, at the bleakest end of the business strip, the part built out of warehouses, tire stores, and a kind of gray defiance in the face of low-flying aircraft.

"So those are good reasons," he said. "Sounds like you need some time away. You're getting cabin fever. It's no joke, people treat it like it is sometimes but it's not. Cabin fever'll kill you."

Cheryl-lin crushed out her cigarette in the van's already full ashtray. "Actually, those aren't even the biggest reason for me to fly to Taiwan."

The van surged forward. "What is?" the driver asked.

She looked over at him, looked for the first time into his small eyes. "To ask my mother why *she* left. And also because I was made in Taiwan."

Before the driver could say anything in reply, or begin the frantic process of switching the steering wheel back and forth, she could feel the van moving sideways toward the shoulder of the road. The big vehicle slid as easily as an amusement park ride. He began to pump the brake, and even at the last drifting second, she thought that the wheels were going to catch. They didn't, and the van listed off the side of the road just past the intersection, ramming slowly and deliberately into a ditch, and throwing Cheryl-lin crown first against the windshield.

• • •

There was a moment in which the sound of crunching snow and metal stopped, an almost chemically pure silence, followed immediately by another moment in which they both began to talk at once.

"Holy Christ," the driver was saying, trying to shift his squat body sideways to get at his shoulder harness release. "Frigging thing wouldn't bite," he said, and then as though remembering her, and the previous liability issues, "Oh God, hey, hey, are you okay? You didn't hit your head again, did you? You all right?"

Cheryl-lin, who hadn't had her harness fastened, was turned sideways on the seat, facing him, head in her hands. "I cannot take it," she was saying softly, now stroking the top of her head with one long hand and her temple with the other, "I can't. It's too much now. I have to get out of here. Out of this town. I'll die if I don't. I'll choke."

"Come on," the driver said, out of his harness now, "you okay?"

She held her head out cautiously forward to him. "Is it bleeding?"

"No. Not bleeding."

"What's it *look* like?" She continued to hold her head out to him, as though it were a damaged jack-o'-lantern. "I mean, is it broken, or what? It feels broken."

"It's kind of pushed in, little bit," the driver said, touching the small waxy spot of scalp at the extreme top of her head with his index finger. "Just a little."

"Mushed *in*," Cheryl-lin said, voice rising. "What do you mean? Is it bloody? I can't believe this, I have to get on that plane." She began to cry. A few tears fell on the Naugahyde front seat.

"No, no, no. *Pushed* in, just barely in. Not mushed in. There's no blood. It's just like a small little dent or something. Little tiny mark."

"I don't have time to see a doctor. I *can't*, I have to go, now, this morning. I'm not waiting any more. I have to get something to eat."

"Take it easy."

"I have to eat. I have to eat something."

"It looks okay. I think it'll be fine."

"Well," Cheryl-lin said suddenly, bringing her head upright, "nothing personal, or anything, but why exactly should I take your word for it? I haven't been in this van for twenty-five minutes and I've been banged on the head twice. If it's not bleeding it's no fault of yours. Maybe it's *fractured* or something. I mean, you're a driver, not a doctor." She rubbed at her eyes, drying them. "And I can't say much for your driving either."

The driver ignored the insult. "Hey, nobody can drive on ice like this. It's glare ice under that dust of snow. No traction. I should've turned the radio off this morning." He began to look out the windows. "We better get out and see if we —"

Cheryl-lin was already opening her door. "You know, you can't *always* blame the ice. It's not always nature who's to blame. I've been hit twice on the head since leaving my house, and you can't just claim *ice* for everything. I'm sure some drivers could have gotten me there with one hit." She pushed her legs out into the snow. "Some could have gotten me there with *none.*"

Outside the van, the strangeness of the situation struck her more forcefully. There was no traffic, the hour and the weather being what they were. The light snow cover was nearly unbroken as far as she could see, over road, ditch, intersection. The outlying warehouses and discount part outlets sat mutely. It looked like the wreck of an airplane in a snow-covered bean field, rather than an airport shuttle van that had jolted off the road.

While the driver was kneeling in the ditch, craning his head up under the elevated front end, Cheryl-lin wrestled open the back door of the van. She grabbed her suitcase's thin leather leash and inched the bag toward her. When it dropped heavily out in front of her, the van buoyed up noticeably.

"What are you doing?" the driver yelled, from the other side of the van.

"Getting my bag out!" Cheryl-lin yelled back.

"What for?" he yelled, after a second's hesitation.

"Because I have to get to the goddam airport, that's what for!" She let down the bag's mini wheels, watching her footing carefully, and began to half-roll, half-drag the bag toward the shoulder of the intersection. After three or four feet, the bag wallowed to one side, and she dragged it upright, set out again.

"What are you doing, hey," the driver said again. He walked up behind her, wiping his hands on his pants. Cheryl-lin noticed that he had a small tear on the arm of the new parka. He wiped melted snow from his forehead. "You're not going to walk, are you? It's a half a mile to the airport." He pointed to the bag. "And that thing's like a millstone. Come on, what are you doing?"

She set the leash down on the bag, and took a matching green knitted cap and pair of gloves out of her coat pockets. She began to put them on. "You know, Mr. um, Mr. Driver —"

"Desautels," the driver said. He was patting his chubby hands together nervously.

"Yes, well, Mr. Desautels, I really — I know I've said this before, and I'm sure that you thought it was just plain old-fashioned hysteria — but I have got to get to the airport. Not only do I have to catch my plane and get five or six thousand miles out of this violent little town," she stretched her fingers in the gloves, "not only do I have to try to get through customs carrying a little rack of medicine bottles and syringes, and not only do I have to actually *see* my mother for the first time in almost ten years. But I also have to eat something. I have to put something in my system. And *no*, I'm not just being a baby and throwing a hunger tantrum." The hat went on, and she pulled it down tightly over her ears, the final renunciation of fashion. "I happen to be a diabetic, something I normally don't bring up on the way to the airport, but since it seems to be really appropriate to tell you now, there it is. I planned my morning with a meal in mind, and without all of this stress, like getting my head slammed around two or three times. So if I don't eat something, and don't stop stressing, I'm going to wind up in an ambulance. That's what I'm saying."

"I didn't have any way to know," Mr. Desautels said softly.

"I know. Because the diabetes was covered by a very tricky thin little layer of snow. Who could see it?" Cheryllin held up a hand to stop his protest. "Don't get upset. I'm just being a bitch. But what I'm saying is it's only half me being a bitch. It's also a background insulin sort of issue."

"Background," Desautels muttered to himself, looking at her carefully.

"You ripped your new blue coat."

"Ahh," he said, waving the sleeve like an arm with a wound, "would've happened sooner or later." Then, looking over her shoulder, he told her, "Hang on, don't move!" and began to dogtrot toward the intersection, watching his feet hit the snow as he ran.

She turned and saw that a black truck was half-way through the process of making the turn that had sent the van off the road. The truck sat on hugely oversized tires, done up in road chains.

Mr. Desautels stood partially in the road, waving his arms. The truck slowed and came — almost enthusiastically it seemed to Cheryl-lin — over to the side of the road. When it had come to a complete stop, he gave a little half-wave to the occupants and then used the showy side mirror to pull himself up onto the running board. He seemed to understand perfectly the procedure for boarding this sort of truck. The passenger-side window came down, and Desautels leaned in toward the cab. Cheryl-lin could see both figures inside the cab leaning over to listen.

It became clear to her, after a second, that she was the subject of the conversation. At one point, the person in the passenger seat stuck his head out the window to get a better look at her. He gave her bag a pointed look too. Finally, Desautels reached into his wallet and pulled out a bill, stuffed it into the window. He jumped down and came running slowly back to her, fiddling his wallet back into place beneath his parka. The truck followed carefully behind.

"They're gonna take you the rest of the way," he said, slowing to a walk.

Cheryl-lin looked at him, then at the truck pulling up in front of them. "What, did you have to pay them to take me?"

"Happy Going-to-Taiwan Day," Desautels said. He smiled, for the second time uncovering the ruined teeth.

"Well, thanks, I appreciate it, but I don't think that's very nice, that you had to *pay* them to do a humane thing that will take them about five minutes of their time," Cheryl-lin went on. "How much did you pay them?"

"Don't worry about it," he said. He patted her on the shoulder. "You gotta make your plane. They're good kids. They go to the University. You probably know 'em. They're out making money pulling people out of the ditch. They'd pull me out, but the way I'm hung up under there it might bend the axle."

The passenger side of the truck opened, and a young man wearing a crimson down jacket, jeans, boots, and a baseball cap jumped down. The cap was worn backward. The bill of it had been shaped carefully into a long, narrow tunnel shape. The cap made the young man's face seem younger, whiter, blanker. It was a fashion badge that Cheryl-lin knew, but had always been puzzled by — a know-nothing look, a pose of good-natured stupidity, yet with something faintly aggressive bleeding through at the edges. She didn't need to look into the cab to know that the driver of the truck was wearing one as well.

As the young man walked by them, she asked him, "Excuse me, I hope this isn't confidential information or something, but how much did you charge him to take me to the airport?"

"Five bucks," the young man said, lifting her bag and carrying it to the truck.

Desautels shrugged, made a face. "It was five bucks.

Big deal. Nothing."

When he had lugged it around to the truck's bed, the young man looked down at the bag, considering it. It seemed never to occur to him to let down the tailgate. He got the bag up in the air with a modified clean and jerk motion, then held it with both hands over his head, looking with elaborate calm for the least snowy place to set it.

"Let me at least give you the five dollars," Cheryl-lin said finally to her original driver. She felt odd just leaving the man, leaving him with his torn parka, by his derailed van that seemed so depressingly like a small plane crashed in a bean field.

"Forget it," he told her. "If one of my daughters was in a foreign country and something crazy happened, I'd want somebody to get her where she had to go."

Cheryl-lin looked at him for a second, hesitating. Then she patted him on the shoulder and said, "Well, I don't happen to *be* in a foreign country, but yes, I know what you mean, and thank you."

• • •

They sat three across in the cab, with Cheryl-lin nearest the passenger-side door. She insisted on that arrangement because she felt odd about riding sandwiched between two strangers, but also because the driver had a small white rat clutching the shoulder of his ski jacket.

The driver was, in fact, also wearing a baseball cap turned backward. He and the young man sitting next to her had done a remarkable job of looking alike, despite the fact that one was swarthy and the other Nordic-looking and blond. They wore their hair in the same very short, over-the-ears style, and their gloves, boots, and jackets had probably all come from the same outfitter on Church Street.

When they were on the road, and Desautels had dwindled in her side mirror, Cheryl-lin took off the green knit hat and stuffed it back in her coat pocket. "I want you to know that I think it was very chivalrous of you to take me the rest of the way to the airport for only five dollars," she said, pulling off the gloves as well.

"No problem," the young man driving said.

"It's not that far," the one in the middle said.

"I *know* it's not that far." She snuck a glance at them. The sarcasm didn't seem to be finding a purchase. "Still though," she smoothed her hair, "I feel like it was almost insanely generous on your part."

"We're charging thirty bucks for a pull out of the ditch. And that's cheap. Tow truck's fifty, sixty bucks."

"Last storm we made a hundred and forty-five bucks in like three hours."

Cheryl-lin deliberately said nothing. Instead she reached into the pocket of her coat and pulled out her cigarette pack. Smoking was the worst thing for her when her sugars were low, but it stopped her worrying about her blood.

At the first sight of the pack, though, the driver said blandly, "There's no smoking in this compartment."

The one in the middle stared at his friend's shoulder for a second, then reached up and flicked something from it with his cocked fingertip. Both the rat and the driver shot him a quick inquisitive look.

"Mickey laid another one on your shoulder," he explained.

"The boy is definitely out of control," the driver said.

"That's only two."

They drove in silence for another minute, with only a

small high-pitched noise coming occasionally from the direction of the rat. And then the driver leaned around his friend. He smiled a bit at her. "So where you flying out to?" he asked.

"Paris."

"Paris, France," the driver said, still smiling and leaning around.

"Actually a little village outside the city. There's a designer who insists that that's the only place in the world where his clothes really *hang* correctly. Something about the distance from sea-level, or the wind or light there or something." Cheryl-lin pulled the skin of her cheeks tight with her palms, then pulled up on the skin of her forehead, adjusting that as well. "But I say let him think what he wants. It's another free trip for me. That's the way I see it. It's just another shot of frequent flyer miles, and some time to walk around and practice my French."

"You're a model?" The driver's smile broadened notice-ably.

"Yes. Among other things. Sometimes a sculptor. But a model when there's work, and when I feel like being stared at."

"*No* shit."

"No shit," she said. She was pretending to tighten the skin on her hands now.

They rode past the large sign that marked the entrance to the airport, and Cheryl-lin felt almost a physical shudder of relief. The one riding next to her seemed suddenly fasci-nated by the shape of her eyes. "If we'd known that," he said, glancing at the driver, "we wouldn't have charged you anything for the ride."

"You didn't charge me. You charged that nice little man in the parka who doesn't even know me."

"Or him," the middle one said. "We don't charge models to ride. That's rule number one in this compartment."

Cheryl-lin shifted suddenly on the seat, coming around to face the two of them. "Well, isn't *that* sweet. You're going out on a snowy day, looking for people in trouble so you can graciously offer to pull them out of the ditch for thirty dollars, and you'll charge some nice little limousine driver who happened to care whether or not I made my plane — I mean, happened to care enough to pay to get me there — but you wouldn't have charged me if you'd known I was a model. If you knew I *posed,* and stuff, for the camera."

"We're not sticklers for the 'and stuff' part," the driver said, after a second.

His friend kept a straight face. "You just have to model. In order to be considered for the free ride."

"You know, people like you two amaze me."

"Mellow out. It's a joke. We're almost to the airport."

"Seriously, you amaze me. I mean, here you are at college on Mommy and Daddy's money, and here you are riding around in your big firebreathing new *man-truck* that Mommy and Daddy gave you as a going-away present, and it would never occur to you to give something back with it, to just help people who need the help. No, you go around using it to *blackmail* people who are desperate to get themselves out of the ditch and can't say —"

"You aren't a model," the driver said flatly. His face was blank and angry at the same time. "You're a fucking wannabee. That's all. And a wannabee sculptor. That's all."

They had pulled up to the loading and unloading zone. Cheryl-lin had her hand on the door handle, but she turned and said, "I may not be a model but at least I've gotten where I am at this point totally on the strength of who and what *I* am, and what *I* can do, and haven't had everything," she opened the door, let herself spill out into the snow, "handed out to me on a goddam silver platter as soon as I snapped my fingers for it."

The driver looked at his friend, smiled. "I think somebody's got a complex," he said.

• • •

Whether it was the last comment from the driver, or the adrenalin involved in sluicing her bag through the thickening cover of wet snow, she began to remember things, bursts of things. She was walking toward the automatic door of the airport, and it was winking open and closed in front of her. She remembered the first time her father had taken her to see the immense IBM manufacturing plant in Essex Junction. There were twenty-one right or left turns before you reached his new little office in the development wing. She had counted. It was the family's second day in Vermont. It had seemed to her then that no one lived here, in Essex Junction, in Vermont, in the United States. It was all woods and vast, kempt yards and never enough people walking or passing to form a crowd. It was hushed, somehow.

Her mother had never grown accustomed, and had returned to Taiwan seven years later, without her huband and without her daughter. That was a time of screaming and crying fits that left Cheryl-lin breathless, drained, ribs sore. She remembered the first days in the house without her, with only her father, for whom trips to the ice cream store remained the way to signify family harmony, no matter how much she grew or what fissures had opened between them. It was a measure of his own laboring to span the cultures. He might order her to eat ice cream. There

was a day when she announced to him that she had
changed her name and her sexual identity: *Cheryl-lin,* one
name, one person, one culture, dedicated to one sex. And
there was a day when he asked her to move out, asked her
and went upstairs, closed his door and put on a Billie
Holiday record. She could hear it, remembering.

The automatic door winked open, and she wheeled the
bag through it. There was the immediate, captivating sense
of airport, even though the Burlington airport had only five
gates and one snack bar. People were moving in heavy jackets and boots. One man went sprinting past with his ticket
clenched in his fist like a baton, boots banging the tile. She
felt tired, and she glanced across the lobby at a row of
chairs bolted to the wall.

In the next instant — without a conscious interval
between — she was seated in one of the chairs, and a red-
headed young woman in a blue blazer was kneeling in front
of her. It seemed to Cheryl-lin like teleportation.

"Are you all right?" the woman asked.

"What?" Cheryl-lin heard herself say. She blinked at the
overhead lights.

"I'm just asking if you're okay. I mean you seem, I mean
you're sweating —"

She felt the hand touch her forehead, briefly, and felt
the impulse to say or to tell something, but she could not
bring it to mind.

"What's the matter? What's wrong?"

The voice was growing urgent, and Cheryl-lin stirred
herself to answer. "I think I have a complex," she said, hearing her words come out heavy and slightly slurred.

The woman began to say something else, still questioning, wiping gently at her forehead and face.

Cheryl-lin could feel a sense of coldness moving over

her feet, coming to her legs as well. She made a larger effort. She said, "Juice, please."

• • •

She stayed right in the chair, as the juice began slowly to pump consciousness back into her. The woman in the blazer stayed in the chair next to her. She was an airline agent, but she seemed to have no better place to be. She sent an attendant named Brad with a walkie-talkie to find out about Cheryl-lin's plane; he came back to say that it wouldn't board for another twenty-five minutes, and they could hold it another ten if need be. There was something additionally reassuring about the fact that the chairs were bolted down. It was strange but not new for Cheryl-lin, waking up somewhere with strange people standing over her. Between being a teenage alcoholic and being a diabetic, she had long ago come to terms with lost memory and the debts she owed people who picked her up when she fell.

"I saw you weave a little bit," the woman in the blazer said. She seemed to be a year or two older than Cheryl-lin, maybe twenty-three or twenty-four. The hair was a brilliant raw-copper color. Cheryl-lin watched it with the sense of absolute newness and fascination that always accompanied her coming out of a low-sugar episode. "And I watched you and you dropped your bag and you just sort of ran over to this chair, but almost like you were falling."

The woman had a roundish face that developed classically high cheekbones only when she smiled. But the moment of the smile seemed to become the frame through which you saw all other moments. She dropped her voice. "And — now don't get embarrassed — but I could *see* you break out in a sweat, from across the lobby. I swear. These lights are so bright. All of the sudden you were just shining."

"Oh my *God*," Cheryl-lin said. She sat up straighter and pulled her wallet from her coat pocket. She snapped it open, studied her face in the small mirror. Her temple looked puffy, very slightly swollen. "Oh, I look like I died and came back."

"You look great. More than good enough to get on a plane."

"Don't lie."

"I'm not. Your skin doesn't get that skim-milk look mine does when I'm sick. You look just great."

"Well," Cheryl-lin snapped the purse shut, "good enough for coach class."

"That's the spirit."

"You would not *believe* the disaster this morning has been. I've only been up for two hours and it's been more hellish than any day I can remember. Total trauma. I haven't lost consciousness in like a year." She opened a bright package of peanut butter cups the woman had also given her, popped one whole into her mouth, then offered the other.

The woman took it, bit off a small piece daintily. "You came out of it really fast."

"I'm just glad you happened to be watching. I could have passed out in that chair and everyone would have assumed I was asleep. That's what happened the first time when I was eighteen. I was in a bar. Everyone thought I was taking a nap in the booth." She gave the woman a smile. "You're one of the nicest people I've ever woken up to."

"Actually, I kind of know you, in a roundabout way. That's why I noticed you when you came in. You tend to stand out in any Burlington crowd, you know. I moved here last summer from New Hampshire, and I used to see you that summer down at Pearl's with that woman who tends bar at the Metronome, with the long brown hair. I don't know her name. I'd see you two there all the time."

"Alison," Cheryl-lin said.

"Right," the woman said. She ate the last of her chocolate, rubbed her hands together. "You two were always quite the happy couple."

"Alison's just a friend. Just a sister friend. She's straight," Cheryl-lin laughed the wound-up, almost desperate giggle, "for the most part, in spite of her own wanting to experiment to the contrary."

"Oh," the woman said. She looked at Cheryl-lin almost coyly. "So to think all that time I had the wrong idea." She checked her watch, put her hand on Cheryl-lin's arm. "You gotta go, my dear. I had Brad haggle around and tell them your condition, so they're going to make the great sacrifice of giving you one of the empty first-class seats. And first-class boards first, so you need to get moving." She stood, straightened her blue blazer. She was a shorter than average height, but straight and strong looking.

Cheryl-lin stood and reached down for her bag, then impulsively hugged her. "You are so sweet. You're just the sweetest thing."

"Where's your final destination?"

"Taiwan," she answered quickly, "but only for two weeks. I just have to go see my mother, who I haven't seen in a solid decade, but that's a very long story. I wish I didn't have to go, but at least it'll be limited."

"Right," the woman said. She brushed her hair back, looking up at Cheryl-lin. "Well, on your way back through stop at the United Airlines counter and see me. I'm Sarah."

"I will, I will. I'm Cheryl-lin, by the way."

"I know." Sarah continued to look. "I know all kinds of

stuff about you."

Cheryl-lin slapped her arm. "Now don't make me blush." She got her bag by the leash, then stopped. "Just for the record, this *sweating* thing is very rare for me, I also want you to know."

"Stop by the counter. Maybe we can go do something some night." Sarah gathered her hair in her hands and twisted it up over her head. "I love this town so far. It's just always got something going, you know?"

Cheryl-lin nodded quickly, then began to roll the bag out of the small puddle of melted snow it had formed for itself. "I know what you mean. I really wish I never had to leave." She hesitated for another second.

"Bon voyage," Sarah said, and then resolutely leaned forward to kiss her brown cheek.

The Past: 1971-1976

Leon & Monica

They had suspected Leon of being the original Burlington arsonist, for a space of some months, fourteen years before. It was in 1976. It was a time when buildings in Burlington were simply going up. They went up in larger-than-life, five-alarm blazes every few months. The most imposing structures would shudder and die, vaporize. When you walked by the absurd ruins of these buildings, the gasoline odor hung in the air, pungent and repulsive as urine.

The Strong Theater, an opera house in the old style, went up on a very cold Sunday night. The arsonist would have seen his breath. It was between three and four in the morning that the opera boxes fell to the stage, and the stage fell to earth. Then a warehouse. Then two churches, one after the other like localized judgments: Church of the Immaculate Conception, Episcopal Church. Then a bottling plant.

The structures went up with an infuriating relentlessness. It was as though the city were being teased by a cruel little brother. Most of the buildings were prime real estate, and people talked in the diners about who might benefit from these fires. It began a strange form of local napkin Monopoly, with people theorizing endlessly, linking plots of land with boxes sketched on napkins, using broken lines and salt shakers to render views of the lake.

The arsons produced three documentable outcomes in the 1970's. First, the Episcopal Church was rebuilt as a massive concrete phoenix. The new angular structure had no wood in it and no front door — a concrete baffle led Episcopalians around the side, to a small entryway that seemed, insistently, like the rear entrance. The featureless hulk sat at the very foot of Pearl. It gave off a penal air. Spotlights trained on its sides, it sat brooding over the lake, across the street from the halfway house the Episcopalians ran for Leon's benefit, among others.

Second, the napkin Monopoly game made partial believers out of most of the town, right or wrong. People believed that money was to be made from the fires, and they responded to the logic of the new legend with a bitter stubbornness. They put up Courthouse Plaza on the site of the Strong Theater, opting expensively and dramatically for justice. And for years they thwarted development of the waterfront in a sort of generalized snub to all developers, who might or might not have paid the man to scatter the gas and light those six matches.

Third, last, least, the police came to see Monica to ask her about Leon, and about his poetry.

• • •

Because Monica had grown up in North Carolina, and had spent her married and post-married years writing in New England, she had a uniquely dual air of gentility, a stain and a varnish of lettered graciousness. She wore bonnets and rode horses in the summertime, and she skied aggressively cross-country in the winter. Both landscapes appeared in her verse. Her hair, prematurely grey, rode in a large, flat bun behind pretty ears.

Her smile and her poetry were of the same mix: beautifully done, shadowed by some lineal southern gothicism, and — at forty-six, nearly forty-seven years old — stirring, disturbing. She had somehow become known as Vermont's second-most famous female poet, and it was a title she always carefully managed to receive as an honor, rather than a taunt. "It's just their way of saying they're proud of me," Monica would tell her daughter, when Alison insisted that it was an insult. "Just one little notch below as proud as they can be."

Now she was standing behind her kitchen door, squinting at the policeman through one of the small panes in the kitchen door. He was standing, black and silver, on her porch. It was ten-thirty in the morning. The policeman seemed to be about forty-one or forty-two, a somewhat small but solidly-built man, and with hair so short that none appeared below his hat. Although set close to the head, the ears looked abandoned. She could see the breath leaking from his mouth. "Can I help you?" she asked through the glass.

"Mrs. Reed?"

"Yes. I'm Monica Reed."

There was a pause in which the officer seemed to be waiting for something. Then he said, "Can I come in, ma'am? Or can you come out here for a minute?" The policeman leaned into the glass pane slightly. He rubbed his gloved hands together.

"I'm sorry to be a pain, but in regard to what?"

He leaned back. "To some questions for an investigation." He put up a hand, in a stationary good-bye wave. "You're busy. I'll come back."

Monica opened the door and stuck her face out into the chill. She smiled briefly. "I am not busy at all. I'm cutting carrots, but I'm just asking what you'd like to talk about. I think that's standard procedure for someone on my side of the door."

"You're right. I wanted to ask you some questions about one of your students, Leon Charlebois. We're asking people questions about him in connection with an investigation we have going about the church fires."

"Leon?"

"Yeah. Leon Charlebois. We're just gathering information at the moment."

The officer had the sort of face that benefits from extremely short hair, and although he was not handsome, as such, his features were well-cut, presentable, and Monica had the impression that women ordinarily opened doors more easily for him. His lips were his finest feature, perfectly, classically formed. He grinned without showing his teeth. He seemed to be waiting for the moment when the military spruceness of his uniform would frame his more-than-passable face, and she would see him in that flash as an attractive man and act accordingly.

"Leon Charlebois is not one of my students. But please, do come in, it's ice cold out there today," Monica said. "I made a pact not to leave this house today." She opened the door, moved aside and the policeman walked into the house. She addressed him as he passed her. "Leon is an auditor. He's participated in two of my workshops, but they weren't official courses. It may not matter, but there's a distinction there, of sorts."

She closed the door, immediately picked up a cigarette curling smoke in an ashtray, dragged from it, and exhaled through politely pursed lips, slightly to the side opposite the policeman. The ashtray was sitting directly beside a pile of wet, peeled carrots, and she moved it to a decent distance before replacing the cigarette.

"And now that I've shown you how *rude* a person I truly am — I am sorry but my mother drilled it into my head when I was a little girl that a man standing outside the door is probably best let stay outside the door — let me at least try and be civil and offer you something hot to drink."

She didn't wait for an answer but opened a cabinet and put her head in, continuing, "I have herbal tea, and regular, English Breakfast and Earl Grey. I have some Asian Trick Spice tea. I sometimes like a cup of that for a change. I think I'll have a cup of cocoa." She looked at his belt, weighted almost clumsily with weapons and tools. "That is a loaded gun, isn't it? Your gun there?"

"Yes," he glanced down, as though he'd never considered it. "It's loaded. That's just standard procedure. On my side of the door, I mean."

"I could tell it was loaded. You hold yourself a little away from it, if you know what I mean. That must be subconscious. I imagine it's easy to shoot yourself in the leg, right set of circumstances."

The policeman had propped himself up against a kitchen stool with a small pad and pen in his hand. He nodded, without really smiling. "I have the safety on. Nothing to worry about. And we don't drink, Mrs. Reed, anything. Just a policy." He took off his gloves, stuffed them in the pockets of his jacket. The jacket he folded neatly on the floor. Then he took off his cap, set the notebook on the top of it like a little desk. "I'll just ask some of this while you're fixing yours. Is that all right?"

Monica turned around, cocoa tin in hand. "You go right ahead." She turned back to the stove, turned around again. "You know I almost said shoot?"

The officer looked up at her. "So, to start off, you do know Mr. Charlebois."

"Yes I do."

"Mr. Charlebois has participated in two of your courses, you said."

"Workshops. Courses are offered at university, and this

group that Leon attended was not at university, by any means."

"Sorry. My mistake. Workshops, then. He's attended two of them."

"Yes he has."

"How did that come about?"

Monica took another drag from her cigarette. The cigarette was bright red at the tip, from her lipstick. "I beg your pardon?"

The officer looked up again. "How did it happen that he took your workshops, or don't you know?" He scratched at his short reddish-brown hair. He had obviously given up waiting for his limited charm to clear the way and was focused almost entirely on the mechanics of transferring what she said to notes in the small book. Monica liked the man better now that his machinery was switched off.

"Oh, I see." Monica put the tea kettle over the flame and turned to the carrots. She began to slice them in short strokes, glancing sidelong at the policeman while she worked. "Well, the first was at the Episcopal Church. You know, Officer —" she looked down in a squint at his nametag.

"Masseau."

"Masseau," Monica repeated, nodding. "You know, I am a poet and I try to do things for the community sometimes that the university cannot do. The university is a big, wonderful place and God knows it does its share in the world, but it isn't much for poor people and it isn't much for old people." She motioned off over her shoulder with her knife. "I have taught up there on occasion, and I think I'm entitled to say it. So I try, every year, to do a little bit around the edges. I go to a lot of churches and libraries. I do readings out in the little villages, sometimes to four housewives and a mechanic. Things like that." She had been staring for a minute at something on his belt, and she pointed to it with the knife tip. "You know I am fascinated by this stuff on your belt. All this filigree. Is that a flashlight, that skinny thing? It looks a little like a piece of piping."

"This thing?" the officer said, laying a finger on it. "Yeah, that's a light. Puts out a lot of light, surprisingly enough."

"Oh, I wouldn't be surprised at all." She dragged finally from her cigarette, ran the butt under a stream of water from the tap, then dropped it in the garbage can beneath the sink. "Is the smoke too bad in here? Winter time it's terrible for people who don't smoke."

"I smoke."

"You do? Really, well go ahead and have one if the feeling takes you. There's a pack on the table if you left yours in your car." She picked up another carrot. "You won't ruin my image of the police force, I can assure you." She smiled again, chopping. "So I was running a workshop on I think Tuesday nights at the Episcopal Church. This would be about two years ago. And a friend of mine who works with schizophrenics — mild schizophrenics, functional people — told me that she had a client who was writing some poetry and who wanted to see about learning a little something about it. She told me that Leon was somebody who tuned in and out, but was pretty much normal."

"Tuned in and out. You mean of reality."

"Well, I don't know if I'd say *reality*. Supposedly, Leon tunes in and out of day-to-day necessities. He'll tune out water, say, just forget to drink for one or two days. Liz said she thought he gets thinking too much or too hard, and the sound of his thoughts drowns out the little water alarm everybody's got, or the food alarm, or the whatever alarm.

Don't cross against traffic alarm."

"She was his psychiatrist, your friend."

"No, she's a human services worker. She's a counselor, I guess you'd say. She had counseled Leon for about a year at that point." The kettle began to boil, and Monica poured steaming water into the mug she had prepared. Small marshmallows struggled to the surface. "That's part of what I was saying before, Mr. Masseau. People like Leon don't have real classes, so you can't call them students. I say workshop. And they can't afford psychiatrists, so they can't be patients. They get haphazard help and learning, and haphazard money too. They're too indigent for proper titles. You can only call them temporary things. Passing things."

The officer paused. "I understand that, Mrs. Reed. I was just asking if she was in a position to know his state of mind, what kind of understanding he has. Things like that." But before she could answer, he added, with what seemed almost like pique to Monica, "I'm part of the people who provide the help, too. Even if it is haphazard. I know what you're saying. We're on the same side."

Monica took her mug and sat down across the table from him. She put a hand to her forehead, with some drama. "Oh, I know, I *know*. And I wasn't implying other-wise, and I did not mean to lecture you. I did not. It's just that sometimes I find myself on my high horse," she smiled again, more genuinely, "without even realizing I've left the barn.

"But in any event, Leon turned out to be what I would call simply a confused man, or a troubled man. I don't see why anybody would label him a schizophrenic. He was as polite as could be, and he could converse like you or me. I think he had some problem with drinking in the past and that's all. He needed some attention, that's it. And all of that is a roundabout way of saying that if you think that Leon Charlebois burned down two churches you are barking up the wrong tree."

"Well," the officer smiled at her, and she felt the machinery coming back on, the ego asserting itself. "Well, we have some things that point his way. Mr. Charlebois attended workshops with you at the Episcopal, and the Catholic Church, about six months apart. Both those burnt. He lives — and I don't know if you know this or not, Mrs. Reed — he lives in a rehabilitation house across the street from the Episcopal Church of Saint Paul on Pearl Street. That was the last thing that burnt. People see him walking around that neighborhood, at night. So he had access, that's one thing. He had a history of frequenting those places."

Monica stared across the table. "Why would I know where Leon lives?"

"I wouldn't have any way of knowing if you do or not. That's what I said."

"I heard you, Officer Masseau. I was asking because I thought from your tone, and from your diplomatic choice of words, that you were implying some sort of question that you wanted answered."

"No, I wasn't implying anything."

"Fine." Monica dragged from a new cigarette. "You know, I am absolutely charmed to have you in my house, because I've never had the chance to really look a policeman over before. I mean, what you wear and all. Can I ask you just a couple of questions, because I may in fact write a poem about a policeman someday." She lifted her eyebrows in a sort of innocent second request.

The officer kept his face unnaturally straight, unwilling to show the pleasure she sensed the question gave him.

"Sure. Go ahead. I'm almost done."

"Great," Monica said. She got up and went to the cup-
board over the sink. She took down a large blue ceramic
bowl and began to sweep the cut carrots into it. "I marinade
these in oil and vinegar for a garnish." She continued to
arrange the carrots, her back to the table. "Now, this is it.
Have you ever shot anybody with that gun? Shot a human,
not a mad dog or something, but shot them while they were
stealing something or something?"

He hesitated. "No. I've shot over top of people before.
But no, I haven't had to shoot anybody."

"You ever punch anybody?"

"What?" He shook his head a little, as though it were a
crazy question.

"I mean have you ever had to render someone uncon-
scious, with your hands, I mean. Or with one or more of
those little tools there on your belt."

"I don't see what you're getting at." The lines of his face
had turned down.

"I'm not getting at anything," Monica said lightly. "I'm
curious."

"I don't like the question. Sorry."

"Skip that one. I have another question."

The police officer was putting his hat on. "Yes," he said.

"If Leon lives in a rehabilitation house, where would he
keep all of his arson stuff? People would see, wouldn't
they? You can't just lug gas around."

He was getting up. She could see that in his mind, he
was already out the door and back in his car. His voice was
more or less impassive now. "Arsonists a lot of time cache
their materials. In a garbage can, or somebody's shed. Or
sometimes they siphon gas out of cars. All kinds of things."
He held the notebook up. "One more question I'm sup-

posed to ask you. What kind of poetry did he write?"

"Leon? He wrote pretty much his own kind. But have you ever read William Blake, Mr. Masseau?"

The policeman shook his head, a touch defiantly. "I didn't go to the university," he said.

"Well, you don't need to be in college to read William Blake." Monica watched him get his jacket, shoulder it on. "If you ever heard of the rock and roll group The Doors, they got their name from a quote from Blake." He wasn't even looking at her now. "Blake writes out of a very wild genius. He makes up his own scripture, and man is his own God in his poetry. It isn't pretty, and it's damn hard to read. But you feel a powerful air there, and I've always thought of Leon in my mind as similar to Blake, because his poetry is strange but there's a lot that's true and strong in it."

The man was putting on his gloves. When he'd done so, he made an obligatory note in his book. It could only have been a word, or possibly two. "Thanks a lot."

"Well, you're very welcome." Monica kept talking at him as he seated his gloves. "I have to tell you again that Leon is nobody's firebug. He is a very good man. And it all sounds kind of thin to me. Sounds like you haven't really got any reason to think he did it. *I* have more of a history of being at those churches than poor Leon." She looked him over again. "I'm sorry my daughter Alison is in school right now. She is just recently turned sixteen, and quite a hand-ful, and I would have loved for her to see what is waiting for her if she doesn't mend her ways."

The policeman turned and looked at her for a second. He looked at her eyes.

Then he said, "You're funny."

Monica stared back at him. "I *beg* your pardon," she said.

He smiled. "Thanks again. Hopefully you'll read about all of this in the paper, when we catch him." He stepped through the door, said "Bye now," as he closed it.

Monica watched the man get in his car. He snapped the interior light on for a second, and she saw the small radio set-up, the wire cage behind him, the shotgun racked below the dash. He turned around to check behind him, then strapped himself in with a shoulder harness. His movements were sure. The car was like an exoskeleton, surrounding him, lending him the power to do most anything. He accelerated out into the little street.

After he'd gone, Monica thought of calling Leon, but she was sure that his phone would be unlisted, or listed under the name of an organization she didn't know. Whenever they had met, at odd intervals over the past year, he had always called her.

• • •

From her friend Liz's description, Monica had originally expected someone who would need help moving from place to place, or who would remember her one day and not the next. There would be outbursts, possibly, episodes. Her knowledge of schizophrenia was entirely intellectual, and a part of her looked forward to being confronted by a grim, spectacular reality.

Instead, he was a quiet man. After three sessions in the basement of the Episcopal Church, with the other six members of the workshop treating him unerringly as an equal — hating his verse or slathering it with praise — Monica could only think of him in that way. He was a quiet man, mild and unassuming, sometimes confused, but without pretension, scrupulous of the workshop rules. He was scrupulous even to a fault, waiting outside the church doors for ten or fifteen minutes rather than risk being late. He wore short-sleeved white shirts and rumpled slacks, with an air that said this was dressy for him. He was clean. His beard seemed regularly trimmed.

There was an occasional wandering. She would watch him, on and off, during the hour and a half each week. Now and again he became lost in thought. When he lit a cigarette, he exhaled with his head leaned back, and his eyes rolled back in his head for an instant. Monica would look up from talking and catch it. He seemed always a little tired, but then everyone was tired, everyone worked day jobs.

It was a book, finally, that opened things up to her. She took out a short stack of books on schizophrenia from the University library. There was a new volume that talked about the disease in a way that amazed her. It suggested that the schizophrenic loses the ability to filter out self-conscious thought, to speak unguardedly or plainly. The consciousness became full of extra tracks of thought, all questioning the validity of the central track. They became carping, these consultation patterns. The result was irony. The mind became steeped in it. It became the default mode of thought.

Once she had the hint, it was like there was an eighth person in the workshop. There was the Leon that the others saw, and a new Leon, one who was saying almost too much about what was going on rather than too little — one given to commentary.

One night he was asked about one of the men's more hackneyed verses on ice and winter, and how it mimicked the coldness of a dying love. "Like it," Leon said deliberately. He caught her eye as he did so. "Very original. Really original."

"Original," Monica repeated slowly, her nostrils flaring slightly with the effort to avoid bursting into laughter.

"Yuh," Leon said, even shaking his head a bit in appreciation. "It's like you feel like you should have heard that idea before, it's so good. It gives you déjà vu."

She allowed herself to smile at him, to share the layered meaning with him, although it felt enticingly wrong somehow, to conspire against one of the other participants. Even if it wasn't a classroom, even if it was volunteer work in the basement of a church, it still felt like a step off the straight and narrow.

"Frozen snow, frozen heart," she said. "That does seem fitting enough, once someone thinks it up, I suppose, doesn't it?"

He was looking at her, his eyes with their shadowed underlids. "That's what you need a poet for. To make it up in the first place."

"So you like it then, Leon?"

"Sure."

"Well, I do too," she said impulsively.

He looked around at the rest of them sitting around the table, blushing from the attention. "It's gotta be good then," he said.

• • •

Once — only once, but still, once — she saw him in the church hallway outside the seminar room, while the others were on break at the candy machines, squatted down on his low black heels, rocking slowly and holding his head in his hands.

• • •

He was a fine listener. They slid slowly into a habit of having coffee after the workshop. He would have coffee and chocolate pie, she would have spearmint tea. Monica began to tell him things without any plan. It had been three years since her divorce, and she told him about her new money problems, with a certain queer pride. They talked about her daughter Alison, who had taken to smoking pot and staying out until two or three in the morning, offering some insultingly thin excuse in the morning. "Children should be had before thirty," she told him, shaking her head. "That's when you have the strength of will, and of body, to keep on battling it out."

She did draw him out, but it was like working against a stiff headwind, always. He had worked at a wire-making plant in New York for years and years, as a threader. He had moved back to Vermont and worked for a short time as a ferryboat mate, then worked his way up to captaining the small boat. He had plied back and forth between Grand Isle, Vermont, and Plattsburgh, New York.

And then, after some dim interval, he was where he was now. His life story never made any more sense than that.

But once she encouraged him, he began to tell her stories from the factory and from the boat — a man losing an arm to the threading machine, how it was snapped and thrown away from him, and a time when a car had bumped over the blocks and nearly fallen into Lake Champlain. He wrote a long poem about falling off the ferryboat once in a storm, dropping down through the black water, and meeting the bodies of everyone who'd ever drowned in the lake, one by one, until they were thick and white as a school of fish.

He eventually followed her from the Episcopal Church to the Catholic Cathedral of the Immaculate Conception, sat in on a second workshop. She gave him her telephone number and they went two or three times to see matinees at the cinema. They'd see a horrible action film, one where the actors ran down one street, and appeared in the next shot wearing different clothing. "How'd you like *that*," she'd say, when they came blinking out onto the street.

"Oh, first-rate," he'd say, smiling slightly, folding his arms critically. "Loved it, really loved it."

They'd begin to walk toward the car. "Oh, me too, me too," she'd go on. "Haven't seen anything as well-done as *that* in a decade. Such talented actors."

He'd walk beside her nodding, a small smile on his face. "Yeah, I really enjoyed that," he'd say. "That's a *film*. That is a film."

"You're teasing, Leon. Tell me you're teasing, now."

"Who's teasing?"

"You didn't seriously love that film."

"Seriously?" he'd say, giving her a little side look, chuckling. He'd rub his gloves together in a happy little gesture. "Seriously, yeah. Dead serious, Monica."

• • •

Monica considered an affair on and off for a year and a half. At first it was with a little shock at herself. She forced herself to think of him from time to time as an almost-student with an almost-mental condition. She hadn't been with anyone since her divorce, or for more than two years previously, for that matter. But he was more and more attractive, in his own impenetrable hangdog way, and she knew that he was interested. And in the eighteen months she'd known him she thought she could see a change in him. He seemed much clearer when he talked to her or looked at her, quicker. And, too, she was curious. She had imagined him, undressed and pressed silently against her, and it worked, mentally. The naked images meshed. Sometimes the imagining took on a furious, even manic rhythm that transfixed her.

But finally — though she made him dinner once when Alison was visiting her father in January, and they sat in her dining room talking around a candle until very late, and though she'd neatened her cavernous upstairs bedroom, on the extreme off chance — finally she didn't. She just didn't. She pulled back.

There were a number of reasons, but only one really mattered. It was the same thing that had drawn her closer to him all along: she could never convince herself completely that what she heard him say was what he, in fact, had said.

She wanted and needed to believe that after all of the months talking, it was him she knew so well and not her own involuted method of reading his silences and threads of conversation. But time didn't break down the lack of certainty. She saw that there would always be a small residue of doubt. And the doubt soured her passion. She suspected herself of making a mirror of him.

Since they had never said anything overtly romantic to one another, nothing had to be unsaid. Monica simply began to be a slightly different person with him. She was still friendly, but she restored all of the invisible limits. She was suddenly too tired to go out after dark. They stopped sitting in the man-made after-dark of the matinee. She would suggest coffee, or lunch, rather than dinner.

This small change began in February. And when the Cathedral of the Immaculate Conception went up in March, incinerating the basement room where she and Leon met for poetry class, she had thought nothing of it except that it was a waste and a criminal shame.

• • •

The policeman had been gone for fifteen or twenty minutes before Monica got up from the kitchen stool beside the telephone. The kitchen phone was tomato-red and wall-hung; at two or three points during the minutes of sitting, she had reached up for it, and then drawn her hand back nervously to her lap. Each time she did so, she would mutter to herself, or bite her knuckle. Once she bent over and hugged her knees, so that her head rested for about five minutes in her own lap. To someone watching through the kitchen door, her distraction would have looked like insanity.

She lit another cigarette. She stared at the telephone as she smoked. Finally, she went to the refrigerator and took out the bowl of carrots she had cut. Bringing them to the counter beside the stool, she sat down and called information.

When the operator answered, she asked for two numbers, suddenly stretching to a counter drawer for a pen. She found the pen in time, and took down two numbers on the wall beside the phone, juggling her cigarette. The blue numbers were the only mark on the otherwise spotless white wall.

Monica dialed the first number and, as though clearing her palate for the conversation, she popped three or four of the carrot wheels into her mouth and chewed them quickly.

A woman answered the phone. "Burlington Central, this is Ellen speaking."

Monica swallowed some carrot. "Hello. My name is Monica Reed and —"

The woman's voice rose slightly. "Oh, sure. I've read

some of your poetry. I think it's just great. My name's Ellen Martins. I'm new at BCS."

"Well, thank you very much. Nice to meet you, Ellen. Sort of meet you."

"I read that piece you had in *Yankee* a year or so ago. It was about those teenagers that lock themselves in the sugar shack, won't come out for anything. Just ate that maple candy. That was wonderful. And where they burned their clothes."

"I always liked that part myself, tell you the truth."

"And the part where the pastor tried to get them out. But they were in *love*."

"I'm so glad you liked it," Monica said, then went on, "and I do hate to be a bother, and I know that my daughter Alison is just now in her Social Studies class, I'm pretty sure, but I was wondering —"

The woman's voice became confidential, tactful. "Has there been some kind of an accident or something? Is everything all right at home?"

"Everything is basically fine. I mean, no one's died or sick or anything, but I was wondering," she dragged noiselessly from her cigarette, "there is a thing or two I really feel I have to tell my daughter, and she's going right from school out to a friend's house in Milton tonight. Do you think there's any chance I could have a word with her, without disturbing or alarming her or anybody?"

"No problem," the secretary said. Monica heard a chair scraping. "If you'll hold the line, I'll go spring her from class. It's right down this hall. Just a minute."

While Monica waited, she began to jot short phrases beneath the two numbers she had written next to the phone. Something about this particular call seemed to have erased a long-standing tradition of not writing on the phone wall. The new marks looked like miniature grafitti. She wrote *Some strange curving firewall heart* and beneath that, after another second, she wrote the word *asteriated.*

"Hello," Alison suddenly said. Her voice was out of breath, suspicious, a dramatic bit fearful.

"Hi, baby," Monica said. "How's school going?"

There was a pause, then a short exhalation of breath, a little laugh of disbelief. "Mom, they just came and got me out of Social Studies. Tell me what's the matter."

"Nothing really is the matter. Everything's fine. I just felt —"

"Well, there *better* be something the matter. I mean, I hope you're not just calling to say hi, because they scared the hell out of me."

"I'm sorry, I told them to tell you it wasn't an emergency. That no one was sick or anything." Monica let it come out in a rush. "I was just thinking about how much of a hard time you and I have been having lately. And I'm," she ran a hand over her damp forehead, then laughed, "I'm sitting here in this house feeling like things could change so fast, you're at the age. And I worry about losing you. To some drunk driver. To some wife-beater who'll knock you up and then marry you, God forbid."

There was no comment from the other end. Monica went on, "Or to *cocaine* or whatever the hell it is people are into now. Or to some arrogant," she got up and made the stretch to the cigarettes on the table, "mean-hearted cop. Some thug. Some Nazi storm trooper who can get you because you made some stupid mistake."

"Mom," Alison began, with exaggerated patience, "I don't want this to be the kind of thing where I come home and then you tell me, like, Dad *died* or something. So just tell me if you really called for something bad."

"Alison, I told you. I called because I'm having a horrible, horrible day, and something made me feel like you could, just anytime," she lit the cigarette, and the smoke hit the mouthpiece of the phone, "I just had a bad feeling about you, baby. I just got worried that something stupid is going to take you away from me. I am so sorry for the fight we had last night. I don't care how late you came in, I just want to know you're safe. That's all. Ever."

There was a silence. In it, Monica could hear an announcement being made over a loudspeaker, a hollow voice echoing slightly. "I'm standing right in the *office,* Mom. There's people sitting here. So I can't really talk about this. Okay?"

"I know. And I didn't mean to call and embarrass you in front of your friends."

"You didn't embarrass me." Alison laughed. Her voice was lighter with relief. "They just think somebody had a heart attack. But you didn't embarrass me. It's kind of cool to get a phone call during class."

"Well. Good, then. Tell them it was a Hollywood agent." Monica was rubbing her eyes. She pressed her fingers against them. "Are you, ah," she began, and then forgetting her words, began again. "So, when am I goin' to see you? You go to Ginny's tonight for a sleepover."

"Yeah."

"Oh, my gosh. I just remembered, I am supposed to do a reading for Barre Literary Club tomorrow night. Everything drove it out of my mind. So I won't see you until, what, Sunday *morning?*"

"Maybe I'll see you late Saturday night." There was a considered pause. "Some people are having a party, so as long as you're going to be away anyway, maybe I'll just stay there until you get back. I'll call you from the party." Alison laughed, in spite of her own show of earnestness. "I promise."

Monica hesitated, then cleared her throat. "Well, we can talk about that. But why don't you come out there with me? Come back in to Burlington, late afternoon, and then we'll have supper and drive out there. I'd love to have you go. Really."

"No thanks."

"You used to love my readings."

"No thanks, Mom. Nothing personal."

"You did. You'd sit and listen, just like a lady. You did like them."

"Yeah, that's the way *you* remember it. I never liked those people, really, and I never liked the five or six hours of talking when it was over. I liked the ice cream afterward." Alison told someone something, hand over the phone. "I have to go, Mom. It's lunch time. Plus I don't think they like me tying up the phone line."

"I know."

"So I hope the rest of the day goes better. Take a nap or something."

"Thanks a *lot*," Monica said back. "I will, maybe."

"Okay, bye. I'll see you tomorrow night, late." Pause. "Probably pretty late. And I'll be completely careful."

"All right. Goodbye," Monica said. When she'd hung up the phone, she sat for another second on the stool, smoking silently. Then, clearly having decided something, she put the cigarette out and went around the corner into the small bathroom off the kitchen. There she ran a brush through her hair, looked at her eyes in the mirror, fingers touching the skin beside her eyes lightly. She applied a small amount of lipstick.

Then she returned to the stool, and immediately uncradled the phone. She dialed the second number written on the wall. It was the Human Services Office where her friend Liz worked. Liz chatted as she searched for Leon's telephone number, but there was a silence when Monica told her about the policeman, and how Leon couldn't have burned those churches.

Liz's voice was froggy, almost blues-singerish. "Look, all I'd say is stay balanced, Monica. Don't start assuming things about Leon. That way lies disappointment." She read Monica the telephone number, then added, "Use your head, babe. That's all I'm saying. You don't know who did what to what."

"Yes, I do. Thank you much, Liz. I'll talk to you this weekend."

"All right, Monica. Remember. Your head."

Monica hung up the phone. She got up from the stool and walked directly to the living room, where she lay down on the shorter of the two couches, legs and arms tucked close into her body. She lay with her eyes open for a little over two hours, watching motes of dust fall in the light from the front window, recharging.

The phone calls made her realize how unconsciously crafty she'd been, crafty to the point of dishonesty. She'd never gotten Leon's telephone number, in a year and a half. She'd never seen where he lived. They'd always met out somewhere, at her suggestion. He had always looked, more or less, like a man who might own and operate a used book store, and she'd let that impression remain. She'd never told Liz. She'd never introduced him to Alison, never — as far as she could remember — even shown him a picture. She'd set the rules and they were the rules of an affair, an affair conducted behind the back of her innermost life and his psychologically classifiable, halfway house self. She'd been lying when she'd told herself that the invisible barriers had to go back up. Because they'd never really come down, and she found herself overcome with distaste and fascination for herself.

• • •

When she finally steeled herself and called, it was almost laughably ordinary. An older man answered the phone and said "Just a second" when she asked for Leon. And when Leon picked up the phone, he sounded as low-key and as sane as ever. Midway through her small-talking, he stopped and said, "Funny for you to call. Great, but it's funny."

"Why is that? What's funny about it?"

"Ah, nothing."

"No, really, Leon, what strikes you funny?"

"Well," his voice trailed off, as though it was too obvious to need saying, "you just never *did* before. Maybe funny's not the right word." Monica heard voices in the background arguing and laughing. She imagined people cooking dinner together in a big, communal kitchen. Leon lowered his voice a bit. "Maybe pleasant surprise is what I'm trying to say."

It was the closest thing to an out-and-out compliment he had ever given her. "Well, that's nice of you to say. I'm calling, Leon, I guess to ask you —"

"If the police came to see me. Is that it?"

"Yes," Monica said.

"Yeah, they came by this morning, two guys. I guess I talked with them for about an hour. It wasn't a big deal." He cleared his throat. "They said they were going to talk to some of my acquaintances." He chuckled softly. He seemed not to be bothered by it at all. "Now you know what you get for being my acquaintance."

"I'm more than your acquaintance, Leon," Monica told him.

"Oh yeah," Leon said, still chuckling a little. "That's right."

She wasn't sure how he meant what he said. She felt her face get a little hot. "It may not have *seemed* like it the last few months, I've been so damned busy, but I am, and you know I am."

"I know," he said.

Monica brushed a strand of hair from her face, patted it into place. "You know, Leon, I have had the most *horrible* day, and I could use some long, drawn-out mechanical cooking process to clear my mind. Are you free for dinner? Because I have some, uh," Monica swiveled her head toward the refrigerator door, trying to think quickly of what she had on hand, "well, anyway, I have some lovely carrot wheels that took me most of the day to prepare."

"Fine. Love to."

"Do you want me to come by and pick you up?" She found that she was almost looking at the phone as she asked it. "It's no trouble."

"Nah," he said. "Don't trouble yourself."

• • •

At two or three points during dinner, when she had passed him the broccoli or when he broke the back of a chicken breast in his thick hands, she told herself, *this man has been accused of arson.* He would look up at her, meet her eyes and smile, then bend over his food again. Then he would glance up a final time to make sure everything was all right before resuming his meal.

When he had finished, he leaned back in his chair. He'd worn an old dark sport coat over his uniform white shirt and dark slacks, and he crossed his hands in his lap. There was something about the fact that he'd worn the old sport coat that saddened her, if she thought about it too much, almost to the point of tears. "Enough," he said. He held up his hand. "Any more and I'll pop like a balloon."

"I'm glad you enjoyed it. It was thrown together, as you saw."

"Good throwing. Major league throwing. Couldn't have been better."

Monica poured herself another inch of the chardonnay that Leon had brought with him. It was sweeter than she liked but perfectly drinkable. Leon was drinking seltzer water, another thing that affected her more than it should have, properly speaking.

"So, I know you told me before dinner, Leon, but these men didn't mention any other reason why they wanted to talk to you than that you live across the street from the Episcopal Church? That seems like just harassment to me."

Leon wiped his forehead, ran his hand down and over his salt-and-pepper mustache and beard. It was a gesture that carried finality. "They don't have anything on me, Monica," he said, looking down at the tablecloth and then up into her eyes. He grinned, without showing his teeth. "They can think anything they want. There's no evidence."

"They told me that people saw you walking, or something, one of those nights."

"I walk at night. I walk every night. It's beautiful out. There's no crime."

There was something that had been bothering her since the officer had come that morning. She had no idea how to broach it, or even how to formulate it to herself. The thought ate at her, sitting across the table from him. She smiled instead of expressing it.

"They got nothing," Leon said again.

And then it simply came out her mouth, without any real planning or forethought. "You know, Leon, this is very, very silly of me, I know, but ever since that policeman was here this morning it has occurred to me that — well, you and I stopped really, I don't know, really palling around just before that first big fire in March. And I was thinking about that, and — although I know that you would never do such a thing — there's been a weird little voice in my head all day that's wanted to ask you, you know, about that."

He drank the rest of his seltzer, pulled his lime wedge out and began to bite at it. His face had clouded over. "About what?" he asked.

"Well, to say it once just as blunt as I can," Monica looked him straight in the face, "if you were angry about that. Our becoming, you know, not such close friends. And if so, I guess," she started to giggle, out of nowhere, "how angry were you? You know what I mean? It's just, the timing seems, I don't know. Uncanny."

He put the cleaned rind back in his glass, a perfect white crescent moon. He folded his hands again. "Was I angry? Was I angry enough to burn down half the town, is what you mean. That's what you really think."

"No, Leon. No, that's not what I'm trying to say. Not at all. But it is something I feel like I need to ask you. How you were feeling then."

He smiled. His eyes were bright white beneath the black brows. "Sure, Monica. I burned down those churches. I did it," he toasted her, "to express myself. I was sending you a signal. It's all Morse code. All a big poem, for you."

"Leon, please, I'm trying to —"

He was laughing a big, booming laugh now. He clapped his hands. "Every time I'd light a match I'd say, this one's for Monica. Dedicate them to you."

Monica started to cry. She leaned forward and put her arms and head on the table and felt herself move almost instantly from single tears to small, fast sobs. And then his voice stopped, and after a moment she felt his hand on top of her head, patting her hair. He was leaned all the way across the table.

"No, no, no, no." He was crooning, almost. "Monica, no. Of course not. Come on. I was mad, I guess. For a little bit. When it seemed like you always had something better to do. But no. Don't think that way about me. God."

"I don't," she said when she had her voice back. "I just wanted you to say it."

"Good," he said. "I'm glad." He continued to touch her hair, a very gentle pressure. "What a serious kid you are, Monica," he told her.

It was the first time he had ever really touched her, that moment leaned all the way across the table. He seemed to know intuitively that she needed the barrier while she was crying. He had a rough genius for these intuitions, she told herself, or she had a genius for attributing it to him, one or the other. One or the other, one or the other. He patted her hair for a few minutes. "Now if you *wanted* me to burn down a church, that'd be different. I might just do it then."

"Leon!"

He chuckled. "No, I'm kidding. *Kidding*. Don't you know a little kidding when you hear it?"

She had ruled out candles before he arrived and settled on bringing the dimmer down to halfway in the dining room. Now, she reached up behind her and clicked the round button, shutting off the light altogether. The only illumination was the spillover from the overhead kitchen light. "I don't want you to see me crying," she said, wiping at her face. "Nothing worse than an aged woman with a streaky face."

"Fine. It was too bright anyway."

They resumed their positions, her head on her arms on the table, his hand passing lightly over her hair. They stayed that way for awhile.

"You've got a movie star's name," he said finally. "Did I ever tell you that?"

● ● ●

And, finally, she just did. She led him up to her neatened, cavernous bedroom. She pulled the hand behind her, towed the silent presence behind her, almost afraid to look back at him. One of them would be turned to salt, who knew which.

While she was taking off her blouse, she was thinking that she had been insane to demand certainty, when everything required faith. Putting your car into first gear required faith. God, breathing, pen on paper, tapwater, everything, as well as taking a man inside yourself. He watched her with the buttons. "It's probably been eight years," he whispered when she came up to him, naked from the waist up. He was shivering. Their bodies were a milky white. "Six for me," she said in his ear.

He put his arms around her and hugged her, and the feel of his chest against her breasts knocked the wind out of her. "That's almost fifteen years, total," he said, pressing his lips to her shoulder, almost exactly as she had imagined it.

Later, she lay on the bed with him moving between her thighs. Although she had her arms laced around his back, it was as though she were lying spread-eagled, unmoving, while he moved in her and at her. She felt him that way. He was changing her, and the familiar uncertainty of him pushed at her, working her toward an uncertainty of her own. She lay, head rocking and eyes closed, beneath him. She let the uncertainty build and release, *one or the other,* gripping it inside her, *one or the other.* He whispered her name in her ear, and it sounded glamorous.

Then he rolled up to her and kissed her neck. He smiled and whispered something, she couldn't tell what, something low and sweet-sounding, and it wasn't one or the other, for once. It was both.

• • •

In a small room off the public library in Barre the next night, she gave them every love poem she had ever written. She read things she had been ashamed of for decades, giddy things, rondelets and rhyming couplets. She read the sugar shack poem, and a few people clapped when the couple burned their clothes.

During the coffee hour, she went up to a small girl in a green dress with white boots, maybe six or seven years old, with hair the color of dark coffee. She had been drawing pictures on her program throughout the reading, amusing herself quietly and completely. Monica reached out for her hand. The child could have been Alison, ten years previously. "How are you tonight?" Monica asked.

The girl looked at her, brown eyes serious.

"You're a beautiful author," she said.

Monica kissed her cheek.

• • •

It wasn't any one thing that caused the accident. A bit of light rain settled on the Nova's windshield, followed by stray needles of ice. Monica turned on the wipers. She was thinking her way through various strands of thought, working her fingers through the stuff of her purse for a cigarette. The night before was playing over slowly in one part of her mind, a part that she would cut to every few seconds to renew the pleasure across her memory and her body. Each time, she would almost laugh out loud at herself, at her fresh new hedonism.

And she was going over, for the hundredth time, something that had happened the previous summer: she'd been walking behind the University hockey rink, in the wilting heat, and had come across a perfect snowbank of white snow, shavings shoveled out by the rink cleaner. For the last seven months she had pulled the image out periodically to see if it had been rendered usable, finally, by the rock tumbler of her mind. She was running through these thoughts when her fingers found the pack of cigarettes, and she tugged at them. Her foot slipped from the gas pedal, and she pushed at it again a little awkwardly, her glance falling from the road to the floor.

When she looked up, the road was brighter than before. And before she realized that the sheen was ice, she had stroked the brake, just once, freeing the car. It seemed to pick up speed as it left the road, moving faster as it rolled out into the dark and over the chasm created by a small, snow-slung creek. She could see through the windshield the fields and tight hills turned upside down and suffused with force. She was astounded.

• • •

The police, ultimately, had nothing. They bluffed him for a few weeks. They would ask him to walk the few blocks up the street to the station. A man in a shirt and tie would ask him a few questions. And then they would tell him he was free to walk home again. Sometimes they watched him from their patrol cars when he went out at night for walks. They shadowed him, radios muttering.

But for the most part, during the fourteen years following Monica's highway death, Leon was left very much alone.

Chris Masseau

In middle May of the year of Monica's death, 1976, Chris Masseau made a day trip to a small parcel of land he owned in the Northeast Kingdom. It was a trip he had made each of the previous four Mays, and one which he would repeat for the next five years until his death at the age of forty-eight. It was six hours of the year that he physically dreaded. His stomach would typically go soft on him one or two days before, acidic, and his breath would come funny if his thoughts took a certain quick turn. This uneasiness that worked at his body couldn't be discussed. Because the official story, the family understanding, was that he loved the parcel of land, and needed time once a year to dote on it, to build mental homes and outbuildings.

Actually, of the six hours he only felt pain during two: the hour and a half drive up from Burlington to above Albany, and the last quarter hour up into the foothills to the logging road that accessed his plot. The last minute of the fifteen would be close to unbearable. He'd churn up the muddy rise to the flat spot that marked the site of the future house. As the truck swung right, he would be able to spy a long stretch of sloping ground, at the far end of which stood a particular copse of spruce.

One of the spruce trees had branches curled down and in, like an oversized toadstool. If the stretch of ground beneath it seemed undisturbed, he would feel a swell of gratitude like nothing he had ever felt, not even at the birth of his first son.

And for the next four hours Chris would eat from a little feast spread out on the tailgate of the truck. He'd throw his chicken bones all around him at random, like a king, just as soon as he'd sucked the meat off. He'd eat grapes. He *would* love the land. He *would* run the house up in his mind, and he'd giggle to himself while he shook the cold coffee from his cup. Usually at some point he'd find a stick that felt long enough and heavy enough in his hand. He might swashbuckle a little.

When he left he'd lean the stick firmly against one of the spruces, but of course it would never be there the following year. The sticks seemed to vanish into the ground, year after year, along with the pine needles and the new leaves.

• • •

This year, this morning, he had decided to take his two sons, Reuben and Maurice. They were thirteen and eleven years old. He had never before considered having them along, especially the first several of the May trips. But he told himself it was all right now. He felt somehow that they might ward off even the last minute of the worst fifteen. He wanted to share the four jubilant hours with them, and to have them see the future stand up out of the forest that now occupied the parcel of land.

But the optimism he had about bringing them along had begun to fray by the time he finished loading the bags of tupperware and foil packets that made up their lunch. Chris brought the tailgate up, and the window of the truck's cap down. He looked in through the back window at the welter of tools he'd decided to take, the limb cutter, the shovel, the rake, saw, hammer. He never knew what to take, really.

He raised his voice to the house. "Suzanne!" After a moment his wife appeared behind the screen door. "Tell the boys let's go."

"They're in the middle of a tournament," Suzanne said, shading her eyes.

Chris looked at his watch. "Well, they're gonna have to break it up. Come on, it's almost eleven o'clock. Tell 'em let's go."

Suzanne went back into the house, and Chris began to go over his little patch of front lawn, examining rents and bald patches. He looked back at the tall old wooden box of his house, and he considered it for a second nothing more than a box that held his family. He could feel where they were in the house this morning as he looked at it. He felt as though he had x-ray eyes because he could see them in there, Maurice and Reuben in the basement playing pool, and his wife moving toward them through the small slanting wooden passage of the stairwell.

The thought brought a clarified sense of himself, as regarded his street and his neighbors. He saw himself as a young husband and crew-cut father, a policeman, someone who occasionally answered calls in his own neighborhood. There was something magisterial in that sense of himself. He was occasionally addressed as "officer" on his street, and now, in his sweatshirt and a pair of jeans he'd owned since high school, he looked at the close-set houses across the street and wondered if they saw him there on the lawn, Saturday morning in his sneakers.

Suzanne came back to the door and opened it just enough to put her head out. "They say to tell you it's for the Coz."

"What game are they on?"

"This is number six. Maurice is up three to two."

Chris dug his toe into the grass and heard the roots pull. "Tell 'em they can finish this one, but if they tie up, they can play the tie-breaker when we get back."

"Chris, come on," she said.

"Chris come on what?" He was widening the hole with his toe, squaring it.

"Chris come on, I'm not Western *Union*. You tell 'em yourself. They're not listening to me. Watch Maurice play."

He looked up directly into her face to find her looking at him from the shade of her hand. He smiled at her, in a way that she had always said she liked. The hungry smile, she called it. *Just give me the hungry smile one time, Christopher Robin*. She recognized it and gave him a smart look back. He knew that for the past several weeks he had been more affectionate, more attentive, and although she was suspicious of it, the change changed her perceptibly in turn. She could sense some real contrition, real new love. As it did every spring, it called back the air of the girlfriend she had been, who trusted implicitly and expected only good from him.

He came into the house and stopped as he went by her in the kitchen and turned her around to kiss him. "That's my boy," she said, grabbing his face hard in her hand as he went to turn away and bringing it back to her mouth. She kissed him again, then said, "That was for trying to be the boss, Masseau."

On the cellar stairs, he heard the touch of pool balls and smelled the faint dampness that the dehumidifier could never leech out of the air. The boys looked up as he came down. Even though they were in sweatshirts and cut-offs, and Reuben was casually tilting a big bottle of Pepsi into his mouth, it was clear that it was a serious game, and that both of them were watching it like hawks. The pool table was an eight-footer that Chris had bought from a man in South Burlington, and it had taken him and three friends a solid

afternoon to break it down and cramp it through the stairwell. Now it seemed as if it had always been in the cellar.
There were rusty circles in the floor where its coasters had
dug into the linoleum like sharp toes.

Maurice looked up at Chris. "It's for the Coz," he said.

"Well, then pay attention," Chris said, going to one of
the bar stools and sitting down. He could already sense the
way that his presence had doubled the stakes. It wasn't
usual for him to watch their games.

"That's right," Reuben added, then burped out one flat
note. "Pay attention, pal."

Maurice glanced up at his brother, then deliberately
went back to the balls. "Paid pretty close attention last
three games, didn't I."

"I put the eight ball in last game, or I'd be ahead."

Chris looked at Reuben. "Well, you did put it in, and
you're not ahead. Close your mouth and let your brother
shoot."

Maurice let a smile drift over his face while he walked
around the table. His red hair was longish on the sides, layered over his ears, but spikey on top. With his thin, boy's
arms, he looked like a sprite. There was something almost
too vibrant about him. Once when he was six, he had had a
fit at the dinner table, laughing at some joke and then
laughing and shaking, his body twisting, unable to stop
while Chris held him in his arms. The doctors had run some
tests, and it had cost a good chunk of money before they
decided it was hyperventilation. It had never happened
again, but Chris thought he could still see the fit in him
sometimes, when he laughed, or when he leapt on Reuben
on the fresh-mowed front lawn.

Maurice was choosing between two difficult shots: cutting the four ball almost the length of the table — catching

just a hair of it and knifing it into the corner pocket — or a very long bank shot on the six, complicated by the need for english to spin beyond a dead ball of Reuben's.

Reuben was chalking his cue audibly, a little piece of flim-flam Chris had taught them both when they were children, a way to say, *I'll need to be good and ready for when you blow this one, friend.*

"Coming back for the six," Maurice said finally, with a flick of a glance at Chris.

"Good call," Reuben said, smiling a little himself now.

Chris shifted in the swivel stool. He was going to keep quiet, and then he couldn't. "Mo, why you going with the six? What's the matter with the four? Why don't you go with that one first?"

"Can't see it."

"Yeah you can. Look, you got a little teeny spot to hit either shot you pick. Why don't you take the one you're gonna hit *direct,* instead of the one where the cue ball has to come off a bank and hit the teeny little spot."

"They're both a bitch."

"One's easier," Chris said.

Maurice looked stubborn, started to say something, then obviously changed his mind. He looked at Reuben. "Okay, I'm going four ball."

"Good call," Reuben said again, smiling.

Maurice bent down over the table and made the awkward little openhand bridge that Chris could not get him to close. He sighted, then hit the purple four with a pretty slicing motion, dropped it directly in the far corner. Chris felt a quick bubble of pride, and Maurice's face took on the slightly manic smile again. He had two balls left, neither a difficult shot, and he bent almost immediately to the table again.

"Chalk your cue," Chris said. "Make some time, Mo. Don't rush it."

"Dad, I *know* how to play."

"Then take your time."

"All right."

"Willie Mosconi chalks his cue just to keep from screwing up," Chris added for good measure. "He says he doesn't need the chalk, he needs the time."

Maurice smiled, stood back up and chalked his cue. Reuben cracked his knuckles impassively. He was much taller than his brother, two years of fast growth ahead. He had a more smoothed-down appearance than Maurice; his hair was slick, seal-colored, and the height he had so far matched broadening shoulders. He would be a fighter, Chris could tell. He walked that way, and he pushed himself up into trouble when it offered, even at thirteen. Reuben kept his face placid while his brother set up. Then he said, "Well, anybody can win with Dad picking their shots for them."

"Yak yak," Maurice said from his crouch. His eye was squinted down the length of his cue. It could have been a rifle in his hand.

"Maybe you should have Dad point out the little spot on the ball for you to hit. I don't mind, go for it."

"Yak yak," Chris put in, and Maurice stroked the cue, pocketing his second to last ball. He got the bounce he wanted, and the cue ball drifted back to the one solid remaining, the seven, which he made, but just hesitantly enough to leave himself a longish, straight shot at the eight. It was a deceptively exacting shot, as easy to miss as to make.

"Don't say anything," Chris warned Reuben.

"There's nothing to say," Reuben said after a pause,

then forced a giggle. Maurice wouldn't be rattled much by any of the little digs or distractions, but Reuben was running through them anyway, almost methodically.

"And I'm *chalking* the cue, Dad. Look. I'm chalking it," Maurice said.

"Attaboy. It's chalk or choke, nine times out of ten."

They had started out playing for titles because Chris wouldn't let them play for money. He didn't want them to be gamblers; he simply wanted them to want to win. So originally the tournaments decided who was the house champion, but almost immediately it became All-Time Champion; then — after a few Saturday afternoons of the three of them watching Mosconi and Misczerak duel it out on television, on bright pink lounge tables — it was the Pro of All Vegas. By the time Reuben was ten and had begun to beat Chris maybe one out of every three games, they were shooting for U.S. Master of Billiards. Then Best Stick on Earth, Best in the Galaxy.

It was only when Chris lost the Galaxy title that he invented the Cosmos, the last ambition. He had raised the number of games to best of seven, favoring his own greater consistency, and when he'd won the title the first time they played for it, he kept it for awhile. The boys would come to him nights after he'd gotten off duty and was lying on the couch, and they'd beg him to play them for the Coz. He'd stretch and tell them to go beat a couple of contenders and then get back to his agent. They'd grouse and go back down the stairs and scrap amongst themselves and get better and hungrier all the time.

Of course he'd had to defend every so often, just like in the World Boxing Federation, or get the title stripped. When Reuben was twelve and a half, he absolutely smoked Chris, four games to one. For the last five months now, he'd been holding his younger brother off contemptuously, telling him to go out and beat Chris a couple of times and then get back with his agent. He'd squeeze Maurice's bicep and tell him to go pump some iron, lose the chickenwings. He was worse than Chris had been when he was the Coz, more of a needler. A couple of times after school he'd driven Maurice into screaming fits, according to Suzanne, talking about how he'd just love to play for the title if only someone with some real *balls* would come along.

Today was the first time in a long time the title had been loose, as far as Chris knew. Reuben had probably meant to get the defense out of the way quickly, before they left, to get his brother off his back for a month. Now it was all about to fold up on him.

Maurice sighted the long but straight shot. "Sorry, Reuben. I think this is it."

"That's okay," Reuben said, drinking from the liter bottle again. He looked at the shot. "Some people can hit these, and some people can't, no matter what they do."

"Thanks for the tip."

"I'm just saying watch tv sometime. Some people choke on these straight-aways."

"All right, Reuben," Chris said. "He's ready to shoot, close your mouth."

"Yeah. Silence, please," Maurice said, half as a taunt it seemed to Chris, and half as a way of talking himself into believing he was in control of the shot. He ran the cue a few times along his bridge and then touched it off, knocking the eight ball off the bank and only lipping the pocket. He'd hit it too quick, trying to beat his nerves to the punch. The cue ball rolled clear, leaving Reuben an easy finish on his last ball and the eight. Reuben exhaled loudly and laughed.

"*Fuck*, piss!" Maurice hissed, and in almost the same

instant he brought the stick down with a solid whack on the bank of the table.

Chris came off the stool. He was yelling before he thought about it: "Hey! You hit that table one more time, and I'm gonna smack your fucking *head*! What the hell do you think you're doing? You think this is some kind of god-dam community center down here? You don't *ever* hit this table, you understand me? Ever."

Both boys were silent, Maurice red-faced and eyes down, and Reuben with his eyes wide and his lips pressed tightly shut, to kill nervous laughter.

Chris stepped over and shoved the eight ball into a pocket with his hand. "You forfeit, smart guy, that's what happens." The boys still weren't moving. The three of them were in the space again, he realized as he was speaking, the space where they watched him like a madman, where they were afraid of him. They watched his hands. He softened his voice deliberately. "You screwed up the shot. Big deal. You screwed it up, not the table. Hit yourself if you wanna hit somebody."

"I'm getting in the truck," Reuben announced, moving toward the stairs, making a big show of staying out of it.

"We're all getting in the truck," Chris said.

Maurice still had his spikey red head down. Chris wait-ed for him to say that he was sorry, but after a few seconds it obviously wasn't coming. Reuben shrugged his shoulders silently and started up the stairs, and Chris followed him without saying anything else. The way he felt then was more or less the reason he'd stopped watching the boys' games. They'd gotten good enough and cocky enough that they couldn't be taught, and he'd lost enough in their esti-mation — as far as the game went — that he felt compelled to coach and show them that they lacked maturity. More often than not, he disliked himself after the games. He would think back on his temper as though it belonged to someone else.

Reuben stopped to pick up a baseball cap from the bedroom he shared with Maurice, and then he and Chris walked out and got into the truck. After another minute, Chris hit the horn and heard Suzanne yell to Maurice. "He's being a baby," Reuben whispered. Chris ignored the remark, touched the horn again.

Finally, Maurice came out of the house with a can of soda. He walked grimly over to the truck and climbed in beside his brother. Chris said only "Attaboy" when Maurice had slammed the door, although it seemed senseless when he'd said it. Then there was silence. They drove out of the Old North End that way, past the leaning wooden houses and bars with no windows like the Steer n' Stein and Eddy's Pub.

They crossed the invisible line into the larger, more affluent part of the city, where college girls with pony-tails jogged in the street and tourists sat at outdoor cafés. Chris found himself watching in the rear-view. He tried to look at them as someone who in another situation might be handing out a citation. He glanced over and saw Reuben watching the girls, while Maurice deliberately read some tiny contest rules on the back of his soda can.

They continued to drive in silence, until Chris snapped on the radio. Someone driving behind would have seen them riding in implicit order in the cab of the Dodge: Chris behind the wheel, then Reuben, and on the extreme right of the cab Maurice, the only one of the three who'd never been the Coz.

• • •

On the Interstate he could see nothing but forest, and occasionally the dollhouse charm of a village below them, in the distance. Chris would catch sight of a steeple and feel stirrings of both guilt and intense love for the white churches. They were signposts for him on the yearly trip; they seemed to speak directly to him.

They passed through the mountain resort village of Stowe. It was like coming across the southern trail of Burlington's affluence again, after losing it in the woods and hills. It was May and warm for May, but men walked in expensive suit coats, packages in their arms. The streets were lined with freshly washed new cars. They passed an Italian restaurant where Chris' precinct had held a yearly dinner once. It was the only time he had stopped in the village.

Reuben punched the button for another radio station. "Dad," he said, nudging Chris' arm.

"Dad what?"

"Did you bring your gun?"

Chris glanced at the glove compartment. "Yeah, I brought it."

"Can we shoot when we get to the land?"

"No, we're not shooting today."

Reuben waited a second before pursuing it. He had his eyes on the road. "We always shoot when we camp. You said there wasn't anybody around up there."

"There isn't anybody around," Chris said. "But that land's not for shooting. It's for building a house, for when Burlington gets too big and scummy."

"We could shoot now, though. Come on, Dad, why not?"

They were out of the village now, the truck passing over lowlands, green fields on both sides of the road. "Because that's the rule," Chris answered, poking his finger into

Reuben's still bony chest. "The rule is no shooting up there. Just rein your horses in, buster. The rule says no shooting, and no questions from skinny little farts like you. Observe the rules."

Maurice perked up a little. He shifted to face Reuben. "Yeah. Rules must be observed, and no questions from skinny," he too poked his finger into Reuben's chest, smiling for the first time since they'd left the house, "little *farts* like you."

It was something he wouldn't have done unless Chris was there. Reuben would have taken him down any other time. As it was he only grabbed Maurice's wrist and pushed it away from him. "Don't be talking about little, okay? Because you're really little. You're puny little."

Chris was glad to see Maurice light up again, and he kept it going. He made a little curlicue in the air with his finger, then poked it suddenly into Reuben's leg. "That's right, Pastrami Reuben, rules must be observed."

Maurice poked the other leg, laughing out loud now. "Rules *must* be observed."

"Knock it off."

"Rule number one, no shooting. Rule number two, *no* skinny farts."

Maurice began to laugh louder now, and Reuben's serious face evaporated into chuckles as well. Chris felt himself laughing, felt it thrilling inside his chest. The cloud that had come down on them after the pool game was gone. "So just please observe the rules at all times!" he half-shouted out his open window.

"This means you, skinny farts!" Maurice shouted out his.

Reuben stopped giggling for a second. "No really," he said, then giggled again, "why can't we shoot up there? Just cans, cans and targets."

It's working, Chris thought. The anxiety he normally felt on the way up to the parcel was almost unnoticeable, and he felt vindicated for bringing the boys with him. He stopped laughing. "Because it's very peaceful up there, Reuben. It's quiet. You'll see. It's just a place to think and to get away from all that kind of stuff. I'm on duty all year in Burlington, I don't need to have the gun out up there."

"Well, what'd you bring it for then?" Reuben muttered.

Maurice leaned over into his brother's face. He smirked just enough. "Just try to rein your horses in, okay buster?"

• • •

The village of Albany was as different from Stowe as it was possible to be. The small highway wound out of the woods of North Wolcott, up a hill, and suddenly the truck passed a gas station and a small desperate pizza and sandwich shop next to a service garage. Those were the only three signs that you'd reached the village's center. Other than that it was country farm houses, some restored, most not. Houses had signs reading Fresh Eggs.

Chris took a left after the service garage and angled up the road into the foothills. Reuben and Maurice were talking about some boy from school that both of them hated, what they would do if they caught him alone sometime, and right in the middle of it, with ten minutes or so to go to the parcel of land, Chris felt a strong premonition of wrongness about the trip. It went through him like fever chills. He felt sweat. He had the sharp, clear sense that something was disturbed up there, that the snow and ice had somehow shifted and rifled through the frozen turf. He saw himself pulling up the rise with the boys beside him, and one of them pointing at a flash of pale color through the trees.

Almost without thought, he pulled into a driveway with a sign saying, *Syrup*. The boys looked over at him quizzically. "This guy has the best syrup in the state," he lied quickly, then slid out of the cab. "You guys wait here. I'll be quick."

"Why can't we come?" Maurice asked, reaching for the door handle.

Chris looked at him for a second, fixed his eye. "Because you're waiting here."

Reuben turned to Maurice. "Deal with it, freak," he said.

Chris rang the front door bell, and the bearded older man who came out took him through a side door into the barn attached to the house. Chris had expected to see the sap boiler at work in a corner, but the barn was empty except for stacked firewood, a large gleaming riding lawnmower, and a wall of syrup cans. He chatted with the man a little, about the land he'd bought up the hill and how he planned to build a house there some day. The man didn't show any signs at the mention of the land, and Chris relaxed a little.

Without the man really asking, and without directly telling, Chris made it clear that while he lived in Burlington, his family was French Canadian by extraction and had lived in the northern part of the state for several hundred years. After that the man seemed to open up a bit. "Burlington's getting too big," Chris said, shaking his head dramatically. "Turning tax-happy. And getting a lot of bums downtown."

"I can't stand the traffic," the man said. "That's what gets me. I don't go in but five, six times a year, and it seems like I'm always fighting traffic. You'd think you were in Boston, try to get into Burlington four, five o'clock."

"You folks got the right idea up here."

"I think so." The man was wiping a fine film of what looked like sawdust from the chrome-bright syrup can. "But Burlington's got its advantages. You know what's the best thing about it, they say." The man was hiding a smile.

"What," Chris asked.

"Best thing about Burlington is how close it is to Vermont."

Chris bought a gallon of syrup and then, as an afterthought, some hard maple candy the man had sitting in a dusty pile. "For the kids," he said, although he knew the boys only liked soft candy. "Someday we'll be neighbors," he said as he left.

"Don't wait till then to come back," the man said.

He felt better when he came back to the cab. He handed the syrup in and then tossed the candy into Reuben's lap. Reuben's face brightened a little, until he stuck his thumb down through the plastic into the candy. "Hey, this is hard," he complained.

"Yeah," Chris said, settling into the seat, "well deal with it, you little freak."

"*Hey,* man," Reuben said, punching him in the shoulder.

"The land," Maurice began to repeat, "the land, the land, the land."

• • •

He felt better, and he chattered with the boys. Still, as the truck surged up the winding incline, Chris found himself asking forgiveness inside himself. The old sin, the big sin, was complicated by new ones. He had made a little over eleven thousand dollars in the last year, secretly, for setting two fires. One had been small, all but unreported by the paper, a summer cottage out on the edge of North Beach. But the other was the biggest he'd ever done, a bottling plant in the industrial section down Pine Street. That one had been a four-alarm fire, late at night when the second shift had gone home. He'd been paid cash. He'd set up trust funds for the kids, as well as a fund to pay the taxes on the new property. He'd done responsible things with it.

There were ways of looking at it. The bottling plant was an old factory, probably unsafe, but now in two or three years a new industrial park would stand in its place. Nicer looking, more and better jobs. The cottage was just something that the owner no longer wanted. It was demolition, more than anything, but done at a stroke, without having to limp through paperwork, and zoning and insurance and environmental impact studies.

And he had quit now, that was the other thing he offered up in his mind. He'd told the man who sometimes steered people his way that he'd quit. He had the land now, and some money to build. He had his place to retreat, when Burlington went the way of New York City, and that was all he'd ever wanted.

It was like playing pool for double or nothing; if you kept playing, you were bound to lose, even to a terrible opponent. Chance would do it. So he'd had the sense to walk away while he was up.

But he could not explain away the worst of the new sins. It was the fact that he'd started to investigate his own fires, that he'd set his friends on the force to catch suspects who didn't exist. In that, he'd marred the best part, the civic part, the magisterial part of himself that he most loved.

• • •

The rise was muddy, and when Chris headed the nose of

the truck up over it, he felt the wheels slide a bit. He felt it almost as vertigo, the sliding. But the tires bit after just a second. And then they were sitting up on top of the flat space, in what would someday be the family room. Chris looked down to the spruce and it was perfectly neat before the little copse, not riven as he'd imagined. It was tough grass and sticks, shot through with wild flowers, as it should be. All of the good sensations rose up in him. As every year, he felt like an idiot for worrying, for babying his superstitions.

He pushed open his door. "Come on," he told the boys. "It's all around you. All this on both sides."

They scrambled out of the truck, and as they jogged to catch up with him he noticed as if for the first time how skinny their arms were. Reuben had just suggestions of biceps. All of their growth was still going up, not out.

He stopped at a point further into the trees, slapped his hand against a trunk. "This is your room, Reuben." He walked next door, around two slight trunks. "This is yours, Mo." He pointed at various spots around them. "That's mom's and my room. There's going to be a sewing room right next to it — your mom's been pushing for that for a long time — then the family room beside that. Family room'll have windows looking down over that little drop there. We'll widen out this cut in the trees, into like a base-ball diamond shape, give ourselves a view." The boys looked out and down the fall of land to the small copse of spruce. It even looked peaceful. "And down there we'll have a big vegetable garden, grow vegetables."

"Where's the garage go?" Maurice asked.

"Right there."

"Where's the pool table go?"

"Family room," Chris said, smiling and pointing, "right

square where the truck's sitting now."

They ate lunch off the tailgate and scattered the chicken bones. They had a nice few hours, pacing off distances and marking trees with spraypaint. Chris let them drink beer with him, and they each had two cans from the six-pack.

The only bad moment was when Chris looked up and saw that Reuben was coming toward him with his revolver, wrapped up in the thick belt. Reuben had a half-smiling, half-begging look on his face. He began, "Dad, can't we just —"

Chris grabbed the gun from his hand and before he could stop himself, he'd swatted at the back of Reuben's head, as hard as he could. His hand only glanced off, though, as if Reuben had been expecting it. "No, Reuben, no! You understand me?" Chris took another step toward him, and Reuben stepped back, hand flinching up to cover his face suddenly. He brought the hand down even more quickly, stood tensed, eyes on Chris.

"What the hell does *no* mean? What does no mean, Reuben?"

"No," Reuben said.

"Well fucking remember it, then! *No* shooting up here. Not even cans and targets. Understand me?" Chris said, looking down at the coil of leather and the gun in his hand. "We'll go shoot somewhere else sometime, but don't keep bugging me, all right? Let's just enjoy it."

Reuben nodded, while Maurice looked on with wide eyes and a small, quashed smile, and it was the same moment they'd had in the cellar after the game, the moment they were always drifting into without warning. Somehow everything led to it, even up here, walking like little emperors through the walls of the new house.

They stopped for ice cream on the way home, and ate their cones on picnic tables outside the dairy. And while they ate and goofed off, the strange air between them lifted again, vanished one more time. By the time they got home, he felt like their father again, the way he felt when they were babies, and they'd run to him at the door, falling in their eagerness.

• • •

But the strangest thing happened that night, when the boys had gone to bed and he'd finished telling Suzanne about the way the land had looked to him this year. He couldn't sleep, so he'd gotten out of bed and roamed through the house, straightening and rearranging things. He'd bagged the garbage and carried it out beside the house. He'd lifted the lids of the cans, finding each all but full and so he stamped his foot down in the last one, crushing the green bag already in it.

The bag broke under his heel and split open. Little wheels of wood came spilling out, about an inch thick, like cut-up hot dogs. He glanced at them. They were glossy on the outside but raw wood on the flat tops and bottoms. He picked a bunch of them up in his hand, but couldn't make out what they were until he saw the number "21" printed in small black type on the side of one. It was a pool cue. Maurice must have run it through the band-saw Chris had in his wood shop in the cellar, just before they left that morning.

His thoughts went black, but some quality of the day made Chris decide to wave it off. He put down the immediate violent impulse to yank Maurice up out of sleep. He rebagged the garbage and said nothing.

Starting the next morning, he began to carry the wheel with the number "21" on it in his pants pocket, like a piece of thick change, a lucky charm. Eventually he polished and drilled it and made it into a sturdy key chain, so that when he and Maurice rode in the truck together it hung there between them. Neither ever mentioned it. It remained for the five years until Chris' death by stroke a queer little statement of kinship, something each really knew about the other.

Suzanne Masseau

Suzanne stood holding the curtain in the dining room window and watched very intently as the Dodge pulled out of the drive with Chris and Reuben and Maurice in the cab. Framed that way the three of them were not of two generations but more simply the assembled males of her family. She shook her head at the way they were playing their parts, at their soldiering. So serious. There was absolutely no waving or smiling, although they all three knew she watched from the dining room when they left for somewhere. Chris did not even toot the horn.

Suzanne pulled in and held her breath, hardly believing that there was no last-minute change in the pulse of the day. The truck had been loaded, and now the truck was in fact leaving. Chris and the boys were off to the land for the day, and Suzanne watched them from the front window, hissing "Oh Jesus, Suzanne" aloud to herself because their leaving meant that she would be meeting a younger man at the Motel Brown to have a short, friendly, cobbled-together affair after all.

The truck signalled left at the end of the street, and then vanished. Another car turned onto the street, erasing even the after-image of the truck. Suzanne waited and watched for about twenty seconds and then half-ran out of the dining room. She took the stairs to their bedroom two at a time, her sneakers banging loudly on the wide old boards.

Because she knew herself well enough to know that she would be slightly fuzzy and fainthearted when the time came, she had made and memorized a list of things to do, and now she started to hurry her way through them. She changed into a new silk blouse and a pair of white walking shorts she had pressed and hanging behind the bedroom door. From the closet she took a gym bag which contained a swimming suit, a towel, and some assorted toiletries.

Opening it, she took the swimsuit and the towel into the bathroom adjoining the bedroom; she ran the suit under the faucet, soaking it, then wrung it out and wrapped it in the dry towel. These she carried back into the bedroom and put back into the gym bag. She had already showered and shaved her legs and underarms that morning, before Chris was up, so she had only to brush her teeth. She thought about perfume but decided against it, even though she would take a second shower later, after, in the motel room. The perfume might linger in their bathroom or in the station wagon.

Today was the day because during the days when Chris worked, his patrol car could be anywhere in the small city. Worse, his friends in other cars would sometimes radio him that Suzanne was parked by Mirabelle's bakery or that they had seen her getting onto I-89. It was always done in the spirit of a joke, from what Chris told her — "She appears to have a cakebox with her, Chris, copy that cakebox" — but it was also a part of the buddy system, and in return Chris kept joking tabs on the wives of his friends as well.

When they had first married, that was one of the things Suzanne loved about him, that he would turn up in the Price Chopper and kiss the back of her neck suddenly. She had been flattered to be looked for and had felt a sense of her own new position when a cruiser tooted its horn as it passed her. Now it was just another reason why she seemed to have nothing private, why everything of hers was open to scrutiny and contingent on her family's needs. Now it was surveillance. And in the evenings, if Suzanne wasn't working a dinner shift, she had to be home with the boys.

So when Chris announced that this year he would take the boys with him to the Kingdom — that they would have a Saturday of house-planning and get away from women and the city — she had begun to premeditate, to lay out her own plans.

She carried the gym bag down to the kitchen and left a note on the refrigerator marker board: *Gone on a shopping spree, guys. Might stop at the Y for a swim. Hope you had a good day.* The note, like all the other preparations, was in case the truck broke down, or she unaccountably ran later than they did, or Chris blew up at the boys and cancelled the trip altogether. It wouldn't be the first time that his temper had come up out of nowhere to singe a day beyond recognition.

On her way out to the car, she went over the last few details in her mind. For one thing, she had to drive past Motel Brown to the Sears on Shelburne Road, where she had four big bags of miscellaneous items — including shirts for the boys, chalk and talc for the pool table, a replacement bulb for the refrigerator, a pair of slacks for Chris — on hold. It had taken her some hours, here and there during the last week and a half, to assemble it all. It would take her a little less than five minutes to pay for it, and the salesgirl would staple the bags shut with today's receipts.

For another, she wanted to stop at Brooks Drugs and buy a package of condoms, if her nerve held. She wasn't sure if she was expected to bring them, but she wanted them to be brought, in any case. She was not only cheating on her husband, she reminded herself roughly as she started the station wagon. She was cheating on a police detective as well.

• • •

Chris had had several affairs in the fifteen years since they were married, several that Suzanne knew about. When Reuben was just about one year old, Suzanne had come down with walking pneumonia and wound up spending two nights in the hospital. She came home to find a message written in careful lipstick cursive on the fold-out mirror attached to her dressing table. Whoever wrote it had folded it back in so Chris wouldn't see, but it read: *He was a stud! See ya!* And a handful of years later a woman called in the middle of the day — Suzanne was ironing and watching a baseball game on their little black-and-white set — and said that she and Chris were in love and planning to start a life together. Later that night Chris tried to soothe her by telling her it was only about sex, it had nothing to do with love, that was all wishful thinking, and that the woman who called had once even been in a mental hospital. That was the only time they had ever separated, for three weeks.

There were other threads of evidence snagged here and there in the fifteen years, scents and unexplained absences, but after a while Suzanne stopped pursuing the threads. Because tugging on them meant an unravelling, and it seemed never to be Chris that came apart, but rather herself and her sense of her own place, the feeling of her family lodged carefully in a corner of the world.

But it wasn't the infidelities that prompted her to have one of her own, at least not directly. It was a night five years before, in 1971. Chris and Avery Yandow were still partners then, working the third shift, on at eight p.m. and off at four a.m. Ordinarily Chris crawled into bed beside her and she moved quickly from light back into deep sleep, but that pre-morning she woke up and went downstairs. It was part of the mystic sense of their married history, that she had actually gotten out of bed, because she was a notoriously heavy sleeper. She thought she heard Chris out in the garage, but when she looked she saw the back door hanging open.

Then, as now, it was middle May and warm. Chris wasn't in the yard, which was fenced with tall redwood slats for privacy, but the fire barrel beside the garage had a fire going inside it. The fire made no sense to her, sputtering unattended in the rusted barrel in the dark yard. The flames were still growing, and she could see plywood sticking out at odd angles, waiting to be consumed. She went over and glanced down into it. And there was Chris' dark police uniform, half burned away, a pant cuff and a sleeve clinging to a cock-eyed board. She looked again into the white and orange heat to be sure. Then her vision penetrated another chamber of the embers, and she saw Chris' uniform oxfords were in there too. One was all but gone, the regulation heel a gelatinous, tarry mass against the coals.

She made her way inside and found Chris sitting in the dark on the couch in his boxer shorts, a glass of scotch in his hand. Even his socks must have been in the barrel. She stared at him. He seemed startled to see her, but only for an instant. His face was slack, and smudged along the jaw line with dirt or ash.

What's your uniform doing in the fire, she stage-whispered, incredulously. Chris?

Nothing, Chris whispered back. I had a bad day. Keep it down. Don't wake up the boys. Go back to bed.

You had a bad *day*? You're burning your uniform. That's a sixty-five dollar uniform. What are your *shoes* doing in there?

Look, Chris said softly, turning on the couch to face her, I had a bad fucking day and I'm not going to want to talk about it. It's over. So please, let's stop the talking about it right now. I mean it. Just forget the shoes, Suze.

Suzanne cinched her robe. Chris, she began.

Stop, Suze.

Chris, for Pete's sake —

He came up off the couch and toward her, and she took a step back, which didn't stop him but made him come forward with his hands out, palms up. He stood to one side of her and said it for only one of her ears. All of the sudden she could hear a whistle of fear in his voice: Look Suzanne, if you don't shut up now, I'm going to walk out the door and I'm never, ever fucking coming back. I don't want to talk about it. Drop it.

With that he went back and sat on the couch, where he would sit to watch television if it were daytime and the set were on. He put his feet up on the coffee table, going through the motions of suggesting that none of this was lunacy. So she had gone back to bed. In the morning she looked in the barrel, but the ashes had been bagged and removed. She looked in the papers for weeks, not knowing what she was looking for. She had never asked Chris. It was another thread that could not be pulled.

But she knew things about that night, knew them mystically. Whatever had happened had reached as far as the land in the Northeast Kingdom, and Chris' trips there each spring were a part of that. Whatever had happened had involved Avery Yandow. She could feel it suddenly when Chris and Avery were together. They looked at one another with slightly widened eyes; there was a new enormity to their significance to one another. Their way of saying hello shared a secret. And whatever it was, the last five years had diminished it, although each spring Chris went through his brief fever of guilt again. Suzanne's heart would go out to him each time, carefully, gingerly, an eighth of an inch at a time. But he never shared it.

So now, in 1976, what the fated and mystic history of their marriage amounted to for Suzanne was that she was tired of being the one whose life was waitressing and mothering and glimpsing the backsides of other people's secrets. It wasn't a thing of grudges. She was thirty-five years old and she wanted a thread of her own, to be the only one who knew what it was strung to. Just recently she had managed to admit that to herself.

• • •

True to Saturday form, upper Church Street was packed with people, and Brooks Drugs was nearly empty. Brooks had windows onto the street but inexplicably the industrial-style blinds were always shut tight. The strategy seemed to be to prevent prospective customers from seeing the goods. But like a patient, heavy-lidded snake, Brooks seemed able to survive on one customer every several hours. Suzanne had chosen it as the place to buy the condoms for just that reason, and because she could make the actual purchase from the pharmacist at the back of the store, risking only one pair of eyes.

She entered and went into a little act she had ready. Without slackening her pace, but without hurrying, she went to the shampoo aisle and picked up a bottle of conditioner. She looked for a second at the hair combs. As she came out of that aisle, she glanced down and saw that the pharmacist had no one at his single register. She walked to it, pausing to lift a pack of condoms at random from the display on the back wall. When she set them down on the little rubber mat beside his register, Suzanne saw that they were the same sort she used to find in her brother's room when she snooped there as a girl. They had the words "Ribbed For Her Pleasure" printed across the box. She felt her ears go hot, and she turned the box over.

The pharmacist was finishing a prescription, but he looked up and nodded. "Be with you in a sec," he said. Suzanne nodded and looked casually around her and then looked up. There was a large convex mirror above her, and Suzanne could see the two cashiers up front gossiping together. She got a ten-dollar bill out of her wallet to be ready to pay.

And then, as the pharmacist stapled the prescription shut and came toward her, she heard a hissing sound, rising and falling. It sounded exactly like someone snickering faintly from somewhere behind her. She craned her head around and saw no one else at the rear of the store. Her eyes went automatically to the shoplifting mirror above her, but again she could see no one except two young girls at the front in Makeup.

The pharmacist, a pleasant older man, picked up the conditioner and held it closer to his eyes. The nametag on his smock read *JIM, Your Brooks Neighborhood Pharmacist.* "Three-eighty-nine," he said, punching the register keys.

Without warning, the snickering sound started again. The pharmacist heard it too, and he paused to look before ringing in the condoms. As he did so, the sound abruptly ceased. Suzanne told herself that no one in the front of the store could decipher the small red dot reflected in the mirror — no one could know that it wasn't a package of antacid being thrust into the bag — but she was grateful when the pharmacist folded the bag shut, took her money and made out the change.

It was as she turned down the far aisle to leave that the

sound began again and Suzanne realized what was happening: about midway down the aisle, a young girl was spraying a can of something onto a pair of black leather boots she was wearing. The girl was crouched down, almost huddled against the display of shoe polishes and medicated inserts. It was obvious that she knew the store's blind spots.

Suzanne got within about five feet of the girl, close enough to see that she was of Asian descent and that she was spraying waterproofing compound on the boots, when a short, heavy woman in a Brooks smock appeared in the other end of the aisle. The Brooks woman had permed blonde hair and wore squarish glasses with mod plastic frames. "Jim, can you come out here please?" she called out toward the pharmacist's desk in a loud voice, before addressing the girl more directly, "You can't apply that in the store, miss. Please put that can down."

The girl stood up as Suzanne went by her. Her almond-shaped eyes seemed to lack focus. Although she had her black hair painstakingly curled and sprayed, she couldn't have been more than fifteen. "Here it comes," she said to Suzanne, out of nowhere.

The pharmacist came into the other end of the aisle, and he and the woman in the smock converged on the girl. Suzanne stopped at the end of the aisle, unable to leave.

"What are you doing over here?" the woman in the smock asked.

"Waterproofing my boots," the girl said.

"But *why*," Jim put in.

"Because I don't want them to get stained if it rains," the girl explained. "They're brand new."

The woman in the smock reached out and took the can from her. "Weren't you in here yesterday? Didn't I see you yesterday?"

"Yes. I mean, you have to wait twenty-four hours between applications."

"Look," the woman in the smock said, obviously growing angry, "are you planning to pay for this stuff? Because if you're not, I'm going to have Jim watch you while I call the police. You can't just use this stuff and not pay. That's stealing just like taking it out of the store."

The girl put out a hand as though to steady herself on the display of shoe products. There was a pause, and then she said, "I forgot my wallet."

"I thought so," the woman in the smock said. "Jim, will you watch her for a second?" The woman came back up the aisle toward Suzanne. The girl called after her, "What's the big deal? Everybody uses it once and then saves the can under their sink and never uses it again!"

Suzanne touched the woman's arm as she came to the top of the aisle. "I'll pay for it," she said quietly.

The woman's face was reddened with purpose. "You'll pay?"

"Really, I'd like to."

"Actually, ma'am, I think it's better if we call the police for this one." She lowered her voice. "She's been in here before. If she gets away with it, she's probably got fifteen or sixteen brothers and sisters that'll be in here next. That's nice to offer, though."

The woman started to move by her, and Suzanne touched her arm again. She looked the woman in the eye this time, possible now that the condoms were bagged and momentarily beside the point. "Actually, my husband's a police officer, and I'm not positive but I don't think there's any crime committed unless the person leaves the store without paying." Suzanne opened her handbag and took her wallet out. "And I'm paying. Tell me how much it is.

She's my son's classmate, and I'm going to see that she gets home."

"Ma'am —"

Suzanne opened the wallet and took a five-dollar bill from it. "Will this be enough?"

"Jim," the woman yelled finally, "how much is that can of Mink Oil?"

"Four-ninety-nine," Jim yelled back.

"You know, Jim," Suzanne heard the young girl say, "just because you're a *pharmacist* doesn't make you some kind of deputy sheriff. You can't keep me here."

The woman in the smock took the five-dollar bill and stepped back into the aisle. "Send her up, Jim. This lady's gonna pay. We're gonna do it the easy way." She turned back to Suzanne, and Suzanne could tell that she was now on the list of undesirables as well.

"There's gonna be tax," the Brooks woman added petulantly.

• • •

Suzanne came out of the store expecting that the girl would be gone, but instead found her seated on the large marble planter outside the store, wetting the boots down with the mink oil spray. Suzanne could smell the sour tang of the spray as soon as she stepped outside. The girl was bent over her dangling legs in such a way that the fumes from the spray boomeranged straight back up in her face. She would spray vigorously for a second, turn and cough a bit, gagging, and then return to the job. Suzanne had planned merely to wave goodbye but the sight of the girl leaned over in the fumes pulled her immediately to the planter. She put her hand on the young woman's shoulder. "Hello," she said.

The girl brought her head up, coughed once, clearing her throat. Her eyes, in their smooth tan folds, were screwed almost shut from the fumes. "Hi, thanks, really," she said, wiping at a tear that spilled suddenly from the corner of one eye, "I mean, I could have paid if they let me go get my wallet. It's in my drawer. At home. But it was decent of you. Seriously." The girl closed her eyes, turned her face up to the sun. "God, that stuff stings. Shit."

Suzanne watched her for a second. "Are you all right?" she asked finally. The girl seemed almost to be swaying as she sat, as though her sense of balance was deteriorating.

"Whoo!" the girl said, shaking her head, and laughing as she looked around at the people passing on Church Street. "Yeah, fine. Absolutely fine. Just the spray, in my eyes, and inhaling and everything."

The waterproofing fumes had dispersed, and suddenly Suzanne had a clear whiff of liquor, bourbon or scotch, strong enough for her to smell it standing at arm's length from the girl as she spoke. "You should take the can, seriously," the girl said, pressing it into her hand. "Like I was saying to those *fascists* inside, this is my second coat on these boots, so I'm done. That's all I need. And after that the can is just, like, dead weight." The girl was drunk, and now that Suzanne knew it she could hear the hesitations and slurred consonants. Suzanne couldn't believe it. The girl was maybe a year or two older than her son Reuben, who had just turned thirteen.

"Look, you seem — I don't know — not okay. Do you have friends downtown today, or your parents?"

"My father's working."

"How about friends? How about your mother?"

"My mother's in Taiwan. She went back. Re-crossed the ocean."

Suzanne sat down on the planter as well, tucking her bag in carefully beside her. "You're from Taiwan," she said.

"I was born in Taiwan. But I'm from South Union Street. I'm a Burlington girl." She opened her eyes, and smiled dreamily before closing them again. "And don't you forget it."

"Where are your friends?"

"I don't know. I called them. They weren't home."

"Oh," Suzanne said, looking at her watch. It was twelve-fifteen. The plan was for her to be at the Motel Brown somewhere between twelve-thirty and one. "What's your name again? I didn't catch it."

"Cheryl." The girl pulled a pack of Marlboro cigarettes from her jeans pocket and put one between her lips. Nothing could have signalled her still lingering childhood more clearly; she looked awkward lighting the cigarette, pursing her lips tightly, and she exhaled immediately without even tasting the smoke. She held it dramatically off to one side.

"Cheryl, I'm Suzanne."

"I'm quite charmed, Suzanne. To make your acquaintance."

"I just have this feeling like something's not okay with you, Cheryl."

"That's what my father says."

"No, I mean now. Physically, I mean. Have you been drinking today already?" Suzanne tried to say it as matter of factly as she could, but she could see that the hint of judgment made the girl stiffen. Cheryl looked as though she were considering ignoring the question, and then she took another drag from the cigarette, quickly blew the smoke back out. Her brown cheeks had tiny, almost imperceptible freckles. She patted her hair down with her free hand, checking it. "I had a cocktail with a friend, if that's what you mean."

"That's what I mean."

"It was a small party, celebration. This friend had something to celebrate."

"Still," Suzanne said, looking around her at people passing, "it's early, though."

"I don't even feel like thinking about it," Cheryl said, and then abruptly doubled over, coughing two or three times between her legs. She put her hand to her mouth tightly and held it there for a long minute. "Oh god," she said when she straightened up. Her face had lost some of its color.

"Look," Suzanne said, helplessly. Something about watching the girl smoke, after watching her inhale the waterproofing spray, had gotten under her skin. It was like watching someone chew tin foil. "Look, do you need a ride somewhere? Or is there somebody I can call for you? You don't look good."

"Thanks a whole lot," Cheryl said, clearing her throat.

"No, I mean, you look completely drained."

"I feel horrible."

"I can see that."

"I feel like I'm gonna ralph. I swear."

"Here," Suzanne said, standing and then holding out one hand a little uncertainly to the girl, "how about if I take you to your house. My car's right on Cherry Street. You said you live on South Union."

"But still a dual citizen of Taiwan," Cheryl said. She stood and it was clear that Suzanne would have to take her arm for her to be able to walk to the car, and so she took her arm. "And don't you forget it."

"Where on South Union, Cheryl?"

"We live at three-fifty-seven, like the gun. And by the way, don't try that joke on my father, because believe me, he won't get it. I tried it. He didn't get it."

"So I'll give you a quick ride home?"

"Sure. I should lie down for a little bit."

Suzanne got them moving, trying to make it seem as much as though she were strolling and window-shopping with the young daughter of a friend as possible. She found herself extra conscious of the well-dressed tourists and shoppers passing them. As they passed a trash can, Suzanne tossed the can of waterproofing compound into it. Cheryl looked at her knowingly. "I told you what happens to those cans, didn't I," she said. "Nobody wanted to admit it, but it's true."

They walked for a second. "When does your mother come back from Taiwan?" Suzanne asked.

"She doesn't."

"Oh. I see."

"Well, if you see it, tell me. Because I sure don't see it," Cheryl said. "Nobody told me a thing about it."

Suzanne saw her car as they rounded the corner to Cherry. She had had an irrational fear that it would be gone, towed, because she needed it, needed to make up lost time. She tried to pick an easier topic. "Your father's working today, you say. On Saturday afternoon. That's pretty dedicated."

"No, it's more like that's pretty pathetic," Cheryl said, leaning more heavily on Suzanne's arm without seeming to be aware of it. Suzanne wondered how often this happened to her. Cheryl seemed strangely comfortable with the situation, in spite of her physical discomfort.

"More or less pathetic. I'm serious," Cheryl repeated, throwing the cigarette in a long arc toward a trash can. She stumbled slightly throwing it, and it took them a second to resume. "You'd have to know the guy."

"Where does he work?"

"He works for IBM and — what did you say your name was again? Susan?"

"Suzanne."

"Suzanne, that's right. Well, Suzanne, he works for IBM in Essex, and he just loves it there. Can't get enough."

• • •

Three-fifty-seven South Union was a somber but fashionable brick house in a neighborhood of even larger and more impressive homes. It had dark green shutters folded back against the old brick, and the yard and gardens at the top of the drive seemed professionally tended. And also, Suzanne thought as she swung her station wagon into the driveway, there was no strong sign of personality to the house, no toys in the yard, no skid marks on the driveway or cat in a window. It was a come-on picture from a real estate listing — charming, manicured, lifeless.

When Suzanne stopped the car at the top of the drive, it became clear that Cheryl wouldn't or couldn't get out by herself. She had chattered for a minute when they left Church Street, and then lapsed into silence as the car's motion reached her, her eyes screwed shut and her face showing her nausea. Only once did she break the silence, opening her eyes to stare at Suzanne as she drove and remarking, "You've got very nice facial bones."

Suzanne got out of the car and went around to the passenger side. She looked down the street as she did so. There seemed to be no one at home in any of the houses, on a sunny Saturday afternoon. No lawnmowers, no bikes.

Cheryl looked up and focused briefly when her door

was swung open. "We're there?" she asked, starting to unfold herself from the seat. She was tall and gangly for her age, and there was something distinctly coltish about the way her thin arms and legs swung out of the car first, looking for balance.

"I got you," Suzanne said.

"I have to lie down," Cheryl whispered to her as she stood.

"Just one more minute. This is your house, right?"

Cheryl looked around her. "Right. This is Magnum House."

Suzanne walked her to the door. There Cheryl fumbled in the pocket of her tight jeans for her keys, and Suzanne had to reach out and steady her as she started once to fall. There was a discreet black metal mailbox beside the door which read, *Mr. Deng-Xin Lin and Family.* When the door was finally opened, Suzanne hesitated as Cheryl stepped inside. "Nobody's home," Cheryl said, turning to face her. "No problem. None."

"Are you going to be okay going in?"

"I wanna pay you," Cheryl said, turning to give her a pleading look. "I have my wallet upstairs. Seriously, I'll feel bad. I'll feel like shit. Seriously."

"You don't have to pay me. It was only five dollars."

"I have the money, I swear."

I just want to make sure that you get —"

Cheryl ignored her response and launched herself up a set of stairs directly in front of them. She took the steps slowly but two at a time. Watching her list slightly on the boards of the stairs, Suzanne felt the same sense of hanging danger she had on Church Street. She found herself closing the front door and walking up the stairs a few feet behind the girl, the way she had with Maurice and Reuben when they were small.

At the top of the stairs, Cheryl turned right and went into a doorway. Suzanne followed her. It was obviously her room, an explosion of disorder in a house otherwise meticulously ordered. Her dirty clothes were strewn about the floor, aimless knotted lines of them leading to larger piles near the walls. And pasted over her bed, so closely cut and fitted together that no ceiling or wall was visible, were hundreds of pictures of women from magazines, models of all kinds, women from hair coloring ads, underwear ads, runway models. The bed rested in an alcove, with the ceiling curving gently over it, and the mass of women's faces looked down on the bed from nearly every angle. Cheryl was lying on the bed, eyes shut, legs thrown over the side and one foot resting flat on the floor. For some reason, the bed and the chamber of women's eyes above it reminded Suzanne of the CAT-scan machinery they had used on her when she'd had fainting spells.

"Cheryl," Suzanne said softly.

"My wallet's in my desk. I don't want to move, okay?"

"Okay. Just stay put."

Cheryl stirred her foot, as though to raise it onto the bed, and then left it where it was. "There's stuff in the fridge," she said heavily, barely awake. "And there's a bar downstairs. If you want cocktails. I'm just gonna stay here."

"You're going to be okay, then?"

"Yeah, fine. I'll probably puke later sometime, when I wake up, before five o'clock," Cheryl said.

Suzanne looked around the room again, and then on an impulse brought the metal wastepaper basket from beside the small pine desk and placed it next to the bed. "I put this can right here," she said, "if you need it."

"Great," Cheryl said, face still immobile, eyes still shut.

It seemed to be all the goodbye that there was going to be, and so Suzanne walked carefully out of the room and shut the door.

She was about to take the staircase when her curiosity flared and she opened the door to what had to be the master bedroom. She poked just her head in. It was a pretty room, well-lit and with what looked like a small balcony beyond french doors that would overlook the backyard. A grand old Vermont sleigh-bed dominated the room. It was covered by a brilliant patchwork quilt, full of color and folk design. To her eye, the bed and its cover had the look of a gift, an expensive and complex gift from a man to his wife. And still the wife had left. The gift, and the daughter, had stayed. Suzanne pulled her head back, went back to Cheryl's room once more, opened the door a crack to check on her, then closed it.

When she reached the bottom of the staircase, Suzanne stood in the small entryway. She felt no rush to leave, no fear that Cheryl's father would come and catch her there, in his house. She had a feeling bordering on certainty that he would not return until five o'clock, and that she could sit and watch television if she wanted until five minutes to five. And she felt in no hurry to keep her own appointment. She felt unhurried, in fact.

She went over to the couch and sat down. There was a dish of butterscotch lozenges beside her, and she unwrapped one and put it in her mouth, sticking the wrapper in the pocket of her shorts. The house had a strange air. The furnishings were all well chosen, and as far as she could tell most of them were authentic New England antiques. There was an ancient oak jelly cabinet standing in an alcove that seemed to have been scooped to fit it. Whoever bought the furniture had taken their time and clearly had a distinct look in mind, a time and a place. On a hunch she lifted the cushion of the couch next to hers, and found that the interior of the couch was newly vacuumed. A maid, she was certain.

There was a phone sitting on the far end table. Suzanne crossed over and sank into the couch's other end, picked up the phone and dialed a number she had memorized that morning in case she needed it. A receptionist at the Motel Brown picked up the phone, and Suzanne asked for a last name — Bove — that was the same as the name of the restaurant where she and the younger man worked.

There was the sound of a connection being made, and then he said, "Hello there."

"Hi, it's me," Suzanne said.

"I knew it." There was a pause. "You're not coming."

"No. I'm sorry. Something happened, and I can't."

"Something," the young man lowered his voice, "with Chris?"

"No. Not something with Chris. I had to put one of my kids to bed. Some kind of stomach thing."

"Oh."

Suzanne heard the confusion, but she sensed that he was about to try to make it okay for her, because he was a good-spirited, agreeable person, half the reason she had been planning to go in the first place. "Well," he said, "I'm glad you said it first. I was having doubts too. But now I'm going to make you pay for half of this room."

"Okay. Look, I'm really sorry. If I could have with anybody it would have been you, but whatever, I can't. I'm sorry. I'll tell you more about it later."

"Don't worry, Suzanne. I'm a big old boy. I'll still lust after you from afar. I'm on the bar Monday night. You're working, right? I'll see you then. Okay, Suzanne?"

"Okay," she said. "Don't be mad at me."

"Nobody's mad. I'll see you Monday."

When he had hung up, she hung up. She found herself staring at a picture of Cheryl in a small silver frame, standing behind the phone on the end table. It was a picture of the girl in a tennis outfit, when she was a bit younger and smaller. Her jet-black hair was straight in the photo, uncurled. Cheryl was smiling, but the sun was in her eyes, making for a half-grimace as well. Without hesitating, Suzanne picked up the frame and turned it over, drew the photo out with the ends of her fingernails. She put the frame back and held the picture in her hand. She was going to steal it, she realized. It was a wallet-sized shot, and she took a minute right then and there to put it in one of the plastic sheaths of her wallet, where Chris would almost certainly never see it, right behind Reuben and Maurice and right in front of the children of other families.

Smooth Water Gabriel Francis

When Smooth Water made the move from St. Albans down to Burlington in middle spring 1971, it was a revelation, like being a deaf guy sitting alone in a big dark field on the Fourth of July and turning around to stretch and seeing that the darkness is full of green and red fireworks, and that there's a mass of people pointing at the sky.

In St. Albans, 1971 was like 1961, which is to say it was like 1951. His mother went to work at the Farmers' Cooperative Creamery every morning at six until four, and she wore more or less what women wore thirty years previously. His father worked at track maintenance for the Central Vermont Railroad all day, then fished on St. Albans Bay until six at night, pretty much rain or shine, clear water or ice. The guys he'd grown up with — the guys who'd instinctively, mercifully, shaved his name down to one clean syllable, *Smooth* — those guys lost their edge somewhere between junior year and graduation; they'd snuck off to the Creamery or walked with their fathers down to the Administration Building at the railroad yard to see about work. All their plans slipped away from them. But Smooth kept his plans active, helped out by the fact that he had always been repulsed by cows and fish, and had always felt that when it came to trains he'd much rather ride them than sweep them.

So when he was twenty, when he'd reached his full height of six feet three inches and his full muscular heft of two hundred and sixteen pounds, Smooth was gone south to Burlington.

And that was where the fireworks were happening. He

got hired his second day in town at a new suburban construction site out on Spear Street, and within two weeks the
labor union had launched one of the biggest strikes in
Vermont history. The company had provoked it, announc-
ing that it would no longer pay the men for the twenty minutes it took them each day to sharpen their tools. They were
trying to nickel-and-dime the union into a strike, by
demanding give-backs. All of the sudden Smooth was getting up each morning and going off to help man a siege, a
semi-circle of men surrounding a thicket of naked wooden
house frames. The union brought food out to the site and
speakers yelled into a bullhorn and guys would beat out a
rhythm on their idle Snap-On toolboxes. He was a warrior,
without half trying.

From college kids who came to the picket line to drop
off donuts and help carry signs he learned that demonstrations were also taking place in town, on campus, once or
twice a week. Not huge demonstrations, not Berkeley, but
respectable, two or three hundred people yelling and
cheering and sunning themselves on the green. A professor
had been fired from the University for giving a speech
while a flag was burned in front of him; for added measure,
whoever lit the flag had thrown it up onto the iron statue of
Ira Allen, where it rested like a flaming three-cornered hat.

So some days Smooth Water would leave his own picket line, if things were slow and the weather was hot, and
hike in to the University and walk right into a whole different battle. He could watch, he could join in or he could just
hook up with a circle of people passing a pipe around. Life
had a lot more buttons to push now.

Sometimes as he was hiking toward the University,
Smooth would think about the way his father saw St.
Albans. His father was Abenaki, and he would talk about

the land up in Swanton, north of St. Albans, where the tribe existed in greatest numbers. He would tell Smooth about the swamp land there for hunting, and the fishing on the Mississquoi River. To his father St. Albans was the city, the hustling machine you loved and hated and couldn't leave. When Smooth went south through Winooski and then down into the bigger city of Burlington, he was just continuing a drift his father had begun thirty-five years before.

But his old man always dreamed of recanting, returning north to the quiet of the Nation. And that was where Smooth had to laugh. He himself, after a riotous month in Burlington, was already thinking New York, New York.

• • •

One thing about Smooth Water's life that was true was that the good and the bad came in elegant cycles. Not the way that life shakes out for most people, and not what they mean when they say they're having a rough time of it, or that things are looking up. Smooth's cycles were truer and more relentless and more sharply defined than was natural. When things got bad they nose-dived and nothing could keep it off. Part of the reason he left home was that he'd lost his driver's license in a DWI bust, and with that went his job and the rest of his money and his father's last bit of patience with him, one thing leading to the next.

But when things pointed skyward, it was as swift and certain as the upswing of a ferris wheel. He could just about feel a wind in his hair, it was so pronounced. And he always knew, infallibly knew, when he had stopped heading one way and was headed now the other. He knew it in his stomach the way your stomach gyroscopes the ferris wheel. When he left St. Albans and stuck out his thumb and immediately caught a ride straight into downtown Burlington, he knew his bucket was going up.

And in the last days he had sensed that he was hitting the sweetest part of the upturn, the place where he was sometimes a magical man.

Two days before, for instance, he had been worried that with the strike he wasn't making enough to pay his minimal rent, forty-five dollars a week for a room at the cheap Wilson Hotel just off lower Church Street. Then he went in to the picket line at the construction site and found that earlier that morning a large bunch of guys had built a little shack out of scrap wood piled near the dumpsters. It was stuck in the trees just to one side of the entrance to the site. The shack was part lean-to, but it had one side that was more or less walled-in, just big enough for two to sleep abreast and play watchmen at night. They'd even put a quick floor and a quick window in it. Somebody had written *Our Clubhouse Local #1120* in marking pencil across the overhead beam. Strike signs had been stapled to the walls.

One guy, a funny fat kid about Smooth's age named Bobby Dinardo, had already volunteered to keep watch; Bobby had parents who thought it was a good time to beat up on one another and then bring it to him for arbitration. As a result Bobby's jokes always came with a quick laugh and a backward head-flinch, just in case.

So the first thing Bobby had said to him the previous morning was just the sort of thing he needed to hear. "Hey, Smooth," Bobby said, slapping Smooth's upturned hand. "What'd you think about sleeping out here for a while, being a watchguy with me? They want two of us out here at nights, now that we got someplace to keep the weather out. Case they try to sneak in some scabs under cover of dark- ness. The married guys can't do it. Come on, you got no wife. You got no life."

Smooth just looked down at him. Bobby was only about five foot six.

"Come on, we can spritz it up a little, put in one of those big redwood hot tubs. Maybe some fuzzy carpeting. It'll be chick bait. What d'you say?" Bobby had this pudgy smile the whole time he was running it down.

Smooth resisted breaking into a smile himself. He was already planning how to spend the forty-five he'd been budgeting for next week's rent. "I don't know. How much is it gonna pay?" he asked, thinking this would get a big laugh out of Bobby.

"Twenty bucks a night," Bobby answered. He was serious, too. "The Union wants to make sure the ground stays occupied at all times. They want to show how committed we are, how we're dug in. What d'you say?"

"I say call me watchman. When do we get paid?"

"The guy from Regional just left, my friend." Bobby brought out a crisp twenty, folded it and stuck it in Smooth's t-shirt pocket, then patted the pocket.

Smooth Water just smiled. He'd had a job where he worked for two weeks. Now he had a job where he wasn't working, but for *not* working he was getting what amounted to room and board and cash over top of that. It was laughable.

That night he and Bobby broiled cube steaks over the fire and sat up drinking until almost three. Smooth listened to the woods and the looming silence of the construction site, and he felt fantastically contented. The air was crisp, campfire air. He reached over and pulled an oatmeal cookie from a package they had lying open beside the cooler.

"Hey, Smooth," Bobby said from the other side of the fire.

"What's that?"

"Where you from? You from Vermont?"

Smooth rummaged in the bag. "St. Albans. I call that Vermont."

"Funny. Hey, Smooth. You an Indian? I'm guessing."

"Part."

"Which side?" Bobby asked.

"My dad's Abenaki," Smooth answered. He bit half the cookie away.

"But you're not."

"Part."

There was a short silence, just the fire sparking. "What's your mom?"

"Goddam nice lady."

"You know what I mean. Don't be a prick."

"French-Canuck," Smooth said, throwing the uneaten half of cookie into the flames. There's more where that came from, he thought. The powers that be will just send more.

"Abenaki got it tough," Bobby was musing, dragging a long curved stick through the flames. "They don't even get recognized officially as a tribe, I heard. The government tells them they're not a tribe, and to go pee up a rope. No land for you."

"Anybody should have their head examined, going to the government and asking for land anyway," Smooth said disgustedly. "You don't get anything except pissed off that way." The cookie was now glowing neon-blue. "There's other ways of getting what you need. Even my old man, droopy as he is. Doesn't ask for shit. Goes out and takes fish out of the lake every fucking day. *Takes* them. Never had a license in his life."

"What if they can't take what they need?"

"They can. Anybody can if they use their head, if they're hungry."

"Oh yeah?" Bobby hunched up to look at him over the flame. "What about you, smart boy? What's your plan for getting over on the world?"

Smooth smiled a lazy smile. He ran a hand through his hair, then brought a glossy black hunk of bangs down before his eyes and looked at it for a second. "The plan is New York, fool. The City, if you know what I'm saying."

"That's where my dad's from, Queens. So New York. *What* in New York, specifically."

Smooth leaned back. He almost lied, then said it and as he said it he truly believed it. "Making movies. You ever watch *Psycho*? That was something that was far out. That scared the absolute living shit out of everybody in the whole world. People in Italy were shitting their pants when they watched *Psycho*."

"So you're gonna be Anthony Perkins?" Bobby tossed his stick into the flame. "Big-time actor. I got a great big picture of that happening."

"No, man. That's backward. I'm gonna be Alfred Hitchcock. He's the guy that's doing it all. The rest of them are just running around and doing what the fat man says."

"Yeah, well it takes a lot of money to make a movie. Lot of money, my friend. Lot of luck too."

Smooth inched his sleeping bag up around himself, felt warmth engulf his body. He had to smile at a guy like Bobby. Bobby was a hell of a nice guy, but Bobby was going to be building other people's houses his whole life, whistling to himself while he built their breakfast nooks. "If luck's all it takes, Bobby, I'm the boy. First thing you did today was hand me twenty dollars. And you didn't even know I needed it." Bobby snorted. "Like you hide it so well," he said. He pulled up his own sleeping bag. "Shows you how much you know. Good night, answer man."

About a half an hour after dawn, they woke up to two pickup trucks pulling into the site. A man got out of the lead truck and came walking resolutely toward the shack. He was a wiry older man with white hair and heavy black glasses. Two words popped into Smooth's mind: *gym teacher.* Bobby was out of the little shack before Smooth had his shirt on; he stumbled after, thrusting his feet into his sandals.

"Well, it's coming down," the man with the glasses was saying by the time Smooth came up behind Bobby. "That was built with company materials, and you damn well know it."

Bobby was scuffing one sneaker in the dirt of the site driveway, looking down and shaking his head. This was when Smooth learned that Bobby's home environment had produced a division-one liar. "Actually, sir, no, actually that's not so," Bobby said. "These materials were *scrap*, it was all on the scrap heap on the east side of the site. You know the scrap heap. Now if they'd been taken off the scrap heap directly, I'd say you were right. I would. But what happened was that Simonetti Brothers came with a salvage truck evening before last, and they picked up a load, which they were paid to do and which they did. Now once they had it back at their yard, it's true that we made another transaction with them to bring the scrap back here," Bobby pointed to his own rusted Ford pick-up, "in my vehicle — "

"You're so full of shit your eyes are brown," the white-haired man shot back.

"That's a good one." Bobby turned to smile at Smooth, then turned back. "That's a really good one. I never heard that one before."

The man turned in a small circle in the driveway, in agitation. It was obvious they had thought they'd dismantle the thing before anyone made it out to the site. When he spoke again it was with barely restrained anger. "Well, how about this, huh? How about if we pull it down, and you can just argue with my boss about whether that wood's scrap or not. I'm not going to sit and listen to your line of bull."

Bobby shook his head. "It's not much, I'll admit, but it is the headquarters of our Local for the time being. If I were —"

The man stepped close to Bobby. "Clear your shit out. Now. We're gonna pull it down."

At that point, Smooth leaned over Bobby. He looked down at the man's top shirt button instead of his eyes. "No, you're not. Believe me," he said.

The man looked up at Smooth, his face tight behind the glasses. Of all the things Smooth could have said, those five words seemed designed to jam the man's sense of his own options. After another look at the shed, he simply spun around and left, signaling the other truck to follow him out of the lot and back down Spear. It was all done with the air of someone who plans to come back with the police. Bobby started for his own truck.

"Where you going, fool?" Smooth yelled.

Bobby jumped in the cab of his truck and rolled the window down. He was laughing at Smooth. "I gotta hit a pay phone and tell Steve Simonetti what he did with his old man's truck the other day. He's got no idea at this point." He cranked the radio and pulled a pair of mirrored sunglasses from the visor. With his fat sideburns the glasses made him look like a hillbilly rock star. "No you're not, believe me," he repeated as he angled by Smooth Water. "Here I'm going to all this trouble to lie and shit." He laughed, and the truck scraped onto the road, and Bobby yelled the words back over the music one more time: "No you're not, *believe* me!"

• • •

It just intensified that afternoon and evening, the elegant lucky streak. Steve Simonetti not only agreed to lie the lie, but invited Bobby and Smooth to a party that night organized by some of the demonstrators on campus. It was going to be a mansion party, Bobby said, in the house of some rich couple gone to Europe. Lobster and ladies, Bobby said.

But that was just the day's opening play. The guy from Regional — who made Bobby look thin — drove out to the site to tell them that he'd been on the phone the whole day with the Company and their lawyer about the little watch house. Finally, he'd told them to shove it, and he was so keyed up about it all that he gave Bobby and Smooth another twenty on top of the money they'd already been promised.

Bobby told him that it was Smooth who'd really put his foot down, and before Smooth could deny it the guy from Regional was telling Smooth that he could have a big future with the union, that rank-and-filers sometimes made president on the strength of what class they showed during a walk-out.

You're interested in working for the union, the guy said, you let me know. I'll show you around, show you the ropes. Never hurts to be a big guy in union work, believe me, Smooth. People tend to get exercised. Some bulk lets them know there are boundaries. Think about it. You let me know, kid.

When the guy was gone, and Smooth pulled the two

twenties out of his pocket to stare at them, one felt thicker than normal in his fingers. He rasped at the edge with his finger and it divided in two; it was two twenties, all but glued together. Now he was looking at three twenties in his hand.

And that evening at around eight-thirty, while Bobby and Smooth were sitting in the lean-to with George, the older carpenter who'd agreed to watch the site during the party, they heard two of the caterpillers fire up, one after the other. At first they could see nothing, but then they saw lights go on at the north end of the site. It took a minute or two but finally two bulldozers crawled toward them, each with an overlarge spot craning down to cast a moving pool of light. It was hard to tell, but it looked as though a man was walking beside each of the bulldozers, just blue-black suggestions in the dark.

"Fuckers snuck back through the woods," Bobby whispered. "They're just gonna run it right over."

It was funny. When the idea leapt into Smooth's head, he considered only whether he should do it, never whether he could. It was as though he was straddling opposite sides of the moment, both knowing it as an accomplished fact and deciding whether he wanted to give birth to that fact. He decided, when the cats swung around the last foundation hole and throttled loudly toward the shack, that he wanted to. They were about seventy-five yards away, most of the length of a football field.

He bent down and picked up a piece of slate that nestled itself knowingly between his thumb and forefinger, and then he sidearmed it. The triangle of slate disappeared, slanting upward into the darkness. It should have fallen short, or banked and tailed off to one side.

The first spotlight shattered with an abrupt crash, there

was a shout, and after a few more seconds the engines suddenly went silent. Then the second light was quickly snapped off. There was the sound of hushed voices and then the bulldozer drivers disappeared back into the woods. Word passed afterward that the men on the dozers thought they were up against a hunting rifle with a scope and silencer combination.

Smooth Water got the reaction from Bobby and George that he tended to get when the lucky moments started to pile up too quickly and too visibly. They started to act like his high school friends in St. Albans. They cheered with him under the lean-to, and they retold the story of it when they'd gone back to their beers, but they gave him sidelong glances as well.

• • •

By the time it was time to go to the party, though, the mood had purified itself, and they were all jubilant with the victory. Bobby offered to stay at the site in case the dozers came back, but George said that as long as Bobby and Smooth were back by twelve-thirty it'd be fine because it'd take the dozer drivers that long just to dry their tears and get a change of underwear.

Bobby started his pickup and then looked over at Smooth. They'd each had three or four beers, and they were giggling at everything that presented itself.

"Now remember," Bobby said, lecturing, "these are *college* girls at this party. You don't want to look ignorant. If anybody asks, we're not insulation packers or sheet-rockers, we're laborers. If they want to know where you went to college tell them you decided not to go because the whole thing seemed like a cop-out. Tell them you felt like it was

time to really live inside your *body* for a while. That'll move
things in the right direction."

The whole way into Burlington Bobby continued to talk
about meeting girls, and Smooth was excited about the
thought, but when they got to the party it was the house
itself that captivated him. It was in the Hill section, and it
was massive, an honest-to-god four-story Victorian mansion, dwarfing the expensive homes around it. It sat back a
bit from South Willard Street, on raised ground, and it had
porticos and balconies and widow's walks at regular intervals, designed to take advantage of the view of Lake
Champlain it commanded. At the very top was a small
tower that looked as though it might contain a bell or a tele-
scope, but it was too dark and too far away to be sure.
Music pumped from the house, a vibration Smooth could
feel in the soles of his sandals.

"Twelve bedrooms," Bobby said as he locked his truck.
"That's bedrooms. That's not counting bathrooms, drawing
rooms, spanking-the-maid or whipping-the-butler rooms."

"That is *so* fine," Smooth said, looking up at it.

"That's nasty old Burlington money, what it is. The guy
that owns this was the heir to the guy that used to own one
of the spinning mills over in Winooski. The man spun himself one hell of a home, I will say that for him."

Although the front lawn was empty, the flat expanse of
grass behind the house was full of people, dancing, standing, spilling in and out of the house. Bobby pointed out the
brother and sister who were hosting the party, whose parents owned the house: the brother wearing a stylish silk
American flag shirt, and the sister combing her fingers
through a head of brilliant copper hair fanned out like a
peacock's tail.

Overall, it was the same crowd that Smooth saw at the

campus demonstrations, the long-haired men, the unshaven women, but tonight there was another different contingent, the prep kids with short hair and even tans and expensive walking shorts. The two groups didn't mix well; as Bobby and Smooth went into the house and through to the kitchen and the keg, each room they passed was dominated by one group or the other.

"The hippies can't wait to get out of college and join a commune in Jericho, and the prep kids can't wait to get out of college and join a country club in Shelburne. And you know what, Smooth?" Bobby turned and asked. "In twenty years you won't be able to tell 'em apart. Just like when you were in tenth grade you thought ninth graders were kids. They're the same, the frat boys and the granola types."

The kitchen, next to the keg, was the only real melting pot, and that was where Bobby pulled up a tall stool and sat down. A woman with knotted black hair was reading tarot cards on one of the countertops, and he stuck his head into the midst of it, whispered politely, "Can I be next? I've got some serious life issues I need resolved."

The woman with the cards looked up with a little annoyance, but Bobby's fleshy face was so earnest — he had on what he called the harmless goomba look — that she smiled and nodded. Bobby pointed a finger around at the people sitting on counters and chairs. "I'm next," he told everyone, getting smiles from nearly everyone, insinuating himself in a way that Smooth had to love.

Bobby was content to stake out the keg, to farce around with the other people who had staked out counter space. "Look, man, why mess around on the edges?" he argued, hand cupped around Smooth's ear. He was already well on his way to being good-naturedly drunk. "Everything swirls through here sooner or later. You got your pick of whatever the tide brings in. Why put together a salvage mission when you can kick back on the beach?"

"I want to check out the house," Smooth said, patting him on the shoulder and picking up his beer glass. "I want to see the big rooms. I can't believe you get in a house like this and you sit in the kitchen. You got no class."

"Yeah, well mind your manners up there." The tarot reader signaled Bobby and he edged himself heavily off his stool. "Stay out of the people's sock drawers. Don't go trying on clothes. These are respectable people we're dealing with."

• • •

It took him several minutes, once he got to the fourth floor, to figure out which door would take him up to the little tower. Although there were fewer and fewer people on each successive floor, still there were a few meandering and gawking on the fourth and Smooth went into a bathroom and waited until the hallway was clear before trying random doors. He didn't want to be caught fiddling around; he had the impression that exploring the top floors was bad form. But the tower was what he really wanted to see. It seemed to him, somehow, that he was meant to see it.

The last door he checked was a small closet, with shelves that ran in a spiral pattern along its back wall. It took another minute for him to recognize that the shelves were also stairs. He stepped into the closet space and began to climb. When he pushed on the closet's ceiling panel, it lifted smoothly and locked into position.

When he finally stood upright in the small tower, which had room for only a high-backed antique love seat and a small glass table, he almost burst into laughter. The view was astounding. Music surged up at him from the yard below and vibrated through the fibers of the structure. The little love seat looked out over the entire, brightly-lit town and took in as well the entire sweep of the Adirondacks over the black water of the lake. The tower saw everything. It had only a lattice on each side, and through the slats he could see to the north and south the diminishing of the town's lights, its descent into forest and wetland and farmland. He could see three sides of the irregular square that was Burlington, he could take it all in at once.

Smooth sat down in the love seat and put his feet up on the little glass coffee table and marveled at the speed with which he'd won through to this place. Four weeks ago he'd come to the city for the first time, knowing no one, and now he was sitting in an improbable position. He had a job, friends, some money, and he could imagine with absolute clarity a set of circumstances under which he would come to own this house, whose secret was that it was built as a pedestal for a love seat.

It was a throne, not a house. Smooth had known that just looking at it from the street. It was his kind of place, the opposite of the low-roofed series of additions his father had cobbled together and insulated and called a house. This home on South Willard spoke to his sense of his own potential, which, while he was rising in one of his cycles, was limited only by Smooth's own vocabulary. He needed to learn new words and images for what he was capable of and what he was worth, and this structure spoke to him in that necessary new language.

He sat there for more than an hour, watching the lights of the town and listening to the building. It said, Smooth, this is the house in the uncut movie of your life.

• • •

He descended the stairs into the false closet, unable to shake the sense that he had tapped the nerve, stumbled into the clarified setting of his life. He stepped out of the closet and walked to the spiral staircase and then, nudged by certainty, looked down to the floor below. Sitting on a plush settee was the red-haired sister. She was alone, smoking a cigarette, legs crossed and one sockless, sneakered foot jogging up and down, as though she were waiting for someone. She smoked with her left hand, her right occasionally combing back and forth through the thick copper hair.

Smooth looked down at her and felt the unhurried spooling forward of the next few hours. She would look up and they would see each other from a cockeyed angle, like something from Hitchcock's *Vertigo*. There would be a stamp of the exotic in that way of meeting. They would talk, she would take him back through the house, give him the tour.

But before he had finished scripting it in his own mind, the sister got up and pushed her cigarette into a small stand-up ashtray next to the settee. Then she ran down the stairs, two at a time, never looking up. When she reached ground level, she crossed the polished entryway floor and disappeared, the mane of hair swishing. He never saw her face.

And just like that it was complete, the cycle, and Smooth felt his ferris wheel bucket calmly heading down, as it always did. It saddened him a little. He'd hoped this one would last longer.

• • •

He searched the kitchen for Bobby, then the backyard, and

finally the first floor, where most people had moved inside and made themselves at home. He went out to the street and found Bobby's truck still parked there. But he could not find Bobby. He asked a few people he thought had been standing in the kitchen with him, but no one seemed to remember. After a while there was nothing to do but drink and wait. He sat at one end of the back porch, speaking to no one and feeling a new discomfort with himself. He'd lost the sense of himself as someone favored by events. Suddenly he was tired of the music and tired of himself, a man-sized half-Abenaki kid from St. Albans who hadn't gone on to anything after high school, hadn't gone on even to the Creamery or to the railroad yard.

At a quarter to one, Smooth had the sense that Bobby wouldn't be back until morning. He'd found someone or something, and he was gone for the night. Smooth thought about sleeping in the cab of the truck, but it was locked.

At about one-thirty, when the party had begun to thin out, to reveal the really hard-core drinkers and the people with nowhere else to go, Smooth decided to hitch back to the site. George was the kind to wait for them, he wouldn't just leave.

But before he left, Smooth went into the kitchen and wrote a note telling Bobby that he was heading for New York City, and thanks a lot for everything. He stuck the note under one of the wipers on Bobby's truck. He meant it half as a joke, as payback for leaving him stranded, but also Smooth wrote it as a kind of charm. Once he had it down on paper it seemed to him more and more possible that he'd really go. It was an argument he could make to himself, that he'd actually already begun the trip. He had the note to live up to.

• • •

He got no rides at all, not one, and he walked from the Hill section up through the University and down Main Street to Spear, and then he walked for another forty-five minutes into the countryside, up and down dark hills and past the occasional new housing development. But he felt much better walking in the open air, in the coolness and the silence. He did what he always did when this turnabout happened, he laughed at it.

Because it *was* funny, and there was no other way to respond to the downturn, it would happen no matter what. He laughed at the way he'd been ready to squander the wave of good fortune on a big house overlooking a big lake, how he'd have hexed his way into that if he could have. For as often as the magic had insinuated itself into his life, he'd never learned how to bridle it, direct it to any real good. He just got drunk on it, and then mourned it later, when he was hurting. It happened over and over again and again because he was lacking something. He thought about his father taking fish from the lake. Day after day, his father — who was a small man, only five foot seven — brought a handful back from the water. Smooth could almost never remember a day when his father opened the screen door empty-handed. His father told Smooth once that luck had nothing to do with fishing, or with anything. Luck was an excuse for lazy men and dreamers.

And then for no good reason, as he walked, Smooth thought of something entirely different. It was a movie about his father that would begin with his father sitting in his little rowboat on St. Albans Bay at sunset, coming home with the string of fish the way he always did, coming into their small homemade house and tossing them to Smooth to clean the way he always did. Although Smooth had always detested doing it, gutting the things and dressing them for the frying pan, it would be different in a movie. It would mean something. It would say something to people about what his father possessed and what Smooth Water lacked, the ability to cast luck to one side and take what was needed.

And the film would end with his father doing what he'd always said he would do: he'd return north to Swanton and trap and fish and fix cars, and Smooth's mother would leave the Creamery and never look back. His parents would both leave St. Albans, the place in the middle that was too fast for his father and too slow for Smooth himself.

Smooth stopped walking and stepped off the road into the tall grass to take a leak. He was a little drunk still, and he wavered slightly as he stood. Before he realized it, he heard a car swoosh by him, and he half-turned.

He heard its brakes set up, the crunch of gravel, and then the car swung back to him, blue neon flashers lighting up the darkness. Smooth Water buttoned his jeans and smiled at the way things were. Of course it had to be the police, cruising by. Where you from, son? the cops would ask him. New York, New York, he would say. And where you headed, boy? Swanton, sir, he would answer back. I'm on my way to the Abenaki territory to direct a full-length feature movie, and my name is Smooth Water Gabriel Francis.

The Past in the Present: 1993-1995

Reuben Masseau

Maurice's very favorite night with his brother Reuben was one of the last nights before the jury returned a verdict in the Outreach arson case, and it was also the night Maurice discovered the whisper booth. He was in Nectar's having an early dinner, at about a quarter to seven. It was Thursday, the twenty-eighth of October, 1993. He was working on a ham and cheese omelette he'd talked the cook into making; it was overly browned, sooty-tasting, and he was wishing he'd simply ordered a club sandwich. Ordinarily he'd have taken it back to the cook, told him with a smile that it was a foul piece of work and gotten something else. But asking for special orders and then sending them back was pushing his luck, even with this cook and in this place, and so he was eating the omelette.

He was also paging quickly through the *Free Press* as he ate. Maurice knew that once Reuben showed at seven they'd talk or take a walk and meet some people, and he'd have no time to finish the paper. So he was scanning for names of people he knew in the Crime Log, and without admitting it to himself he was studying the local and state legislative news. These last things were routine: his studying so that his brother couldn't catch him in ignorance, and his failing to admit to himself that he was studying at all. What was different about tonight was that Reuben was out on bail and his case went to a jury on Monday, the day after Halloween.

As he was turning the page, he heard a woman next to his ear say in a high, soft voice, "He was lying the whole time." The words were very distinct.

Maurice turned his head, thinking the waitress must have come quietly to his table. But there was no one there. In fact, the restaurant — mostly a late-night hang-out — was nearly empty. Except for the cook standing at the grills in the front of the long room, and two women in a booth in the very back, Maurice had the place to himself. There was no one within earshot of him. Someone would have had to shout for him to hear.

"I came over to his house, and I *seen* her car right there in the driveway," the voice went on suddenly, intimately, as though from someone whispering into a hand cupped around Maurice's left ear.

Involuntarily, he spun around in his seat, suddenly realizing that the woman might be standing behind his booth, in the space between it and the wall. But the narrow space was empty, just smudgy white walls and an empty beer cup.

By now he had put down the paper and was sitting tensely in the booth. He and Reuben had an old uncle in Florida who was supposed to be crazy, the sort to hear voices out of nowhere telling him to quit his job, and Maurice felt a quick, nauseating fear that the flooring of his own mind was giving way. He took a sip of his Coke, chewed the ice. He ran his thumb and finger over the bars of his goatee. He tried to sit casually, but he had his ear swiveled and cocked like a cat.

A fragment drifted by his ear: " — so I look at him and I go, *my* fault!"

He waited, not moving.

"My sister saw him that time," the voice said.

And then as he happened to glance at the back booth, he saw the young woman facing him hold up a hand in a stop gesture, and he saw her lips form the words he heard in a close whisper, " — that's what you mean by straight with somebody, I'm gone. You can mail me my crap." The woman's lips all but popped on the last word, and the sight of it matched up almost perfectly with the sound beside his ear.

Maurice sat back, absolutely delighted. The woman had to be forty feet away from him and talking softly. He looked around at the construction of the place, something it had never occurred to him to notice before. The roof was built in a smooth cream-colored arch that melted down into walls fitted with turquoise and emerald decorative panels that looked like the lids of barrels. It was some 1950's architect's tribute to the galley of a ship, and the booths running down either side only added to the nautical feel. He could almost see the woman's words rising up to the ceiling and traveling its slope, then stooping to fall to his ear, in the corner of the room directly opposite her.

Discovering something like this in an obscure bar out on the highway would have been novel enough. Burlington was a small place, with a correspondingly small share of local miracles. But Nectar's was a main nerve center for the downtown; he and Reuben had both been eating and drinking there since they were kids. They knew every inch of the place, all of its legends, and all of the people who'd invented all of the legends. And now he'd stumbled onto a brand-new thing. It was like finding another, cannier burial chamber in a pyramid already completely picked over by grave-robbers and archaeolgists.

Maurice leaned forward, trying to find the right position again. "Can you hear me, baby?" he whispered, watching the blond woman.

She didn't react, but continued listening intently to the other woman.

"I love you, baby," he said just a little louder, in a phony

French accent. "Can't you hear my words of love?" Maurice started to giggle, and he looked back toward the open kitchen area, caught the cook giving him a look. Maurice smiled. "Killer omelette," he yelled over.

• • •

By the time Reuben arrived, at a few minutes past seven, Maurice had determined that the whisper booth only worked one way. He happened to be sitting in the receiver; the blonde in the back was sitting in the mouthpiece. As Reuben came up to the booth, Maurice stood and, without explaining what he was doing, took his brother by the shoulders and steered him down into the receiver seat.

Reuben started to protest. "What, have you got a bucket of water rigged up or something? You just discover whoopee cushions?"

Maurice patted him down into the booth. "Just take a load off your feet. I want to show you something." He could hardly control his excitement, and his grin made Reuben more suspicious. Maurice laughed. "Bok, just trust me, okay? You are going to fucking love this, but you have to sit in that seat. Just sit there and listen for a second."

Maurice sat down across from him. Reuben was taller than Maurice and broader, with sober eyes and long, thin brows that still managed to seem brooding. He sat straight and listened, and Maurice thought that except for the scarf and the jean jacket he looked like a Secret Service agent, sitting there listening and glancing around. Reuben didn't have much in the way of a sense of humor. Maurice had gotten the sense of humor and the red hair.

"You mean the sound of the lights?"

"No, not the lights. Keep listening."

"I don't hear anything, Mo," Reuben said, shaking his head.

Maurice leaned across the table. "I gotta adjust you a little bit," he said, and when Reuben started to slap at his hand, Maurice pulled back and looked his brother in the eyes. "Reuben, come on. Just please humor me." He reached out and took Reuben by the shoulders and pulled him forward a bit, trying to recreate his own position leaning over his omelette. Reuben watched Maurice's face as he let himself be inched forward.

"There," Maurice said, leaning back. "Now just stay like that and listen for a second."

Just as he said it, he glanced back to the women in the rear booth and saw that they were preparing to leave. "Stay there," he said quickly to Reuben, as he got up. Without waiting for an answer, Maurice turned and walked back to the rear table. The blond young woman was about to put her coat on. Her friend, a chubby brunette wearing a Hinesburg Volunteer Fire Department windbreaker, was finishing the last of her beer.

Maurice stopped in front of the blonde. She looked about twenty-one or two and both naive and highstrung. She was awkwardly smoking a cigarette. He tapped his forehead. "You ladies are leaving. I can't believe it. I was going to ask you to let me buy you a round. I've been over there for an hour trying to work my nerve up."

The two looked at each other, and the blond woman covered her obvious pleasure by looking skeptical. "You were gonna buy us a round?" She snuck another stagey look at her friend. "And just why were you gonna do that?"

Maurice narrowed his eyes and looked at her carefully. "Because even from all the way across the room I can tell that you haven't been treated well recently. I can tell that somebody thought they could walk on you." The young woman's eyes widened. "I just wanted to let you know that while it's true that ninety-six percent of men are, in fact, assholes, there's still the other four percent of us out here, just struggling along and trying our best." Maurice smiled, and the blonde's face turned up into a smile as well.

"Oh my god," she said to her friend. "He can tell just by looking at me."

Maurice gestured her back into the mouthpiece seat. "I'm not gonna bother you. You two just continue your evening, and I'll send a round back. Just go on like you were. What are you drinking?"

"Heineken," the friend said quickly.

"Me too," the blonde said, sitting down with a barely controlled flourish.

The bottles on the table were cheap domestics. Maurice nodded in appreciation. "Right. Have a nice rest of the evening," he told them. On his way back to the table, he stepped through the side door into the bar half of Nectar's and ordered the beer. When he got back to the table, Reuben was leaning back in the booth, looking annoyed.

"Mo," he began, "I'm not in the mood for some sort of half-assed double date. I have some other things on my mind, you know what I mean? If you want to go out and go hound-dogging, just say the word and I'll let you be. I'm tired."

Maurice settled into his half of the booth. "Reuben, believe it or not, I'm *trying* to give you a thrill here. If you would just give it a chance. Just sit up a little bit closer to the table and humor me for a few minutes."

Reuben didn't move.

"Bok, come on. I'm telling you you'll love it when you

hear it."

Reuben slumped further toward the wall, pulled a menu out and began idly going over it. It was for show, as both of them knew Nectar's short menu well enough to recite it.

Maurice stared at him. After looking at the menu for a second, Reuben stared back.

"Fine," Maurice said. "Don't hear it. Don't learn something."

"I'm just not in the mood for games, that's all. Whatever the hell it is."

"You're just not in the mood to do something I ask you to. That's more like it."

"That's extremely deep, Mo." Reuben put a finger up, and when the waitress came over he ordered a ginger ale. He saw Maurice look at him as he did so, and when the waitress had left the table, he leaned forward. "I'm not hungry. And I can't seem to get worked up about the idea of drinking for some reason."

"I didn't say anything," Maurice said. "I just don't think I ever saw you order a ginger ale before."

"Well, suddenly you've seen it."

Maurice leaned forward, put a hand on Reuben's shoulder, overly sympathetic, just barely grinning. "You feeling okay there, champ? Got a little stomach ache or something? Ginger ale's just the thing for a weak stomach."

Reuben simply looked at him. There wasn't the grudging smile that Maurice had expected — just obvious fatigue, with something still jumping and worried back in the eyes, like a nervous tic waiting to take control of the muscles.

Maurice pulled back slightly. "Reuben, don't tell me you're worried about Monday. Come *on*. Your lawyer destroyed that woman. She started out saying she saw your car, and by the time she was done, she was saying she saw a *blue car*. She didn't even stick on the model of the car."

"She said she saw a small blue car with a bumper sticker on the right side, that could easily have been a Skyhawk," Reuben corrected him.

"Could have been," Maurice repeated.

"More likely than not, was how she put it."

Maurice's face broke into a big smile. "The woman is sixty-four years old, man. She wears big thick black-framed, fat-assed Poindexter lenses just to get a view out the window," his smile widened even more when he saw Reuben giggle slightly in spite of himself, "I mean, face facts. She looked like a fucking Alzheimer's case up there. Catherine had her eating her own tail."

The waitress came with Reuben's ginger ale. Maurice held out what was left of his Coke in a toast. "To good lawyers, and to whoever did burn that place down."

Reuben didn't raise his glass. "You know, Mo," he said, looking down at the water ring his glass had left on the table, "what really put the fear of God into me was when I looked at the judge at one point — I think it was when the prosecutor was reading some affidavit into the record, and the judge was rubbing his eyes and staring off into space. He was cleaning his glasses, cleaning his ears."

"Cleaning his cleaver, more like. Jerk-off."

"The guy wasn't *listening*. That got to me somehow. I just had this image of getting hauled off to jail by a bunch of people who were only half awake during the trial. It was like the judge is driving this big eighteen-wheeler, and he's just forgotten how much force and power he's got going." Reuben looked up. "That's what I'm really scared about. Getting run over by somebody who's fiddling with the radio stations instead of watching the road. Somebody who's thinking about lunch."

Maurice watched his brother talk and could only remember one other time when he had seen Reuben truly, cold-in-the-bones frightened. At fourteen, Reuben had borrowed their father's police revolver one weekend while he was away on a fishing trip, and Reuben and a friend had gone out to a stretch of Lake Champlain below Ferrisburg to shoot. Maurice blackmailed his brother and was paid a full two dollars to keep his mouth shut. But Chris Masseau had scented something amiss somehow, and he knew that the gun had been moved and fired. He'd chased Reuben out the house and up North Avenue, both of them sprinting, and finally yelled to Reuben not to come home. That night, Reuben tapped on Maurice's window, looking haunted and miserable. They'd talked through the screen, with Reuben starting at every creak. Eventually, he came home and took his punishment, a genuine beating that left him unable to go to school the next day. But it was the jumping white eyes outside the screen that Maurice remembered most vividly, that and Reuben's failure to believe that Maurice had in fact kept his mouth shut, and the lesser beating he had given Maurice as a result.

"Catherine said the jury would have to be insane to convict, Reuben. She knows what she's talking about."

Reuben leaned back into the corner again, let himself smile. His hair, shaggy and brown, hung about his face, as though it hadn't been combed in a day or more. "You're right. I've just got the shakes. But I figured this would be as good a time as any to tell you a few things, as though I was going to jail. As though I might never see you again. For when you become acting-oldest-male in the family."

"Reuben," Maurice interrupted. "Don't be a dick. Please."

Reuben held up his hands. "I said as though."

Maurice nodded slowly, and Reuben continued. He seemed to have turned some kind of corner in his mind, and his voice was less anxious, more conversational. "I've been thinking about it and I think I've got three things to tell you. One about Dad, one about you, and one about me, basically in that order."

"How cool," Maurice said.

"The thing about Dad is really pretty interesting." Reuben cleared his hair off his forehead. "I got this from Avery. He and Dad used to be really tight when you and I were kids, I don't know if you remember that. They used to be patrol partners before Dad took the desk job. But one night a couple of years ago, Avery was in the Steer N' Stein, just drunk out of his mind. And I went over to say hello. First he kept reminding me that he was my godfather. He was very sentimental over that fact. Then he started telling these cop war stories about him and Dad, and before he realized it, I think, he started to tell me some secrets. Apparently Dad was a bad man before he died, Mo." Reuben came forward, and Maurice did as well, without thinking. "Avery said that Dad used to — guess what? — burn stuff down, for money. He didn't say so, but I think he was hinting that Dad burned down some of those churches and buildings back when we were kids."

"You're shitting me," Maurice whispered.

"I didn't believe it at first."

"But you believe it now."

Reuben shook a finger at him. "I started thinking about it. I can remember this point where it seemed to me we got richer when we were kids. When we started to have better cars, and vacations, and the land up north. Dad had the house up there half-built when he died. All that took money. So yeah. I believe it."

Maurice took off his baseball cap and ran a hand over his short red hair, put the cap back on. It was a little display he didn't have to think about anymore, but automatically put into motion when he was bored or perplexed. Finally, he said, "Well if he was, I call it pretty ironic that Dad actually was what you're on trial for being. That's pretty trippy."

Reuben nodded and met Maurice's eyes. "I agree," he said softly. "Very ironic."

They sat in silence for a moment and then Reuben spoke again, his voice still lower than before. "Anyway, I could see that part of what Avery told me. Dad was Dad, after all. A guy to make the world into what he wanted it to be, and get pissed off if it didn't happen fast enough. But the part that was even weirder was when Avery said he and Dad had done some nasty shit together, when they were partners. He kept hinting around at something, like he wanted to tell me but just couldn't. You know how Avery nods the whole time he talks to you. He was drunk and nodding and he winked at me and said, your father and I shared one dark little secret, Reuben, that he took to his grave and I'll take to mine. He wouldn't say anything else, even after I bought him another beer. I tried asking him the next time I saw him, and he just put me off, said he'd just been raving the first time."

"Sounds like they got together and knocked someone off."

Reuben laced his fingers together and said nothing.

Maurice finished the last of his watery Coke. "Well, knowing Dad I'm sure it was some hard-core secret. Dad was a fucking hurricane when he was pissed."

"You're right, brother," Reuben said. He was about to say something more, and then he stopped, a look of sheer puzzlement on his face. He was in approximately the same position Maurice had been in earlier, leaned out over the table. He looked at Maurice, and then turned around quickly to look behind himself.

It was the whisper booth. Maurice clapped his hands delightedly when Reuben swung back around. "Freaky, isn't it?" he asked, twitching his eyebrows. "And brand spanking new."

● ● ●

Once Reuben found out about the whisper booth, they had to leave Nectar's. Reuben didn't want to talk private matters in a place where the air seemed suddenly whimsical, exposing whoever it chose to expose with no regard for tradition or everyday physics. Maurice tried to convince him that they were in the receiver booth, but Reuben wanted to walk down to the lake.

They came out onto Main Street and the soft, chill darkness of late October. They walked through the milling crowds in front of Muddy Waters Coffee, and Maurice stared in through the plate glass windows for a second at the people playing chess and drinking cappuccino. He saw a short-haired woman inside catch sight of Reuben and point him out quickly to her date. The woman had a nasty look on her face, as did the man when he turned, and Maurice glanced at Reuben, but he had his eye on the street and seemed to have missed it. Maurice quickened his step a bit and said to Reuben, "Pick up the pace, guy. It's getting tough to hold myself back."

They walked past the courthouse and City Hall Park, which was dark and empty except for three homeless men with sleeping bags unfurled around a large oak.

"Parasites," Maurice said, looking to Reuben for confirmation. But Reuben said nothing. "Scare everyone out of the park," Maurice added for good measure.

In the people that passed them, the bar-goers and late shoppers, there was here and there a single person in costume, a skeleton carrying a jack-o-lantern, or a woman with her face painted with stripes and tabby whiskers. They didn't blend in, and they didn't clash with the evening. It was the Thursday before a Sunday Halloween, and the ghouls were just beginning to enter the city's pedestrian bloodstream. They would be thicker every day until Sunday, when Church Street would be swarming with extra police patrols and the perennial costumes, the vampires and serial killers and college girls self-consciously playing prostitutes.

As they passed St. Paul Street and began the slope to the lakefront, Maurice punched Reuben mildly on the shoulder. "So what's the thing you wanted to tell me about me," he asked.

Reuben looked over at him as they walked, and then his fist shot out and he smacked Maurice's arm just at the dip beneath the shoulder muscle, knuckles finding the bone, just hard enough to smart. But he smiled affectionately when Maurice rubbed the spot, looking ruefully over at him. "I'll tell you if you promise not to say a word," Reuben said. "If you can't promise that, we'll skip it."

"I promise, freak."

"All right. I've been thinking about this a lot. I started thinking about it when you wanted to get on the stand at the trial, and Catherine wouldn't let you. She's a pretty sensitive person, and I thought it was interesting she said no. So what I've been thinking has to do with how you do what you do, the organizing, the politicking, interacting with people. That's really your talent. You *are* good at what you're doing, that's something I've told you before. In some ways — not all — but some ways you're better at it than I am. You feel people's dissatisfaction, you can pick them out of a crowd. I've watched you, and you pick it up like trace radiation."

Maurice felt his poker face begin to dissolve into a smile in the dark, and he scowled to chase it away. What Reuben was saying made distant connection to the way he saw himself, and the obscure, local sense of destiny he felt. He had known for years that he had the power to move other people. That he could make someone on their way out of a bar stay in a bar, or make someone determined to hate him like him. But hearing his brother say it was intoxicating. He continued walking in silence until Reuben went on.

"You could probably be as rich as you decided to be, Maurice Earl Christian Masseau," Reuben held up a hand to silence his protest at having his full name strung out, "if you went all out selling real estate or riding lawn mowers. I mean it. I think you understand intuitively how human beings make their choices — what to do, how to live, who to trust. Now if you could make them *like* doing what you want them to do, you'd have something really powerful going for you."

"Can I talk now, swami?" Maurice asked.

"No, you can't. That was the easy part. This next part is the part I'm really trying to get you to see. You can move people, yeah, but there's a part of you — the mean part, maybe even the bitter part — that likes to let them see at the last possible minute that they're doing your bidding. Likes them to know they got worked."

"*Bull*shit," Maurice coughed into his fist.

"Shut up, Mo. I've seen you do it. And eventually that realization pisses them off and they develop their own grudges and then they're useless to you. If you can get over that, give up that cheap kind of thrill, you'll have it made. But right now it's like that stupid open-handed bridge you use on the pool table. It's holding your game back. You play damn well with it, but it's holding you back."

"Can I talk now?" Maurice repeated.

"Sure."

A couple walking up from the lake passed them, holding hands and murmuring to one another. Maurice waited for them to pass, then spat on the sidewalk. "This mean streak I have. Since you see all and know all, tell me where this mean streak came from. I'm curious to know. From Dad?"

Reuben shrugged. "Maybe you were born with it. I think it's more the case, though, that I built it inside you, spit dribble by spit dribble, BB gun wound by BB gun wound, broken bone by broken bone." He walked for a second, rubbing his hands together against the cold. "Remember that time when you were like eight and I was ten, and we were wrestling in the living room? I was about twice your size — "

"Goddam right, I remember," Maurice put in. "You used to sit on my chest until I couldn't breath, push your knees right into my ribs."

Reuben was smiling and nodding. "And I was holding you down and slapping your cheeks — just playful little pimp-slaps — and letting a little dribble of spit hang down out of my mouth almost to your face and then sucking the stream back in at the last minute. It was this talent I had. I could have gone pro. You were basically having an epileptic seizure underneath me, you were so mad — "

"I think if I wasn't afraid Dad would kill me," Maurice broke in, "I'd have gotten his gun and killed you."

"And I'll never forget, it was the closest to slow-motion

I've ever come in real life — I saw your hand reach back and grab one of the wooden slats from the coffee table, pull it out of the fixtures, and then you broke it right in two against my forehead." He rubbed his forehead with a finger. "Remember that? You can still feel the mark right here. Little moon shape."

Maurice found himself laughing, but he had no real memory of the incident. "You *definitely* deserved it, you jerk."

Reuben was laughing a little too. His face looked hollowed out in the dark, shadows at his eyes and cheeks. He seemed as though he were finally at ease, and Maurice was glad they'd gotten off the main drag.

"I know, Mo. I always told myself it was cool because I was your older brother, and that's just what we older brothers did. That's my point."

They crossed Battery Street and entered the waterfront park. The lake was calm and indigo black, sparkling brilliantly only where it lapped at the lighted boardwalk.

"I don't think I get it," Maurice said.

"I'm saying that I worked out on you when we were kids. When I pulled you on the saucer behind the snowmobile, I used to build up momentum and swing you into trees on purpose. My friends and I used to throw you the ball when we were playing Smear the Queer so we could dog-pile you. Try out kung-fu moves on you."

Maurice looked over at him, keeping his features flat, blank. "So what's your point? I'm dense, I guess, as well as having the mean streak."

They detoured around some skateboarders practicing jumps on the curb.

Then Reuben said, "The point is I'm sorry for that."

• • •

They walked down the lighted boardwalk. It was punctuated by large wooden bench-style swings, each filled by couples rocking slowly back and forth on noisy chains. They reached the end of the boardwalk and picked up the bike path, which took them out of the lights and onto the thin tarmac path that followed the shore of the lake to the North Beach woods. There was more than enough moonlight to walk by.

They walked just past the water treatment plant, to a small weedy lot to the left of the bike path, empty except for a series of granite blocks standing here and there. Some of the blocks were tall, others just knee-high. Some were put together in rough table shapes, and it wasn't until you had walked into the midst of them that they coalesced into a design. It was a miniature Stonehenge, made out of Barre granite by some guerilla artists in the early 1980's. It was laughable and grafitti-spotted in the daylight, but when the sun had gone down it took on a little dignity. It was a Stonehenge you could walk through and tower over, and both Reuben and Maurice had spent hours there growing up, drinking beer and heaving the bottles out over the lake and into the sunset.

Now, they each picked a medium-sized stone and sat down. Maurice pulled a joint from his pocket, one that he had rolled with special care, one that he had not admitted to himself was being rolled with special care. But Reuben waved it away. Maurice shrugged, lit it for himself.

"Last thing," Maurice prompted.

"What?" Reuben answered, startled out of a thought.

"Last of the three. The one about you."

"Oh." Reuben kicked a foot at the dirt beside his obelisk. He hesitated for another minute. "I did burn it down, Mo. The AIDS center. Surprise." There was a long pause. "We all bitched about it so much, how it was just going to attract more of the wrong kind of people to the county, and one night I drove past it and it just came to me what somebody had to do. What Dad would have done. I did it and I didn't tell anyone, not one person. That way everyone could get indignant. That way nobody had to go into court and tell lies except me."

Maurice let out a hit he had been holding for a half a minute or more, and when he did his vision stretched and swelled in a way that he liked sometimes. Now it seemed for an instant that he and Reuben were giants or gods, lolling in the dark on ruins that would dwarf a man, resting before striding across the lake to the Adirondacks. He blew on the ember of the joint. "Jesus, I knew that Reuben. I thought you had a revelation for me."

Reuben said nothing, and then he reached for the joint. "You knew that."

Maurice handed it to him. "Oh yeah."

Reuben dragged the joint and then flicked it onto the ground in front of him. It continued to glow next to one of the stones, and again Maurice felt that he was looking down on a campfire made by figures too small to see. It was a crazy feeling.

"Bullshit," Reuben said softly.

"I knew soon as I saw you, day we read about it in the paper. Knew it."

"And just how did you come to that conclusion?"

Maurice picked up a handful of sand and threw it at the ember, extinguishing it. "That's just how younger brothers stay alive, freak."

Cheever & Deng-Xin Lin

To those who had never set foot inside it, the white, green-shuttered building was known as Pearl's, but otherwise it was known simply as the bar. There was no need to distinguish further, as it was the only one of its kind. It stood discreetly between tall brick book ends — the five-story Masonic Lodge Building and the more modest Community College — looking new-painted and carefully tended. It had a dark green awning with *Pearl's* written across it in an elegant cursive. There were flower boxes outside the upper windows, and they were kept up. The doors and shutters were always closed, and except for the seepage of techno-rhythm onto the quiet stretch of lower Pearl Street it could have passed for anyone's grandmother's house in any residential area of the city.

Traditionally there was only one day of the year when the bar came out from behind the shutters, and that was the Pride & Unity Festival in early June. On that day there was a raucous parade, with people spilling openly in and out of the white clapboard house; the shutters were thrown open, and the techno played at one in the afternoon as well as one in the morning. Men who on other days brought their outfits in gym bags to the bar and changed in the bathroom, on Unity Day walked from their apartments in their ironed skirts and careful makeup and heels. Women held hands out on the street, in the sunlight.

But the year before, an arsonist had destroyed the AIDS Outreach offices, and it had created a new memory that had to be both honored and defied by public celebration. The first anniversary of the fire, August 13, was called

Outreach One. It was a day of tables set up on the sidewalk in the shade of the dark green awning, of collecting donations and signatures on a petition to stiffen the sentence of the arsonist, who had been caught and given five to seven years in the state penitentiary, and who was eligible for parole in as little as two. There was music all day, and there was even dancing under a tent in the broad alley beside the bar, but it was celebration with a very sharpened sense of purpose.

On that first year's anniversary, Outreach One lasted until almost two-thirty in the morning, when some policemen on black mountain bikes rode up and said they'd have to wind things down. The police were in uniform shorts, and they took the whistles and jokes about their legs in stride, even looking secretly pleased with the attention. They helped pull the tables off the sidewalk before mounting their bikes, and it was clear from the way the cops rode away that they felt slightly more dashing than they had riding in. The organizers counted the donations, and then a little drunkenly they struck the tent.

• • •

By three a.m., there were only four people left in the bar. The basement-level bar known as the Dungeon was empty. In the office-attic on the third floor, the bartender, the waitress and the owner were going through the extra-large mass of receipts and tickets. And on the second floor — where you went if you wanted some peace and conversation — Cheryl-lin sat perched on a bar stool, smoking a cigar and sipping ginger ale from a brandy snifter. She had the lights way down low, the way she liked them. She was waiting for the waitress, Sarah, her girlfriend of five-and-a-half months.

The owner of the bar was fussy, and although he knew Cheryl-lin well by now, he still insisted that she wait in the middle bar for Sarah while the receipts were counted.

Cheryl-lin had never smoked a cigar before, but she was in a tired, mellow mood now and it seemed like a good time to experiment. She was wearing espadrilles and a stretch mini-skirt and had her long brown legs slung out over another stool, and she felt very much like a young Gertrude Stein. The ginger ale in the snifter clashed with the image, but she was a recovered alcoholic. She'd been on the wagon for two years and eight months. There was still a ghost part of her that considered the bottles lined behind the bar, that focused out of habit on the Jameson's Irish Whiskey, but it was such a weak impulse now that she could laugh at it almost, point at it with the cigar and make fun of it.

A very tall young man walked around the corner from the stairs. He had slightly horn-rimmed glasses.

"Excuse me," Cheryl-lin said, giving him a quick profile shot of her with cigar, "but they're closed."

The young man kept walking toward the bar. "I can see that. Thanks," he said in a deep voice. He was probably six-foot-four or five and like most very tall people he walked deliberately and with a slight hunch to his shoulders. He had on sloppy sandals, khaki shorts and a white t-shirt. Printed in very small black letters on the front of the shirt — letters that Cheryl-lin couldn't read until he was almost to the bar — was the word *Rigorous.*

"Well if you can see that, why are you still walking this way?"

He pulled a stool out at the other end of the bar, propped himself on it. His legs still rested on the floor, bent at the knes. "That's a good question. I was just asking myself

the very same thing. You know how sometimes right at the
beginning of some long heart-wrenching affair you have a
sort of shudder of premonition?" He began to spin the rat-
tan stool slowly on its axis. It creaked under his weight.

"Really, they are *way* closed and —"

"I'm waiting for Steve the bartender," he said, shying a
hand at her as he spun.

Cheryl-lin ashed the cigar. "Does he know you're waiting for him down here?"

The young man broke into a big, disbelieving smile.
"*Yes*, he knows I'm waiting down here for him. God, who
are you? Who made you the gatekeeper?"

"I'm waiting for Sarah." When the young man showed
no sign of recognition, she added, "She waitresses here."

"Well, I outrank you then."

"Pardon me?"

"You're waiting for a waitron. I'm waiting for a bartender."

Cheryl-lin just looked at him for a second. "*And?*"

"And so when they leave tonight, who tips out to
whom? That would be my question to you. Clearly your
waitress tips out to my bartender. So how about a salute for
your superior officer." He got up suddenly and, with a
quick look at the door, began to move around the bar.

"What are you doing?" Cheryl-lin asked sternly.

"Looking for some beer nuts," he said. He pulled a
rocks glass from the shelf beneath the bar and before she
could say anything, he'd pulled the yellow bottle of
Drambouie down and begun pouring a shot. He seemed
very at home behind the rail. He glanced up. "Need anything while I'm back here? It's no trouble."

For some reason Cheryl-lin was almost speechless.
"You are really, I mean, you are going to get thrown right

out of here on your ass when —"

He gestured with the glass at her snifter. "You helped yourself, didn't you?"

"This happens to be ginger ale."

"Really? Ginger ale?" He came back around the bar and propped himself back up on the stool, began the slow spinning again. "That's pretty nihilistic. But my point was just that you didn't actually *pay* for the ginger ale. I'm just guessing. But those sodas go for about a buck fifty a pop."

Cheryl-lin brought her legs down off the adjoining stool and sat up straighter. She puffed the cigar a little, then she said suddenly, "Sarah and I have been going out for six months. What about you and Steve?"

He hesitated an instant. "Actually, I just met Steve tonight. We got to talking baseball. Little baseball."

"Oh, I see," Cheryl-lin put in quickly.

The young man took a long sip of the liqueur. "What is it you see exactly?"

"So you're more or less a pick-up, then."

He snorted at her. "This is the late twentieth-century, in case you don't have CNN. Pick-ups happen on networked terminals, not in bars. He's taking me to some post-Outreach after-hours yacht party out on the lake."

Cheryl-lin nodded wisely, eyes slit at him. "Yes, well, I have no doubt that he is. That would be Steve." She crossed her legs, noticed a bruise on her calf and touched it lightly with her finger. She was a diabetic and bruises were something to notice. "In my book, a half-year relationship with a waitress beats a one-nighter with a bartender any time, and I don't care if it's one night on a Carnival cruise ship. So if anybody's going to salute — " She punctuated the remark with a showy little comedian's puff on the cigar, but the smoke struck her throat wrong, and she coughed convulsively two or three times.

The young man watched her, then said, "*That's* attractive."

"Oh shut up," she shot back.

"Save your strength. Concentrate on taking small, manageable puffs."

She coughed determinedly, one last time. "Shut up," she said. "Just shut up."

When she was over it, she took a long sip from the ginger ale and shot her hand up through her black bangs twice quickly, putting herself back together. She sized him up. "You know, I'm not surprised. I could have told the minute you walked through the door what you'd be like. It's such a common pattern. Every really tall gay man I've ever known has been exactly the same. Little straight guys get Napoleon Complex and buy Rottweilers and run around in big four-by-four trucks beating their wives, and you guys get the same thing but in the reverse, or the converse, or the *obverse* or whatever. But every tall gay man I've ever met has just been plain nasty."

He considered the comments. "Maybe they're only nasty to you, because you start running your little rosebud mouth at them the minute they walk through the door. Maybe you've got Motor-Mouth Complex, but it only gets activated when you see a tall, graceful gay man making his way through a room." The young man toasted her half-heartedly with the glass and looked down at his watch.

Before Cheryl-lin could say anything in return, he tilted his head back and gave a little wail. "*Jesus*, what is taking them so long? I mean there's three of them up there. They've been at it an hour now. What, are they making some kind of microfiche archive of the register tapes or what?"

Cheryl-lin couldn't help but let an explanatory note creep into her voice. "Well, there's more to it than just totaling the register tapes. She's got to put the tickets in sequence, and break out the food from the liquor, and then match the —"

"Thank you very much for the explanation. But I happen to *be* a bartender, and I know pretty much exactly how to settle up at the end of the night. But thanks, though, like I said."

"Forgive me."

He gave a benediction with his free hand. "Forgiven."

She slit her eyes at him again. "So where do you tend bar? Exactly."

"I pour drinks at the Metronome. Three nights a week."

The minute the words left his mouth, Cheryl-lin felt the familiar sinking feeling, the feel of the town reaching around to bite its own tail. Just when you thought it was safe to make an enemy for once, it turned out that they owned a half-interest in your restaurant, or they turned out to be the man your sister was about to marry.

"So you work with Alison, then?" she asked, a little more courteously.

"I'm usually on when she's off." The young man's face also got a little more guarded, and he pushed up his glasses with his pinkie. "Why, do you know Alison?"

"Yeah. We're like best friends. She's like my sister."

"You're bullshitting me."

"Actually I'm dead serious. I used to come pick her up every night when she got off work. I haven't been doing it as much since I met Sarah."

"Oh."

"I can't believe I haven't met you before. But I guess I only go in on nights when she's working." A name floated up out of her memory. Now that she thought about it she'd heard Alison say it a hundred times, here and there, telling stories from work. "You must be Cheever."

"Cheever, exactly."

"I'm Cheryl-lin."

Cheever looked a little pained, but smiled. Alison was at least nominally his boss. She was the one who assigned his shifts. "Oh right, right. I've heard Alison talk about you."

There was a short silence. Cheever spun back and forth, seemingly lost in thought. A little film of disappointment hung in the room.

"I wonder how many names they got on that petition," Cheryl-lin said abruptly. "I'd like to see that sleazy little arsonist punk go up for another ten years at least."

Cheever picked up the topic. "You and everyone else in here tonight. I wouldn't count on it though. The *Free Press* had this article about how the guy was really innocent, a victim of circumstantial evidence. They had his lawyer and his mom and his college professors, everybody still saying he didn't do it. And he's got some kind of defense fund set up, because his dad was a career cop in Burlington. But the last part was about chances for parole, and I guess he could make parole at the minimum. Two years. He's being a model prisoner, supposedly."

"Yes, well, I'm sure he is," Cheryl-lin said. "I'm sure he's fitting right in." She stubbed out the cigar with a grimace. "These things are just foul," she said, stabbing at the ashtray again. "I always knew they were without even trying them." She dusted her hands off. "You know, Alison is always talking about how desperately straight and violent this town is just under the surface, and I tell you, when I think of that guy getting out in two years, I start thinking she's been right all along."

"What if he is innocent?"

"What if he's *guilty?* That's *my* point. What if he's guilty. That doesn't reflect very positively on what's going on in this little place in the world. Two years for destroying an AIDS Outreach center out of just plain malice. It's scary to find that out about the place you live in."

"Don't blow it out of proportion," Cheever said. "That was half the problem in here tonight. There weren't five people who wanted to be realistic about the situation. He was a head case. Not Hitler."

"I am being realistic. That's why it's very, very scary," Cheryl-lin said. She pointed to his Drambouie. "You know, that looks like urine. I'm sorry, but it does."

Cheever was obviously still trying to be accommodating, especially as Alison's name had just come up again, but he still shook his head briskly. "Come on. If you're scared of *this* town, let me suggest you stay out of the rest of the contiguous United States. My car's unlocked even as we speak."

"I'm just talking about the plain nasty bitterness people can have for other people. People like, for example, you and me. Maybe a little more for me than for you."

Cheever snorted again. "What's *that* supposed to mean?"

Cheryl-lin flicked a glance at herself in the wide bar mirror. "Let's just say you can blend when you want to. You're the default color. A few of us in this town never blend."

The truce was fraying, almost audibly. Cheever crossed his long, thin arms, then said, "Oh, the ability to blend. Look, if you want to talk blend*ability,* you and old Sarah up there can go to any club in town any night of the week and dance all night and no one will say a word to you. You know where Steve and I could go and dance, if we had a date, which we haven't yet? We could come here. Period. So put away the violin. You've had it light."

Cheryl-lin hung her mouth open. "Light?"

"That's right. Comparatively light. Yes. People find lesbians quite cute." He held up a finger as though he'd just remembered something else. "And sexy. At least every good red-blooded American boy. Very few are repulsed. Very few."

"Yes, well, at least when you go into a shop, and you're filling out your charge slip, they don't kill time by asking where you're from. They assume you're from here." She pulled a pack of cigarettes from her pocket, lit one. "You don't have to run through your ancestry and place of birth every five minutes for people."

"What's so horrible about that? People are *friendly* around here. They're a little nosy and curious, but it's well-intentioned. They think you're exotic. You're an instant celebrity. You must have women dripping off you in this town."

She gave a significant nod of her head. "It can be more than a little friendliness and nosiness. Believe me. I could tell you some stories. Take my word for it."

Cheever grinned and got up from his chair, walked behind the bar. He was nodding his head slowly as he moved. He took down the bottle of Drambouie and poured himself another, smaller shot. Without asking, he pulled the soda gun out of its plastic holster and re-filled her snifter with ginger ale. Then he ambled back out and stood beside the chair he had been sitting in. "Could you now? Tell me some Burlington stories?" he asked finally.

"You bet."

"Well, I'm dying to hear one. Really."

"I bet you are." She smoked for a second, thinking it over. "Fine. I'll tell you why my mother went back to Taiwan. It's not directly about things that happened to me, but indirectly it's very much about me. Very much."

"That sounds perfect. Don't hurry in the telling. We apparently have several more hours to kill."

"This is a true story, I swear. As my father told it to my mother, and as my mother told it to me, when I visited this past winter. I asked her why she moved back overseas when I was little — why she basically deserted me — and this is what she told me."

"Heard and understood."

"This happened in 1976, the year of the Bicentennial. I don't know if you remember, but they put out these hokey commemorative coins and bills that year." Cheryl-lin stared into the mirror behind the bar, focusing on the reflected ember of her cigarette. "My mother kept saying, This happened in the year of the different money. She still speaks English pretty badly. And I speak like no Mandarin now."

He looked at her for a second, smiled big again. "So begin already," he said.

"I *will*," she said back.

• • •

It was the year of the different money, 1976. Both the radio and the television were broadcasting clever minute-lessons about the Revolutionary War, Valley Forge, Ticonderoga. It was the year in which Deng-Xin Lin moved his family from a more or less temporary apartment the company had scouted for them when they moved from Taiwan three years earlier.

The company was named International Business Machines, Incorporated, but was known in the United States as IBM, except in the Burlington area. There — because it employed more workers than any other company, and because it flew its own aqua flag over its own village-sized manufacturing center — it was known as Big Blue. Big Blue had treated Deng-Xin very well. It made him a middle-executive, with a large salary and a car leased by the year. They had suggested but not insisted that the car be blue.

They had found him the original apartment, and their personnel people had worked with him on making the transition to the States. Finally, in 1976, they had helped him through the suspicions of the loan process, and he purchased an old but elegant brick house on South Union, a tier of fashionable homes that rested just below the level of the University. In exchange for all of this, Deng-Xin's Taiwanese business connections and language skills were added to IBM's effort to open the Far East to the early growth of computer culture.

Deng-Xin was thirty-six years old, and he was amazed at what had happened to his life. More than fifteen people worked under him, and each night he turned off the lights in what seemed a brick mansion before he went to bed. On his drive to the Essex plant in the autumn mornings, he drove through shivering forests, with reds and oranges that touched his sentimental side.

Only three things took away from his contentment. His wife seemed not to be adjusting to the new country. His daughter Sun-Yin, on the other hand, seemed to be adjusting too quickly and too essentially. And finally, he had a problem with the little boys in the neighborhood.

They were lawless little boys, from his perspective, riding their small bicycles in front of his house and leaving long black marks on his sidewalk with their tires. They were always shouting in piercing voices. There was a small gang of them — all between six and eight or so — but there were three who seemed particularly to enjoy troubling him. Though almost all of the children looked the same, Deng-Xin could distinguish these three because they were never apart. They formed their own inner group and their parents cut their brown-blond hair in the same layered style. And they all looked at him the same way, as though they disliked him. The tallest had freckles covering his pale face. Where the freckles clumped together, his skin was nearly the same shade as Deng-Xin's.

Deng-Xin would look out his window and they would be tramping across his lawn with something huddled between them — a donut or a pellet gun or a captured toad — and they would catch him looking and glare back, these seven-year-olds. Deng-Xin once asked them politely not to walk across his lawn and they said nothing, just glared at him as they retreated. The next day they were back. They were little boys, but somehow not.

The problem grew. One morning he came out to look for his newspaper and saw immediately that something had happened to his company car. He walked out to the driveway in his bare feet and terrycloth bathrobe. The car was caked with something white and sickly yellow. All around the car on the blacktop was the same dry white-yellow stuff. When he got closer, he saw that it was eggs, what looked like two dozen or more smashed with some precision over every square foot of the vehicle. He even found an egg resting unbroken inside his tailpipe.

Deng-Xin cleaned the car immediately, pulled out the hose from inside the garage and spent his morning reading time washing and waxing instead. As he worked, he glanced surreptitiously at the neighboring houses. The little boys were nowhere to be seen. He did see the father of one of them come out of the house and get into his own car to go to work. Deng-Xin waved curtly as the man drove by, gave the ghost of a scowl at the soiled car. The man didn't notice, however, and simply gave a short friendly blast on the horn. But the son was hidden away somewhere in the large brick house down the street from Deng-Xin's.

He told his secretary at work, and she laughed and told him that American boys all pulled pranks every now and then, and that there was even a kind of honor in being the one chosen. She told him a story about how friends of her daughter had once swathed her entire house with toilet paper.

That night, Deng-Xin told his wife and daughter about the egging over dinner, as something of an amusing incident. He asked Sun-Yin if any of her friends might have been involved, but she seemed offended that he would even ask. By the time he went to bed, he had forgotten all about it.

The next morning in the same bathrobe he opened the front door on the same scene: his car crusted with dry yolk and ivory fragments of shell, the blacktop covered with smashed eggs. There was even another fresh white unbroken egg resting in his tailpipe, and this time there seemed something obscene in that gesture. Deng-Xin stood looking at the car for a minute. All of the brick houses opposite his own were sleeping still. All of the landscaped yards were quiet.

The confusion he'd felt the day before ripened quickly into real anger. He dismissed the idea that some honor was implied in the vandalism. After a minute of examining the car and searching the driveway and the yard for tracks, he walked into the house and called the police. Then he changed into his best Italian suit and waited for the police to arrive.

When the policeman pulled up, Deng-Xin met him in the driveway and explained in his precise English what he thought had happened. The policeman seemed neither overly friendly nor helpful. He did get down on one knee to see the egg in the tailpipe but other than that he was uninterested by the spectacle.

"This is kid's stuff, Mr. Deng," he said after he'd looked for a minute.

"Mr. Lin," Deng-Xin corrected him after a pause. "Deng-Xin Lin."

"Mr. Lin," the officer repeated. He had a notebook out and began to jot something down in it. "There's really nothing we can do. Kids are a pain. Happens all the time. But unless you catch them doing it, that's all she wrote." He looked up at Deng-Xin and smiled. "Kids sometimes just go for whoever's different."

"In what way different?" Deng-Xin asked carefully.

The policeman smiled to himself and shook his head. His reddish hair was cut very short, and he ran his hand over the inch of growth. "Look, kids do this kind of stuff. They'll stop after a while, they'll get tired. Probably just me driving up here is enough to scare them away for awhile."

"But this vandalism is illegal, certainly," Deng-Xin repeated the word and pointed to the car, "certainly. How can you say to wait for it to happen again?"

The policeman's face slowly became a mask. "Look, Mr. Lin, I told you what I can do. If you want us to drive by once and a while, we'll be glad to oblige. I'd suggest you sit up late with a flashlight. That's what I'd do, flashlight and a hose with some good water pressure."

Deng-Xin thanked him, and the man turned to go. As he walked away, Deng-Xin heard him mutter something that sounded like the slang term "Ding-a-ling."

That night Deng-Xin did sit up and wait, at a card table inside his small garage, next to his wife's little-used sedan. On the table were a flashlight, a Polaroid camera, and a small baseball bat that he had bought on a trip to the Baseball Hall of Fame in Cooperstown, New York. While he waited, Deng-Xin turned his other worries over in his mind, mostly those concerning his daughter Sun-Yin. She was just turned eleven years old, but she seemed desperate to be grown up, and to be American. Recently, changes had begun to crowd in upon his awareness of her. He saw the coal crumbs of mascara occasionally on her lashes, and her straight black hair, forever drawn into a single ponytail, she had now curled and permed to the point where she was unrecognizable.

There was still his overpowering love for her. He attended her tennis lessons, at the University courts, and there were moments, under the dogged instruction of the old pro he had hired, when she would flash across the court in pure aggression, pure contest, to take a point. He watched her work on her forehand, that same stroke end-lessly duplicated, while at the other end of the court the tennis pro pulled ball after ball from magic pockets. That bit of legerdemain always enchanted Deng-Xin.

Yet these same sessions began to worry him, once he realized that she was bent on becoming something new and foreign to him. She drove the old coach oftener to the point of stumbling, put the ball routinely in the one corner he had left unguarded in his fatigue. She went to the net with-out being instructed to do so. Deng-Xin felt that he knew that Sun-Yin only dimly, the fierce one, the one who tacked up glossy pictures of thin blonde models over her bed and who suddenly demanded to be referred to as Cheryl.

No one came that night with eggs. Deng-Xin sat up the next night, and again no one came. But four days later, he came out late for work, having overslept and missed his breakfast, and found the yolk again covering his car like flaking skin.

And while he was washing the car, he saw the ringleader of the three worst little boys — the one with the freckles — ride by on his undersized bicycle. The boy pedaled vigorously by, saying nothing. But Deng-Xin had the crystal-clear sense that he was laughing.

That night after work Deng-Xin walked down the street to the ringleader's house. He felt both foolish and angry, but he rang the doorbell and waited. The father came to the door still in his tie, a large man with the broad shoulders, square jaw and loud voice that Deng-Xin associated with American businessmen. Deng-Xin quickly explained the problem. The man was very friendly, very apologetic. He said that he would take care of it, and he even apologized for not having come across the street earlier to introduce himself and his family.

About an hour after Deng-Xin returned home, his doorbell rang. He peeked through the curtain and saw the three fathers of the three boys, their sons standing meekly in front of them. He opened the door, himself embarrassed. All of the fathers wore white dress shirts with the top two buttons undone. One of them was partially bald, but still they all three looked much alike. All of the little boys wore jeans and t-shirts.

The ringleader's father stuck out his hand, and Deng-Xin shook it. "Mr. Lin," the man said, "our boys have something they'd like to say to you." He propelled his own son forward, but the boy twisted his head back.

"I didn't *do* it," he moaned.

The father squeezed him by the shoulders, brought his large face down close to his son's small freckled face. "You had best say what you came over here to say, young man," he whispered fiercely, "you had best say it right now."

The boy was silent. Beside him, the boy of another of the men began to cry, the small shoulders shaking. The father spanked him once hard on the seat of his pants. "You're going to get a reason to cry in about one minute," the father hissed at him.

The third man stepped forward and reached out his hand. "Mr. Lin, I want to apologize for my son here. I can assure you he's gonna be severely —"

"We didn't *do* it, Dad, I swear to *God*," the third man's son said, twisting around to plead with his father. "It was some *other* kids."

Deng-Xin wanted desperately to shut the door on them but he couldn't. It was torture to stand while the boys squirmed and cried. The fathers continued to threaten the children quietly for another moment. "Please," Deng-Xin said, waving a hand, "I simply would like that there be no more eggs."

The large father nodded humorlessly. "There won't be, I'll guarantee you that." He looked down at his son, then spoke very quietly. "You will say you're sorry right now for throwing those eggs."

There was a silence. "I'm sorry for throwing the eggs."

As though it were a signal to capitulate, the two other boys confessed as well, the one through sobs that shook his small frame. The men shook Deng-Xin's hand again, and offered to have their sons do yardwork in exchange for the time Deng-Xin had expended in cleaning, but Deng-Xin emphatically declined.

The next morning the car was clean, and the morning following, and the morning following that. Deng-Xin began to enjoy his mornings again, the brilliant autumn foliage, the snappy lessons about American Revolutionary history that came over the radio on his ride to work. He began to pass sly allusions to Thomas Paine in his conversations with American executives abroad, to the effect that going with Big Blue this year was simply a matter of Common Sense. He now knew several of his neighbors, and the men waved pleasantly to him when their cars passed.

But one night a few weeks later he woke out of a sound sleep with the overwhelming feeling that his family was coming apart. His wife had been complaining about her feelings of isolation, her discomfort with the landscape itself, and the egging incidents had only increased that urgency. Sitting up in bed in the dark, Deng-Xin had the sudden certain sense that she would return to Taiwan. He could put his hand on her sleeping form and feel it in her shallow breathing. In a similar way he felt the coming loss of his daughter. He had finally, in some desperation, begun to call her Cheryl, because she would otherwise refuse to speak to him. He knew he would lose her.

He wandered downstairs, thinking to make some tea. As he passed the large front window, he noticed movement in the drive. He went to the curtain and inched it aside. Coming silently down the street were the three fathers, carrying each a carton of eggs. He could barely make them out in the dim glow of the streetlight.

He said nothing as they went through the routine, first the car itself, quarter-panel by quarter-panel, then the driveway. The eggs exploded in perfect silence, one after another.

Finally the large father, the father of the freckled boy, leaned down behind the car to place the last white egg in the tailpipe.

Deng-Xin wanted to run out screaming, but he was transfixed. His legs would not move. He wanted to call to his wife sleeping upstairs but he couldn't.

All he could think of was an image he had seen the previous week on public television, a painting of men in war paint dancing around a tall-masted schooner, throwing crate after crate of tea leaves into the sea.

• • •

"That was mildly impressive," Cheever said when she'd finished.

Cheryl-lin shook her head. "You know, I don't know why I bothered telling you about my family and my childhood, because it's obviously lost on you."

Cheever patted the air with his hands. "Calm down. Nothing's lost on me. I said it was an impressive story. It's just that it sounds like it's gained a little in the telling. You know. From your dad to your mom, and then to you. Just sounds like it's been magnified a bit." He smiled at her. "And I don't think that's Burlington. No offense to your parents."

Cheryl-lin couldn't help but smile back. She ran a hand through her straight black bangs. "All right, fine, you're probably right about my mom at least touching up the story. I mean, that's her. Fine. She accentuates. But the nuts and bolts are there."

"Well, of course, the nuts and bolts. Nobody's questioning any nuts and bolts."

Cheryl-lin giggled. "Fine."

"All right," Cheever said.

There was another silence, and then Cheryl-lin said expectantly, "So?"

"So what?"

"So you dissed my story. I'm assuming you have a better one. I'm assuming you're not just talking out your butt."

"Why sure." Cheever looked very confident. "But I can't just *launch* into something. I have to think. It's very difficult to launch."

"I did."

"Well, sure, and look what happened to your story." He sipped the Drambouie. "It came out all enhanced and everything. Don't forget that." He stroked his chin. "I guess I could tell you this one story that happened to me, just about a year ago tonight, the day after the Outreach fire. How I got over my own little depression about it. I mean, it's amusing, anyway."

Cheryl-lin giggled again. "Fine. But just the truth. Just the facts."

Cheever nodded, picked up the front of his white t-shirt and held out the small black word *Rigorous* printed on it. "Don't worry, that's my thing," he assured her.

• • •

All right, then, this will be my story, if everyone in the bar only gets to tell one. This entry is mine, and I will try to make it righteous.

It was the day after the Outreach fire, and I was more than ordinarily upset about it, I think. They knew almost immediately that it was arson. People were calling to talk about it all morning. I started to feel like a Berlin Jew on the morning after *Kristall Nacht*, you know, *targeted*. You need to add into the equation that I had been dating a guy named Rick for about a year, and we had broken up the week previously. He broke up with me, actually, I'm not ashamed to say. So I was fairly blue before the fire. But the day after, I was dark, dark blue. I felt as though in one week this whole pretty community that I'd felt safe and secure in had been blown to shards, by Rick from the inside and by some lunatic from the outside. I felt as though I'd just moved to town all over again.

If you've lived in Burlington for any time at all, you know the drill when you break up with someone: you immediately section the town off into spheres of influence and — at least if it's a civil break-up, one in which you ritually exchange chattels — you each stay strictly out of the other person's zones. Because neither of you wants some random, brutal Sunday morning confrontation in front of the bagel store. Neither of you ever specifically mentions zones to the other, but it's understood. It's Geneva Convention.

And the zones are great or small depending on how integral, how frequented they are. The Metronome was my biggest zone, obviously; he worked at the computer room at the University, so the whole campus was his; I couldn't come down the length of Lower Pearl because that's where he lived; he had to avoid South Winooski where I lived. I pretty much knew, and Rick pretty much knew.

So the afternoon following the fire, I was sitting at home and I decided that only a long, meditative bike ride was going to have any effect on my state of mind. One of those endless rides out on the bike path, lake off to the left, woods off to your right, seagulls tilting. Honesty resides in bike rides like that.

The problem was that the bike path, while it wasn't

actually a Rick zone all the time, was a p.m. Rick zone, as he was given to walking his dog there maybe three nights a week. Ordinarily I thought of the thing as mine until five, and his after, his and the dog's, who I liked one hell of a lot by the way. That dog and I had no problems, and if Rick thought even half as logically as the dog, we'd be together today. Or if he loved me a quarter as much as the dog, same thing.

It was about five-twenty in the afternoon, at this point. You can see it was a judgement call. Protocol was only very weakly in force. So I went for the ride, with the general sense in my mind that people were now actually blowing up facilities designed to stem an epidemic and the epidemic's effects — in other words, people had taken to *helping* the epidemic — and I was not going on that day to have the bike path taken away from me for any reason. I needed it.

I was just past North Beach, at that stretch where it's just green trees and ivy on either side, and things were fine: it was hot but low humidity, and the sun was hanging over the water, just beginning to redden on its way down to a very hot-coal orange. You know this sunset, I'm certain. I had just about gotten to the point where my legs loosen up and piston without my really having to think about it, and I saw Rick and the dog walking about fifty yards ahead of me. There is no mistaking the dog. It's a Great Dane big enough to sit its back end on the couch while its front end watches television. And Rick has an idiosyncratic walk, it would be kind to say. Because — let's face realities — Rick Borcini has an extremely fat ass from sitting at the computer all day.

So I'm coming up fast behind them. I'm in eighth gear, and rolling. I have about four seconds to decide a course of action, and there are three possibilities. One, I can brake fast and head back, just chop three or four miles off the ride, but of course those are the miles with the scenic over-looks. Two, I can stop and talk and know the entire time that he's pitying me for arranging what can only seem like a faked chance encounter. Or I can speed up and shoot by, bent down over the handlebars, and be fairly certain he won't be able to recognize me.

So, needless to say.

Now the dog's name is Diane, or Dydee. She's tan all over, but with a black muzzle. By and large she's a docile animal, even desperate to please sometimes. She's really a good animal. But for whatever reason that afternoon — whether she was cranky or frisky or what — she was in the mood to bite her leash and tug. This motion brings her big tan backside swinging slowly left, out toward the center of the bike path.

I have some decent bike reflexes. Before I'm even aware I'm doing it, I squeeze off on the brakes and kill about thirty percent of my speed. I'm looking to the left, even eyeing the grass shoulder and the trees beyond. I'm still coming fast and my back tire's drifting just a bit, but I've got room and time to make sure I sweep through the gap between the dog and the edge. The only trouble is that fast braking gives off this little whistle, an unmistakeable ten-speed brake lock-up whistle, and everyone who's ever walked that bike path knows it. Rick hears it, and he sees Diane swinging to center, and he goes quick to grab for her collar.

Unfortunately — I'm guessing here now — Diane thinks she's about to be hit for something, and she flinches left, a big haunchy flinch. I crush the brakes, my back wheel shoots forward so I'm perfectly perpendicular to the path, and I wish I could say that I don't but I undeniably do.

I cream Diane, or we cream each other.

And when you take the two of us together that's a lot of leg to send whipping through the air. It is a serious collision. And she makes that sound of injury and absolute recrimination that only dogs can make. My head and forearm catch the ground as I'm pinwheeling.

Then I'm in the grass, flattened out. At rest.

When I could, I lifted my head a few inches and saw Dydee, limping and whimpering, but standing, walking. That dog is like cut granite. But before I could move or reorient myself or check my wounds, Rick was leaning down over me screaming his head off. He was livid. I'm saying that he was flailing his arms. I can still see his apoplectic little face. Rick is not a very large guy, excepting the butt, but he can be a terrier when he's upset. He was screaming that I'd *deliberately* stalked him and targeted his dog, that I was going to pay for the goddam veterinarian bills, and so on. I just lay in the grass, too weak to tell him not to flatter himself.

Finally, he and Diane walked away. About fourteen people on rollerblades and mountain bikes must have stopped to see if I was okay, because I was bleeding down my forehead as well as down my arm. I just kept waving them on. I was smiling for some reason, almost laughing, the way you get when you've suddenly sunk way below what you thought was the lowest point. It becomes funny in a way that gives you a glimpse of insanity.

And while I was lying there in the grass bleeding, I was thinking three words, *Fuck this town*. It seemed like a very true poem, those words. Fuck a town so small your ex-boyfriend practically leaps out of your refrigerator every time you open the door. Fuck a town where there's a geeky little arsonist. Just fuck a town like this right up and down. It's time to move on, I was thinking.

And that thought got me up and moving for some reason. Denver, Colorado, I was thinking. St. Paul, Minnesota. These are large, good places to live. I managed to start walking the bike back down the path, but I had to stop after five or ten minutes because I caught sight of the blood from my head dripping onto my shirt, and it gave me the shakes. I'm not ordinarily squeamish. It's just that I had no way of knowing how *bad* it was, big cut, little cut, I couldn't see it.

I was passing that little fenced complex that has the water treatment plant on one side, and that new Coast Guard station on the other. There was a Coast Guard guy out shooting some hoops at this basketball net they have up in the parking lot. He was in a dark blue, short-sleeved uniform that looked almost like a SWAT uniform. He was goofing around, backward lay-ups and behind-the-back stuff. As you might have guessed, I've played some basketball in my day. So for an ex-athlete who was half-scared and half-looking for some kind of official to take a quick look at their head — but who didn't want to make too big a deal out of it — a basketball-playing Coast Guardsman was made to order.

Basically I went over and stuck my head out at him and said, "Sorry to interrupt, but just how bad does this gash look to you?"

He was about an inch taller than me, if you can believe it, with one of those eagle noses, a real solid hook on it that makes its own kind of fashion statement. I've always liked guys with prominent noses, an embarrassing fact. He had his name stitched onto his uniform: *J. Balfoort*. And when he answered me, his voice came out in a real syrupy Southern accent. He was from Georgia, I found out later. Bremen, Georgia, which is about fifty miles south of Atlanta. I know because the next day I looked it up on a map.

J. Balfoort just snapped into action the minute he

looked at my head. He was one of these extremely earnest guys in uniform. He started asking me questions about the impact, did I lose consciousness. Before I knew it he was taking me into the Coast Guard station.

I'm guessing you've never been in there, but apparently the whole little station cost something like four and a half million dollars, and it is quite elegant. Quite. Those boys have perks. Big windows looking out over the water everywhere you look, views for which developers would prostitute themselves. Radio rooms full of equipment, day room with a fairly massive television, ping-pong, pool table. And a first-aid room, which is where he took me.

"You tore the skin on your head up a good little bit," he told me while he was stacking some supplies next to the chair I was sitting in. The word *head* came out *hayid* when he said it. "But I think I can just bandage it. I don't think you're gonna need stitches." And *think* came out *thank*.

He cleaned my forehead off, even swabbed my arm where I'd scraped it. Then he started putting together this makeshift bandage. It was held on with two extra long crisscrossed band-aids, so I had what amounted to an oversized Manson-style X right between my eyes. "I think that's gonna hold," he said, pressing it one last time with the tips of his fingers. "You didn't hit anybody else out there on the bike path, did you?"

I thought about it. "People, you mean?"

"Well *yeah*, people."

"No."

He screwed up his face a little. "You didn't hit a animal, did you?"

"Unfortunately." I patted the bandage on my arm. He'd done a neat job. "And as if it had to be made worse, it was a dog, and the dog belonging to my ex. That's not easy to do.

That's world-class bad luck."

Balfoort whistled under his breath. "Well, I hope you didn't kill that dog, else I imagine she's gonna be stalking you but good."

I thought about it for a good couple of seconds, taking recent events into account. And then I just said it anyway, looked him right in the eye. "He, you mean."

"He the dog," Balfoort said.

"No, he the ex."

"Oh." He didn't look perfectly surprised, you know. He looked like he'd had some inkling, who knows why. But he didn't look comfortable either. He started gathering up the first-aid supplies. When he turned around I noticed this red streak up the back of his neck, and I thought, either this guy's such a prude that the mere mention is making him blush, or he's a gay-basher with a quick, mean temper. He turned around, and I smiled the way you do when you're caught looking hard at somebody and wondering about them.

"What kind of a dog was it?" he asked me. His expression was normal enough now. He had a nice smile, a little lopsided, disarming.

"Great Dane."

"Damn," he said, snapping his fingers. "I was hoping it was a poodle. I can't stomach poodles. Too Frenchified, you know what I'm saying."

And then I had the feeling he was shuffling me out of the station. He wasn't rude about it or anything. He'd stop and show me this or that little thing, but always as part of the move toward the door. I may have imagined it, but he seemed anxious not to be seen with me all of the sudden. I was thanking him as we walked, asking him where he was from, and he was answering but not really looking at me anymore.

He brought me out the side door, the one fronted by their little dock. It was turning dark, and there was just enough cool breeze to start to cut the heat. There was a rescue boat tied up at the dock, you know, white with one thin blue and one thick red slash down the side. Little enclosed cabin for the pilot.

"That's one snappy boat," I said. I figured I'd try to make whatever little bit of parting conversation there was going to be as easy as possible for him. He'd been damn nice, after all. "What's that, like thirty feet long?"

"That's a twenty-five footer," he corrected. He scuffed at the dock with his boot. Then he picked up a rock and pitched it at the water. "You like boats?"

"Love 'em," I said, which is true enough. I can't swim or sail, but I've always thought boats were righteous.

He gave me a funny look, or rather, he gave me a normal look with a funny look hiding directly behind it. "You ever been on a Coast Guard rig?"

I shook my head, then said, "Well, actually, just that time off the coast of Baja. We got run down with a boatload of opium. But just that once."

He didn't really smile. Maybe they don't like to joke about contraband. "Well, I gotta make a patrol sweep," he pointed south, "go down as far as bottom of Shelburne Bay there, then back up this way out as far as Grand Isle. Just a lookey-lookey trip." He gave me the funny look again, but this time it was almost like he was daring me. "You feel like coming, I'll get a life jacket on you, and we'll take a ride. Anybody asks, I'll tell 'em you're showing me where your boat ran onto rocks so I can tag the area."

I thought about it. He squinted an eye at me. "Okay," I said.

"Okay, then," he repeated.

So in about fifteen minutes I was headed straight for New York in the cabin of a Coast Guard rescue boat, the wind on my bandage. Balfoort turned into a Coast Guard pilot machine, checking dials and making observations. If I asked him a question, he'd answer, but it was like all of the sudden he didn't want my company. So I looked out the window. It was a great ride, even in silence. Those cutters are God's own motorboats, even I could see that.

At one point, I turned to him. I liked the fact that we were almost exactly the same height. That simply never happens to me. At that second I felt like a person, instead of a very tall person. Balfoort's face had a greenish tint from the displays in front of us. "So what's the *J* stand for?" I asked.

"Jefferson," he said. He gave a small grin.

"Like Thomas Jefferson."

"No, sir. Like Jefferson Davis." He went back to sighting some point of land out his window. Then he turned back. "You know who that was, son?"

"Sure," I said. "I had my history, even if it was Yankee history."

"Well all right."

"No offense," I said.

"None taken."

I went back to looking out the window. It's funny, for the five years I'd lived in Burlington, I'd never been out on the lake, except walking on it when it was frozen. I'd never been in a boat, never looked back at it like looking back at Earth from a space capsule. But that's exactly what it was like. It was just a small, neat body of lights. I could trace streets if I tried. Pearl Street I could see running straight up College Hill like a glowing spine.

While we were slapping over the water, I was looking at the lights, and out of nowhere I felt this surge of tenderness for the town. It was where I lived, and I was sorry I had cursed it. I was sorry I'd sworn to leave it. Because it looked blameless from the water, absolutely and perfectly human-sized, in fact smaller and finer than human. It was a miniature.

We'd started back up from Shelburne and were just passing Juniper Island on our way out north when Balfoort killed the engine. He fiddled around putting his log book in a little compartment. "Come out on deck, man," he said and turned without really looking at me. "Come out here for a minute."

I followed him out onto the small reardeck behind the cabin. The boat was rocking slightly, and it was very dark out there. I remember I was walking toward him, and he had his back to me, and I could see when I got close that he was holding himself rigidly. I had a flash of warning, the kind of caution that runs through your body outside of thought. It had to do with the fire and his uniform and the dark, all shot through with the realization that I couldn't swim.

Then he turned around and looked at me, his face set and serious. It was one of those country-boy faces — freckled skin, small bright eyes and overlarge nose and teeth — that you associate with both star centerfielders and axe murderers. He put his hand out toward me. I looked at it for a second. He looked down at it too, then back up at me, determinedly. I could see he was willing to be laughed at. That was the rigidness. And then I took his hand.

With him half drawing me, and me half walking forward, I came up to him and he turned his face slightly and we kissed.

That's more or less where the story ends. We stayed out on the boat for another half hour or so, and once or twice he came to my apartment, never to spend the night and never to do more than a little furtive kissing and quick fumbling with the lights off. He was one of those people stuck so tightly in the closet it's killing them. Even with no one else around, he was miserable with what he wanted, and he was deathly afraid that his Coast Guard buddies would find out. He was more comfortable kissing my cheek than my lips.

He was transferred to the station in Juno, Alaska this past April. But he said some things before he left, and they're things I keep close at hand mentally. We had coffee his last day, down at Muddy Waters. He kept apologizing for being hung up, and I kept telling him that was a stupid thing to apologize for. He said that he'd never forget me, or the night on the cutter, that it was something he'd always dreamed of doing. And then he told me — looking out that big picture window onto Main Street as he said it — that I was beautiful, and that's something I don't hear very often.

● ● ●

Cheryl-lin said nothing. She had a cigarette going now, and she shaped the ash against the side of the ashtray, but said nothing. She was at a loss for words. She couldn't really say why, what in the story had prompted it. For no good reason, she almost felt as though she wanted to cry.

"Well?" Cheever asked in his deep voice.

"What do you want me to say?"

"I want you to respond. Come on. That was my *story.*"

"How exactly do you want me to respond?"

"Say if you think it was a nice thing."

Cheryl-lin rolled her eyes. "Yes, okay? I think it was a nice thing. I think it's nice you got to be on a boat. I think it's nice he didn't tie an anchor to your leg and give you the heave-ho." She thought for another second. "It sort of reminds me of how I met Sarah. In a screwed-up way they're kind of the same."

"Do tell." Cheever seemed to have forgotten his impatience. He had his fingers locked behind his head, and he was leaning as far back as the metal legs of the stool would allow. He was looking around the middle bar with the air of someone who realizes that he may or may not be seeing a lot more of a certain place. "Let's hear it. I'm in the mood, now. Let's do another round."

"Another time," she said.

"Fine," Cheever said.

They sat in what was perhaps the fifth prolonged silence since he'd entered the room forty minutes before. At one point, Cheryl-lin looked up to find that he was grinning at her, staring at her.

"What?" she said finally.

He offered his glass for a toast, silently. She looked at him, then rolled her eyes. He didn't seem to be kidding. When she'd relented and clinked glasses, she glanced back at his face to find him still grinning. "*What?*" she asked again.

"That story warmed your heart, didn't it?"

"You wish," she said softly. "You enhanced, didn't you?"

"Never," Cheever said. He twirled in his chair, his grin still working. He patted his hand over his heart. "That's my one good and true story."

James (reprise)

It lifted, all of the sudden, more or less just like that. James was kneeling in front of a new window frame, through which he could see the stainless steel bones of the condominium. He was kneeling and pulling Tyveck housewrap taut with his hands, the whole process made awkward by thick work gloves, when he felt the last of the depression lift somehow and burn off in the sun. He had been feeling better since the night before, had felt better still on the way into work. And now he felt normal, and well. He felt *good* even, and that was what had snapped him out of his work routine — the realization that he was humming.

James looked out toward the lake. It was still miraculously unfrozen in early January. The sun was shimmering on the water. He looked down through the unfinished building and into the floors below. He could see men moving and working, striking out in all directions with their tools. Their laughter drifted through the steel and wood skeleton. He sat down on the joists beneath him, then let his breath come out suddenly in a rush.

There were white clouds over him, hung up in the air like kites, and the sun and the cold both played on his face. It was gone. He took off one of his gloves and ran a hand over his cold forehead. He straightened his hat. He felt almost as if he would smile. It was as though his stomach and his heart had been wrapped tightly with twine — bound tight enough to cut, the way his mother used to tie up a roast — and someone had snipped the strings. It was gone.

He felt like climbing down off the frame of the condominium and running to the water, but he reminded himself where he was, and what he was doing. He had only another hour to go, in any event. But the feeling bubbled in him. James took a step or two to one side and squatted beside a large square hole in the future condominium roof. He could see a big, paunchy man working below. It was Bobby Dinardo, known around the site as Bobby Drill. He was drilling holes for the new window frames on the second floor. Bobby was one of the few guys who had tried consistently to be nice to him, in spite of James' silence, his never-ending mood. The others had pretty much ignored him. James picked up his nail gun, for no good reason, started to twirl it on his finger.

"Hey, you fucker," James yelled down suddenly through the hatch. It was the first thing that came to mind.

Bobby looked up at him, puzzled. His leather tool belt pulled at his big stomach, elongating it and giving the impression of an oversized girdle. "What's your badness," he said by rote, looking back at his bit. The drill whined, and wood shavings curled to where the floor would one day be, then vanished between the joists.

James pointed the nail gun down into the hatch. "Dance, man."

"Hey, don't fuck around, James."

James squatted there, grinning down at Bobby. It occurred to him that he really liked this fat man some fifteen years his senior. He hadn't allowed himself to know that. "I reckon I been workin' here three months, Bobby," James drawled, "and I ain't seen a man dance yet. That ain't right. What say you dance now, Bobby."

"Don't fuck around."

"Don't make me shoot one of them big foots of yours."

Bobby pointed the drill up at him. "Don't fuck around,

James. I don't want a nail in the arm, okay? Point that thing somewhere else, okay?" He fired up the drill, and the bit spun shrilly. "Or you get a drill enema. I mean it, don't fuck around. Put that thing away." He was shading his face now with one hand, face screwed up. "Seriously. Come *on,* James, Jesus."

James brought the nail gun up. "You're a good guy, Bobby." He stood up and went back to the sheet of house-wrap he had partially fixed to the penthouse wall.

"You moody fucks are the worst," Bobby yelled up. "You have no consistency."

James yelled down pleasantly, "Yeah, right. Screw consistency, Bobby." The whine of Bobby's drill floated up at him, and James started even laughing a little. He noticed that he could not only see his breath in the cold, but that it came out thick and white, more than ordinarily visible.

He spent a solid three minutes blowing fake smoke rings.

• • •

What had happened is that he had been beaten up. Almost four and a half months previously, in the last hot days of August. That night, the air had been full of cottonwood pollen, floating everywhere in slowly billowing sheets. Like a snowstorm, but the snow coming slowly on a hot wind, and sticking to you if it touched you, clinging like fine white hair.

They had been out at the Metronome drinking, he and four other guys. One of them — a redhead named Maurice — James had met playing pool one night, right after James moved to Burlington, not so long after his divorce. It was a time when he wanted friends more than anything.

Maurice was an organizer. He was the kind of guy who collects other guys, almost aimlessly, over time, and designs things for them to do once he has enough of them. James had seen organizers before. It might be gang fighting. A guy collects a gang and matches them with other gangs like fighting cocks, just for sport, just to see blood and the desperate looks on the faces. Or it might be politics, all of the sudden the group of friends realizes that they've become a grassroots movement, and the organizer is their candidate. It would come complete with the illusion that the movement pre-dated the candidate. And although James had spent two or three afternoons and evenings with Maurice and the people Maurice was collecting, he could never get a clear sense of what they were for.

But he had gotten an inkling, that last night in August. Maurice had been buying the drinks, and when they were all good and drunk, he had taken them down to a little access road off the lakefront. There was a new Vietnamese restaurant on that road, and while they stood there drunk a group of Vietnamese waiters came out of the restaurant. Maurice began to talk about chasing them, talking up the idea of throwing a scare into them. One of the other guys, a big gangly Southerner, had started making sounds like a dog. And before James really knew what was happening Maurice had all of them running toward those three small scared young men in waiter's black-and-whites. James ran too, for a second, he couldn't have said why at the time.

Then he stopped running, and Maurice came back furious and struck him so hard along the side of his head that he'd fallen over. James was so surprised that he never even flinched. He was only half-aware as the rest of the curses and punches and kicks connected with his back, side, and face. One kick put his tooth through his lip.

The police never came, although James lay on his side in the road for nearly an hour. The Vietnamese waiters ran away. Maurice and his new recruits ran away. When James finally dragged himself up, he was almost covered with the airy white pollen. He could remember the feeling of looking down at himself, seeing the ghost layer fall away.

It turned out that he had a fractured bone in his wrist, as well as a tiny chip and a stress line across his zygomatic arch, the bone socket for his right eye. The doctor said there was nothing really to do about it, except to know that it was there.

So for the last four and a half months, James had known it was there, and the town had seemed dead to him — worse than dead, at once menacing and perfectly uncaring.

When he found out that they were going to build a small row of condominiums right next to the spot on the access road where it all happened, he applied for work as a finisher, and it was part of the menace and the sense of brooding cruelty that he was hired. Some days, working on the top of the new structure, he would look down at the spot and then have the panicked sense that someone was running up behind him to push him off.

But now the feeling was gone. He understood why, in one of the very few flashes of insight that people get about the composition of their own lives. He had slipped so far down into dullness and depression that it was either death, in one way or another, or regeneration. He could have fumbled his way to suicide, he saw now. Apparently his body and the shuttered part of his mind had flipped a coin.

• • •

After work, he left his truck down by the lake and walked

up the hill to Church Street. It was the first time he had been on the pedestrian mall in months, the first time he had been *any*where in months. He had forgotten the sense of invigoration. The sun was seducing everyone. It was bright enough, in spite of the cold, that people were walking with their coats half-unzipped, their heads and hands bare. There were people moving briskly, the shoppers, and then there were people standing and shuffling their feet, the smokers and the high school kids and the bullshitters, the people killing the whole day. All of the shops and restaurants had their fair-weather racks and signs standing out. Music was playing from speakers somewhere up above his head. The tall white church at the head of the mall looked so stark and pure against the blue sky that James swore under his breath.

He got a cup of coffee from a coffee shop wedged in like a record album between two normal-sized shops. It was strong, carmel-flavored coffee that fixed its smell to his hand and mouth almost instantly, so that all he could smell was coffee and caramel and cold, bright air. He sat down on one of the benches outside the shop, sipping and feeling his legs and backside grow chilled and not really caring.

A tall, rail-thin kid in a black leather jacket walked up to the bench. The jacket said "FEAR" in white letters on the back. His hair was bleached, and he had a slightly portly dog on a leash, an obvious mutt. Its back end looked like a Corgi, and it had the mottled blue-gray of an Australian Shepherd, but there was some air of Collie in the face, in the tall, sensitive ears. The kid in the leather jacket told the dog to sit at the end of the bench. The dog sat slowly, working itself down on bad joints.

"Hey, citizen," the kid said to James suddenly. "You gonna be here for a couple minutes?" He had thermal underwear on under the bomber jacket, and a skirt of the dirty ribbed material hung down below the leather.

James nodded.

"Think you could hold her leash? I don't like to tie her to garbage cans," the kid said, without elaborating.

"Sure," James said, accepting the leash. "I don't blame you."

"Dreyfuss, get up. Move over here. Meet the new boss," the kid said. The dog dutifully worked its way up onto all fours, took a few steps closer to James, and sat again where the kid pointed for it to sit. "Her name's Dreyfuss. I'll be out in, like, four minutes."

"Hey, Dreyfuss," James said when they were alone. The dog squeezed a little closer and flipped his arm up expertly with her nose, so that his hand landed on her head. He began to scratch behind the long ears. "What's your badness?"

Almost immediately a woman walking slowly by stopped and made eye contact with the dog. "Well, isn't she the sweetest thing," she said, coming forward to pet her. The woman was in her sixties, short and impeccably dressed. She had on a black cashmere coat that immediately picked up the white dog hair. "She's got some Dingo, looks like." Dreyfuss leaned in to her, turning her face up adoringly, and the woman broke into a beautiful smile. "What a lover! What a lover girl. She's definitely got some Dingo, doesn't she? I have some friends who had one flown over straight from the Outback, and they've got that same wild look."

A week previously James would have said that the dog belonged to someone else and that he didn't know. Now he said, "I think you're right. I mean, I got her from the pound, so there's no way to be sure. But I think you're right." He told the white lie, and the woman pursed her lips in satisfaction, nodding down at Dreyfuss.

James had to smile. There never was a dog that looked less wild than the plump thing at the end of the leash he was holding. But that was what mutts were good for. They let everyone be right, they made everyone a sleuth. People loved themselves more after petting a mutt.

Someone moved up on the other side of James. He turned reflexively, and he saw a man with short red hair, a small red beard. For a second James thought it was Maurice, and he felt adrenaline pulse inside him. But it was a slightly older, fatter young man in a parka, with something about his eyes and face that suggested retardation. He stood beside James, looking down at the dog. "Does it bite?"

"Nope," James said, then amended it: "Never known her to before."

The man continued to look down at the dog. "I've seen that dog before," he said.

"Probably around town," James replied.

"I think. Or maybe it was on tv. It was a coyote like this one." The man bent his knees and put his hand out to the dog, who moved forward just enough to make contact, but without losing contact with the first woman. "Nice coyote dog," he said, looking up at James. "Where'd you get him?"

"Her," the woman in cashmere said gently. "She's a little lady, can't you tell?"

"At the pound," James answered. The lie seemed to get more palatable every second.

"And I think she's actually Dingo dog," the woman added to the man in the parka, but again softly and gently, as though she understood that his disability might make him unable to determine breed correctly.

The man looked at her and then gave two slow shakes

of his head. "I think it's a coyote. I've seen her before."

"Yes, well, Dingo dogs can look a lot like coyotes, I'm sure."

"Nope," the man in the parka said, patting his mittens together. "Not on tv."

The woman gave James a quick look. Just then, the owner of the dog came out of the coffee shop with a large paper cup. He came over to the bench and set it down. He didn't seem surprised at the impromptu party around his dog.

The woman looked up at the FEAR jacket, then smiled and said to James, "I guess no one can resist your fat little pooch today, can they?" Then she looked into the dog's eyes and said firmly, "No they can't."

In another few seconds, they had all spun away from him, fragments of acquaintance, but fragments that would reappear at intervals, around town. Already they were *déjà vu* waiting to happen, because names wouldn't be remembered, or exact circumstances. James knew he could hold his seat and someone else would come along to talk, to chat just on general principles. He could feel the connectivity of the town around him, the determined easiness of people's relations. It was the way the town had elected to be. People who moved in had to pick up the habit, or continue to misfire, like a bad cylinder. And he had the reassuring sense that he sometimes got around the Christmas season, that even if people were buying and giving and visiting on cue, or because they thought they should, they were still wrought up in the process of loving. They were still possessed by the right emotions underneath it all. Mercy was still loose in the world.

• • •

He spent the afternoon drifting through the downtown, sticking his head in doors and stopping for a beer, a sandwich, a sundae, a hot dog, whatever and wherever he felt a tug. But he still had a ghost impression that his black mood of the last months was dogging him, waiting to catch him alone.

And thinking those thoughts brought him down Main Street, which he had avoided when possible, and into the doorway he had thought he would never use again. He found himself on the stairs leading up to the Metronome, the bar where he had met Maurice and where Maurice hung out and bought people beers, where he seined for people like James.

Except for the spot by the lake — which James had come to terms with by working three stories directly above it, week in and week out — the Metronome was the place in town that disconcerted and frightened him the most. He couldn't believe, in a way, that it was possible for him today to climb the stairs. He held his breath, walked around the corner and into the bar, saw that it was empty except for a pair of wasted looking guys at the far end, and let his breath come out finally in a soft whistle.

The bartender was watching a cartoon on the overhead television, with the sound off, one foot propped up on the ice cooler. The cartoon featured some near-sighted animal with thick glasses that James couldn't place. James waited at the bar rail for a second, politely.

He glanced around the bar. There was no trace of the menace he'd assigned to it in his memory. It was a bar where he'd happened to meet one sick person. There were neon beer signs in the windows and a huge plastic bottle of beer in a huge plastic ice cube hanging over the pool table. It could have been any bar, except for a strange tracery of neon tubes on the black ceiling. The bartender didn't take his eyes off the set, and after another minute, James walked down to his end of the bar and into his field of vision.

The bartender took his sneakered foot off the cooler, laid a napkin down on the polished wood. He pushed his glasses up with his pinky. He looked like an intellectual basketball player. "You're customer number three for the entire afternoon," he said slowly. "Congratulations. You can have anything you want for regular price." He waved at the liquor behind him.

James ordered a half-pint of beer. The bartender brought it to him, and then turned his head back up to the cartoon above James' head.

There was a determined silence, determined on the part of the bartender, who seemed to be dreading small talk. James drank his beer, ordering his memories like a hand of gin rummy, positives and negatives, goods and evils. He had met another bartender here the night he met Maurice, a woman who'd reminded him in a wistful way of his ex-wife. She'd had the same dark hair and eyes, and the same blunt approach to the world. Her name was Alison, and his memory of her was both positive and negative — he felt somehow that Maurice had introduced her to him as a lure, somehow, that he'd blown her up like an inflatable doll and put her away when she'd done her job of drawing James in. His curiosity poked at him.

"Does Alison still work here?" James asked after a minute.

"Yes," the bartender said carefully.

There was another determined silence. The bartender even crossed his arms to ward off conversation.

"But she's not working today," James said after another pause.

The bartender nodded just perceptibly, eyes still locked on the space over James. Then he seemed to give up the ghost. "Yes, she certainly is. She's in the totally far corner of the dance floor. She's making posters." He pointed through an archway leading into the larger space connected to the bar. There was a black curtain on the customer side of the bar, closing it off. When James didn't move, the bartender dropped his eyes down from the cartoon. "You want me to tell her you're here?"

James held out a hand. "No, she doesn't really know me. She wouldn't remember me."

"So you don't want me to go get her."

"Right," James said. "I met her like once or twice."

They stood in their respective positions for another moment or two, and then the bartender walked out from behind the bar and through the archway. Almost immediately he came back followed by Alison. Her dark hair had been cut short, close to her head.

She stared at him for a second. "What do you mean I don't know you? You're King somebody," she said to James, walking over to the mixer gun.

"Sorry," the bartender said, going back to his position in front of the cooler. "I told."

Alison took a rocks glass from a rack by the sink and filled it with ice. She started to shoot different sodas into it, mixing them. She looked up at James. "I met you in here one night, and you were with Maurice. I know that for a fact. I just can't remember your name. But it was definitely King somebody. I know it's not Solomon, but that's all I can think of."

"James," he corrected. "Actually I think we met twice." He remembered her more clearly now. She was a kidder.

She nodded rapidly, mouth full of soda. "Right, *right.*

The bible. You wrote the bible, I remember now." She slapped the bartender on one of his folded arms. "This is the guy that wrote the bible, Cheever."

"Stupefying," the bartender said without shifting his gaze.

"Just my version," James added modestly.

Alison came over and leaned against the bar in front of him. She seemed perfectly content to kill time. She began to wipe down the bar, cleaning the rings from it in a reproach that the bartender behind her ignored. "So how is the great Maurice Masseau these days? Not in jail is he? Not working nine to five in some lingerie store, is he?"

James shrugged. He tried to look casual. "Couldn't tell you."

"I remember you guys as being buddies."

"Never," James said.

She hesitated. "Maurice didn't give you the big pals-for-life routine, then."

"Nope." James felt his face get hot, but he shook his head and took another sip of his beer. "I hardly knew him."

She was looking at him carefully, with her head cocked slightly, as though she were watching for something that had flitted across his face. "Well, join the club. I went out with him for a couple of months — when I was a child, mind you — and I've known him ever since, and *I* hardly know him." She started to fold the damp white cloth into precise quarters. "But I know that of the people who meet him, about fifty-one percent come away saying, 'You know, excuse my French, but that guy is a world-class prick.'"

As she said it, she had her eyes on him, and when he smiled in spite of himself, she smiled back. She looked like she'd won a bet with herself. "So in what particular way was he an asshole to you?" she asked him. "You can tell *us*.

We're all family here."

James glanced at the bartender, who was watching him now. He looked back at Alison. He couldn't think of what to say. "What?" was all that came out. Somehow he sounded guilty to himself. Alison nodded. "I thought so. Come on, grab your drink." She started to move toward the arch leading to the dance floor, then looked back when she realized he wasn't following. "Come on. You aren't doing anything. We're gonna put you to work. I have to make posters. I was *supposed* to have help, but no help ever showed." Alison waited for him to walk around from his side of the bar. She reached over and pulled the black curtain aside. "I mean, I'm assuming you can draw a straight line."

"I hope so," James said. "I'm a carpenter."

"That was Jesus' big pitch too," the bartender remarked without looking over at them.

Alison shot him a sour look. She turned back to James. "Well, that must have made it a heckuva lot easier for you to write the bible, I bet, huh?" she said brightly as she let the curtain drop behind him.

• • •

They made posters. Alison had her posterboard and markers spread out on the dance floor, and the two of them sprawled there for an hour and a half, James working meticulously with a ruler until Alison told him to stop, it was making her nervous. The posters read, *The Memorial Auditorium Restoration Fund presents The Marvelettes & The Coasters.* At the bottom of each was a list of songs the groups had made famous in the fifties and sixties — "Don't Mess With Bill," "Yakkity-Yak," "Playboy," "Charlie Brown," "Please Mr. Postman." Alison drew dancing musical notes at odd intervals around the margins. She chattered as she worked. James sipped his beer, and drew, and laughed at her jokes. It was like being shunted back in time to high school, the good moments in high school. There was a very complete sense of warmth and satisfaction and excitement made up of poster-making, the coming event, the hardwood floor that could have been a gymnasium, and the sudden nudging sensation of a new crush.

When his beer was finished, Alison got up and took the empty mug around the other side of the bar and filled it from the tap. She came back and set it on the floor. "That's your shift beer," she told him with a small smile. "So don't think you're getting something for nothing." She picked up a purple marker, uncapped it, tested it on the bleached denim covering her knee. "You know, I have no idea where they got these groups for this benefit from. These guys were popular like forty years ago."

"I like 'Don't Mess With Bill'," James said. He had his eyes down, concentrating on keeping his lines straight. "Don't knock 'Don't Mess With Bill'."

"All right, I like 'Rudolph the Red-Nosed Reindeer' but that doesn't mean I think we should get Burl Ives to sing at a benefit at Memorial. I mean, you want people to *come*." She pointed at him with the marker. "Correct me if I'm wrong, but there is some idea of wanting people to actually show up."

"That's what I'm saying. They'll come to hear 'Don't Mess With Bill'."

"You know," Alison began, eyes back down on her poster, "the horrible thing is that you're kidding, but you're probably exactly right." She bore down on the marker. "Exactly right. It's exactly this town's speed. The audience will probably be jam-packed with a whole crew of sixty-year-olds clapping their hands and humming along. A nice safe nostalgia trip from these nice *non*-threatening," she looked up at him, shaking her head in disbelief, "squeaky-clean Motown black performers. And it will never dawn on them that it's the Cotton Club all over again, that Burlington's all for black entertainment and traveling troupes of black performers as long as they don't stop traveling when the show's over." She looked at James. "Where'd you move here from again?"

"Southern California," James answered.

Alison sipped from her mix of sodas, began to talk with ice cubes in her mouth, chewing them as she talked. "So you know what I'm saying. I grew up in this town, and it's flat-out amazing. I mean the rest of the world has changed, it's *gone* somewhere. People have learned to live together, you know? All kinds of people. But here it's just blah, it's just, like, *white.* I don't know. There's this conservativeness that goes way beyond politics. It's like everybody who lives here all send out their secret thoughts and it all collects and runs together and forms one big huge mental shield, like a time capsule. So nothing changes. I detest the fact that I still live here. I should have caught a bus or something."

James picked up the ruler, gave her an apologetic look when she raised an eyebrow. "California's no paradise, either, you know," he said. "There's all different kinds of people, but that doesn't make it any better. Nothing stays the same there. Every place is a different place every ten years."

"So why did you come here, James?" she asked suddenly. "I'm curious. To know what makes somebody actually move in to Burlington."

James hesitated. Alison started to tap her marker against the hardwood. She put up a hand to silence him.

"Okay, let me guess. You followed a girlfriend here. She was some kind of middle management in the dairy or syrup industry."

"That's very funny."

"You'd be surprised how often I'm right."

James sat up, tailor-fashion. He thought about making up a story, and then he just told the truth. "Actually, it was the opposite. I got divorced, and I couldn't handle living in the same town as my ex-wife, and so I zapped around for awhile, wherever there was work. And I had some family here." He held up his hands innocently. "An absolutely true story."

"How long were you married?" Alison asked.

"A year and seven months."

"What happened?"

He hesitated again. "She said she needed room to grow." After a second he smiled and held up his thumb and forefinger about an inch apart from one another. "She was only about *this* big, was the problem." It was the first joke he could remember making about the divorce.

They sat there for a second in silence, Alison shaking her head slowly. Then she sat up too, also tailor-fashion, mimicking him but not mocking him. "Okay, James, I'm not dying of curiosity, but I make it sort of a hobby to keep up with Maurice's fuck-ups in life. Maybe it just confirms me in my decision to dump him all those years ago. Or, I don't know, maybe it's none of my business. But when I asked you before, you looked like something happened. And if something happened, knowing you and knowing Maurice, I'm betting he did something shitty." She was looking into his eyes. "So what did he do?"

Again, he considered a story, found himself telling the truth. "He beat me up."

Her face went blank. "Beat you *up*?"

James smiled at her reaction. It seemed the more he talked about it, in this place he had dreaded for months, the less it bothered him. He started to giggle. And then he pointed to the skin just below his eyebrow. "Feel right here," he said.

Alison looked suspicious, then reached up to the spot. She moved her finger a bit, gingerly, until she found the chip in the socket. She snatched her hand back and made a face. "Oh my god," she said, staring at the spot. "I cannot believe he would do that."

"He did."

"Why?"

"I have no idea."

"But I mean what *happened*?"

James leaned back on his hands. He felt good enough — from her company, from the beer, and from the feeling of being favored, allowed to sprawl in the closed part of a bar and draw posters — that he could actually consider it. He could muse a little. "I think he felt like I wasn't doing my part for that big shield you were talking about before. I think he thought I was somebody totally different than who I was. I think he was disappointed in me."

She looked at him, one eye closed, appraising. "I'll give you another beer if you tell me what actually happened." She waited, then said, "*And* a shot."

"I'll tell you some day," James said. He couldn't help smiling a little at her obvious disappointment. "Not today."

"But he was disappointed, you said."

"I think he was. But I really have no idea." He let his mind flash to it, just for an instant. Finally he said, "No one has any idea."

• • •

When they'd finished, Alison took the posters into the back office, holding them out in front of her with stiffened arms. She came back and handed James an envelope. "Ticket to the show," she said. "Somebody else was supposed to help with the posters and get the ticket. But you were the one who showed, so it's yours. It's next Friday night." She ran her hands up through her skull-short hair. "This other person is supposed to be my best friend. But *now* my best friend has a new girlfriend. You know how that little deal goes. All of the sudden you're on the C-list. You start getting their machine when you call."

"You never see him anymore," James filled in.

"Her," Alison said.

"Oh. Her," James amended.

"No, I don't. And I'm really pissed off about it." She looked down at her hands. "I'm such a grub. I have to go take a shower before my shift. Thanks for the help."

"It was the most fun I've had in about six months." He wished immediately that he hadn't said it. But it seemed to be his day for truth-telling.

"God forbid," she said, with a horrified look.

• • •

Memorial Auditorium was Burlington's second-tier, second-rate venue. It housed the acts and events that would have felt out of place at the Flynn Theater, the restored opera house on lower Main. Memorial sat two blocks up from the Flynn in a kind of perpetual darkness; it was dark old brick, brick with the visual tang of prison to it, and it showed only its back end to Main Street. There seemed to be no streetlights anywhere near it, and James had lived in the Burlington area for six months, driving right past it almost every day, before he finally became aware of it. The Flynn was Shakespeare and vaudeville and *Les Africains* African Dance Troupe. Memorial was the World Wrestling Federation, one-hit wonders, the rawer comedians and the New England Golden Gloves.

It was the Golden Gloves that caused Memorial to register in James' field of vision for the first time. He had met Bobby Drill and another guy from the site there one night for the matches, in the first few weeks following the incident with Maurice, when he couldn't have cared one way or another about making friends. His memories of it were nauseous memories. It had been a mistake to go.

He remembered three things about it. The referee wore bright blue surgical gloves, a new pair for each of the thirteen matches. Everything else in the auditorium — the klieg lights over the fighters, the darkened, screaming seats, and the boxers' brilliant silk shorts and shoes — everything seemed familiar and known in the blood but those blue latex gloves. They were a barrier to the blood, and to the history of the sport, to the animal and to the human. James had found himself watching the gloves as they broke the fighters, then called them immediately back to fight.

The second thing he remembered was the last of the heavyweight matches. A kid came out of maybe nineteen, pasty white and flabby, black greasy hair. He had a look of unease on his face that deepened as his trainer set up the corner. His opponent came out and stood in the facing corner, a beefy young black fighter, with a somber expression. The crowd began to murmur at the sight of the black fighter; he was the first and only black on the card, and James could feel the energy in the room begin to tune, seeking some new fix. The kid's expression had turned very nearly to open fright.

When the bell sounded, the crowd strained forward to see the black fighter advance and jab experimentally at his opponent's face. The kid went down immediately, on all fours, shaking his head as soon as he touched the canvas. *Are you okay,* the ref yelled down at him. The kid shook his head wildly. *You want to fight,* the ref yelled again. Again, although clearly unhurt and fully aware, the kid shook his head violently. *You sure? You can't fight?* The kid shook his head, still on his hands and knees, eyes wide with panic. The blue latex gloves waved once, disdainfully, and the match was over. It had taken 2.5 seconds official time.

And when the pasty white kid climbed out of the ring, almost fell out in his mental exhaustion, the crowd screamed at him, *Go eat another donut! Have another burrito, you fat piece of shit!* The kid couldn't look into the seats. He was holding his elbow for some reason, trying vainly to suggest an injury. But he knew, and James knew, that if he had fought and won he would have been loved, truly and lastingly loved, by the crowd. He would have been remembered. But he hadn't fought, he hadn't at all.

And the last thing James remembered was his own growing feeling of nausea, the more he watched young fighters be swarmed and overwhelmed by faster, older, smarter, crazier, stronger opponents. Bobby sat on his one side and drank beer after beer, occasionally cracking a joke to James. But the other guy from the site, whose name James had forgotten, and who had since quit the job, kept screaming, "Rock his world!" "Nail him, *nail* him!" or "Put some salt in his fucking shaker!" And he would scream these things with such obvious malice that James suddenly flashed on his own beating three weeks before, and felt — for one instant before he got his legs under him again — that he was going to lose consciousness.

• • •

But the night of the Marvelettes and Coasters concert, Memorial was a different place. James stood outside in the line that stretched down the concrete steps, chin down in his jacket to keep his neck warm. The crowd was good-humored, and he didn't feel like he wasn't with anybody for some reason. Somebody had fixed small blue and red spot-lights to the outside of the building, small enough to be a little laughable, but big enough to begin a mood, if you were willing to have one begun.

There were two kinds of people filing into the drafty, vaulted old gymnasium: couples in their fifties and sixties, silent but smiling placidly, and with the look of people from the outlying farm areas; and a much younger crowd, most-ly in their twenties. For the most part, the young people shared an air that James couldn't place, except to say that it was celebratory, far more excited and eager than he would have expected. It was like they were coming to a party.

Most of them were much younger than he was, and he could barely remember the Marvelettes' songs, at thirty-five. And *he* only knew them because he had learned them from a fifties nostalgia collection he'd talked his mother into ordering from a television advertisement, when he was about eleven years old.

Where the boxing ring had been, and the judges' tables, there was now row after row of metal folding chairs, each with a small white sticker on its back, with a handwritten number and letter. There was a concession stand in one cor-ner, selling soda and hot dogs and candy bars. The gym's bas-ketball nets had been folded up and back, so that each point-ed into the darkened balcony. On the walls hung overlarge cardboard cut-outs in the shape of musical notes, guitars, and saxophones, the shapes covered with metallic glitter.

The stage was empty except for a few speakers on each side, some musical equipment, and a small white banner hung from the center of the faded tan backdrop: *Let's Restore Memorial!* Like the spotlights outside, it was all underdone and nakedly low-budget, but with the same parallel feel of pluck and good intentions.

His seat was in the third row, bordering a space left open for dancing right in front of the stage. There was one empty seat to his left, and he glanced around at the milling people for Alison, but he couldn't see her. James looked down his shortened row. Next to him sat a couple of about sixty, both with pure white hair and glasses, heavily lined faces; then came a group of women a bit younger, but still in their fifties; and at the end were four young men in their twenties and early thirties, very stylishly dressed, laughing animatedly and clapping their hands, waiting for the show to begin. He had the sense again of duality in the audience, of crowd within a crowd.

The woman next to him spoke just as the lights began to dim. "I've never seen either of 'em, Marvelettes or Coasters," she informed him. "He did, though." She gave a nod of her head toward her husband, who sat duly watching the empty stage. "He saw the Marvelettes one time in New York City. Right when he was gettin' out of the Navy."

Some people in the back began to yell in high, crazy voices.

"I've never seen either of them either," James whispered back.

"Well, it'll be something."

"Yeah it will."

The woman seemed as though she were going to turn back to her husband, but she whispered again, eyes on the stage, "He had to see 'em. The minute he heard they were playin' in town, he said he was goin'. He doesn't know the Coasters from Adam, though." She patted her hair with her hand, then turned to James and smiled. He could see she was very happy to be there, sitting in the half-light. "Not much he'll go out to a concert for."

Four men in jeans and work shirts came out onto the stage and picked up their instruments without ceremony. The drummer perched himself on his stool, then blew his nose as surreptitiously as he could, re-settled his handkerchief in the pocket of his jeans. None of them really tuned or warmed up. They all simply looked at one another and began to play. The young screamers in the audience began to scream again.

And then the Marvelettes made their entrance — three black women in tight-fitting, spaghetti-strap dresses. The first two of them had the straightened black hair, cut to eyebrow length bangs, that once marked the Motown woman. The third woman was taller and slightly younger-looking, with a high headful of dull platinum curls that almost looked like a wig. She wore more makeup as well, and smiled brilliantly while the other two kept their expressions sultry-straight. They all began to move to the song in Motown unison.

It was "Don't Mess With Bill," a dreamy, sexy number, and James sat up in his seat. It had always been his favorite, a song that got under the skin. The minute the women opened their mouths, the flawed rendition that the band was working its way through changed into something purer. Their voices melted almost seamlessly into his memory of the record. It was a moment of authentication, undeniable as a voice-print. The audience responded with a ripple of applause, strengthening into whistles and cheers, and all three of the women suddenly smiled as they moved through what must have been the number's original choreography.

There were moments, if James squinted his eyes and let the harmonies rush him, when he could imagine what these women must have been and felt when they were at the pinnacle, when they were driving a whole new medium and when they were absolute style in the flesh.

The old woman next to him leaned over. "Now *I* remember this one," she said.

"Leave my Billy alone," the first singer, the leader, sang with her finger pointed into the dark audience.

"Don't mess with Bill," the other two sang back. They were pointing as well.

"Find a guy of your own."

"Don't mess with Bill."

James looked down his row again. The older people were watching and politely clapping, really more patting their hands together than clapping. But the four young men at the end were rapt, whispering excitedly. One of them was pointing at something; he seemed to be explaining something to the man beside him. The other was nodding his head and smiling.

James looked back at the singers, and as he did so, the three of them executed a little stage turn, arms over their heads. And then — like spotting a set of lost car keys that had been lying on the table in front of him the whole time — he saw that the third Marvelette was a man. His arms were too long and muscled, hands too large. The hair could only be a wig. James looked back at the heavily made-up face and wondered that he hadn't seen it immediately.

"Because he's mine all mine," the leader continued, signaling behind her for the band to pick up the tempo.

"Don't mess with Bill."

The older woman next to him whispered something James couldn't hear, nodding her head again toward her husband. The husband wasn't moving or clapping, but he had his head tilted slightly and his eyes closed. James shook his head, and the woman spoke closer to his ear. "He's lost in a little dream world. Look at that."

• • •

They ran through "Playboy" and "Please Mr. Postman" and six or seven other lesser hits. People filtered out onto the dance floor. In between songs, the leader would insert a minute or two of patter. "Ver*mont*," she said at one point, scratching her head. "This is a strange damn place up here. It's beautiful, but, you know, it's strange. We went to Stowe today, to do some shopping." She waited a beat. "You want to talk Stowe, well they *Stowe* from me down there, they charged me thirty-five dollars for a hat to cover my head up with!"

"That was a bad joke," the second singer said as the audience groaned. "That was really bad."

"Well, I *mean* it. It was a robbery," the first one said, smiling and snapping her fingers absently behind her. The band picked up the cue without a change of expression. "This is a Tina Turner song, not one of ours, but all's I can say is I wish that it was."

The third Marvelette answered all of the lead singer's stagey questions and gibes with little mimed movements, go-on-with-you waves of her man's hands. Only once did she speak, and then it was in such a breathy falsetto that James inadvertently swung around to the old couple next to him, to catch their reaction. The old woman was looking at him when he turned.

"What," James asked her hesitantly, "what do you think of that singer on the end? With the silver hair."

The woman paused in her clapping. "Oh, he's a pip," she said confidentially. "You'd just about never know."

The Tina Turner song turned out to be "Private Dancer," and the lead singer had just begun it — snarling her lip in what wasn't a half-bad Tina Turner imitation — when Alison sat down next to James. She was wearing a black mini-skirt over black tights. Her short hair was fluffed a little, and she was wearing a fiery lipstick that made her white face seem paler. She looked fabulous. "Hey, so what do you think of Mr. Marvelette?" she asked without saying hello.

James glanced back up at him, then said, "I think he maybe needs hand-reduction surgery."

"He's really good though, don't you think? I mean, hands aside. And speaking voice."

"He is," James said. "I'm still not a hundred-percent sure looking at him right now. Maybe a he, maybe a she."

Alison almost jumped in her seat, and she slapped her hands down on her thighs. "I am so absolutely *glad* that he's up there, oh my god! I just love it that all of these people are sitting around mooning over two Marvelettes and some guy with fake boobs and pouty lips. I was up in the balcony before and all you can see down here is people just groov-ing away. I just love it." She started to drum her hands on her thighs and kick her heels against the hardwood floor. "Oh man. Everybody was telling me, but I just didn't think I'd come here and it would be real."

"Who told you?" James asked. "How'd they know?"

"I guess the word had been going out for like a week." She looked around at the house. "Every alternative

Burlingtonian is here, as far as I can see. Remember my friend I told you about, that I never see anymore — the bitch — because she has the new girlfriend? Actually I shouldn't say that. I like her new flame. And I'm like that when I get a beau too. Well, that's her out on the floor, with the straight black hair, dancing with the redhead." The woman she pointed to was a tall, slender Asian woman, dancing and laughing with a short young woman with carrot-red hair and a green party dress. "That's who I heard from. But apparently somebody knew somebody who knew somebody, and the word spread that there'd be this man-woman Marvelette tonight. That's what everybody kept talking about it as, this *man-woman Marvelette.* I mean, at first I thought it was some rumor planted by the Restoration Fund people, just to up the attendance. Look at how packed this place is. You can almost believe it was a PR deal."

The white-haired woman sitting next to James could obviously hear their conversation, and she turned and smiled at Alison, then politely turned away from them again. James lowered his voice a bit. "Well, who is he? Is he just some guy or what? How'd they wind up one Marvelette short anyway?"

Alison lowered her voice too, but she was still smiling wickedly. "I've heard about six different stories. Either he's some guy from New York that the two original singers saw one night at a transvestite bar doing one of their songs," she waved to someone out on the dance floor, "or he's the gay brother of the original singer, or — and this is my favorite — he's really one of the Coasters who doubles. I mean, the two groups travel together. It would make so much sense, when you think about it."

"That would be pretty bold," James said.

"Bold is right." Alison nodded slowly. "That's it *exactly.* That's what this town needs and has never had the whole time I've lived here, and that's every minute of my life. It has never had any boldness." She pointed to the third singer. "There's not a spot in this whole country that needs that great big black transvestite up there more than we do. He's like a godsend."

Her voice had risen just enough so that the woman next to James turned again and quickly held a finger to her lips, then gave a nod to her husband who seemed now half-asleep. She whispered, "He doesn't know, you know."

"Sorry," Alison stage-whispered.

"Oh, that's all right," the woman whispered back.

James looked at Alison again. He couldn't really see the resemblance to his ex-wife anymore. And more, he felt that he had never really seen it, but that it had been some kind of show of loyalty by his subconscious. He hadn't wanted to admit that his more durable love was gone, as well as the weaker love of his wife, that their marriage was better ended, and that there was nowhere to move but forward into a more violent uncertainty. He realized he knew nothing about Alison except that she claimed to despise the town she'd lived her entire life in. He didn't really know if she was gay, or straight, or both or neither. He knew she'd had a boyfriend once, someone they'd both rather never see again. He felt a fragmentary kinship with her. "Let's dance," he said, impulsively for him.

"Okay," she said, standing up and reaching for his hand, "I will, if you absolutely won't have it any other way." She yanked him standing. "King James."

He thought about telling her not to call him that, but it didn't really matter. "Please," he did say, "just call us James."

She gave him a look. "The awful thing is, you're probably

serious," she said.

They found a place on the floor and it was perfectly crazy, the people dancing, the two different audiences mixing irreversibly on the old hardwood. Alison introduced him to her friend, and her friend's new girlfriend, and the four of them danced in a square that got smaller and smaller as the audience realized that this was to be the last song, and more people crowded onto the dance floor. But it seemed that the more people that came onto the floor the politer everyone got. People danced with their elbows tucked. It was crazy, the group on stage singing like a living riddle, and the sense that the town contained, and had always contained, a thousand back doors and counter-conspiracies. At one point, Alison asked him if he knew how to run a circular saw because she wanted to re-do the house that had once been her mother's, turn it into the city's only really cutting-edge art gallery, and James said yes, sure, but inside himself he was thinking, *this is crazy*.

Avery Yandow

By eleven o'clock it was clear to Maurice that something was off-center. His nose and his sense of calibration told him that before he began to reason it out for himself. He was in the Metronome and, number one, there was no one to challenge him on the pool table. He had to keep practicing bank shots in the dead time between what few games he could get.

That was simply wrong. Unless a name act was in town, or unless it was the County Fair, the place should have had anywhere from thirty-five to three hundred people milling around on a Friday night, and of those ten or twelve would have had their names on the chalkboard waiting to play. He should have been ruling on the felt. There weren't that many fewer people, but fewer enough to twitch his antennae.

Number two, the few people who were in the bar that night were the dregs, the sort who would graduate to being full-scale losers after a few more years on the stool. And number three, when he signaled the bartender over to ask what the hell was up, the bartender was some young kid with a lip ring Maurice didn't know. It was Friday night and Alison wasn't there and Cheever wasn't there. *Ipso facto,* Maurice thought, watching the kid shuffle his way over, *something's kicking and no one bothered to tell old Maurice.*

"How you doing, friend," Maurice said to the new bartender.

"Not so bad," the bartender said, his face not friendly and his eyes landing everywhere but Maurice's eyes, looking at Maurice's red goatee, the freckles on his nose.

Maurice thought, *Please tell me this young prick is not giving me the once over.* But he smiled and said, "Where's the party tonight? I'm looking around and there's nobody here. I can't even get a game tonight."

The bartender ran his hand through his shoulder-length hair. "Oldies show at Memorial," he said. "Marvelettes and the Coasters." He wasn't going to exert himself, Maurice could see that.

"Well, yeah. But let's face it, it's an *oldies* show. The Marvelettes? Even my *mom* wouldn't go catch the Marvelettes, even if she won tickets on the radio. So what's up with that?" Maurice tried to smile as he said it, but the kid's attitude was getting under his skin just a bit.

From the look on his face it was clear the bartender knew something else about the little mystery, but he wasn't going to give it up. "Go figure," the kid said, moving away, and in some strange way it sounded like an order.

• • •

He thought about walking up Main Street and poking his head into Memorial, but for some incoherent reason his pride was involved, and instead he walked over to South Winooski, cleared and scraped the windshield of his car, and then drove up the quiet, plowed length of Pearl and over the hill to Winooski.

He made the turn into the New Social Club's narrow driveway and ran down the length of the building before he could see the back parking lot. Only Avery's car was there, a chocolate-brown Lincoln Towncar, sitting in the fresh snowfall. Maurice sat in the middle of the lot for a second, engine idling, fingers drumming the wheel. "Well, fuck me," he said a couple of times to himself.

Taped to the door was a small note in magic marker, *Club Closed — Owners Meeting*. It was the sign that Avery put up every two or three weeks when he met with his three partners. It was considered bad form to buzz in if you saw that sign; that just put Avery to the task of telling you to go away. But those meetings ordinarily ended before ten, and so Maurice picked up the phone receiver next to the door. The phone buzzed four times. Then Avery's voice said, "We're closed. Regular hours tomorrow night."

"It's Maurice, Avery. You all by yourself in there?"

"Yup," Avery said.

"Well, if you don't let me in, I'll huff and I'll puff. I'm serious, now, don't get me started."

"I haven't got the bar stocked, young blood. Go on downtown. Regular hours tomorrow."

"Let's you and me have a game of billiards."

"I don't feel like playing." There was a pause, and then Avery said. "You can come in for one draft. A glass, not a pint. Then I gotta think about going home."

The door buzzed, and Maurice pushed his way in. All of the lights were off except the light over the bar and the wide-screen television playing around the corner from the doorway. Avery was heading back to the couch in front of the television. "Your beer's on the bar," he called over his shoulder. "And you're in here on the understanding that I don't feel like playing pool."

"That's cool," Maurice called back, walking to the bar for the beer. "I haven't been able to get a game anywhere tonight. Better people than you have already turned me down tonight, believe me."

On the wide-screen women were figure-skating. Avery had the sound down almost all the way. The skaters were all wearing fairly revealing outfits, lots of transparent panels in their uniforms, a really tartish look, and Maurice realized that it was one of those professional skating matches, the kind that were rigged like wrestling and piped all over the world by satellite for people like Avery to watch. The camera kept making these fake cuts to backstage, where all of the skater girls were adjusting themselves, supposedly worrying about their performances. He shook his head as he sat down, laughing to himself. "This is pathetic, Avery. Why don't you watch some *shopping* or something, some Value Shopper's channel, something that would show a little class."

Avery smiled lazily. "No sense showing class if there ain't no one around," he said. He was scooted way down on the couch, his arms folded and the diminutive legs stretched out on the coffee table, glossy black cowboy boots crossed. "You must be losing your touch, you can't get a game. That happens when you get older, son. Lose your edge."

Maurice nodded, settling into the couch on the other wall. "I see that. You start spending Friday nights looking up girls' tutus. That's hard-core, Avery."

"You done with that beer yet?"

"Almost," Maurice said, taking a sip. "So you had a meeting tonight."

Avery nodded, lips drawn in so his clipped silver beard filled in his mouth.

"What'd you folks have on the agenda?"

"None of your damn business."

"Don't give me that. I'm curious."

There was a pause. "Usual shit. Lot of talk about that grant the government gave for developing the North End. Enterprise Zone money. You read about that. That's three million dollars, or near enough." Avery nodded his head almost imperceptibly again. "So people are pretty interested in that. How they're gonna chunk some out for themselves."

"Anybody interested in selling their share of this place?"

Avery laughed. "Hardly. We're making money, young blood."

"How much?"

Another laugh. "Not hand over fist. But more comes out than goes in. Every month."

"I'm first on the list if somebody decides to sell out their share. No shit, Avery."

"You got no assets but your mouth."

Maurice gave him a look from under the bill of his baseball cap. "I got sweat equity. This place could use somebody to do some serious renovation. And if you all decide you want money, just give me first dibs and time to raise it. That's all I'm saying. I can get money."

"Don't get yourself in an uproar," Avery said.

"I'm not. I'm just drinking my beer and watching this skating competition."

They watched without speaking for a minute, and Maurice could hear the commentators' voices talking excitedly even with the volume down. Avery turned his head and gave Maurice his full attention. "How's your big brother doing? He doing all right?"

"He's hating it in there, but he's doing all right. I go up and see him every three or four days. We got a little letter-writing going. But it's prison. It can only get so good."

"It isn't for long, tell him."

"I told him."

"I already talked to those folks over at the parole board."

"I know it. He appreciates it, believe me, Avery."

Avery scowled at the television. "They didn't have no evidence to speak of."

A woman was skating in a pair of ripped jeans and a man's shirt knotted beneath her breasts. The audience was straining forward in the stands, clapping along to her music, some sanitized piece of rock and roll.

"Yo, Avery," Maurice said.

"What do you want?"

"Reuben was telling me one night at Nectar's about a serious conversation you and him had one night, about Dad."

"Oh, yeah?" Avery said, looking over at him. He took his cigarette pack from his shirt pocket and shook out a cigarette for himself, took it neatly between his lips and came up with his lighter. He let out a gray bloom of smoke. "I must have been about nine sheets to the wind, to be talking serious about Chris Masseau."

"I guess so," Maurice agreed. There was a pause and the announcers chattered, barely audible. Avery seemed determined to sit silently. Finally Maurice started again. "Reuben was saying Dad used to torch shit, burn things down. Make extra money that way." He kept going with it, because he needed to hear it from Avery, not just delivered second-hand from Reuben. "Somebody wanted something torched and they'd get in touch with Dad. That's true, isn't it? I never knew that about him. I can't believe I never knew that."

Avery ashed his cigarette with a stretch of his arm, then just left it burning in the ashtray. "It wasn't that often," he said grudgingly, quietly, after a minute of silence. "And shit, every town's got someone to do that job when it needs to be done. Every town in the country's got somebody to clear old buildings, and do it so the owner doesn't lose his shirt in the deal, just like every town used to have somebody somewhere could do an abortion. Sometimes there's just something in the way that people want *out* of the way, nobody getting hurt, but just getting it out of the way. But I shouldn't have said nothing to Reuben about it. That's all gone with your dad. Doesn't matter how he made his money."

Maurice took a sip of his beer, as casually as he could. "I didn't say nothing, Avery."

Avery gave him another hard look. "And it wasn't always for money. Your dad wasn't a greedy man, and you know that better than anybody. Sometimes it was for sending a message, when one needed sending. One of them churches was falling down anyway, and it was a place where all kinds of trash were hanging out, not because they were Christians but because the church was giving them hand-outs and sponsoring their families to come over from Mongolia and who knows where. So sometimes it wasn't for money at all," Avery looked for the word, "but for his conscience."

The buzzer for the door phone sounded, and Maurice jerked his head toward the bar. "Just ignore that goddam thing," Avery said. "I shouldn't have answered it when you buzzed through."

The buzzer fell silent, as though whoever was standing outside the door was afraid of pressing the point. Maurice imagined whoever it was going back to their car, finding it already grown cold. He felt a rush of pride, having been let in sign or no sign. And the pride made him feel like pressing his luck. "Reuben said there was something else you were talking about, something you didn't go into. I was just curious about that. That other thing about you and Dad."

Avery nodded. "Yeah, well, lot of times I think your

brother Reuben can't hear things quite right because his head's so far up his ass."

"That's pretty true," Maurice said, draining half his glass. "He's got it right up there."

"Got an imagination on him."

"Yeah, he's pretty much of a fucking idiot when you get right down to it," Maurice added, and both of them broke up into laughter for a second. Maurice finished the last of his beer, stood up and, without asking, went over to the bar and came back with a second draft. Avery kept his eyes on the television, not acknowledging Maurice's full glass. They watched a replay of a woman missing an axel, her muscular legs whipping, skate blades whirling and her head striking the ice.

"Still, though, Avery, what was that shit all about?"

There was silence, and then Avery said, "Nothing important. Leave it alone."

Maurice took off his baseball cap and scratched his head. "Bullshit."

"Bullshit yourself."

"What, did you and Dad knock somebody off or something? You take somebody out of the game?"

"Finish that beer."

"You could tell me, Avery."

"I could slap your monkey ass, too."

"I only ask because he was my father, and I figure I should know the things he did while he was around."

"You know everything he did."

"Obviously not. Come on, Avery, you should share it around, and you know it."

Avery said nothing, mouth tight, eyes fixed on the television, motionless.

And suddenly Maurice had the sharp, uncanny sense

that all of the layers of evasion were clear, that Avery had thrown up all the dust he could throw, and that all he, Maurice, had to do was ask once again, the same question asked one more time. He could tell that asking it now would be a simple thing. So he asked. "You got rid of somebody, didn't you, Mr. Yandow?"

Avery looked at him. Avery was in his mid-sixties now, and in the last five years or so the veins in his cheeks had begun to rise up to the surface, like fine red streams on a map of the county. He wiped at his cheek with his hand, for no obvious reason. "Yup. We did."

It lay in front of them both for a moment, the admission. "No shit," Maurice remarked and then gave a little whistle.

"You don't tell Reuben this, understand?" Avery said softly. He leaned back into the cushions, his hands flat on the couch. Crowd noise came up from the television, and Avery touched the remote. The word MUTE appeared in the corner of the screen. "Not even your big brother. Understand?"

"No, never."

"You better mean that when you say it."

Maurice nodded. He had known this also, that when it was told it would be told to him alone. It was something that made clear intuitive sense, and he knew also that he wouldn't tell Reuben, ever. It linked up with his feeling about his own singular future, and the singular nature of the city, and how the two were indivisible.

"Because I can about stand one other person knowing about it, but not two. So now Chris is gone, it'll be you. I guess I sort of figured it might wind up that way." Avery picked up his cigarette and looked at Maurice. "And that's all right. That's a good thing." He seemed eager somehow to Maurice, like a married guy who'd bagged a beautiful woman from his office and who couldn't tell anyone, just had to walk around with it held inside. And now Avery was getting to tell.

• • •

Your dad and I were out one night about ten o'clock, out on Spear Street. This was back in the early seventies. In those days Spear Street only had a few housing developments. They were all just getting started being built, all those houses that are out there now. But mostly it was still just one long dark country road. We were out there because a guy that owned a big old farmhouse and sugar house and barn wanted to go out of business in style. He was losing his business, mostly because he was a lazy son of a bitch, but he was losing money, and he looked down the road two years and he saw Chapter Eleven coming there. He'd sold his livestock, and he was living in town with his brother, and that farm was eating him up. Couldn't get a buyer, and couldn't bring himself to actually work.

So I knew this guy, and the place was way out in bumfuck Egypt where there wouldn't be anybody around for miles and I thought your dad could pick up a bit of change, and I could get a little off the top too. Now you know your dad, Mo. He was a smart man. I mean he could be shrewd, shrewd like a lawyer and a soldier all in one. He was that, and he had a way he went at this fire-starting that he called operating according to procedure. He'd made up all these rules about how to do it so he wouldn't get caught. He thought up these rules in peace and quiet, see, when he had time to think, when he could check and recheck himself. He had thirty or thirty-five of these damn things.

Like he wouldn't do it if he thought the person paying for it had a big mouth. Like he wouldn't give a specific time when it would be done, just say that it would happen when the time was right. Like he alternated accelerator, gas then charcoal lighter or whatnot. On and on. The place had to be scoped out, and he had to do that in his own car. He never used the patrol car.

That was procedure. It was like the procedures we had to go by down at the station house, it was just exactly that *picky*. He was serious about this shit. And it worked. No one ever come near to tipping that he was involved in this sort of thing for the ten, eleven years he worked it.

Now that night out on Spear I'd pulled off some kind of a miracle, son. I'd shamed Chris so much and busted his balls so much about *procedure* and being a procedure pussy that he finally agreed to just swing by and scope this job in the cruiser, with the lights off. It was so far out of town, I mean. Wasn't any risk to speak of. I still say that.

And we swung out there, and we were in stealth mode. Flying below the radar. No lights once we rolled into the driveway, just dead-reckoning by the moon. We sat there in the drive for a good fifteen minutes, and your dad got out and explored a little, looking for the sweet spot where he could put the package and get the most coverage. The house and the barn were pretty close, and Chris thought he wouldn't even have to light up the house. He said that'd go up all by itself, sympathy fire.

We didn't say much while we were there, both of us just keeping our eyes open, and I remember I was kind of relieved when we hauled out the driveway. We hadn't even gone twenty yards — hadn't even clicked the headlights back on — and we float right past some guy standing in the weeds by the side of the road, taking a leak. I about jumped out of my pants. I mean, he was standing right there, where he could have been watching us right through the trees and brush. I don't know if he was but he'd only had to walk in a bit to do it. Probably he wasn't, but that's the thing, you can't know.

I looked over at your dad, and I could tell the whole thing was off. Permanently. That was procedure, too. If Chris Masseau got seen casing some place — even if the person passing didn't know what they were seeing or turn their head even — it was just off. He wouldn't even do it a year later, not for nothing in the world. And I knew that for a fact, especially since he'd gone back on procedure once already that night, and maybe got spotted for it. Your dad was driving the cruiser, and I looked over and I said kind of sarcastic, "So I guess that's that," and he just nodded once, not really answering me. Wouldn't even look at me. I mean, he was mad at *me* all the sudden, I could tell, for shaming him into taking a risk. And so I felt myself getting hacked off too, not at him, but at this deadbeat in the weeds.

Right then I told your dad to swing it around. At first I thought he wasn't gonna do it, because he gave me a look, but then he jerked the gearshift lever down and he hung a three-point turn, not saying nothing. He was doing a slow burn, like he used to do, because I'd fucked up holy procedure.

So when we rolled up, I hit the blue lights. By now the guy was done relieving himself, and he'd kind of stepped back off the road, into this little kind of clear space under this row of pine trees. He's back in there in that little alley of pine needles, kind of like he don't know what's going on. Drunk. I clicked off the flashers. I told Chris to hold off on calling us in, and to stay in the car, and just to let me know if anyone was coming. Just blip the siren quick if someone was coming or if we got a call on the radio. See, I had it in my mind I was going to have a little discussion and find out what the boy thought he was doing out there. And Chris probably knew I meant to hassle the kid some, but he was in a snit. He didn't say a word, not a thing, when I told him to stay.

This guy was Mexican, I could see once I got up to him. He'd given himself some kind of free-love name, too, the way they used to then, but his real name was Gabriel something. Kind of a big bastard. He said he was from New York City. I told him to keep his joint in his pants, he wasn't in New York City any more. I could see right away he's drunk, and the bastard was just all smiles. Seemed like he thought the whole thing was a funny little game.

I was quizzing this kid, and you could tell he was a draft-dodger, making his way up to Canada. You better believe we got a lot of them in those days. They'd stay up in some commune for a little, and then make their break for Quebec. I asked him for his driver's license, and he said he didn't have one. I asked him where he was headed and he told me he was going up to St. Albans, but he was looking to slip over the line somewhere out in the woods, I guarantee you. All the dodgers had this look. Long black hair and a cheesy little moustache. I decided to cuff him, give him a night in jail and run him through the system. Check him out with the draft board, just to make his day. And if he was telling the truth then send him on his way the next day, because God knows we don't need him stopping here.

But he started giving me a hard time. He started asking for my badge number and that noise. Finally I told him I didn't have to give my badge number to some dickless Mexican, and all of the sudden he starts laughing. Right out loud, right in my face. And I lost it.

After I hit him with the night stick and knocked him over, he turned around and looked me right square in the eye and called me a pig.

Shit, Maurice, back in those days that was like getting called nigger. You didn't say that unless you wanted major trouble. And I didn't have no patience to speak of when I was young. You're a patient man next to the way I was, young blood. I just remember wanting to destroy that son of a bitch, wanting to wreck him. I was gone out of my head. I hit him, and my arm felt like a flame-thrower. I hit him like the flat hand of God.

• • •

Chris had one hand gripped around the wheel, and with the other he cranked the car's side spot, playing the beam over the bank of trees across the road. There was no one else, no friend crouching in the trees. The thick bank of leaves shimmered in the wind, the leaves showing yellow backs, predicting rain. He looked back out the passenger window. Avery was standing off the road under some pines, and he was right up in the taller man's face. It was the way Avery always handled bigger perps. Chris couldn't hear their voices over the fuzz of the radio and the car's engine, but he could tell from Avery's posture that the kid wasn't giving him as many yessirs as Avery was looking for.

He knew he should go out and stand back-up, but part of him didn't feel like watching Avery's back. He felt himself boiling inside, felt his anger pressing against the wall of his chest. If they hadn't seen this man, and if he had seen them, it could have all collapsed in a day, his family, his job, his home, everything that he was and had made. The same fire that eliminated the farm could have eliminated

Christopher Masseau entirely. He'd always felt the risks, but felt that he could control them by being precise, by inspection and detail.

Now he'd gotten lax, and he was fiercely angry with himself, but it bled over into anger too at Avery. Avery was his partner, and they were partners also in this shadow business, but Chris had always kept him at arm's length and insisted that things proceed according to some kind of predetermined logic. Avery sometimes brought people to him, but only Chris knew exactly where and when and how things would happen. Because for all his good trooper's instincts and his heart, Avery took shortcuts. Avery didn't think, not clearly and not deeply. He reminded Chris of his son Maurice, who had never had his older brother Reuben's brains or self-control. Both Avery and Maurice thought that their intuitions were the only true compass in the world.

He swung the spotlight once straight back down Spear Street, to pick up anyone standing or walking down the unlit road. There was no one, not even a tomcat. There was not a light or a house silhouette visible on the horizon. He turned back and glanced out the passenger window, but Avery and the man in the weeds were gone. Chris snapped his head to the right and the left, and he saw only pines and blackberry bush. He shoved himself toward the open passenger window.

A flicker of movement near the door lock caught his eye, a little finger of black rising and falling like a piston, and only then did it occur to him that the two men were at ground-level.

By the time Chris was out of the car and crossing under the overhang of pine boughs, Avery and the man were lying in the needles. At first it looked like an adult lying next to a child, the difference in their sizes was so pronounced. The man, who looked younger up close, was lying on his stomach, arms and legs spread, with blood soaking his mat of black hair and his white tank-top. Avery was lying perpendicular to him, on his back. His hand still gripped his night stick tightly. Avery's chest was pumping spasmodically, and Chris could hear him pulling in shallow breaths, a sound almost like a high whine. Chris felt nausea curl in his stomach.

Of all the things that rushed his mind one was the clearest, the sense that something had leveled both men, something as violent as gravity, more powerful than either of them or both of them put together. Something undiscriminating had crushed them down flat against the soil and the pine needles.

• • •

Avery cleared his throat, coughed violently into his fist. He hesitated, eyes down now on his own hands in his own lap. Then he went ahead with it. "So by the time your dad was out of the car and over to where we were that guy wasn't ever gonna call anybody a pig again. It was over and done with in five, six minutes. Right out of nowhere."

Maurice took a drink. "Goddam, Avery," he said. He had no idea what to say.

"Goddam is right."

After a minute, Maurice prompted, "So that was that."

Avery ran his hands over the fabric of the couch, watching his hands trace across the slightly faded stripe pattern. "It was. Your father saved my ass that day for sure. We set there and figured out all the angles. Both of us were about shitting our pants, but we kept it together. And then he helped me put that bastard away where nobody wouldn't ever find him. And I'll tell you something, young blood. And you remember this, because it's the only sensible thing. You know you did the right thing when something like that stays down in the hole you put it in." Now his eyes looked watery, bloodshot, and his voice was earnest and genuinely imploring. "If it wasn't righteous, God would have that thing come back on you, and it never has. Knock on wood, but it never has."

Maurice took a sip of his beer, and glanced at the screen. Women were playing volleyball now, somewhere in Southern California. "That's intense, Avery," was all he could manage as a comment. "That is truly hard-core."

Avery touched the remote, and the trickle of crowd noise and shouted signals came back up. He yawned and stretched, and Maurice realized again what a physically small man Avery was, when you subtracted the personality and the beard. Avery turned his eyes back to the spectacle, but he kept murmuring quietly, more or less to himself. "The Taco Hippy, we always called that bastard, whenever your dad and I had any reason to refer to him."

• • •

It had snowed while Maurice was inside, and when he pulled out of the Club lot and turned right to head back into Burlington, it felt like he was in a hovercraft moving over a clean dark expanse of snow. There was no sense of traction at all, no sense of connection to the road, and yet the car was responding perfectly. He wasn't sliding, he was gliding. For the hell of it, he put the car into a short spin right in the middle of the quiet street, and brought it around to almost exactly the orientation he'd begun with.

He started to laugh out loud to himself. Before Maurice left the Club, Avery told him that he saw Maurice as like a son to him, with Chris gone. *You remember,* Avery had said, gripping his hand and giving him a look, *you keep that secret for good, even after we make you the mayor, you don't tell anybody.* Now Maurice banged on the steering wheel and whispered out loud to himself in a television voice, "Maurice Masseau. Keeper of all secrets."

The story Avery had told him was there in his mind, but he was concentrating on a new sense of purpose and seriousness he could feel smoldering. Both his father and his brother had put themselves at risk, had broken the law and sacrificed, and Maurice had a new larger sense of his family and the way it connected to the land they had grown up on. He had always loved stories of Ethan Allen and the Green Mountain Boys as a kid, and once the shock of Avery's story had rippled through him he'd begun to feel like those books were coming alive all around him. His father had done as he saw fit, stepping behind and around the law like it was a set of props put there for other people. He had the sense of his family working for something, warring for something.

Out of habit, he caught himself angling down Pearl to cut over to the Metronome, but he remembered that it was deserted tonight, everyone was up at Memorial listening to oldies. He felt like organizing, like running his mouth a little, getting some of this feeling out in talk. He really felt like talking to Reuben, but he remembered suddenly that Reuben was in jail, and that he'd promised to keep this for himself.

And then he realized that it had been a long while since he'd checked out the skateboarders, the fourteen-through-seventeen crowd who were too young to drink. In the summer, they hung out in cliques on Church Street and in front of the Social Security Office, practicing rolls and wilsons off the side of the low concrete walls, banging their wheels and talking trash and scaring the shoppers. But in the winter, they still hung together on clear nights up on the second floor of the Chittenden Bank parking garage. They'd have on their thermals and their gloves and they'd be practicing, seriously practicing, right in the middle of February. Crazy-ass skateboarders.

He banked the hovercraft left on South Winooski, aimed it at the center of town. It moved silently over the cover of snow. He'd go scout the skaters, he decided, pass out a couple of joints and talk it up. They were the future, Maurice knew that. They were most of them punks, those kids, but you had to give them credit for single-mindedness and devotion. Those boys had heart.